On the Make

by

Margo Hoornstra

Brothers in Blue, Book 3

On the Make

Cover Art by *Diana Carlile*

The Wild Rose Press, Inc.
PO Box 708
Adams Basin, NY 14410-0708
Visit us at www.thewildrosepress.com

Publishing History
First Crimson Rose Edition, 2020
Print ISBN 978-1-5092-3060-0
Digital ISBN 978-1-5092-3061-7

Brothers in Blue, Book 3
Published in the United States of America

As he drew closer, more details became evident. Pleasingly evident. Blond hair, long on top and shorter on the sides. A square, firm chin. Lips, not too full, not too thin. Perfectly matched to the rest of his features. There was only one problem. Aviator sunglasses kept her from seeing his eyes. Did they light up when he smiled? Crinkle at the corners?

Get a grip, woman. Naturally he'd be devastatingly handsome. According to Cameron, he was a movie star. And no doubt played the part well.

"Wow. You remember me." All one hundred and fifty pounds of star struck boy fell across her as her son did all he could to get closer to his newest idol. "That is so awesome."

The man flashed another smile. This one within inches of her face. Perfectly straight, white teeth. Perfectly shaped mouth.

She blinked again as a streak of longing she hadn't experienced in Lord knew how long burst forth to trickle across her stomach. Like a peaceful flock of butterflies startled into frenzied flight. *Overwrought emotions.* The only explanation for her extraordinary reaction.

"Sure I remember you. You made quite an impression." His voice was like smooth, hot caramel flowing over a scoop of chilled, vanilla ice cream.

Her mouth dropped open as if she'd given up all control. Maybe so, but she absolutely refused to swoon. To her credit, she retained the presence of mind to not release the huge sigh that inched its way up from her heart to recline at the back of her throat—sitting there, waiting to be freed.

Praise for the Brothers in Blue Series:

ON THE SURFACE

"If you like a heavy helping of romance with your suspense, this book is for you."
~Alison Henderson, Author of Second Wind

"Ms. Hoornstra didn't disappoint me with this one."
~Brenda Whiteside, Author of The Love and Murder series

"There was action from the beginning, and I was hooked right in. I loved that the characters had such serious issues and secrets."
~Lacey Clary, Romance Reader

"*On the Surface* is a well researched, slow burner of a read that will keep you turning the pages and staying up late at night."
~Sharon B. Buchbinder, Author of The Hotel LaBelle series

ON THE FORCE

"I enjoyed witnessing the suspense building in a relationship while danger kicked up the plot. Lots here to appreciate about our men and women in blue. A great read!"
~Rolynn Anderson, Author of When Mountains Fall

Dedication

To Barbara Kerns Johnson.
The glass will forever remain half full.
Rest in peace, my friend.

Other Wild Rose Press Titles by Margo Hoornstra

Chapter One

"Let us pray."

Madison Clark dutifully lowered her head, along with scores of other mourners, in the main hall of the Guards Park Convention Center. Though she did so more for show than reverence. Known for its panoramic views of the magnificent Rocky Mountains, the center was perhaps an odd place to hold a funeral. Then again, nothing about her marriage to Joe, short as it was, could be construed as normal. Why should anything change now that he was gone?

In one sense, this cavernous auditorium was particularly fitting. Somewhat cold, decidedly impersonal—very much like her late husband.

"Dear Lord, we humbly commit Joseph Edward Clark to your compassionate care." Pastor Gregg's voice invaded that line of thinking, only to create a new one.

Closing her eyes, she issued her own silent prayer. *Dear Lord, please don't let Joe run across Dave in the hereafter.* Second husband meeting first, Dave would probably deck him. Perhaps for good reason. Shortly after their vows were exchanged, their intimate partnership complete, it became clear Joe had no real investment in their marriage. A total one eighty for the handsome, full of life man, attentive to her every need, who had courted her relentlessly until she fell in love.

One would expect I'd have outgrown starry-eyed stupidity at this stage in my life. Thirty-five and counting.

Pondering what might have been, her throat burned, and tears threatened before anger charged in to sweep them away. To think she gave up building a successful law practice, uprooted her family from Chicago and moved west, to become little more than a glorified event planner. As a respected real estate attorney, she assumed at least some of Joe's attraction to her was for her brains and expertise. Not so. The sole companionship Joe Clark sought was convenient eye candy on his arm in the form of a woman who could also host his myriad of necessary functions. Mostly business. Occasionally social.

"Almighty God, we ask that you grant the means to understand and the patience to accept Your decision for those left behind to grieve."

With her head still down and eyes shut, a sigh escaped. She and her two young sons knew all too well about being left behind to grieve. Three short years before, she had buried her soulmate and the boys had buried their father. Heart-broken and bewildered, Dak and Cameron sat on either side of her at Dave's service. Stoic and silent in their grief.

A mere thirty-six months later, front and center in this jam-packed amphitheater, a classic Black Widow in the making, *she* prepared to bury spouse number two.

Both her sons on either side of her again.

"Bleep! Blip!"

Faint flashes of light accompanied the noise to her left. Opening her eyes to mere slits, she glanced over. Typical teen, Cameron had his cell out. Head bent, deep in concentration, he moved his thumbs across the virtual keyboard with incredible speed.

Her jaw clenched as irritation sparked. Inching stiffened fingers his way, she touched his arm and squeezed, fully prepared with a stern look of reproach when he glanced up at her. Which, of course, he didn't. She firmed her lips to hold in a verbal reprimand. Squeezed harder. Still not acknowledging her, he pushed one last icon, slid the device into the pocket of his suit coat and sat back.

"In Your name we pray. Amen."

"Amen." Her murmured response joined the rest of the chorus in the room.

As all heads lifted, her gaze immediately fell on the urn containing Joe's ashes. Set on a pedestal of sorts up front in all its noble glory. Sleek in design. Dignified in its burnished gold finish. An ample supply of mourners, though some no more than morbidly curious, her late husband would be pleased with the final, colossal event she'd planned for him.

"Joseph Clark was a man of many aspects." Slight of build and nearly lost in the folds of his robe, the minister gripped both sides of the dais with bony fingers as he leaned into it. Though Pastor Gregg may have finished praying, he wasn't done speaking. "Real estate mogul by profession. Community leader and philanthropist by choice."

From her other side, an adolescent leg jostled hers. Over and over and over again. She angled a discreet glance toward the disturbance. Nine-year-old Dak had some pretty significant foot tapping going on. Placing a gentle hand on his thigh, she followed up with a slight head shake when he immediately straightened to look over. Heartened, she cast a stern glance left then another right for good measure. For her sake at least, shoulders straight and heads up for a change, both boys appeared to pay attention.

Pastor extended his arms, palms upward. "Our heartfelt condolences go to the grieving little family before us."

She nodded in gracious acceptance of many sympathetic gazes aimed their way. With all due respect though, this loss paled to what she and her boys had already survived. The days following Dave's unexpected and lethal leukemia diagnosis had crushed her. His death came fast, within weeks, to throw her world into a tailspin. More of a bottomless vortex. Fast moving, dark and immeasurably deep. Sucking her into its depths and spinning her life completely out of control.

Grief stabbed her heart at remembering, and she took several shallow breaths. Back then, only the fact she had two young children to raise kept her going. Coping like an aimless robot through necessary days. Suffering agonizing loneliness through endless nights.

Meeting Joe changed that for the better. *Or so I believed.*

A shudder caught her unaware. One tear started it all. Soon others welled up to roll down her cheeks. She quickly blotted them away with a yet unused tissue.

"Joseph was a man of many aspects in his personal life as well." Pastor Gregg let his voice grow soft. "To Madison, a devoted husband. To Cameron and Dak, a loving and benevolent father."

"Beussst!" Cameron coughed into his elbow.

Though thinly disguised, the word *bullshit* rang

4

true to Madison's ears. Heat flushed her cheeks.

"Bless you, son." The good reverend didn't miss a beat, apparently not quite as perceptive as she.

But then, he wasn't Cameron's mother.

Her son coughed a second time in response.

"To everything there is a season, a time for every matter under heaven." Pastor Gregg launched into what she hoped would be the wrap-up scripture of this lengthy memorial service.

Even knowing Joe had held no feelings resembling love for her, pangs of guilt she had somehow failed him speared deep. She couldn't even call on her previous marriage for guidance. Her union with Dave was based on mutual respect and devotion, as well as love. Her brief experience with Joe never even came close.

"...and a time to castaway." Closing the Bible, Pastor Gregg folded his hands on top as he took his sweet time to scan the crowd one way then the other. Apparently with high expectations. "And the people said…"

"Amen." After a few awkward seconds, those assembled complied.

"Amen indeed." He nodded with a self-satisfied smile. "And now Joseph's family asks that you join them in the lobby area for some light refreshments." Tapping his Good Book a few times, he stepped down from the podium.

A dull hum of idle conversations erupted as those who had come to pay their respects stood. The platforms of the seats they vacated folded up with a series of muted thumps. Clasping each son by the hand, Madison stood too, bringing them with her.

The trumpet skirt of her charcoal gray suit flared

around her legs before coming to rest mid-calf. Cameron and Dak looked handsome, so grown up, attired in smart business suits, starched dress shirts, coordinating ties. High-end wing tips.

"I'll go check on the caterer." Her thoughts scattered as she turned toward the familiar male voice.

Just like that, she stared directly into her late husband's eyes. While looking at the face of his younger brother, John. Although each sibling carried the same DNA, for all the power and aggression contained in Joe's, the man before her had proven to be the exact opposite. Pleasant and easy going. Soft spoken and unassuming. Nice to her and her boys.

She offered a warm smile. "Thank you. That's very thoughtful."

"It's the least I can do." His expression remained solemn.

With light touches to the top of her hand and then each of the boys' shoulders, he was gone.

Exuding peaceful repose, Pastor Gregg came to stand before them. "May God remain with you at this time of need."

She gazed into the kind, wrinkled face so close to hers. "Thank you. That was lovely."

"Mine to serve." He reached out to pat her shoulder. Then did the same with Dak and Cameron.

"Joe would have been pleased."

Taking a breath, she glanced at her boys. The three of them walked as a unit beside the cleric out to the lavishly decorated lobby area with its cathedral ceiling and sparkling chandeliers. A number of linen covered tables lined one wall, replete with extravagant appetizers and assorted canapés, both hot and cold. As they passed by one abundantly set table, a particularly offensive aroma, strong and overly spiced, assaulted her senses of smell and taste. Her stomach roiled. She closed her mouth to swallow with little relief.

Oblivious to her discomfort, Pastor Gregg turned toward their little group when they stopped beside the offending cuisine. "If you don't mind, I'll grab a bite to eat. Mingle with your other guests."

"Of course." Madison immediately slid into hostess mode. "By all means, help yourself."

"God be with you all." On a slight bow, he left them alone.

"And also with you." The response slipped out of her without much thought.

Before she could draw her next stomach settling breath, a gloved hand touched her arm.

"Our hearts go out to you." Mayor Edwina Gillespie peeked out from beneath the wide brim of a beige felt fedora. "And, of course, these boys."

"We appreciate your kind words. Don't we?" Glancing on either side of her, the comment had no more left her mouth when Cameron pulled free of her grasp.

"Sure we do. Thanks." Twisting on his heel, he strolled away.

Madison's heart broke at her son's slumped shoulders and bowed head. Still, she willed her cheeks not to flame as she turned back to Edwina. "He's my strong, silent child."

"So I see." Her disapproving gaze followed his retreat.

"Much like his father was." Nerves caused Madison to say the wrong thing. "This one, on the other hand…" She pulled poor Dak forward, not sure how to finish.

"Is, I'm sure, a great comfort to you." On a decidedly tolerant smile, Edwina did the honors for her. "Well. You have many others who wish your attention. I'll step aside to let you get on with it."

"Thank you. We appreciate that." Madison cringed at her hollow remark.

Already halfway across the expansive facility, subtly smiling and nodding as she went, Edwina barely took note. A typical politician, she was more intent on working the room.

"Your late husband was a very kind and giving man." A woman in a black jumpsuit with long blonde hair had quietly approached. Madison recognized her as a contractor's wife she'd met at their company Christmas function the year before.

"What a nice thing to say." With a quick glance down at Dak, totally different thoughts took hold.

Joe *had* been a kind and giving man to many. Particularly those who didn't make the mistake to get too close. Contrary to the public persona he so carefully displayed, the real Joseph Clark the third was a man who coveted his new wife more for how she looked than who she was. While he merely tolerated the presence of the two precious boys she'd brought into his life.

Regret and indignation rolled over her like an unsettled sea and she automatically lifted her chin.

"It's the truth, after all." Prettily manicured nails rested on her arm. "I'm so very sorry."

"Thank you for coming." Madison kept up the congenial smile as the woman moved on.

"I'm going to go find Liam." Dak wasn't quite as abrupt as his brother when he let go of her hand. Though he no doubt harbored the same strong feelings.

"Okay, sweetheart. Just don't go far."

He executed a classic, pre-teen eye roll. "Where exactly could I go?"

"Good point." With a curt nod, she assumed an appropriately somber expression as he walked away.

"Sorry about your loss." Hayden Riley jabbed his hand out to take hold of hers. His entire tall, skinny body came forward with it. He had an abrupt, agitated demeanor which didn't fit with his long-time position as President of the Guards Park Historical Society.

"I appreciate your thoughts." When she tried to free up her hand, he wouldn't let go.

"When you get a moment." He continued to lean in until he and Madison practically touched foreheads. His hot breath blew in her face. "I was hoping we could talk about the Concord Estate."

With a robust jerk, she broke contact and stepped back. "Here?"

"Why not? I'm afraid your husband made a big mistake letting those movie people onto the property. Perhaps now that things have changed, you might be able to rectify the unfortunate situation. Bring the property back to the auspices of the Historical Society as before."

Dumbfounded, she could only shake her head at the man's gall. Though *she* was offended he'd bring up business at her late husband's memorial, sadly Joe wouldn't be. In his world, business always took precedence over everything else.

"Actually, I wouldn't know about that. Joe wasn't

one to share much about his business dealings with me." *Yet one more reason our marriage didn't work out.*

"As I said, an ill-advised deal your husband got himself into."

Bringing out her most tolerant smile, she lowered her voice. "And, as I said, I wasn't privy to the details of my husband's real estate holdings. Though I will be sure to have our attorney get in touch at the appropriate time. Should the situation warrant it."

Narrowing his eyes, he took a pace toward her. "I strongly suggest we meet as soon as possible to facilitate such a move."

If he expected her to shrink back in submission, she was more than happy to disappoint him. Gritting her teeth, she looked him in the eye and forced another smile. "Thank you so much for coming to pay your respects."

"Hey, Mom. Liam wants me to go home with him for a sleepover."

Thankfully distracted, she turned her back on what had become a rude intrusion. "He does?"

"Can I go?" The longing in his tone was nothing compared to the plea coming from deep within his young gaze.

She blinked to escape the intensity. "I don't...I..."

"We weren't sure how you'd feel about letting Dak go for the night." Patty, Liam's mother, trailed behind in an anxious flurry. "Given the situation. But, the boys begged me, and I said it was okay. Provided you agreed."

"That's fine with me then."

As Madison focused in on Patty, Hayden strolled

away in silence. *Good riddance.*

"Sweet!" Dak pumped his right fist.

Madison grinned at his antics before reality hit. "Oh, but he doesn't have anything besides his suit to wear and no overnight supplies."

"Not a problem." Petite and blond, Patty waved away her concerns with a lifted hand. "We always have unopened toothbrushes at our house. As far as play clothes, Liam and Dak are generally the same size. I'm sure we can find him something to wear."

"Excellent." Her youngest piped up again as he yanked on the neck of his dress shirt and slid off his tie. "I can't wait to get out of this damned suit."

"Dak!" Feigning wide-eyed horror, Madison suppressed a laugh.

"Sorry, Mom." He cracked a small smile as his little pal openly snickered. "I meant darned suit."

Glancing down at the two of them, Patty shook her head as her lips twitched. "Liam, you and Dak can go find your father. Tell him I'll meet you at the car in a few minutes."

"Beat you to the stairs!" Taking a leap forward, Dak stuffed the tie in his pocket.

"Let's go!"

The two rowdy youngsters drew a few indignant stares as they raced across the floor, but Madison didn't mind one little bit.

Patty watched them go then looked back at her. "I'm sorry if I overstepped…"

"There's no need to apologize." Madison grabbed her hand and squeezed. "It would do Dak good to get away from all this drama for a while."

"Well that's a relief." Her worried expression

11

eased. "Your husband was a great man."

"Thank you. I'm hearing that a lot." With the assembled business associates and politicians, insincere pleasantries were one thing. Someone as sweet as Patty deserved authenticity.

"Though this is quite the production, if you don't mind my saying." She pulled her hand away to gesture around the room.

For the first time that day, Madison felt it when she smiled. "I don't mind at all. In fact, I completely agree. A necessary production, given my late husband's..." She surveyed the crowded room. "Popularity. I'll be anxious to get our lives somewhat back to normal as soon as possible."

"No one could blame you. Thankfully, it's over for you now."

Madison grimaced even as she agreed. "The worst of it anyway."

"Take care and don't worry about Dak. The boys will have a nice time." With a quick flutter wave, Patty hurried away.

"I'm sure they will. Thank you." Momentarily alone, Madison grabbed a breath she blew out on a whoosh.

Taking advantage of a temporary lull in the constant line of well-wishers, John made his way over to stand beside her. "How're you doing?"

"Holding my own." Casually resting a hand on his arm, her fingers met the rigidity of tensed and tight muscles beneath his suit coat. She immediately recoiled, then wished she hadn't. Poor guy. As the last surviving member of the Clark family, Joe's death had to be devastating for him. Something he kept well hidden by a placid exterior. "How about you?"

"The same." He turned as another acquaintance took his hand. "Thank you for coming. I'm sure my brother would appreciate your presence. Yes. It is a great loss." When they were alone again, he twisted her way. "If you'd like a break, go ahead. I'll cover for you."

Tempting as it was to take him up on the offer, she couldn't do that. Even to Joe. "Thanks. But no. Your brother deserves a properly grieving widow."

With a nod of understanding, he casually flicked out his fingers. "Hope it wasn't too hard on you, the amount of time it took to schedule all of this."

"Considering who Joe was, it couldn't be helped. But then, this whole situation is difficult."

"Especially since the authorities held on to his body for a while."

"That was hard." She nodded her agreement. "It's what conscientious authorities do when a man of your brother's stature succumbs to a massive cardiac arrest. Especially given the fact Joe prided himself on being in excellent shape. Not a day went by that he didn't log at least five hard-fought miles, either on the treadmill in his study, or on the trails and roads outdoors."

"He was a dedicated runner. You certainly can't fault his desire to take care of himself." John lifted his gaze to acknowledge more guests about to descend. "I saw Hayden cornered you. That couldn't have been pleasant."

"You're very perceptive." She reached out to shake an extended hand. "Thank you."

Bowing slightly, for the next few moments, John did much the same.

When the crowd once again thinned, she went on. "He seems obsessed with some Concord Estate of Joe's."

Recognition flashed in dark eyes. "Sounds about right. That property has been in the family for generations. An albatross as far as I'm concerned. Our mother set it up as a historical shrine of sorts to the area. More power to Joe for trying to make some money off it."

"I wasn't sure what he was talking about." She had no problem admitting the short coming.

His eyes narrowed briefly before he smiled. "Why would you? Set on four acres on the outskirts of town, it was first built in the eighteen hundreds as a small village and currently consists of a church, store and two houses. All according to the brochures Hayden had made up."

"Mr. Riley mentioned something about movie people."

The smile became a chuckle. "As I understand, my brother rented the site out to some production company."

"Really? For what?"

"Filming some major motion picture, I guess."

Further private conversation was cut short by more well-wishers. It was no surprise the entire town had turned out to pay their respects to one of its most influential citizens. Or check out for themselves the reaction to his death of the woman he'd recently married. With a slight smile and head shake, Madison acknowledged her cynicism. And put it to rest just as quickly. This was Joe's town. The sooner she and her sons were out of here, the better.

Standing beside John, reciting appreciations by rote, Madison found her mind wandering to another difference between the two brothers. How ironic, while Joe had built structures for a living, a demolitions expert by trade, John systematically demolished them. Yet their personal lives were polar opposite. Joe was devoted to tearing down those around him, while John dedicated himself to building them up.

"Yes. Thank you for coming." Engaged in further appropriate niceties, after more time than she cared to measure, the crowd dwindled to a few stragglers here and there, then down to nothing.

"It looks like we're both finally free." John glanced over with a wry smile.

"Looks like it." Madison let out a sigh. "I'm anxious to track down Cameron. He left rather abruptly."

"I noticed that. Although you can't really blame him. All of us grieve in our own way." He patted her arm. "You go ahead. I'll see to any necessary details around here before I leave."

"What would I do without you?" As much as she regretted marrying Joe, meeting John was one bright spot in the unfortunate situation. "Thank you again…still."

"No need. You're dealing with enough right now." He started to walk away then turned back. "Though I'll definitely be in touch."

"I'll look forward to it." *At least for the length of time we're here.*

As she navigated out of the lavish surroundings and down a few stairs to a short hallway, her black low-heeled pumps were silenced by the thick, plush carpet.

Her stomach twisted then turned as she hurried along. A little jump and flutter came next, and she slowed her pace. *My body's way of settling itself.* Adjusting from all the activity and emotion flung at her the past few weeks.

The brass embossed door slid open in front of her, and she gratefully stepped outside. The chilling winds of an early November afternoon brushed her cheeks. Clean fresh air bit into her lungs as she pulled in a hearty sample. Her suede trimmed jacket and long wool skirt provided ample protection from the cold as she embraced a welcome contrast from the oppressive atmosphere she'd left behind.

Shivering none the less, she didn't have to look far to find Cameron. No farther than the Lincoln Towne Car she'd parked two rows down from the entrance earlier that day. Scrunched down in the back seat, he held the ever-present cell in front of his face with both hands. As usual, his thumbs worked the small screen keyboard with uncanny precision. No doubt engaged in one of the many search and destroy fantasy games he played every chance he got.

Opening the door, she settled in beside him. He'd discarded his suit coat into a crumpled heap. She curled both hands into fists, resisting a strong desire to pick up the jacket to fold neatly. It wouldn't do to touch her son right now either. No matter how compelling the urge.

"Aren't you cold?"

"Naw." The clipped reply was accompanied by a slight shrug.

"You sure?" These days, it rarely paid to question anything this son said. She did so anyway.

The keyboard manipulation continued unabated.

"Yeah."

"John gave you a pass for walking out like you did." She snapped up his coat she draped over the front seat. "That was rude of you, Cameron."

Saying nothing, he gave intent study to the screen.

She inclined her head, attempting to see his face he expertly kept from her view. "You embarrassed me."

Finally, he glanced up as if to let her in, yet never set down the phone. "Sorry. I didn't mean to do that. I just needed to get out of there. It was so hot and stuffy. All those people. I couldn't breathe."

She put a hand on his arm. "I understand. Next time, though, be a little polite. At least say excuse me."

He nodded before looking down again. "Okay, I will. Anything else?"

"No. Just that."

"Got it." Lights flashed as the cell regained his full attention.

Wishing with all her heart he would look up and continue to talk to her, she should know by now he'd do neither. As a sort of test, she slid closer then tried not to resent it too much when he slid an equal distance away.

"Did you enjoy the service?" She silently cursed herself at the lousy word choice. *Enjoy?* "Sorry. I didn't mean that the way it sounded. Naturally it's not something one would enjoy." She ran a hand through her dark curly hair, not caring if a few strands on top spiked up to stand on their own. "I thought they did a nice job. There were some pleasant tributes."

"I suppose."

"Much like those they made to your dad." Desperation made her utter the notably forbidden statement.

"Seriously?" An all too familiar look of disbelief at something she'd said crossed his face.

I know. Would they ever get things right between them again? Sitting beside him in silence, she studied the blond head bent over the device he manipulated with such skill.

"Bleep! Blip!"

The screen lit up in a series of bright spurts. The red, yellow and orange clouds of virtual explosions. Her attention shifted back to her son as the device went dark. Lifting his gaze, he said nothing as he stared straight ahead.

She was running out of options. Ways to get through to him.

"Hey!" Miraculously, he spoke up at last. Only to look right through her out the side window. "It's Adam Pride! Hey, Adam!"

The odd fact his voice was filled with excitement registered first. "Adam Pride?" *The man must really be something.*

"He's the superhero police officer I met the other day."

Confusion sank in next. "The superhero police officer you met?"

Had her oldest transferred those fantasy characters he idolized in the virtual world to the real one? Where she struggled to keep her family intact, any kind of hero, super or otherwise, simply didn't exist.

"Hey Adam! Over here!" Cameron leaned across her to lower the window. "Baddest ass cop ever to walk this earth."

Wincing at his language, she refrained from correcting him. As impressionable as her son was lately, for all she knew he simply quoted some line he'd heard on the internet.

"Adam brings serve and protect to a whole new level."

As a police officer's son, he knew the vernacular, but was probably quoting from somewhere again as he waved furiously. It was stunning enough that the cell was quickly relegated to the seat beside him and apparently forgotten. What really registered for her was the ear to ear smile affixed to his mouth. Unexpected and bigger than any she'd seen on him in quite a while.

"You met him? When?"

He looked at her, really looked at her for the first time in weeks. "The site of the latest Kyle Flynn Super Cop movie. They're making some of it right here in Guards Park. He even came over and talked to us. Talked to me. It was totally awesome."

No you're the one who's totally awesome. The transformation in her son was as amazing as it was heartening.

The sides of her mouth tipped up despite tears threatening. "He sounds like a very nice man."

"Man?" His gaze swung her way. Narrowed eyes signaled surly teenaged son was about to re-emerge. "Shows what you know. That's no man. That's superhero Adam Pride."

More cool November breezes washed over her face through the open window as she followed Cameron's gaze, seeking the object of such an over-the-top reaction. Although, unlike her son, Madison was all too aware of the difference between make-believe superhero and living, breathing flesh and blood mortal man.

"Hey. How are you?" From across the street, after some minor hesitation, an ordinary looking guy in jeans and a leather jacket flashed a smile as he waved back.

Ordinary except for one thing—several things in fact. She took a short breath and blinked to clear her vision, allow herself a better look. If Cameron hadn't pointed him out to her, he was definitely someone she would have noticed. Even from a distance, she could tell he was huge. Wide shoulders strained against the soft leather covering them. Zipped only an inch or two up from his waist, the front separated to reveal a casual shirt pulled equally tight over a solid chest.

As he drew closer, more details became evident. Pleasingly evident. Blond hair, long on top and shorter on the sides. A square, firm chin. Lips, not too full, not too thin. Perfectly matched to the rest of his features. There was only one problem. Aviator sunglasses kept her from seeing his eyes. Did they light up when he smiled? Crinkle at the corners?

Get a grip, woman. Naturally he'd be devastatingly handsome. According to Cameron, he was a movie star. And no doubt played the part well.

"Wow. You remember me." All one hundred and fifty pounds of star struck boy fell across her as her son did all he could to get closer to his newest idol. "That is so awesome."

The man flashed another smile. This one within inches of her face. Perfectly straight, white teeth. Perfectly shaped mouth.

She blinked again as a streak of longing she hadn't experienced in Lord knew how long burst forth to trickle across her stomach. Like a peaceful flock of butterflies startled into frenzied flight. *Overwrought emotions.* The only explanation for her extraordinary reaction.

"Sure I remember you. You made quite an impression." His voice was like smooth, hot caramel flowing over a scoop of chilled, vanilla ice cream.

Her mouth dropped open as if she'd given up all control. Maybe so, but she absolutely refused to swoon. To her credit, she retained the presence of mind to not release the huge sigh that inched its way up from her heart to recline at the back of her throat—sitting there, waiting to be freed.

The persistent November wind became a welcome counter to a rising heat within she seemed unable to keep in check. Even as this Adam was close enough, and large enough, to shield her from further drafts coming in the opened window.

Unfortunately, wedged between an over eager son on one side, and an overwhelmingly hot man on the other, she needed all the help she could get to cool off. Especially when the man leaned nearer as he conversed with Cameron. Subtle scents of definite male layered with a woodsy musk came in with him. She drew back out of sensory range, but its intense effect lingered. Though not at all overpowering, he emitted a warmth that seeped over her.

And they hadn't even touched. *What in the world would happen then?*

She shook her head. *He's a movie star. Duh!* Every woman was supposed to be attracted. It was all part of the package. A visual sales pitch.

The thing was, his movie idol persona aside, the positive effect he had on her sullen son was nothing short of amazing.

That was it. That had to be it. The one and only sensible and sane justification for her swift interest in the man was his apparent influence, in a good way, on Cameron.

Because of him, she'd gotten a brief glimpse of her once happy, smiling, loving son. And she'd do anything she had to if it meant keeping him around.

Anything.

Chapter Two

Adam could hardly believe he stood beside the shiny Lincoln Towne Car in the parking lot of what looked to be a coliseum. Conversing with another fan.

"Cameron. Right?"

He recognized the kid from the location shoot the other night. The one he'd chatted with, briefly. When neither one of them had been where they were supposed to be at the time.

"Wow!! You remembered me. That's awesome." The kid came out with one heck of an enormous grin.

Hoping to do the one he received justice; Adam flashed a wide smile to match. "What's not to remember? I enjoyed talking with you. It's nice seeing you again."

He cringed at the little white lie he tacked on at the end. At first, upon hearing his stage name called, he'd scanned the immediate premises. Anxious to take cover. Definitely the coward's way out. Was it so bad he detested being recognized when he was off the movie idol clock? Out for a walk when his shooting schedule responsibilities had eased up, his plan was to enjoy the sunshine and fall breezes of this little burg that reminded him of his hometown near Detroit. Take in some pretty stunning colors as ordinary green leaves took on cool weather costumes of brilliant red, orange and yellow.

Then the bottom fell out of an otherwise peaceful afternoon when he was recognized by a fan and, God forbid, summoned over.

People expect you to play the movie idol role even when all the lights, camera and action brouhaha isn't going on. How many times had he heard that so called advice when he'd first gotten into this crazy business? No matter how inconvenient to follow through.

It wasn't as if he was necessarily anti-social. He preferred to think of himself as a personable enough kind of guy who liked to keep his personal involvements superficial. No harm in maintaining this conversation though. Now that he was here and all.

"That was one late night. You guys were real troupers to stay until the end."

The kid's brow creased. "Why would we leave?"

"Good question."

In the spirit of being a good sport when it came to interacting with fans, Adam looked directly at the woman he'd looked beyond as he conversed with the boy. The movie persona bullshit aside, all at once he was extremely grateful he'd gone with his gut to walk over. Connecting with the boy was nice, but she added a whole new dimension to the wisdom of his decision.

"Is your phone working now?"

"What? Yeah." Adam pulled his gaze away from her and back to Cameron. "Thanks for figuring out what was going on."

"No problem. You were in a dead spot around that area where you tried to call out. Not a lot you can do about that."

Cameron kept sliding sideways glances toward the woman beside him, as if he expected her to chime in with additional advice or something. Adam figured he did too. Although guidance wasn't necessarily what came to mind. Or even small talk.

Damned if he couldn't help staring. *Good God she's beautiful.*

Dark, curly hair framed a face sent straight from heaven. Smooth skin. Huge, long-lashed, amazing eyes. Cute nose. Fascinating lips. How would they feel pressed up against his? He'd bet warm. Definitely soft.

Trained to read body language and interpret facial expressions, Adam picked up a similar vibe of interest coming from her. One he was more than willing to explore at the soonest opportunity. Once they got to know each other better, of course.

But man, if she was this spectacular from the neck up, he could only imagine what visual delights awaited from there down. He shifted his stance as blood cells rushed to places they had no business going.

"Adam, this is my mom."

"Your…mom?"

All inappropriate thoughts, complete with unseemly ramifications, did an immediate nosedive. While his libido revved him up with some rather spectacular fantasies, his conscience stepped in to toss a bucket of cold water over where it hurt the most. *This is my mom.* Lest he forget, he was standing here talking to the woman *and her son.* Tempting as this was, he never approached married women in that way. Ever.

At. All.

He nodded politely. "It's nice to meet you Mrs. uh Cameron's mom."

Eyes the green of a meadow at springtime met his. On closer inspection, they were troubled in some way.

Even as the mouth beneath curved into a courteous smile. For his benefit he was sure.

She extended her hand. "My friends call me Madison."

He made the most of an excuse to lean in close, though not too close. "Nice to meet you, Madison."

"Nice to meet you, Mr. Pride."

She referred to him by his stage name, and all he wanted was to correct her. Share his given name. The one on his birth certificate. Not the one that had been bestowed on him by an overzealous talent agent. When what was supposed to be a temporary stint as technical advisor for a popular cop drama on television morphed into a movie career that had long ago gotten out of hand. Truth was, he should've said no and stayed with the department when this big screen opportunity came along. He'd always been more in his element, working as the police officer he was trained to be. His true calling and definite first love.

Taking a breath, he blinked. Too late to do anything about it now. He was committed when the actor thing was all formalized with a bunch of legal paperwork. While he was caught up in the moment and, yeah, okay, dazzled by all the attention and hype.

"What are you two doing out this nice fall day?" Shifting his gaze to the boy, he took a cue from the clear skies and cooler temps. When stuck for something to say, talk about the weather.

"They just had a memorial service for her dead husband." Cameron indicated the huge coliseum like structure behind them with the backward flip of one hand. "In there."

"A what?" Dumbfounded, Adam immediately

jerked back to darn near stand at attention. "I'm sorry. I didn't mean to intrude or anything. I didn't realize. My condolences."

"Don't worry about it." The boy shook his head. "It's really not that big a deal."

It's not? Adam reared back more, struck by such lack of emotion.

That explains her grief. Not his cavalier attitude. What kid refers to a parent as 'her husband?' Obviously one extremely disenfranchised for reasons Adam could only imagine. And identify with at the same time.

She glanced at her son, the message in her eyes hard to read. "My husband actually died almost a month ago. It took a while for the memorial to be scheduled."

"I see." Adam nodded as if he understood fully. "My condolences just the same."

"Thank you."

Now that he'd had more than his fill chewing on a significant amount of shoe leather, it was best for him to leave this little family to whatever baggage they had going on. He never had been good at dealing with his own baggage. Why get caught up in someone else's.

"Dead spot by the tower. I'll have to remember that. Such a simple clarification, and yet when it comes to all things electronic, I'm significantly challenged." He let out a snort. "People my age didn't grow up with a phone permanently attached to their hand."

People his age? Mid-thirties wasn't old. Though probably ancient to this kid.

"Not a big deal." Cameron laughed with him.

Enjoying their spontaneous joke, Adam waited for Madison to join in. If not in full out laughter, with a smile at least. Until a drawn down mouth below a suspicious stare deep sixed that little expectation.

Okay then. He cleared his throat. "At any rate, Cameron. I appreciated your assistance the other night."

"Yeah. Like I said. No problem." The response was oddly subdued as, guilt awash on his features, Cameron seemed to key in on the wary expression crossing his mother's face.

"Where exactly was it the two of you met again?" Brow creased, she looked from one to the other before settling a sharp gaze on her son. Apparently detecting some sort of deceit, as a mother, she was determined to get at the truth.

Like it or not, Adam was deep within it now.

"At the casting call the other night." He provided the bare minimum, minus any incriminating details.

Wariness changed to distrust. Her disapproving stare shifted from her son to land directly on him. "Casting call the other night?"

"The movie they're making in town." The excited tone Cameron started out with had dimmed considerably.

Adam gulped again, deciding to pick up the story for him. "We're filming at a compound just outside of town."

"The Concord Estate," Madison supplied.

"Yeah. That's it." Nodding, he purposely moved a subtle distance closer. "As a historical site, it's pretty well preserved. I understand one of the buildings contains a museum. We're using two of the four buildings for our location shoots. The church and the larger of the two houses. The quad area in front is where we're filming most of the action scenes."

"I'd heard the production company was in town."

Her tone was polite, but that was the extent of it, with none of the giddiness he usually got. Had even come to expect. This woman wasn't interested in having silly questions answered. No 'How does it feel to be a movie star?' or 'That must be exciting for you.'

His interest detection meter of a few moments ago must have been rusted up from disuse. Maybe a sliver of intrigue flared briefly in her eyes, the hint of a smile played around her lips. But that was about it.

All of which she brought swiftly under control with a well-placed scowl.

Despite the ho-hum reaction, he dove back in anyway. "We've been here for nearly two months already. And probably won't wrap up filming for at least another month or more."

"And my son was somehow there?" She drilled him with a suspicious gaze. "While you were filming?"

Absolutely sure he'd discover puncture wounds on his forehead the next time he looked in the mirror, he shook his head. "No. Not there during the actual filming. At the casting call."

Put a cork in it, dipshit.

Mindful of another look of warning shot his way, he couldn't seem to stop talking. "We had some time to kill when production was halted for a couple of hours because they couldn't get the lighting right to suit Joel Eggers, our…" He stepped back to air quote. "…it's never good enough to be satisfied director."

Lowering an arched brow, Madison swung a sharp gaze toward her son. "What casting call exactly?"

Cameron's return gaze had rebellious teenager written all over it as he remained silent.

Adam sure didn't. "It does pay decent. But those

things can be brutal. Standing in line for hours, filling out necessary paperwork. Waiting for a call back. If one comes at all."

"Really?" Her eyes narrowed as she turned to regard him.

"Yeah." Adam swallowed before going on. "A hundred dollars a day is some pretty substantial pocket change for someone Cameron's age."

"And what age would that be exactly?"

Blindsided by her question, he blinked. "Eighteen, right?"

Cameron remained mute, as Adam rattled on like some damned idiot.

"Eighteen?" She cast a keen look from Adam to Cameron then back. "Really?"

"That's what he told us." *And we were apparently stupid enough to believe him.*

"More like fifteen." She transferred a stern glare directly at her son. "This was a calculated deception on your part."

When she'd turned away from *him*, an uncanny sense of relief washed over Adam. Not knowing what else to do, he clamped his mouth shut. The last thing he wanted was to narc on the kid. Too late. He already had. Not on purpose, but he had.

"Going to the casting call where you two met." Her tone demanded an explanation.

Adam kept waiting for her to holler holy hell at being lied to. What he'd come to expect when he was a kid. What Madison seemed to be going to great lengths to refrain from. Trying her best to not embarrass either one of them. Her fingers curled and uncurled into her palm, never quite making her hands into full fists. The only betrayal she still carried any anger.

Though Adam had no idea what would happen when she got Cameron home, part of him admired her restraint. Or maybe she was simply one of those mothers who tended to put the needs of her kids above her own. The type he'd heard about but just never experienced.

He pointedly glanced over at her son. "Probably not your best decision to take off without letting your family know where you were going, Cameron. Families worry." The cop in him was coming out. And felt pretty darned good. "Your mother cares about what happens to you. She also has a right to know where you go. Who you go with."

"Yeah." The boy looked up at him, confusion flooding his gaze, only to deteriorate to basic contempt. Before he broke eye contact altogether to stare straight ahead.

Sympathy that had nothing to do with her recent loss poured into Adam as he locked gazes with Madison. Her initial spark filled glare had softened to the clarity of understanding. Possibly to let him know she appreciated his attempt at support. Right or wrong, a signal he acknowledged with a curt nod. It felt good to back her on this.

"It was Phil's idea."

They both looked over when Cameron spoke. He didn't bother to acknowledge either of them.

"Phil." The name she uttered on a harsh breath carried a boatload of resentment. "So this happened last Wednesday. When you didn't have school the next day and I let you spend the night at his father's."

"His dad didn't mind. He encouraged us. Even

31

gave us a ride down there." The terse response contained its own share of resentment.

Everyone else's parents...fill in the blank...why not you?

Evidently not immune to the universal and unspoken teenaged accusation, guilt and disappointment filled her eyes. If only temporarily

"Cameron's friend Phil." While she kept a steady gaze on her son, Adam was pretty sure her words were directed at him. "Is the product of a recent and very nasty divorce. Consequently, both parents seem to be overcompensating by giving their son certain privileges, such as not imposing a curfew. A decision the poor child might not yet be old enough to handle."

"We called his dad to pick us up. Got back before daylight. Around two in the morning. That's not late." Cameron tried hard to hold his expression of stubborn indifference but kept losing ground to the guilt flitting in for split-seconds at a time.

No doubt it was beginning to dawn on him he might well be in some deep shit here.

Still, Adam couldn't leave the kid out there twisting in the breeze. "A lot of the story takes place at night. Hence the nighttime casting calls. A two AM quitting time is nothing unusual."

She glanced over with her lips drawn down and one eyebrow raised. "I'm sure your production company has a good reason for keeping everyone they employ up and out until that late hour. My son, who happens to be a minor, isn't among them, Mr. Pride."

There she went again, using that formal way to address him. He clamped his mouth shut a second time to keep from impressing upon her he preferred the use of his real last name. No matter how much he wanted to, correcting her now was definitely not in any of their best interests.

"Your mother's right, you know. We have certain legal protocols in place. Disclaimer paperwork that needs to be filled out. That kind of thing."

"Phil's dad signed one for me too when he signed Phil's." Defiance flared in the gaze he directed first at Adam then his mother. "He read about the casting call in the paper." To his credit, Cameron stayed eye to eye with his mother's glaring expression. "Phil's dad said it would be cool for us to go."

"You keep coming back to that. Phil's dad thinking it was cool." Some, no, a lot of the previous anger was noticeably absent from her voice. "You think Phil's dad is cool and I'm not. I can understand that, but not the deceit."

Adam stiffened his elbows to hold both arms firmly at his sides. If only to keep from wrapping them around her in a physical show of understanding and support. Accomplishing that, he lifted a hand he was about to place somewhere on her in comfort. Then didn't.

None of which kept him from chiming in again. "I'm sorry if our production company has caused problems for you."

"What?"

While she turned her head to look at him, the confusion in her expression spoke volumes. Even as the sadness remained.

"Is there anything I can do to help?" His hand finally found its way to rest gently on her shoulder. Incredible warmth trickled into his palm and he stilled for a moment of pure acceptance.

"I don't think so, Mr. Pride."

At her use of his formal name yet again he dropped his hand to stop touching her. "Are you sure?"

"I'm sure." Her voice had gained some of its former strength.

Well, I'm not. From out of nowhere, an unexpected resolve emerged to stick around and somehow help these two come to grips with their current issues. Maybe even reach a suitable resolution if his cop negotiation skills hadn't gotten too corroded while he'd been on leave from the force.

The woman's full regard had already returned to her son. "If this movie making thing is that important to you. We'll figure out another way for you to be part of things. Go to watch a day of filming or something. If that's allowed."

"I don't know about that." Making a quick decision, he looked beyond her. "But, Cameron, I just had a thought. Since your mother did mention figuring out a way to make you a part of things. There's a list of minor parts they're casting for some of the extras. Cameos. Nonspeaking. But there is one you might be a candidate for. The part of my character's son."

Same blond hair. Similar build. Cameron could definitely play the part of Adam's…make that Flynn's…son. Since the youngster had yet to look up, Adam kept his gaze on Madison.

Her eyes took on a hint of acceptance before widening. "Oh, I didn't mean."

"For me?" Cutting her off, the boy was back in the conversation. Smiling. Tentatively, but smiling.

That was all Adam needed to spur him on. Plus,

maybe, just maybe, he could bring a smile to his mother's lips too. "With your mom's permission, of course. And full cooperation."

You'd think the caveat was his idea. He had a hunch they both knew full well having a guardian involved was the legal way things had to be.

"Mom?" Hope flashed over the boy's features as he turned her way.

Adam took that as a positive sign and jumped back in. "I'll definitely run the idea by my director. You do understand the decision isn't mine to make." He hit Cameron with a pointed glance. "But I can certainly put in a good word for you."

"I'd have to know the legal particulars." Her gaze never strayed from her son's exuberant face. Until, slowly she angled her attention Adam's way. "It would be nice if you could look into that. Thank you."

"You're welcome." His gaze settled on her where it remained. Even if he'd wanted, he was powerless to look away until he absolutely had to.

As a bonus of sorts, shortly after, his original wish was granted.

Her mouth tipped up at the corners and a true smile emerged, if only briefly, before she straightened to become all business. "Well, we won't keep you any longer, and wait to hear from you then."

"That works." Though it was the last thing he wanted to do, he pulled away from her. "Nice seeing you again, Cameron. It was nice meeting you, Madison."

His voice came out softer than usual. A far cry from the cordial and friendly, yet impersonal voice he reserved for mere fans.

Thing was, Adam was fine with that. Better than fine. He was totally and perfectly okay with it. Because, somehow, he was convinced this relationship was going to turn out to be the farthest thing from impersonal there was.

Chapter Three

"Mo-o-o-m!" Dak's voice reverberated up the stairs to where Madison sat in her bedroom. "I can't find my backpack! I think Cameron hid it."

Here we go again. She set down the hairbrush that was doing a lousy job of taming her unruly curls, anyway.

"I doubt your brother did that." Walking out to the hallway, she made sure her voice was at least a decibel higher than his. "But, I'll ask."

In a few short steps, she reached the doorway to the Forbidden Zone. Her oldest son's latest title for the bedroom he occupied for more hours than most anyplace else.

"Cameron." Raising a hand, she knocked lightly. "Cameron, answer." She took hold to jiggle the knob. Locked, as usual. "Cam, please. I know you're in there."

I know you're in there. Her words echoed back along with all too familiar doubts and frustrations. Lately, when it came to Cameron, she didn't truly *know* much of anything. For all she did know, he could have easily snuck out the window with her none the wiser.

Their drive home after Joe's memorial was a true indication of their current lack of communication. Cameron had talked non-stop about being an extra in Adam Pride's movie as if the whole thing was a done deal. Not wanting him to get his hopes up and then be disappointed, she had countered with some cautious realities about necessary regulations when minors were involved.

Big mistake.

He, of course, bristled, accusing her of treating him like a baby. Never trusting him to make decisions for himself.

She closed her eyes, remembering. His accusations had cut deep. What he saw as not allowing him to grow up, she saw as wanting—no needing—to keep what little family she had left intact.

"Cameron. I'm talking to you."

About to put her knuckles to the door one last time, she held her fist aloft. As metal scratched against wood, she glanced down. The knob turned.

"No. I don't know where his stupid backpack is." One eye peered out at her through a crack.

Madison peered back. From what she could see beyond him through the sliver of an opening, the room was dark except for on again-off again flashes of light. Either he'd set up some program on his computer, or his television was on with the sound off.

"He asked me to check." She breathed slow and deep. Determined to not let on once again, he'd strung her nerves to the breaking point. "I won't bother you any longer."

She backed away, half expecting—or was it more like dearly hoping—he'd throw the door wide and step out into the hall. Tell her he was sorry for being so rude.

"Okay." Clipped. Abrupt. Immediately followed by the click of the latch.

He may just as well have snapped her heart in two.

For a few seconds, she didn't move. Couldn't more than didn't want to. Stunned at how quickly their once loving relationship had deteriorated. Or had they been at odds longer? She was losing track. Almost to the point she wasn't sure their relationship was even salvageable.

"Cameron doesn't know, Dak."

Knots of sadness and frustration pushed up to fill her throat. Unwanted tears followed she refused to shed. For now, at least, she'd share her suffering with no one. Squeezing her eyes shut, she drew a shaky breath. More like she had no one to share her suffering with.

"Mom! Phone's for you." Once again Dak's voice surged up from downstairs.

Jolted into action, she lifted her head, cleared her throat and turned. "Coming!"

"It's some man! I don't know who."

Please tell me you have the mouthpiece covered.

Hearing the word *man*, Madison's thoughts immediately keyed on Adam Pride. Complete with a full color visual she'd be better off to ignore.

Cameron jerked open his door and stepped out into the hall as she passed by. "Then ask." Hollering first, he focused on her next. "I bet it's Adam. Calling to offer me the job."

"We'll see what he says. If it's even him." She left it at that, rather than argue as she barreled down the stairs.

He was right on her heels. "If he offers me the job, I'm going to take it."

Reaching the living room, at the sour expression

from her youngest, she lost a step, and her stomach took an uncomfortable turn.

"You don't have to take this. I can tell him you're in the bathtub or something." He held the receiver in one hand while he covered its mouthpiece—*thank God*—with the other.

"Don't be silly."

He'd obviously listened to Cameron and asked who was calling. For whatever reason, he was trying to protect her. From what, or whom, she had yet to find out. Shaking his head, Dak surrendered the phone but stayed where he was beside her.

"This is Madison Clark."

"I must say it took you long enough."

Hayden Riley. A grimace claimed her features. Cameron stared at her from where he'd stopped at the bottom of the stairs. She shot him an apologetic look and shook her head.

With a shrug of disgust, he turned to walk away.

"You there?"

She dragged her gaze away from the now empty space. "I was busy. My son and I were talking."

"Have you considered our request to kick that movie company off the premises?"

"You do realize we are only a few days out from my husband's memorial. Plus today is Sunday." Pressing her lips together, she quickly counted to ten. "Not to mention the estate is rather extensive and complicated."

"That Concord property belongs to the people. The Clark family has no business demeaning its worth by renting the use of its treasures for commercial gain. As President of the Historical Society, I should have some say in how and when this property is settled."

She'd had it with his steamroller tactics. "As Joe Clark's widow, I have *all* the say in how and when it is settled."

A snort of pure disgust blasted over the line.

Madison said nothing, only smiled.

"Do you know the meaning of eminent domain?"

Obviously you don't. "That doesn't apply here. Your society is not a government entity." She didn't give him the opportunity to reply. "I will let you know when all the paperwork is filed, and the estate is finally and properly settled."

"That could take months."

"Then that's when I'll be in touch."

"I'm not done with this, you know."

"Well, I am." She ended up speaking to a dial tone. "Damn. Couldn't even give me the satisfaction of hanging up on him."

Turning, she intended to replace the receiver to its cradle. Not set the instrument into Dak's outstretched hand.

A major share of the bravado she was riding high on skidded out from under her. "Oh, Honey. I'm sorry. Have you been standing there all the time?"

"I don't like that guy. Even more than I didn't like Joe. He wasn't very nice when I answered the phone. Said you'd better come talk to him if you knew what was good for you."

"He did, did he?" Her blood pressure notched up a few points and she clenched her teeth. *How dare he threaten me. And my child, no less.* "He's not a very nice man."

Saying no more, she wrapped him in her arms.

Simply because she could.

"When's grandma coming?"

She rested her chin on his head. "In a few more days. Why?"

"Just wondered."

"Oh."

It was apparent his young mind had its fill of melodrama as he changed to a happier subject. The much-anticipated arrival of one of his favorite people.

"She'll definitely be here to celebrate Thanksgiving with us." Still holding him tight, she glanced over to find Cameron at the bottom of the stairs again. Watching. Hands on his hips and expectation on his face. Though she could definitely be wrong, and probably was, a strange sense of longing was reflected in his eyes. Momentarily torn as their gazes met, she was about to loosen her hold on Dak to draw Cameron in.

His expression cleared as he regarded her. "What's for dinner? I'm starved."

Something in Madison's chest shifted as her hope for a tender family moment vanished. Even so, she released Dak and faced Cameron. "Dinner?"

"Yeah."

Dinner.

A routine request in most families. Most *normal* families. For her part, she didn't have a clue but thought fast. "I was thinking we'd have Cobb salad."

"For dinner?" Dak spoke first as both their expressions crumbled in disgust.

She quickly brought out Plan B. "We could have beans and hotdogs. I'll whip up some homemade potato salad."

Her second suggestion met with the same scrunched up faces. She smiled when Plan C hit. "Or we could go out somewhere. Say for pizza."

"Pizza!" Dak lifted his arms skyward. "I vote for P-I-Z-Z-A!"

Well halleluiah. Her third try was a winner.

"Dork." Even as Cameron watched in supposed disgust, the hint of a smile teased around his lips.

At the precise second he caught her staring, he stiffened then stilled. His brief, cheery expression flipped to an impassive mask. Her smile immediately fell, leaving her powerless to retrieve it.

"Pizza it is." Clearing her throat, she stepped to the hall closet and pulled open the door. "Well, look at this."

Though it wasn't what she'd gone there for, she knelt down to retrieve Dak's backpack from an inside corner, holding it up for both of them to see.

Dak glanced sheepishly at Cameron. "Ooops. How did that get in there?"

More disgust filtered over his brother's features. "Told you I didn't touch the stupid thing."

"No sense arguing about it now. Looks like someone put this away. What a concept." Unable to hold in her sarcasm, she set the bag back where she'd found it then pulled out her bright yellow University of Michigan hooded sweatshirt, along with fleece pullovers for Dak and Cameron. "We'll need these."

"Thanks, Mom." Dak slipped into the one she handed him without question.

Cameron backed away, head shaking in the negative. "Nope."

Regardless, Madison extended the pullover toward

him. "It's going to get colder when the sun goes down."

Lips pulled tight, Cameron stood his ground. "I don't need it."

Because I suggested it? She held in what had moved to the tip of her tongue as she placed the jacket back on its hanger. "Suit yourself."

Gathering her purse from an inside hook, something fell from the top shelf. Without much thought, she bent to pick it up. The second her fingers touched what turned out to be a knitted hat, her breath caught as she slowly rose upright.

Dave's hat. The one he always wore to snow-blow the driveway. Or walk, holding her hand, in their wintry neighborhood. Engage in riotous snowball fights with their boys.

"Are we going or not?"

Memories flew in all directions at the impatience in Cameron's voice. She jerked her head up. Slapping the hat back up on the shelf, she shut the door. Hefting her bag in one hand and keys in the other, she remained silent as she followed Dak out the side door to the garage.

"Shotgun!"

Apparently unfazed by the mini power struggle between his mother and brother, Dak clambered into the front passenger seat of the Lincoln as Madison slid behind the wheel. The second he slammed the door shut, Cameron flung it open again his fingers gripped on the edge.

"I am *not* sitting in the back seat like some dipshit."

"Cameron, watch your mouth." Her reprimand was sharp.

"Let go! I was here first!" Screaming in a high-pitched protest, Dak hauled on the door to reclose it.

Using stiffened arms, Cameron worked his way in between the scant open space. "Get in back like the baby you are."

"M-o-o-o-m!" Dak tossed his head back to holler at the top of his lungs.

Madison grimaced as his ten-decibel yell pierced into her right eardrum. "Dak! I'm right next to you." Leaving the key in the ignition, she twisted in her seat. "Cameron. Dak called dibs."

"Did not!"

"Did too!"

Jerking the door this way and that between them, both boys continued their stand-off battle as if she hadn't said a word.

"I said get in back." Cameron's expression turned fierce.

"Let go!" The quiver in his voice confirmed Dak was losing ground.

"You let go." He gave the door a tremendous yank.

"No!" Hanging on for all he was worth, Dak nearly tumbled onto the concrete floor.

Madison grabbed a handful of his jacket. On a grunt of exertion, she hauled him back in.

"Boys! Stop! Now!" Her voice hit a decibel level to rival theirs. "I. Said. Now!"

Immediate silence followed. She released her death grip on Dak's coat. Slowly glancing from Dak's resolute stare to Cameron's indignant sneer, she set her face to no-nonsense stern. "That's better. Cameron, for now get in the back seat, please."

Staring daggers at his brother, he let go of the door

with one final jerk. "Forget it. I just won't go."

Madison was up and out of the car before he had the chance to take too many steps toward the back door. Catching up to him, she lunged forward to take a firm grip on his arm.

"Cameron." When he didn't answer, even though it took all her strength, she spun him around to face her. "You not going isn't an option."

A pained expression was the extent of his response.

Raising her chin, she managed to make and maintain eye contact. *He's going to be tall like his father.* The way he was growing, before long he'd tower over her.

Then what?

She released her grip on his arm and blinked. "We decided as a family to go out for pizza, and as a family, that's exactly what we're going to do."

Saying nothing, he kept his face in the ever-present pained stare.

One she accepted head on, more resolved than ever *not* to blink again. "I mean it, Cameron."

"Why should I?" He tensed his arms in challenge.

"Because I asked you to." Hoping he caught the nuance asked instead of told, she reached up to place a palm against his cheek. "No, scratch that. Let me try again. Because we're a family. You, your brother and me. Part of being a family is doing things together."

She lightly stroked smooth skin that would soon be rough with whiskers before dropping her hand. "I know you might not want to hear this right now, but Dak is nine. You're fifteen. It's as simple as that. You need to step up and help your brother because he's having a hard time figuring out how to cope with all the tragedy that has happened to our family."

For the first time in as long as she could remember, her oldest hauled in a breath with enough force to lift his shoulders. His lower lip edged out, and his eyes began to glisten as if he were ready to cry. Instead, he drew his lip back and held his chin tight to stop its quivering.

"And I haven't suffered?"

"That's not what I'm saying. Of course you have. But, being older, you have maybe had the chance to develop better coping skills." She did her best not to wince at butchering the idea she tried desperately to convey.

He blinked several times but remained silent. She could tell he wanted to keep his angry face in place, even as the hard edges around his eyes eased. The rigid set of his mouth loosened.

As her love for him swelled inside, no matter what, she smiled.

Bottom line, sweetheart, I need you to help me stay sane. "How about if I promise you can sit in the front seat on the way home?"

"Fine." He pushed out a huff.

"Thank you."

Shrugging, he walked toward the car, flung the back door open and climbed in. He shut the door behind him with such a force, the vehicle rocked.

Slow, measured breaths matched her slow, measured steps as Madison followed to resettle behind the wheel. All the while counting her blessings Cameron hadn't decided to bolt and stalk into the house. She never would have been strong enough to forcibly haul him back out again. *Was he aware of that, too?*

Thankfully, the rest of their trip to the local Pizza Palace went off without incident.

Surrounded by savory scents of tomato sauce, garlic bread and cheese, they were led to a booth toward the back. Both boys automatically settled into one side while Madison slid in to sit alone on the other.

"I'm starved." Bouncing in his seat, Dak started them off. "We definitely need a large."

"No, we definitely need two larges," Cameron countered. "With pepperoni."

"Lots of pepperoni," Dak agreed in a rush.

"And breadsticks."

"Cheese breadsticks."

Flipping their menus open, the two brothers proceeded to banter back and forth about suggested toppings, along with the merits of each, then moved on to discuss the pros and cons of thick crust versus thin.

Pleased with the newfound, if temporary, harmony between her sons, her spirits rose. Only to hit a downward snag when she inadvertently laid her hand on the vast empty space beside her. Before she knew it, memories drifted in, along with emotions strong enough to clog her throat. Pizza had been one of Dave's favorite foods. Especially when he shared it with their boys. She recalled how he took her out for pizza on their very first date. Big, gooey slices that required lots of napkins.

"You know you can be comfortable with someone when you eat messy, finger licking good pizza together." He'd made the comment as he wiped marinara sauce from her upper lip with the gentle touch of his finger. Then, eyes twinkling, he popped the

48

residue in his mouth and favored her with a playful grin complete with a flirtatious wink.

A smile bloomed as she sank back in her seat. And so began a love affair that lasted nearly fifteen years. *More than fifteen.* She made a quick correction. *Because I'm still in love with you to this day.*

Her chest grew heavy and her heart squeezed. At thoughts of what now could never be, her throat ached. A swallow of ice water helped ease the pain some. But not much.

As she set down her glass, their red headed waitress approached. "Welcome. What can I get you?"

"You boys decide." She pushed her closed menu aside.

Geared up for possible conflict, Madison was pleased when putting in their order went off without incident. Though she put her foot down when the boys wanted a pitcher of coke.

"You'll be up all night with that much caffeine. Tomorrow's a school day."

Half-hearted groans echoed back.

She glanced at the three tumblers of water on the table then up at their waitress. "How about we compromise? We'll get a pitcher for convenience, but limit to one glass each."

Dak's eyes took on a mischievous gleam. "Large glasses."

"Large glasses." Madison laughed her agreement.

"Anything else?" Red curls bounced as she scanned all three faces.

"That'll do it. Thank you." Collecting the menus, Madison handed them over as the two exchanged smiles.

"Coming right up."

Turning her attention back to her boys, Madison talked a little about what their plans should be for the upcoming Thanksgiving holiday. When their food arrived a short time later, Dak and Cameron eagerly dove in. Eating hers with a bit less gusto, she kept the conversation going with specific questions about school.

"You both like your teachers so far this year." She wiped her fingers on a napkin then took a sip of water. "That's good."

"Mr. Howard is so funny in science." Dak went on to describe a specific incident in which his teacher used common ingredients to make some pretty nasty sounding slime.

"Seems like he still has a little fifth-grader in him too." She spoke on a laugh, thankful Dak had a positive male role model in his life. "How about you, Cameron?"

"Old Man Conrad in biology sucks. Always throwing his weight around. Saying how all of his students better do exactly what he says or else."

A lot like Joe was with you. She again took refuge in a sip of water, making a mental note to check out this Conrad at the next scheduled conference.

"Someone needs to give him what he deserves." Cheese dripped from both sides of the next piece Cameron took from the pan. Setting it on his plate, he slid one finger across his throat.

"Do the other students feel like you do?"

"Some, maybe." Cameron rolled his eyes and shrugged. "I don't know."

Staring at her food, she wasn't sure what to say

next. This was so not what their battered family needed right now. Cameron having a difficult teacher. Along with all the other baggage that had been dumped on his young shoulders.

"You have to learn to get along with your teachers." As usual, where Cameron was concerned, the unfiltered comment couldn't have been more wrong.

His upper lip curled. "Yeah. I know. As far as you're concerned, it's somehow my fault."

"That's not what I'm saying."

"Sounded like it to me."

"I'm sorry that's what you heard. Some people are just hard to get along with." When he let out a heavy sigh, slumped back and looked away, she pressed on. "I'm sure you're doing your best with him. You're getting along well with the rest of your teachers, though. Right?"

"Yeah. Pretty much." He didn't bother to make eye contact. "I'm going to take a leak."

He was up and out of his seat before she had a chance to press for details. She absently reached for her water glass. *So what else was new?* When it came to relating to Cameron, Madison was better served to pick her battles. This latest being one of many more to come.

".... so can Liam stay overnight next weekend?"

Dak's eager voice broke into her thoughts, bringing with it a sharp pang of guilt. She hadn't meant to ignore him. But she had.

"I don't think we have anything going on." *Who am I kidding?* She was certain they didn't. She didn't anyway. Outside of the boys' activities, her social life was pretty much non-existent. "I'll have to check with his mother."

"I did." Dak beamed at having taken on the responsibility. "She said it was okay."

Good old on the ball Patty. "Then it's okay with me."

"Mom!"

Struck by the absolute zeal in Cameron's voice, Madison glanced up.

Boasting a huge smile, her oldest hurried to the table, walking side by side with Adam Pride. In all his movie star handsome glory. Or so she imagined. His features were mostly hidden by the baseball cap pulled way too low over his forehead. The Aviators were conspicuously in position. *Inside a dimly lit pizza joint of all things.* At least he was dressed casually enough. Stone washed jeans, well-worn in all the right places, was topped by a matching denim shirt open at the neck. Sleeves rolled up at the elbow revealed solid and nicely corded forearms. She took a breath as the sensory details piled on.

A dark blue, down vest completed the look.

"How cool is this?"

Her visual inventory slammed to a stop as her attention was drawn back to Cameron.

"Awesome!" Dak rubber necked to look behind him then climbed on to his knees to peer over the seat back. "Wow! It's you. Adam Pride!" Suddenly shy, he spun around and plopped down on his butt as Cameron and Adam stopped at their table.

"Guys." Adam spoke in a raspy whisper as he lowered onto the empty space beside her. "Keep it down a notch. Please."

Cameron returned to his seat as he and Dak complied without question. Mouths clamped shut and eyes becoming huge, they awaited further instruction.

"Okay." Cameron hunched toward him, his tone equally hushed. "But why?"

Adam touched the bill on his Tigers baseball cap. "Maybe it's wrong, but I'd rather not be recognized."

As if on cue, diners from a nearby table glanced over then quickly away. He kept his voice low, and the boys leaned in. Even Madison shifted slightly to press nearer. When she did, subtle musk and robust male drifted in to tease her senses. Heat from his closeness sent her internal temperature soaring. Even the air around them took on a taste all its own as she licked her lips then swallowed.

There was no denying the man sitting beside her—the extremely attractive and sexy man sitting beside her—occupied way more than his half of the cushioned booth they shared. And filled an emptiness she'd been painfully aware of since she and the boys first arrived.

"Where'd you find him?" Dak's mouth finally gaped open.

Cameron flashed a monumental grin. "He was standing next to me at the urinal and…"

"Cameron." Though she meant to hold on to a stern tone, Madison ended with a laugh. "I'm sure Mr. Pride doesn't appreciate you sharing something that personal with your mother."

"By the way. About that." Their guest put his arm along the back of the booth as he turned toward her. Taking the sunglasses off, he stuck them in his breast pocket.

Her cheeks burned as she faced him. "About what, Mr. Pride?"

"That. What you just said."

"What, I…?"

"My name." Stunning blue eyes caught her gaze and held tight. "My last name isn't Pride."

"It's not?"

"Nope. My real name, the one I was born with, is Hollingsworth. Pride is supposedly catchier." The warmth of his breath reached out to stroke her cheek. "I wanted to set you straight about my name the first time we met."

"Hollingsworth."

He smiled as she tried out his real name. When the corners of his eyes crinkled in a most appealing way, her heart somersaulted up to her throat.

"It's good I ran into you though." His glance moved from her to Cameron then back to her. "Because I was going to call you."

"Cool!" Cameron lit up as he leaned across the table.

"There's been no decision yet. But I didn't feel it was fair to keep you hanging."

"Oh." His face fell as he collapsed back.

"Take heart though. I should have news for you soon. Be aware, there's going to be a lot of paperwork for your Mom to fill out. Legalities for her to agree to. We have rules to follow when a minor works on a movie set."

Madison glanced at her son and cringed, fully expecting him to argue about being pegged a dreaded minor. Only to find, smile intact, he nodded agreeably.

"I can see that."

Her mouth dropped open at the foreign exchange.

"All that being said, I'll leave you three to finish your dinner. I didn't mean to intrude." He made a move to rise.

"You don't have to leave yet." Cameron reached across the table to grab his arm with a hand he just as quickly retracted. "Do you?"

"Yeah. Do you?" Dak chimed in.

Madison caught herself with a still opened mouth. *Prepared to add to their pleas?*

"Have some pizza, Adam." Cameron shoved over the half full pan.

"Yes. Adam. Please dig in." She was quick to second the invitation. "We have plenty."

"I had planned to pick up something to go." Even as he made a feeble protest, he accepted the spare plate she slid his way.

"Like Mom said. We have lots. It's not that good warmed up either."

Madison shot a surprised glance across the table at the sacrifice of her oldest. Leftover pizza was Cameron's all-time favorite meal. He'd eat it every single day if she allowed it.

"He's right." Quirking a brow at Cameron, she turned her attention toward Adam. "All this will just go to waste."

"Okay. If you insist."

He lifted a piece mounded with pepperoni off the tray he devoured as the boys chattered on about video games they liked and asked for his input. In between bites he obliged, then filled them in on his personal insight about some game just released. The man made incredible eye contact with her boys as he talked. Looked intently at first Cameron then Dak. Listened with interest to their responses. Judging by their rapt attention, her boys felt the connection too.

Adam wiped his hands on a napkin. "You guys are what? How old?"

"I'm in fifth grade. Almost middle school." Dak piped up first. "My brother is in tenth."

"A sophomore," Cameron refined.

Chewing the bite of pizza he'd taken, Adam swallowed. "Fifth and tenth, huh? Sounds about right. Your mother on the other hand, I'd probably mistake for your older sister. She doesn't look old enough to have two kids pushing toward adulthood." As he turned toward her, his gentle breath brushed over her face like the caress of a warm springtime breeze swept in to overtake the cold desolation of winter.

She hardly noticed when the waitress stopped by with a clean glass.

"Here you are, Mr. Pride." Judging by the sparkling eyes and wide smile, the woman was immensely impressed with the customer who had joined their table.

Adam covered the glass she was about to fill with coke. "Just water for me, please. I'm not a fan of too much pop."

"Of course. Whatever you say." Exchanging one pitcher for another, ice cubes tinkled as she filled his glass. Then she leaned down to make definite eye contact with him, complete with another high beam smile. "Can I get you anything else?"

"That's all I need right now." He returned a brief smile, but that was it, before he looked away. "Thanks."

"Can I get anything for anyone else?" Reluctantly drawing back, she took in the others.

"I'm fine for now. Thank you." Madison shook her head, not sure what to do with the look of pure envy sent her way.

A wide-eyed Cameron glanced up. "I'll take water."

Dak obediently pushed his glass forward. "Me, too."

"Sure, boys. Here you go."

Releasing a small smile, Madison counted her blessings for a second time that day.

Once their little group was again left alone, Adam nodded his thanks at another piece of pizza Madison put on his plate, then turned to her boys. "How's school going?"

"Cameron wants to kill one of his teachers." Excitement tinged his voice as Dak blurted the information.

Madison gasped. "Dak. That's not exactly what your brother said."

Adam zeroed his gaze on Cameron. "That's a pretty bold statement. What's going on to make you even talk about doing something like that?"

"Because sometimes I think he deserves it. He's a real jerk." Undeterred, Cameron went on, offering details to justify his blunt take on the situation.

Adam's brow creased as he listened in silence until Cameron finished. "Some people are just hard to get along with. But you can't let them get to you. Think of it as your job to get along with him. Turn it around. Become a model student. My guess is it'll drive him nuts, wondering what you might have up your sleeve."

"That could work." Once again, Cameron's eyes lit up as he nodded in agreement.

"Kill 'em with kindness." Adam flashed a smile as he leaned toward her son. "Seriously though, learning to deal with difficult people now will serve you well later in life. I promise."

Slowly, genuine realization dawned to spread across Cameron's face, and he nodded again. "That makes a lot of sense. I'll have to try it."

"I guarantee it will work. You can practice some of those acting skills you'll be able to put to good use. I could even help you with that."

Madison witnessed the exchange, riding a roller coaster of conflicted emotions. Though gratitude far outweighed any resentment. Cameron's unquestioning acceptance took care of that. Not to mention the unmistakable joy flowing through her at not being so alone.

At least he's paying attention to someone. A definite plus for her side. She couched a glanced at the noted *someone* beside her. Adam Pride. *No. Not Pride. Hollingsworth.* Adam Hollingsworth remained totally engaged with her son.

And yet, Madison reaped certain benefits as well. Moral support related to her sons chief among them. Without really knowing it, Adam provided exactly what *she* needed when those needs were the greatest.

What else could he fulfill for me? A few, less pure options came to mind. Her cheeks flushed and her body warmed at the possibilities.

Glancing her way, Adam smiled briefly then turned away to respond to something else Cameron said. Madison took advantage to quell her many uncalled for thoughts. What her boys required right now took precedence over some impossible fantasy that had their mother so foolishly engaged.

Except, the appeal of truly sharing even small parts

of her life with someone again refused to go away.

"…don't you think?"

Before she could banish yet another idle daydream, Adam once more glanced over. This time, he caught her staring. Incredible blue eyes took hold of hers. Plumbed their depths as if to seek out her most recent thoughts. A small smile curving his lips paired with the flash of recognition in a knowing gaze confirmed her secret was out. The private fantasy had somehow been revealed.

And he agreed wholeheartedly.

"Don't you think?" He spoke again, reminding her she had yet to respond.

As if to urge her on, a large hand covered hers. Bringing an incredible warmth to surge forth and spiral around inside her. He might just as well have reached over to haul her into a full out embrace. The heat spreading through her was that strong. That satisfying.

"Whatever will work best for Cameron." She salvaged enough of her floundering wits to put her son's best interests first.

His face once again lit with delight, to confirm her response was correct. A slight squeeze on the hand Adam still possessed supplied additional proof and she smiled too.

There was only one thing, if she was confused about her true motivations with this man before, she was downright discombobulated now. And loving each and every moment of it.

Especially the uncanny belief Adam seemed to bring out in all of them that, for now at least, when it came to their decimated little family, the future was going to turn out to be okay.

Chapter Four

"All right. The sun is with us for a change. Let's do this." Joel spoke into the bullhorn as he took his seat in the molded plastic chair mounted beside the huge production camera on wheels. "We'll start with the wide shot and go from there."

Various crew members hefted smaller cameras up to peer through their lenses.

Early afternoon clouds had cleared, allowing an elusive sun to emerge and provide just the right amount of light. Plus, their director finally had all the necessary angles blocked out. After more than a two hour delay, filming would begin again.

Standing in the main courtyard of the complex, Adam shook his arms to stay loose as he waited for his cue.

"And…Action!"

Head down, he took off. Sprinting to his mark on the pavement as tiny explosions to simulate gunfire erupted along his path. A hulking figure appeared on the fire escape above him. Pretend Glock in hand, he assumed a crouch position. Arms out straight and finger closing in on the trigger, taking aim, he unloaded a magazine full of blanks in rapid and deafening succession. The stunt man jerked and grimaced. Grabbing his gut where several paintballs burst blotches of red across his shirt, he fell, face-first into a pile of cardboard boxes off screen.

Jumping to his feet, Adam side-stepped, reloading as he went. *If only it was that easy in real life.* Another figure just like the first charged at him from the left. He ducked for cover behind a strategically placed trash can.

Ping! Ping! Ping!

More blanks dinged as they ricocheted off its surface. In the distance, an approaching siren blared and whined. Earsplitting wails rose higher then lower. Higher then lower. Tires screeched and squealed as the squad car careened to a stop amid the chaos. Rotating bubble lights illuminated red, white and blue flashes on the surrounding buildings. With one glance over his shoulder, Adam lunged forward.

This is it. Up and over. He psyched as best he could for the upcoming stunt. *Easy does it. Don't freeze.*

Arms slack, hands splayed out, knees flexed and ready, he tucked his head, pushed off…and prayed. Rolling up and over the hood as he'd rehearsed hundreds of times, still airborne, he shifted his limbs to draw them closer to his body. In the next split second, he cradled his head in both arms and held on tight.

Land shoulder, hip then leg. Evenly distribute the impact. The rubber mat designed to look like more pavement was coming up fast. He hit with a sickening whack.

Every scintilla of air whooshed out of him on one gigantic, *"Oooofff!"*

Damn! The impact was always way harder than expected.

"And cut!"

Joel's voice echoed through the bullhorn to filter into Adam's not yet completely focused brain. As crew members lowered their cameras and stunt men stood, he stayed put.

Not by choice.

By necessity.

Reality check!

Forget the powers attributed to fearless super cop Kyle Flynn in all the publicity material sent out in studio press releases. He, Adam Hollingsworth, was definitely flesh, blood…and mortal. Shoulder to toes, his body tingled from impact. If some part didn't hurt right now, there was a good chance it no longer functioned.

"Great job, Adam. You nailed it. Nice work, everyone. That's a wrap." More terse announcements from Joel vibrated in the air above him.

Fighting a monumental urge to curl into the fetal position, Adam eased on to his back.

"Perfectly executed. Just the way I taught you." The bearded face of his stunt mentor, Frank Hines, appeared above him. Distinctly outlined against a clear sky, and slowly coming into focus. "But, I say we do another take. Just for fun."

"Thought I just killed your ass a minute ago." Adam narrowed his eyes. His voice came out weak and strained. "How come you're not still down?"

A hearty laughed reverberated into the cosmos. "It's make believe, remember? We're all playing pretend."

"Oh, yeah. I forgot." He didn't share there was nothing make believe or pretend about the throbbing in his hip. *Probably went more airborne than I should have.*

Even as Adam struggled to draw his next breath, the man standing over him grinned.

"Only six takes and he calls a wrap. We all must be living right." Frank leaned in to offer a hand up.

He shook it off. "Give me a minute."

Holding in a groan, he rolled to one side. Seconds later, so as not to make a spectacle of himself, or worse, be branded a wuss by his more daring colleagues, Adam cautiously rose to his feet without help of any kind. Placing one foot in front of the other, he did his best not to hobble as he gingerly made his way to the folding chair with his name emblazoned across the back.

Lowering just as carefully to a sitting position, he rested back into the thick canvas. Frank and another stuntman, Rafe, the one Adam jumped over the patrol car to avoid, sat in similar, yet unmarked chairs, across from him.

"It's definitely getting colder around here. That mat I landed on was pretty darned stiff."

"Yet serviceable." Again Frank leaned toward him. "Our esteemed director has his eye on an Academy Award. He isn't about to suspend shooting just because of a little cold snap. He's having a hard enough time giving us all a few days off over Thanksgiving coming up."

"That's right." Adam flattened his lips and nodded. "I forgot all about that."

"Forgot?" Frank raised a brow but didn't press.

Adam reached for the unopened water bottle one of the crew had set there for him. After taking one substantial swig then a second, he set it back down as he slowly began to feel somewhat human again.

"We're going into town later for a couple of beers." Rafe leaned toward him this time. "Care to join us?"

Not quite that human. "Some other time." From his still seated position, Adam waved them off with a lifted left arm. *What do you know? That still worked as it was supposed to.*

"You sure? The Wrangler's Pub has line dancing tonight."

Now I know I'm not going. "Thanks. I'll pass." The idea of having to move his still tender limbs in any kind of regulated fashion for an undetermined amount of time made him absolutely shudder. Not that he'd let on to these guys. "I've gotta run some lines for tomorrow."

And rest my weary body while I do it.

A long soak in a muscle soothing hot tub would be ideal. Too bad, given the limited facilities of his eight foot by twenty-four foot trailer, he'd have to settle for the slightly cramped space of a stand-up shower. Hot, at least. Then a late lunch from the food truck. Chill in front of the boob tube for a while. Turn in early.

"You're missing out." Frank draped one arm over the backrest as he lounged in the chair. "Line dancing is a great way to meet the ladies."

"I'll meet the ladies on my own. Thanks." Adam took another long swallow of H2O.

Even if loneliness is one of the biggest downsides to working on location.

"Your call." Frank tried again as the two stuntmen stood.

"And I just made it. No woman for me tonight I'm afraid." *Not sure if, given the opportunity, I could even get it up anyway.*

"Suit yourself." With a loud snort, Rafe hitched up his jeans. "And here we were going to give you first pick of all the ladies that'll be swarming our way. Especially the blondes."

"My loss."

An image of dark curly hair and sparkling green eyes came to mind. Similar to other visions that had been popping in and out of his head on a pretty regular basis the past few days. Whether he wanted them to or not. Mostly not. A recent widow with two adolescent boys attached? No way, José.

As much as he'd love to have a family of his own, the key was he wanted his own. Not someone else's ready-made version.

"We're out of here to get ready."

"Good luck." Adam bid them goodbye with another hand wave, then closed his eyes. A few more minutes of much needed R and R and he'd get up and get moving. Tend to what he'd decided were *his* plans for the evening.

"Adam. I'm glad you're still here."

Both eyes popped open at the familiar feminine voice. "I was just about to leave."

Tina, the location's chief gopher and Jill of all trades stood over him. Hugging the ever-present clipboard she carried against a well-endowed chest. "Joel says he won't be ready for you again tomorrow until at least two o'clock. Maybe later than that."

"Got it. Thanks." He stood as he spoke, ignoring the flicker of discomfort that shot all the way from north to south. Yep. Hot water running over sore muscles was essential in his near future. "If anyone needs me before that, I'll be in my trailer."

Call him selfish, he turned away before she could engage him in some pointless conversation that inevitably ended with major hints from her to join him. Spend some alone time together. *Unless I manage to get away first.*

Light fingers placed on one arm momentarily stopped his progress. "I'll be off in another hour. Then maybe we could do something together."

Too sure where she was headed, he remained cordial. "Right now, I'm really tired."

Undeterred, she glanced up at him and licked her lips. "We could at least grab something to eat together. You still must eat. We both do."

I've told you before I'm not interested. He shook his head. "I'm pretty sore and tired right now. I just want to take it easy. Probably wouldn't be the best company."

"Let me know if you change your mind."

"You'll be the first." Making the promise with a manufactured smile, he made a hasty exit.

Not that he was averse to exploring the hookup she so temptingly dangled in front of him each and every day without fail. His reluctance to pursue anything even resembling romance was more for her sake than his. Why start something he wouldn't be around to finish? The second shooting wrapped up here in Colorado, and after two weeks doing close ups in LA, he'd be gone with the speed of those shots he'd fired earlier. Headed back to Detroit and his real job. The career that truly defined who he was.

Lost in thought, he made his way across a small patch of grass to the compound where the sleeping trailers were set up. And darned if an image of Madison Clark invaded his mind again. Giving up to indulge in the perfect daydream, with her as the main attraction, his foot landed on some kind of divot in the ground, and he stumbled.

Where that kind of thinking needs to remain. A plain and simple dream with no chance in hell of coming true.

He regained solid footing just as his cell sounded. Pulling it from his pants pocket, he checked the caller ID and smiled, then swiped to answer.

"Hey, Vince. How's it going?"

"Life is good. How about you?"

"Can't complain. It's great hearing from you."

As the first colleague Adam met when he enrolled in the police academy, he and this fellow officer at the Waterton PD had always been close.

"How's the movie business?"

"Honestly? Getting a little old. We should wrap up shooting here in the next several weeks, then a couple of more and I'm home."

"Well within your three-month leave-of-absence window."

"Oh yeah. Easily. Then I'm outa here."

Dark curls and green eyes again filtered into his mind as he walked along. This time complete with the flowery sweet scent she'd carried on her the other night. Way more mouth-watering to him than the competing smells of garlic and tomato sauce in that pizza place. Any idiot was aware it was bad form to hit on a woman in the parking lot following her late husband's memorial service. A few days later in a public place, in the company of her kids. Well, that was different. A lot different.

Right?

Not that hit on her was what he did. Exactly.

"Then you'll be back to work."

Adam came out of yet another musing. "To tell you the truth, I miss my real job."

"I hear you."

"Anything new in your life? Besides the woman you were lucky enough to hang on to after that undercover case?"

"Not much besides her. Except I made Captain."

"Hey, that's great. Congratulations."

"Yeah. Thanks. Sydney's pretty pleased I'm no longer on the road chasing taillights."

"That's good. When's the wedding?"

A low huff came first. "Your guess is as good as mine."

Adam chuckled. His friend did not do baffled well. The straight arrow of their group, Vince Miller had the answer to almost anything. Or at least a good idea where to go get it. Not this time, apparently. "So you're kinda just doing what you're told where that's concerned."

"Yeah. Something like that. And, to tell the truth, I don't mind a bit." His voice was forceful, despite the light-hearted topic.

"Must be nice." Adam surprised himself with the gravity of his reply but went with his gut anyway. "To have found someone to share your life with."

"You have no idea." Pride, even a little joy, colored his tone as he launched into a story about his new relationship.

Maybe not. But I'd sure like to find out. Adam kept

the unfiltered response to himself. He and Vince had discussed the numerous virtues of permanent female companionship before. And no doubt would again. Except not just now. No matter how sorely tempted he was to start that conversation for himself.

Madison Clark was easy enough on the eyes, but her appeal for him had to end there. His temporary residency rule applied here too.

Right?

It took a moment before he realized it was his turn to speak. "What else has been going on at the department since I've been away?"

"Funny you should ask."

A sudden turn to the solemn caught his attention. When Vince Miller turned serious, it paid to listen.

Adam quite walking. "You didn't just call to share the news of your promotion or shoot the breeze about Sydney. How did I know that?"

"The Hawthorn case is coming to trial."

"When exactly?" Stock still, he immediately stood straighter as the adrenaline started pumping. A road rage shooting that resulted in the death of an innocent child. A case he'd put his heart and soul into solving.

"Not sure about the timing. But Chief says the DA has a good shot at a conviction. Your testimony as first officer on scene will be crucial. When I have an exact date, I'll let you know."

"Thanks. I'll wait to hear from you. But I'll alert my director the next time I see him that I need some time off."

"Sounds good. I'll talk to you soon."

"Yeah. Soon."

The screen went dark. Returning the phone to his

pocket, he started walking again. Ignoring savory aromas from the food trailer he couldn't quite identify, he stepped up the steel stairs of his home away from home. The soles of his boots clanged to announce his arrival. Once inside, the brown leather couch beckoned. Taking up one entire wall in the living area, it could easily accommodate his six-foot three height. And quite comfortably. So comfortably in fact, he didn't dare get near it just now or he'd never want to get up. Same with the matching recliner in one corner. If it weren't still littered with his discarded clothes from a few days ago. The last time he'd climbed in here with only enough energy to head to bed. Stripping as he went.

He did pretty much the same now. His shirt came off first, he fisted in one hand. The snap at the top of his jeans opened easily and he moved to lower the zipper, anxious to get under the hot water spray he'd promised himself for the last hour or so. Then a thought occurred, and he stopped short.

First things first. Retrieving his phone from the front pocket, he quickly dialed Joel's number, then ended up leaving a voicemail about the needed time off.

Twenty minutes later, towel dried and hair combed, he pulled on clean briefs and jeans. Taking special care to ease both over the three-inch diameter bruise blossoming on his right hip. Just this side of his butt cheek, the injury showed real potential to turn from its current pastel purple hue to an ugly blue-black mass with yellow overtones.

Hazard of the job. With a shrug, he pulled on a worn Detroit Lions sweatshirt and left the trailer. Conversing with the culinary staff, he collected an amply filled plate at the food truck. His stomach rumbled at the tempting scents of baked chicken, savory dumplings and sweet, fragrant cooked carrots. Despite a chilling breeze, heat from his food conducted through the ceramic plate to burn his fingers. He readjusted his hold to grip the edges as he headed back home.

"Please. I need to talk with someone. It's important." The woman's voice sounded familiar and alarmed.

"Can't let you do that, ma'am. This is a closed set." That deeper voice Adam definitely recognized.

Bill Woodley, aka Woody, the security guard sent over from a local agency, stood his ground in front of said woman, blocking her from his view. A retired deputy sheriff from Denver, Woody took this job protecting their privacy from some loose cannon fan just as seriously as when he worked vice, putting dope smugglers and pimps behind bars.

"I need to talk to someone in charge." Undeterred, she tried again, stepping to one side. Directly into Adam's field of vision.

Madison!

He immediately set his plate down to walk over.

Keeping her gaze trained on Woody, she narrowed her eyes in much the same way she had when she first suspected he'd been complicit in her son's deception. He could only hope his fellow officer was up to countering a coming assault.

"I assure you, sir. I'm not some simple-minded groupie. I have no interest in seeking a glimpse of your so-called stars."

Ouch. Adam stutter stepped as his ego took the unflattering hit.

"This is the only entrance to the property. I understand you're looking for your son, but I swear I haven't seen him."

Son? Which son? Adam picked up his pace.

Still arguing, hands waving for emphasis, Madison peeked over Woody's shoulder and her gaze met his. Immediately, she moved toward him, only to be strong armed back.

"Let her go." Adam was on them in no time. His fingers clamped around the guard's beefy shoulder. "I got this. Thanks."

Woody turned around, saw it was him and immediately released her. "Sorry. This a friend of yours?"

Adam had yet to break eye contact with Madison. "Yeah."

"Okay then. If you got this, I'll finish my rounds. Call if you need anything." Tapping the radio on his belt, he strolled away without further comment.

"Thanks. I will." Adam briefly glanced over before he again keyed in on her. "What son's missing?"

"Cameron didn't come home from school today. Dak said he never saw him. When their bus arrived from the high school, he wasn't on it. I know it was because of our latest fight. I was hoping maybe he'd come here. To see you. He talks about you all the time." She was talking a mile a minute.

Adam was trying desperately to keep up. "Why? What happened?"

"Friday, he went out with friends. One of whom has a brand spanking new driver's license. I told him, I didn't care if the other kids had to be home at eleven, he had a ten o'clock curfew."

How did that go over? No need to ask. He could easily predict what happened. "He got home at eleven anyway."

"I should be so lucky." She ran a shaky hand through her hair. "No. He got home closer to midnight. Said he told Gil, the kid with the license, he could drop Cameron off last. It was no big deal. He made a point to tell me he lied to his friend, telling him his mother was one of the cool ones." Glancing up at him, she shook her head. "Cameron relayed the conversation, sarcasm included. Just before he went to his room and tried to slam the door. He didn't realize I was right behind him to prevent it. I told him from now on he was grounded from traveling in a car with friends and to take the bus home from school. It's obvious he didn't care enough to listen let alone obey me."

Tears of fear and frustration filled her voice by the time she took a breath.

"Parents disagree—" he was careful to not use the word 'fight' "—with their teenaged children all the time."

"Not my children. Not with me."

If you only knew some of the things I've witnessed. As a police officer, he'd seen it all. "It's kind of a rite of passage for both."

"I'll give him rite of passage." She drew in a breath she quickly heaved out again.

"Have you called the police?"

She shook her head. "I thought about it, but I'm sure they wouldn't do anything for at least twenty-four hours. Plus, he's probably somewhere with one of his buddies. Just to show me. Except, I called all his friends' parents I could think of this afternoon. Those I got a hold of said, though their kids were home, they hadn't seen him. I got answering machines for two of them. I can only hope the messages I left weren't too franticly rambling."

Chillier temperatures of late afternoon turned their breaths to billows of frost. Even though she wore a coat and scarf, as agitated as she was, every time she quit talking, she started trembling. Pale skin. Dilated pupils. Though he sure as hell wouldn't tell her, he didn't want to chance she'd go into shock. He put his arm around her shoulders. The best thing to do was get her warm and hydrated. Calmed down.

"Let's get out of the cold."

She didn't protest when he directed her toward his trailer, though she kept talking all the while. "My mother is with Dak right now. She flew here late Friday, arriving at our house by cab right in the middle of the huge fight Cameron and I were embroiled in. It's hard not knowing where he is. Having him not want to come home." Tears streamed down her cheeks, but she didn't seem to notice.

As their feet clanged up the steps, he opened the door. Ushering her inside, he eased her onto the couch and sat beside her, then got up to snatch a section of paper towel off the roll above the sink to hand her. The best he could do under the circumstances as his cop instincts took over. Not to mention that old innate male drive to fix things. Make them better. So long as he remembered to heed his academy training to keep from becoming personally involved.

"When did you see him last?"

"This morning." She dabbed at her eyes, then shuddered. "The boys were running late getting ready for school. Cameron especially. I started yelling at him to keep moving."

"How did he react?"

"His typical display of misguided anger. Stupid bus. Stupid school. Stupid, pick a noun, any noun. It was that kind of discussion." Fisting the crumbled paper towel, she dropped her gaze. "Like many Cameron and I share lately. Pointless and inflammatory."

"He's what, fifteen? Hormones are running pretty rampant at that age. Especially in guys."

"I had really hoped he'd come here. Sought you out, maybe. I hated to bother you." Her gaze returned to her hands, now clutched together as if in prayer. "I didn't know where else to go."

"I'm sorry I haven't seen him." He'd never spoken truer words in his entire life.

Tears glittered in the gaze that captured his. A few even spilled over to trail down slightly flushed cheeks. "When he's around you, rather every time you're around, he acts less defiant. But he's become really full of himself and harder to deal with since you brought up the idea he could be in a movie."

"I'm sorry about that, too." Guilt gnawed at him and the impulse to make things right for her flared again.

Her hair fell forward over her face as she nodded and glanced back down. A flyaway lock it would be so easy to push back into place. Caress her cheek with his palm. Provide the comfort he sensed she so desperately needed.

"So." Putting his hands on his knees to keep them occupied, he stood. And almost banged his head on the cupboards hanging over the couch. Ducking just in time, he turned to open the refrigerator and pull out a bottle of water. Twisting off the top, he handed that over too.

"I'm afraid he's getting his hopes up about something that may not come true."

Her doubt of his intentions rubbed him the wrong way. Hadn't she just come here seeking his help? He drew away from her. "I'm not in the habit of lying. Especially to children."

"I'm glad you see Cameron as a child. That's not exactly how he sees himself. He sees himself as an adult, capable of making all his own decisions." More tears brimmed in her eyes as she went on. "Like wanting to quit school to become an actor full time. Another of our infamous arguments that went nowhere."

Lips shut tight, she met his gaze as she finally quit speaking. Hopelessness crept into her eyes then spread across crest fallen features. Her lower lip began to tremble. His inborn compassion meter swung upwards in response. This woman needed to be held. It was that flat out simple.

Except, if he'd had misgivings about possibly taking advantage of a vulnerable woman in the aftermath of her husband's memorial, similar pangs of conscience were coming at him like gangbusters now. Sirens blaring and red flags waving furiously. Imploring him to resist. No matter how powerful the impulse.

Or tempting the prize.

"The decision of whether or not to hire him has taken longer than I expected. I'm sorry for that. Our cost-conscious producers are mulling over whether or not possible script changes will make it more efficient for us to finish that part of the movie when we're done here and back in LA." *Before I return to Detroit.* He winced as unexpected regret set in, but went on anyway. "It would be great if it all works out on our end and you agree to let Cameron take the role. It will give both of you a diversion from so much contention while still allowing you to do something together. The rules surrounding minors are pretty clear. A parent or guardian must be on set at all times when a child actor is working."

"The idea of doing something constructive with Cameron for a change would be nice." Blinking away her tears, she managed to smile. "That would certainly be doable. Aside from having some legal issues to deal with concerning my late husband's estate, my time is pretty much my own."

"Also, in keeping with the rules, any school he might miss because of the shooting schedule must be made up with the services of a tutor. At company expense, of course." He added the last with a wink, pleased and relieved when her hard fought for smile remained.

"That would also give Cameron a break from the teacher he has so much trouble with."

He opened his mouth to agree when her cell chimed.

Her smile dropped as she pulled it out. "Hello. What? He is?" Clutching the phone to her ear, she closed her eyes on a sigh. "Who? Caleb's mother sent him home?" She flicked a quick gaze up to Adam. "Where is Cameron now?" Her brows drew together as she listened. "Really? In the family room with Dak? Imagine that." Again her eyes flooded with tears. "If I were home, he'd be holed up in his room with his door bolted from the inside." She lowered her gaze and those tears spilled over onto her cheeks.

To go to her and wrap her in the comfort of his embrace seemed like the only logical next step. It took all he had to remain some distance beside her instead.

"Yes, it is that bad, Mother. You've only gotten small glimpses of what we've been going through since..." Her chin lowered as more tears fell. "For quite a while."

She grew silent again to listen, as a variety of emotions played over her face. Sadness and frustration changed to anger and resentment. With a definite touch of defiance thrown in at the end.

Then rebellion hit full force before she spoke. "We'll see about that. No. It's not you. Thank you for being there." Her face softened as she listened. "I'm nowhere in particular. I was all over the place looking for Cameron."

When she brought her gaze up to meet Adam's again, her eyes no longer glittered with tears, but teemed with determination. "Let me talk to Cameron. Please. Call him up from the family room." Her voice was tight to match her pinched features as she stared straight ahead while she waited. When she absently slipped off her coat, Adam was there to set it to one side. "Cameron, I told you to take the bus home after school. No exceptions." Beginning with a strong voice, her stern expression remained unchanged as she paused to listen. "An explanation? Of course. I'd like to hear it." As soon as she grew silent, her features relaxed.

"Mr. Rodriquez can verify this? Because I will be calling him." Pausing again, she drew down her mouth. Pain threatened to creep into her eyes she quickly blinked away in favor of resolve. "I do want to trust you, but sometimes you make it difficult for me to do that. No, Cameron, I don't think that's a good idea." Her shoulders slumped as if something had changed and she was about ready to give up the fight. "As a matter of fact, I'm with him right now. No. Not for that. I came here looking for you."

Determination re-entered her voice as she sat straighter. "We'll discuss that when I get home. No you can't talk to him. As your mother, I'll do the talking for you. Unless your behavior improves immediately, neither one of us will have reason to talk to him ever again." Her voice shook and she drew a quick breath.

Adam cringed, yet understood her need to step up and take a stand in confronting her son. Stay strong.

"No arguing. I mean it. I'll be home soon. We can talk then. Bye."

Madison dropped her phone to the cushion. From the stricken look on her face, Adam was afraid she was going to drop next.

He braced himself, ready to catch her if she collapsed. "Everything okay?"

"You could say that. As okay as it's going to be for now."

"I take it he had a reasonable explanation?"

"Depends on how you define reasonable." She took a long drink from the water bottle he'd given her. "A lost assignment. A teacher who had gone home early. A cell phone with no service. A perfect storm of circumstances that caused him to miss the bus and not be able to tell anyone. All situations the fault of someone else. Not his responsibility." She shook her head on a heavy sigh. "He caught a ride home with a friend. Rather their parent."

"He didn't break your rule of not traveling with a teen driver."

"Pretty much what he pointed out, too." Lowering her chin to her chest for a scant second, she raised her head to glance up at him again. "They were delayed because the parent had to pick up another sibling at practice somewhere. Cameron's home and he's fine. Mad as hell because I called around to some of his friends looking for him, but fine. Thank God."

He couldn't take it any longer. He had to do something to help her feel better. "Maybe he's angry now. But kids his age always get over it."

He had before, hadn't he? Most of the time anyway.

"One can only hope." Folding her hands around the paper towel she'd picked up again, she stared down at them. "Cameron's rebellion has been going on for quite some time now."

"It's also natural for teens to rebel."

"Especially since his father died." She went on as if he hadn't spoken. "His real father. Not Joe Clark."

"That's a lot for someone his age to deal with." He kept up the sympathetic tone.

"A lot for anyone at any age to deal with. That doesn't excuse his selfish behavior."

"No. It doesn't."

"And, right now, I'm mad as hell too." The tightness in her voice confirmed those words. "All I want to do is read him the royal riot act, then take him in my arms. Hug him and never let go. My mother is telling me I need to back off. Let things cool down without constant interference." When she looked up at him again, the pain in her eyes had been replaced by sparks of frustration.

He forged ahead anyway. "It might not be a bad idea. Terrible things, regrettable things can be spoken in anger."

"You're probably right about that. And she is too." Her gaze fell to her lap. A series of tear drops fell there soon after. Heaving a sigh so deep it shook her, she went on. "That's how pathetic I've become. Letting my mother take the lead in raising my child."

"Only temporarily." He stayed far, far away from the clichéd response, 'she did a pretty good job raising you.'

"And you, a virtual stranger, he listens to you." Catching a breath, she glanced over at him, her cheeks and forehead flushed a deep pink before she looked away. "I just have no idea what's the right thing to do anymore. Lately my life has been such a nightmare." This time when she looked down, she covered her face with both hands. Soon, her shoulders began to quake, and soft sobs came out from between her palms.

"Hey. Come on now." Not knowing what else to do, he wrapped her in his arms.

She burrowed close and clung to him as more sobs, harder sobs wracked out of her. "Two husbands dead in a short amount of time. Left with two children to raise, one of whom wants nothing to do with me anymore."

"You know that last part isn't true."

"Do I?" She raised a tearful gaze to meet his. "Everything I try to do to make things at least seem normal again fail. It's all such a waste."

"You're not a failure. And your life isn't a waste. Not by any means. You're a kind and wonderful woman, Madison Clark." Even though he didn't really know that for sure, given his ability as decent judge of character, the list of assurances came naturally to him. "You are intelligent. Giving. Devoted to your children." Backing away enough to take her face in his hands, he stared into her eyes. "I could never lie to you about that."

The faintest glimmer of hope flickered in their depths. Her cheeks glistened where more tears lingered. "If only I could believe that."

"Believe it. Because it's true." He drew her closer, rested his chin on the top of her head and rocked her. Held her tight as a heat seeped into him like none he'd ever felt before.

Too soon, she pulled away to look up at him. "I just wish with all my heart things could be, if not normal, at least somewhat sane for us once again."

"It will be some day. I promise." Capturing her gaze, he whispered the response.

"If only that were true." A small smile crept across her lips. "But thank you for trying to convince me. Whether you meant to or not, you've provided exactly what I needed, precisely when I needed it."

Before he could answer, her mouth touched his, giving Adam no choice but to accept and respond. Her skin was soft. Smooth. Her lips too. Warm. Tender. Flawless. Everything he expected them to be.

Not only that, she was everything he'd imagined her to be. And more. So much more. Until he was lost, hopelessly lost, in all things Madison Clark.

Human nature took over from there.

Kissing. Touching. Embracing. Savoring. In a short amount of time, they experienced it all. Together. Offering and accepting. Giving and taking.

Leather gave a delicate rustle when they slid as one to lie side by side on the couch. Spanning the length of her to share his warmth, he cradled her face in his palms. All the while, his mouth was covering hers again. Tasting. Loving. Yearning.

Clothes soon became nothing more than a minor inconvenience between them to be hastily removed and discarded. Arms circling bodies, they came together once again. Perfectly. Eagerly.

As if in a painstakingly choreographed scene from his movie, Adam rolled Madison to her back beneath him, then wrapped her softness up hard against him and simply held on tight. All the while sprinkling kisses on her forehead, her nose, her cheeks. Here and there along the flawless expanse of her throat.

"You're a kind and loving individual. Important to your boys. Your life is valuable and so are you."

His words were no more than murmurs against her cheek. Her earlobe. Her throat as he tasted the sweetness of her skin while rising above her.

When he joined them as one, her response was immediate and strong.

Her eyes closed as her lips parted to release her breath in tiny gasps as skin slid against skin. Consumed by sensation and driven by need, from somewhere deep inside, near his soul, desire swelled forth until it blocked out all things sane. Everything he'd known to be rooted in reality such a short time ago. Until he was forever lost.

And blissfully so.

Afterwards, breathing in rasps, they clung to each other in a tangled embrace. For how long, Adam had no clue. The only thing he knew for sure was his life had just been eternally altered.

Never to be the same again.

Chapter Five

Madison held the steering wheel in a white-knuckled grip as she navigated out of the Concord Estate property. Icy cold seeped into her palms. *Why not?* That's what happened when you left your car to sit out in chilling temperatures for a few hours.

Was I with Adam that long?

Enough time for daylight to turn to dusk.

Long shadows crept over the pavement in front of her. What had been a clear, blue sky when she arrived, was now streaked with amber that blended into the deep pink streams of another sunset.

Stopped at the main exit, she glanced in the rear-view mirror to get her bearings. Wide and wary eyes stared back at her. Or was terror-filled a more fitting depiction?

Breathing in anxious spurts, each exhale came out as a misty puff in the frigid interior. *Again, why not?* Once she came to her senses, stood then awkwardly dressed, in her haste to leave, she hadn't dared linger long enough to let the car warm up. Especially after Adam walked her out and opened the door for her. Both hands shook as she navigated out onto the two lane highway. Immediately stopped at the blinking traffic light above Fall River Road, she chanced another glance in the mirror. The panic so blatantly evident in her eyes was put there for good reason. The unnerving result of what she'd just done.

That can never be undone.

For the absolute very first time in her life, she'd slept with someone she hardly knew. Willingly. Wantonly.

Despite the cold, heat sizzled from the top of her head to the tips of her toes as she relived the delicious sensation of clinging to the sheer strength in Adam's body. Its warmth and power overtaking hers. The sweet pleasures of their kisses. The unrelenting joy of…

"You have an incoming call."

The voice of her car's computer came at her from the dashboard. On a sharp intake of breath, she jumped, then pressed a button on the center of her steering wheel to answer.

"We were wondering what was taking you so long."

Though her mother certainly couldn't see her, Madison's cheeks flamed. Shame was a powerful emotion. Once embedded, nearly impossible to ignore.

"I needed some time to pull myself together. I was a complete wreck. I was so desperate to find Cameron."

"Now why doesn't that surprise me? You are such a good mother. Always looking out for your boys. Putting them first."

At the familiar tone of pride from *her* mother, humiliation reared up large and ugly. *If only that were true at all times. No exceptions.*

Cruising along the highway, she didn't need to see herself in the mirror this time. There was no doubt whatsoever unbridled proof of tremendous remorse climbed up from deep inside to spread across her features like a firestorm. Paralyzing her so she couldn't respond.

"What time do you think you'll be home?"

Home. Her guilt riddled state of mind set her stomach to churning.

"Madison?"

"Yeah, Mom." She cleared her throat as tears threatened.

"When will you get here? The roast I put in the crock pot this morning is done. Much longer on warm and it will be overdone."

More guilt to deal with. "You and the boys go ahead and eat. Don't wait for me."

"No. We'll wait for you. It sounds like you're in the car. I assume you're on your way?"

"Yes. I should be there in about twenty minutes. I'll see you then." Unable to take the ungodly stress of communicating any longer, she pressed the disconnect button, also on the center of the steering wheel. Then gripped her hands tight at ten and two on its top.

"Call ended." Her car's onboard computer announced the obvious.

Madison lowered hunched shoulders. "Aggghh! Why did that have to happen?"

Her voice echoed back at her as more reminders of Adam came to mind. Solid arms taking hold of her in comfort. Verbal reassurances, recounting her value as a person.

Warm. Caring. Supportive. Affirming. All leading to something they never should have done. No matter how perfect things *seemed* to be between them at the time.

Consumed by regret, the sudden whoosh of air blowing into the vehicle took a moment to register.

Heat poured full blast from the vents on the floor and dash. Her breaths were no longer turning to frost. She flexed her fingers on the steering wheel. Even her hands were warming up.

Maybe, just maybe things would turn out okay.

Convincing herself she was happy to be going home, she focused on the road ahead. Flat. Straight. Stable. Predictable.

Headlights flared in the rear-view mirror. Coming up fast. Nearly blinded, she averted her gaze then blinked several times. With a hand up to shade her eyes, she checked the speedometer.

Was I so preoccupied I've become a road hazard?

Fifty-five, pushing sixty. More than fast enough for this stretch of secondary highway in the mountains at twilight. With her gaze fixated out the windshield, intense yellow light filled her mirror again. Harsh, glowing golden spots burned into her retinas.

The vehicle behind was close. Too close. The interior of her car lit up like a sunshine filled day. She tightened her hold on the wheel, not daring to turn around and look behind her. High beams flashed up to fill the side mirror as well, making it nearly impossible to avoid more glare and see in front of her.

"Pass me then, asshole. Pass me." Without thinking, she stared into the rear-view mirror again as if to actually confront the jerk tailing her.

Contemplating the wisdom of pulling over to the side of the road, she stepped on the gas instead. The unrelenting shine of those lights stayed in place. Chills tripped up her spine as panic rushed in to replace annoyance and anger. Hands still clutched at ten and two, tires squealed as she negotiated a tricky turn.

"Pass me, damn it!"

What the hell is this idiot's problem? Her fingers ached, and her eyes watered as she held her ground. Road rage happened all the time, but she never expected to be caught up in it.

A vehicle coming the other way flashed its lights several times. The interior of her car blessedly returned to shadows. Headlights that had seemed to be attached to her back bumper veered off and disappeared. She loosened her death grip on the steering wheel and let up on the gas. Short gasps for air eased to a steadier, more normal, tempo, and her tensed body went slack.

"Good riddance."

Navigating the rest of her short trip without incident, Madison made it up her driveway within the promised time frame and pressed her foot on the brake. There was only one thing to do now. Despite what she and Adam had discussed before…

Letting out a sigh, she shook her head.

Avoid. Avoid. Avoid. She simply had to avoid anything to do with Adam *Pride* and his collection of movie people at all costs.

The man had indicated his colleagues weren't keen on the idea of using Cameron anyway. *Hadn't he?*

Taking a deep breath, she hit the garage door remote on the visor, drove inside when the door opened and turned off the engine. Then did nothing more strenuous than to sit still and simply breathe. Gather her flyaway thoughts. Compose herself for the immediate future. It was more than a few moments before, reluctantly, she was able to collect her purse, get out and shut the car door.

I can do this. But only with a certain amount of

help. *From myself, and no one else.*

Drawing on a much disparaged inner strength, brick by brick, she constructed a wall of resolve so high and thick, she couldn't see any problems beyond it. She was perfectly capable to bring a sense of normalcy to her life...their lives...again. On her own, with no help whatsoever from one Adam Pride.

Honestly, she really could...do...this. Return all things in her life to normal.

Except, the second she walked across the threshold and into the house, what she perceived as *normal* came to a screeching halt. For the first time in a very, very long time, as she entered the kitchen, Cameron met her at the door.

"What did Adam say? Did I get the job? Did he say what kinds of things I'd be doing? Stunts I hope."

Of course his intention was never to greet me. "Nothing's been decided yet. Adam's...the people he works for are still considering whether or not to hire you." The response came out quick. Followed by totally different thoughts better left alone. The earnest touch of Adam's lips. Strong arms surrounding her, pulling her close. Murmurs citing her value as a person...a woman who...

"Did you explain to him how much I wanted this?" Her son's voice was sharp, accusing even, as if she'd somehow already failed him.

No more than I failed myself.

"Did you?"

She pushed away her guilt, leaving the brick wall and its foundation intact. "I'm sure he's aware how much you want this. But, as I told you on the phone, unless your behavior changes dramatically, whether they want you or not is a moot point."

"Everyone at school already knows about Adam's offer. If I don't get the part, I'll look like a dipshit."

"Please don't talk that way. Maybe it wasn't the best idea to spread the word about something that's not yet a done deal." She reached out to touch his arm. "It's not like you."

"I didn't say anything. Phil did."

Phil again! Dammit. She pried open suddenly gritted teeth. "What did he do now?"

"Only blabbed it everywhere." He shoved both hands in the pockets of his jeans. "Did everything but send it over the PA system."

A fissure inched its way into Madison's blockade of resolve to keep her son, and herself, away from anything to do with the movie production in town. And, especially, Adam Pride.

"Chad Horvath said no way. Said he didn't even believe I'd met Adam in person."

"He did, did he?" She knew the name well. Both from Cameron and some of his teachers. A senior. Captain of the wrestling team who liked to throw his weight around even if he wasn't on the mat.

A larger crack formed in the mortar holding her wall together.

"He announced to anyone who would listen he's taking bets I won't get the job. That Phil and I made the whole thing up." Any confidence present in his voice when she first came in had long ago fallen away. Shoulders slumped, he lowered his head. "I was hoping I could go to school tomorrow and tell him and everyone else where to go."

Desolation settled in eyes that lifted to meet hers.

A wavering heart twisted as what remained of her cement citadel came crashing down. To send dust and debris spewing in all directions.

"I'm sure they'll call and let you know when they make a decision." *Because Lord knows any decision has now been taken out of my hands.*

The kitchen door from the dining room swung open with a bang. "I don't know where that mother of yours has gotten herself off to." Wiping her hands on a bright red apron, *her* mother's voice rose in volume as she walked closer. "Oh you're here." She didn't quit talking until she stopped, toe to toe with Madison. "When did you get home?"

"A few minutes ago. I've been talking to Cameron."

"Have you?" She glanced over at her oldest grandson. "He's been on pins and needles since you told us where you were. What did they say about hiring our own little star here?"

Here we go again. Though the weight of the world bore down on her, Madison refused to let *her* shoulders slump even one iota. Proud Grandma didn't give her a chance to even open her mouth. Let alone speak up, as she rambled on and on.

"I'm assuming a resounding yes, bring him on." Grinning ear to ear, she beamed at Cameron again. "Who could turn down that beautiful face?"

When she reached over to pat his cheek as only a proud grandma can, Cameron didn't back away in horror. In fact, he even let go of a sheepish smile as a light flush of crimson crept up from his neck to spread across those cheeks, turning them rosy red.

"Thanks, Grandma."

"They haven't made a decision yet. As I told Cameron."

When Madison spoke, her mother looked back her way. Then darned near did a double take as she stepped closer. "What in the world happened to you?"

"Me?" Guilt-ridden daughter immediately emerged, all too aware the blood drained momentarily from her face, only to rush back up again. Heart thumping, she matched her mother gaze for gaze, even as her cheeks once again grew blazing hot. "What about me?"

"You look a little…" She tipped her head slightly right, slightly left. All the better to scrutinize her errant offspring with *the look*. The piercing stare that declared *I don't know it all now, but I will soon enough.* One brow lowering, she pursed her lips. "…a little off."

"Off?" Though Madison was smart enough to not break eye contact, she did close her mouth and swallow.

"Yes. Off. Your cheeks are flushed."

Let the game begin.

An expert of observation when it came to her only daughter, Kay Carmichael could spot something amiss in Madison at the cellular level.

The back of her mother's hand pressed against her forehead with its all too familiar gentleness. "You don't seem to have a fever. Are you feeling okay?"

And so the spell was thankfully broken. "I feel fine, Mother."

"As I said, you look a little flushed."

Great sex will do that to a person.

Quick to bury the wayward thought, Madison sidestepped to unbutton her double-breasted pea coat.

"Because I've been standing inside to converse with my son, still wearing all this." She moved farther away as she shed the cold weather gear. Removed the scarf from around her neck. "I was so interested in our conversation."

She glanced at Cameron with a weak smile just before she turned to hang her things on one of the hooks by the door. Adjusting her cowl necked sweater and yoga pants before she turned, Madison became painfully aware she now had her panties on backwards. *That's what happens when you climb into them on the fly.*

She ran damp palms along her hips before heading to the dining room. "Let's eat. I'm starved."

Blessedly, dinner went off without a hitch, where Madison miraculously avoided being grilled by her mother. Said miracle took the form of Dak and his incessant jabber, bless his heart, about some quirky substitute teacher he'd had that day at school.

"He has this puppet he holds who talks."

"A puppet who talks?" Kay's brow creased. "You mean like a ventriloquist?"

Dak stared at her. "A what?"

"Someone who projects their voice without moving their lips, so it seems to come from somewhere else."

"Yeah. I guess that's what he did. His puppet told some funny jokes." He smiled before speaking again. "Why didn't the two fours want dinner?"

Madison and her mother shook their heads.

"Tell us why," his grandma said.

Dak's eyes twinkled. "Because they already eight. Why was the math book sad?"

More head shakes came from his elders.

"It had too many problems."

Kay threw her head back to join her grandson in raucous laughter. "That guy sounds like he missed his calling. He should take his act on the road. Don't you think, Madison?"

Still plagued by worry, Madison joined in with the biggest laugh she could muster. Which wasn't much. "I'm glad you enjoyed your day, Dak."

"He's going to be in our class all week, and…"

Only half listening, Madison's thoughts took her back to earlier that afternoon.

"Mom." Dak looked over at her, eyes still shining, and grinned. "What did one toilet say to the other one?"

Blinking back to the present, she smiled at his joy. "I don't know. What?"

The grin widened. "I'm flushed."

As the jokes went on, even Cameron joined in. "Knock knock."

"Who's there?" Leaning forward, Dak bit.

"Dots."

"Dots who?"

"Dots for me to know and you to find out."

Dak chuckled as, clearly, his enthusiasm grew. "Knock knock."

"Who's there?" The three others answered in unison.

"Alice."

"Alice who?"

"Alice fair in love and war." The phone ringing in the other room coincided with his latest chortle. "Except I'm not sure what that one means."

"Grandma can help you with that." Setting her napkin on the table, Madison rose.

"Okay, Grandma. What does it mean?"

Madison didn't hear exactly what her mother said. Only the pleasant echo of her youngest's laughter followed her into the living room, and she found herself grinning.

She was still smiling by the time she walked to the desk in one corner and picked up. "Hello."

"Madison? It's Adam."

Her grip tightened on the receiver as the smile collapsed. *So soon?* Her emotions were too rocky. Too up and down unstable. The memories of his touch too real and vivid to be forgotten. Closing her eyes, she focused to banish all but necessary thoughts. *I can do this.*

"Hello, Adam." A satisfying sense of cool detachment tinted her tone. Score one for her.

"I hope I'm not interrupting anything."

Great! He's being polite. "We were just finishing dinner."

"I can let you go if you want to get back to it."

The needle on her hard ass resolve meter wavered then dipped a point or two and she opened her eyes. "No. That's okay. What do you need?"

"Nothing in particular. No. Scratch that." Dead air came out next as she waited. "I needed to talk to you. To make sure you're all right."

"Of course I'm all right. Why wouldn't I be?" She shook her head at her own stupidity. *Seriously?* There were thousands of reasons.

"Good. I'm glad to hear that."

A tremor in his voice suggested he doubted she was being totally above board. In fact, she could envision his brow arched in skepticism, his eyes narrowed in doubt.

"I'm sorry for what happened today." She had to be the one to speak up first.

"I am too."

If she was less than truthful with him, she could at least be honest with herself.

I'm sorry for the emotional meltdown you were forced to witness. For the weakness in me that led to it in the first place. For the mess I've let my life become. Sorry for more reasons too numerous to go into here. But not for allowing you to make love to me. Helping me feel alive and vital and wanted. Desired.

"Madison?"

His voice brought her careening back to the here and now. "Yes?"

"I just wanted you to know...um...about today."

Tensed fingers curled around the phone. "I'm not in the habit of doing that."

"That's never happened before."

Each blurted nearly identical excuses at nearly the same time.

After a nervous laugh, Adam let out a sigh. "Ladies first."

Thanks a lot. Unsure what to say next, two distinctly different responses came to mind. *I really don't sleep around you know. That sex we shared was amazing.* Neither truly appropriate. "I've been under...things have been very difficult lately for me." Though she held tight to the receiver, her stomach flipped then flopped.

"That would be an understatement if you asked me." The steady calm of his voice, more a caress than anything else, found its way inside her to spread its warmth. "You've been through more in a short amount of time than most people could handle over a long haul."

How sweet. All she wanted to do was accept the comfort he offered. Let it flow in and melt some of the ice from around her heart. Heal the sore and gaping wounds life had so cruelly inflicted. *But can I? Really?*

Straightening, she found her voice. "While I appreciate your understanding, that's no excuse for what I did."

"What we did. Takes two, as you know."

He was assuming full responsibility for his actions. Unfortunately, such apparent nobleness from him made retaining disinterest more difficult for her. "Regardless, jumping in bed with the first warm body I come to is not what…is really quite unforgivable."

"That may be your take on it. It's not necessarily mine."

Talk about saying all the right things. Not exactly helping her original case for cool detachment.

"No?" The single word left her lips before she could stop it.

"No." When she said nothing more, he went on. "It may be hard for you to believe this, but I don't make it a practice to sleep with women I barely know either."

"I never, ever really thought you did. I'm just saying…um…from my perspective…" She cleared her throat and kept right on going. "There were definite reasons…emotional reasons…why I did what I did."

"And you assume my reasons weren't anything beyond pure animal instinct." His tone had gained a definite bite. "It may be a little accepted fact, but some guys have feelings too."

"That's not what I'm saying at all."

"Sounded like it to me." He wasn't going to let her off the hook so easily.

"Okay." She took a breath and went on. "What emotion were you feeling today?"

"Loneliness." His answer was swift.

"I…ah…" Caught off guard, she verbally stumbled. "And I was beside myself with worry then flooded with relief. Feeling worthless and ineffective."

"Sufficient emotions to justify doing what we did."

"Possibly." Her response was no more than a whisper.

What they'd done was serious, but not life altering. People had one night stands all the time that never led to anything long lasting. Why would things be different for her? Or Adam?

"Madison? You still there?"

"Yes." Another breathless response.

"Just wondered."

"The fact remains, it's unusual…no make that unheard of, for me to become intimate with someone so quickly whom I've just met." Heat rose up her neck.

"Fact is, we can't undo what happened. Nor can we forget."

Her eyes closed. *Nor can we forget.*

Or want to.

When she didn't respond, he went on again. "Nor should we have to. It doesn't mean we can't go on with our respective lives. Maybe even be friends."

"Cameron idolizes you. He'd be devastated at not being able to see you again. Dak too." Desperation leaked into her voice, and she shut her mouth. *As would I.*

"Why would they have to never see me again?" The compassion in his voice was nearly her undoing.

"Because." She couldn't allow her single word to hang in the air between them but wasn't sure how to finish. "Because, it would be…"

"…uncomfortable for you?"

When words failed her at first, she nodded. "Yes."

"I am sorry for that. In more ways than you may realize."

"What if Cameron, or Dak, found out about…"

"…us?"

"Uh-huh." She seemed capable of only simple, breathy replies.

"As far as I'm concerned, there's no way anyone would. First of all, we are two consenting adults with a right to privacy. Second, and most important…" He lowered his voice, and her heartbeat picked up in response. "I consider some things to be sacred."

The sweetness of his words took her breath away. She fought hard to pretend they didn't.

Two husbands gone within a few years of each other. It seemed rather callous to drag someone else into her Black Widow lair. Come to think of it, she wasn't all that familiar with Black Widows in the wild. Was the deadly species promiscuous by design, character flaw, or both?

"This is our secret." Again he spoke when she remained silent.

"Just ours." Again she nodded her agreement.

Her cool detachment was in danger of heating up. She struggled to pretend that wasn't happening either.

"I just wanted to make sure you were all right."

Adam's caring tone, along with his equally caring

message didn't make her the least bit uncomfortable. In fact, the exact opposite was proving to be true with this stranger who had so easily become a friend. And only a friend. Because this certainly wasn't the time to become involved in another relationship.

Not to mention she had her boys to think about. "I am."

"Good. Now that that's settled, another thing I called about was to tell you Cameron got the job."

"He did?" She nearly lost her grip on the phone as elation for her son turned quickly to dread for her. "That's wonderful news...for Cameron. I'll let him know as soon as we're finished here."

Call it a cruel twist of fate. For the next few weeks, she'd be contractually obligated to be in the man's presence. On a more or less routine basis. Unfortunately, this was one parental duty her mother couldn't fill in for her.

"Joel, our director, came by to tell me after...shortly after you left."

"That was considerate of him." She fought to drag back some recently departed cool detachment. Shaking her head, she cleared her thoughts. "When does he start? Cameron will want to know, I'm sure."

"Not for a few days, I'm afraid."

She strained to detect disappointment in his tone. *To match mine?* "Oh."

"Tell Cameron I said to break a leg." He chuckled after he spoke. "Explain to him that's an actor to actor pep talk."

"I will."

"We'll be in touch." While he took a breath, she waited. "Good-bye, Madison."

"Good-bye, Adam. Thanks for calling."

She was pretty sure her response went nowhere as the double beep of his disconnect came back at her. Releasing a sigh, she replaced the receiver and headed for the dining room to tell her family the good news.

Chapter Six

"Good. You're early." Joel glanced up as Adam walked onto the soundstage.

Technically the upstairs main ball room of the mansion their company had converted for that purpose where they filmed close-ups and some more intricate hand to hand combat scenes. Joel liked it because floor to ceiling windows on all four walls allowed occupants to see anyone approaching from anywhere. Friend or foe, as the crew often joked. Even so, with its cathedral ceiling, the space had surprisingly good acoustics. The area was never without activity, and today was no exception. A few crew members staged a section in one corner for an upcoming scene, as cameramen and other technicians blocked out appropriate angles. Across the room, a huge conference table ringed with high backed chairs, where Joel sat now, could easily accommodate basic rehearsals and table reads of upcoming scenes, along with cast and production meetings.

"When the director calls you in, it's a good idea to be on time." Adam took a seat at the table across from him. Ready to discuss the time off he'd asked for. That had to be why Joel wanted to see him. "So what did you need? But make it fast. I'm set to meet Frank in the workout room. He wants to go over choreography for a fight scene Rafe and I have coming up."

"You might have to cancel. Or at least postpone."

Joel didn't bother to look up from whatever was in front of him he studied with deep concentration. "Better yet, I'll have Tina let them know you aren't going to be available at all today."

"I'm not?" Adam held in a sigh of frustration as he lowered his head to try to look Joel in the eye. Talented as he was as a director, the man had a penchant for changing things after the day-to-day calendar was set up and distributed. "Why's that? According to today's shooting schedule, the stunt guys and I have some free time this afternoon."

"Not anymore." A wide grin spread across his boyish, freckled face when Joel finally did glance up. "This Cameron kid we hired. He and his mother are coming here today so you can do a table read of one of your more dramatic father-son scenes. I want to get a feel for his acting abilities before Thanksgiving break."

"Madison. His mother's name's Madison." Adam made the clarification first, protested next. "That wasn't an item on the daily list I was given this morning."

"That's because I put it on after they went out."

Adam clamped his teeth together to keep from saying something he shouldn't. What Joel termed his enthusiasm for their project, Adam and some of the others saw as micromanaging his crew's schedules to suit his personal preferences. Not only that. Adam wasn't sure he was ready to face the woman he'd made love to a week ago today.

And hadn't been able to stop thinking about since.

"Man. This is really something." He looked down at what Adam now recognized as a picture of someone.

"What's really something?" Sitting forward, he craned his neck to get a better view of whatever had his director so fired up.

"This." As he held up the sheet, Adam found himself face to face with an eight by ten image of Cameron. "Where'd you get that?"

Still grinning, Joel brought the paper down to look at it again. "I had Tina print me a copy from that cell phone shot of him his mother emailed."

"Oh."

Brow furrowed and lips pursed, Joel laid the photo out flat on the table to pour over again. "I tell you, it's uncanny how much this kid looks like you." His gaze flicked from Adam to the picture then back again. "If I didn't know better, I'd say he was your flesh and blood son."

"Yeah. I know." Adam hesitated, his tone low. At last forced to openly acknowledge what he'd recognized the first time he and Cameron met.

"We couldn't have gotten a more perfect match." He glanced down again and tapped Cameron's photo with the tip of one finger. "If we'd sent out a casting call nationwide."

Though at first reluctant to hire an unknown, now that the decision had been made by the higher ups to use Cameron in the role, Joel was apparently all for it.

"Sure was lucky." Adam levered out of the chair and came around to stand beside him.

"Yeah. Luck." Glancing between the photo and the real thing then back, his gaze finally settled on Adam as he leaned back in his chair. "You sure maybe you didn't have a one-night stand with this kid's mom a while back?"

"I'm sure." Adam glanced away. When it came to Madison Clark, one-night stand didn't seem to sit quite right. At least for him.

"I lost you there for a minute." Joel's voice yanked Adam out of his thoughts.

"I was just…" It took a millisecond before he blinked and lifted his head.

"Trying to remember if maybe you did?" Joel chuckled.

Trying to remember? Ha! How about trying to forget?

"What's so interesting?" Tina suddenly appeared beside him, a small stack of notebooks held in tightly front of her.

"This kid we hired to play Flynn's son." Joel held the picture out so she could see. "Uncanny resemblance. Don't you think?"

"Maybe." Glancing at the portrait, she followed up with a shrug. "I brought the script sections you wanted."

"Great." He took the one she offered. "Thanks. Pass them out when everyone gets here, if you would please."

"Sure. Starting with Adam, I assume."

Accepting the copy Tina handed him, Adam took his time returning to his chair. Once seated, he thumbed through the pages. "Which scene are we doing?"

"The flashback scene. Where you and your son have an actual conversation." Joel rubbed his hands together like a warlock concocting some vile brew. "Damn I love how that scene reads. Hope its transfer to the screen is just as powerful."

"Don't see why it wouldn't."

Tina said nothing as she set more packets around the table.

Adam glanced at his watch. "What time are they supposed to be here?"

"His mom is bringing him right from school. I promised to only keep them a couple of hours." Joel returned the picture to a folder he slapped down on the tabletop. "This is gonna be good."

Madison. Adam refrained from issuing another correction, simply nodded. *A couple of hours.* He could certainly stand to be around Madison, in the flesh, for a couple of hours. Though he had hoped their first face to face after the events of the other day would be somewhere private. Seriously though. *How awkward could it possibly be?*

As Adam's contemplation continued, Joel glanced up and grinned again. "Mom. Cameron. Welcome."

Adam braced his hands on the table. *Guess I'm about to find out.*

Joel rose to his feet to hurry over. "Nice to meet you both in person. I've been telling the crew how great this is going to be." When Tina joined them, he introduced her as well, along with a brief description of her duties. "If you have any questions at all, Tina can get you the answers." There was a fleeting pause, before… "You, son, could be our star performer's own offspring."

That was Adam's cue. While Joel babbled on, metal scraped plank flooring as he stood. "Cameron, hey. You made it." He slipped his arm around the boy who was all smiles.

"I did. I want to thank you for this opportunity. I won't let you down."

"I know that." Releasing him, Adam turned his attention to Madison. "How are you?"

A soft green gaze caught his and held tight. For a split second, he detected a flare of interest, the hint of a true and honest connection. Which quickly disappeared in favor of caution.

"Hello, Mr. Pride. It's nice to see you again."

So we're back to that. A subtle signal he needed to keep his distance. Regardless, as he accepted the hand Madison offered him, the controlled chaos of a busy movie set at mid-day faded to so much extraneous background noise.

"Adam. It's Adam. We appreciate your willingness to let Cameron take the job." Nothing personal about that comment. *I can do this.*

"He was, rather is, very excited. No way could I deny my son such a wonderful, once in a lifetime experience."

There they were. The lines of protocol distinctly drawn. Not that he was under any real obligation to accept them. Even when she punctuated her statement by turning away to take a seat on one side of the room away from the conference table.

If anyone else noticed they didn't let on.

Especially Joel, who was oblivious to anything but setting up one of his favorite scenes. "Okay. Let's get this table read going."

Retaking his seat, Adam picked up his copy of the script, determined to not let on he noticed either. Or reveal it bothered him as much as it did. To that end, he kept his gaze on the pages in front of him as his thoughts spiraled. He'd assumed his phone call was sufficient to smooth over any possible discomfort.

We all know what happens when one assumes…and I'm the one made out to be an ass.

"Where are my manners? Madison. You don't have to sit way over there." Joel came to stand behind Adam's chair. "Come join us around the conference table. This is informal. We're a pretty close crew. Like family. Take this empty seat here beside Adam."

"Sure, Madison. Over here." Adam put his arm on the chair Joel had indicated as he silently repeated his now favorite mantra. *I can do this. I can do this.* What the hell else was he supposed to do? "As Joel said. We're purely informal."

"Well, okay." Standing, she walked over innocently enough.

Then she arrived beside him, and innocence took a hike. Everything, *everything* in him flipped to friggin' high alert. Her scent caught up with him first. Sweet and at the same time sensual, it drifted over innocuously as could be, then proceeded to grab hold and wrap him up tight. Offering a small smile of welcome as she took her seat, he helped her scoot forward, inadvertently touching her shoulder. Unbelievable warmth riding a sudden jolt of electricity flowed in to settle close to his heart.

"What I want to get out of this scene is some real heart tugging emotion." Joel strolled to his chair at one end of the table where stacks of notebooks and other papers were piled to the side. Giving Cameron an overview of the incidents leading up to this point in the story, he described what he termed his vision. Hands moving this way and that for emphasis.

For his part, Cameron sat ramrod straight, his full attention trained on Joel. Seeming to hang on every syllable coming from the director's mouth.

Only half listening, and as covertly as possible,

Adam ventured a glance in Madison's direction. Eyes wide as she took it all in, her keen interest alternated between Joel's animated gestures and Cameron's unfailing concentration. Certainly none of it on him.

"Cameron. You start."

Joel's voice broke apart his brooding.

"Okay." The teen picked up his script with shaking hands. Taking a breath, he looked at Adam, the pure nervousness on his face hard to miss. Right down to the pale skin and beads of sweat gleaming on his upper lip.

"No big deal, Cameron." He made sure his voice was even. Conversational. "We can just read back and forth as if we're shooting the breeze. Pretend you and I are the only two people in the room." *And if you can do that, you're a better man than I am.* He ventured another glance Madison's way.

Pages of the script Cameron held rustled. "Okay."

Adam brought his full attention back to settle on him. Waited until he glanced up. "You can do it. I have faith in you."

Flipping a cautious gaze up at Adam then down at the script, he took another quick breath. "I'll never forgive you. It's your fault I lost my mother."

Adam's eyes widened at the forceful delivery. The raw emotion in the boy's voice.

"I hope with all my heart you don't mean that." His tone remained soft, in keeping with his role as shocked and beleaguered father. Flynn's vulnerable side. The quality that brought a sense of emotion to the otherwise, wild car chases, shoot 'em up action movie.

"Why wouldn't I? As far as I'm concerned, you're dead to me, too."

Joel sat forward with a huge smile planted on his

face. "Excellent, Cameron. I can almost see your hatred of this man."

He thumped his fist on the table toward *Flynn* a couple of times. Adam shut his mouth as his next lines remained in his throat. *I love you too much. You'll never be dead to me.*

"Hey, Mom." Joel called over to Madison with a wink. "Pretty good stuff, huh? Your boy is showing some real anger here."

"I'm very proud." Her voice came out low. Infused with its own emotion. "The sentiments he portrays are very believable."

"I agree." Joel pulled his attention from her to the room in general. "I knew we made a good decision when we cast this kid. This whole segment is going to be everything we've dreamed."

Long after Joel had gone off on another tangent, Adam kept his gaze on Madison. Though she'd quickly glanced down as she spoke, he'd caught a glimpse of the desolation flickering in her eyes. The way her body heaved as she took a silent breath. He sure as hell noticed that too. So much so, he had to concentrate to *not* reach over to pull her in and hold her close until the pain and sadness went away. No matter how strong his sense she desperately needed it.

Almost as much as he did.

"Okay." Joel clapped his hands. "Although I'd dearly love to hear Cameron run those lines again, let's take it from Flynn's response. Adam. Go."

Out of necessity, all thoughts of Madison scattered as Adam eyed the script. "I love you too much."

The second he realized his gaze remained on Madison, he snapped it back to where it was supposed to be, according to the script. On Flynn's son.

"You're just saying that out of guilt." Cameron's voice wavered. "Wait. I'm sorry." He cleared his throat. "Can I say that again?"

"Sure you can, Cameron." Joel's tone was surprisingly patient. "Go ahead."

After over an hour, and a good ten pages of script, Adam was pretty much tapped out, emotionally. He could only imagine how Cameron was faring.

Even so, he picked up again where Joel asked him to. "So things can get back to how they were before your mother died."

"We'll never get back to the same way we were." Cameron glanced up at Adam this time, tears glistening in his eyes.

Either he's one hell of a little actor, or this really is getting to him. Adam didn't have time to figure out which as his next line came up. "Maybe not the same, but even if they're different, things can still be good for us."

Staring across the table at Cameron, when the boy blinked and lowered his eyes, Adam shifted his gaze to Madison. Though she had been watching her son, as if drawn there for a purpose, her gaze strayed over to Adam. As it had when she first walked in that day and took his hand, everything else going on around them faded to an indistinct hum as the special woman became the center of his world. Time seemed to stand still for her as well when her gaze didn't falter, and the hint of a smile graced her lips.

"And that's a wrap! Cameron, you did a nice job today." Joel clapped his hands three or four times slowly, then kept it up, and the spell was broken. Others joined in shifting all attention to Cameron as Joel went on. "I know this may sound cliché as hell, but, swear to God, you're a natural."

"Great job, Cameron." Adam followed Joel's lead in offering brief applause. "You did really, really well."

"Yeah. Wow. Thanks." Cameron looked around, his grin wide. Expression bright.

"You did do very well, Cameron." Madison stood and came to her son's side. "I'm very, very proud of you."

"Thanks, Mom." The glow on his face remained. "And thanks for letting me do this."

Madison said nothing as she smiled, tears beginning to shimmer.

"So, Cameron. How would you like a tour of the rest of our facilities here? We'll show you some of the equipment. Fill you in on a few of the processes." Joel burst into what Adam considered a tender family moment.

Cameron was immediately on his feet. "That'd be great."

"If it's okay with your mother." Joel flipped his wrist to check his watch. "We'll take a half hour tops. Still within the timeframe I promised."

Both Joel and Cameron double teamed Madison with expectant looks.

"It's fine with me."

Was it his imagination, or did her voice come out somewhat shaky? Adam didn't know.

"Tina can come with us." Joel already had his arm around Cameron. That was one thing about Joel. If you did a good job for him, he was your friend for life. "She knows more about some of this stuff than even I do."

Despite the compliment, Tina gave Joel a definite frown of distaste he missed entirely. Adam didn't. Clipboard held to her chest, as usual, she had no choice but to follow when Joel took off with Cameron in tow. As the threesome walked away and other crew members disbursed, leaving Adam alone with Madison, he wasn't about to argue.

"I can show you around too." He came to stand at her side, though was careful not to make any physical contact. "But, it probably won't be as interesting as the tour Cameron is going to get. I'll try my best not to bore you."

She stared after her son so intently, Adam began to question whether she'd heard him. Or worse, cared to respond.

"With all that's happened in my life lately, boredom might be a welcome change." Despite her words, she purposely glanced around as if seeking a distraction. "That's beautiful."

She raised a hand to indicate the balcony built around the room, above the windows, rimmed by an ancient but ornate bannister.

"The spiral staircase in the corner there leads up to it. Nice to look at, but that's about all. Our instructions are to stay off it at all costs."

"Why?"

"One of the crew went up there to get a camera angle Joel wanted and nearly fell through. It's not safe to walk on."

She tipped her head back. "It is remarkably high up there."

"Easier to stay away from it. Now how about we start our tour."

"Okay. Bore away." As she turned to look up at him, her lips curved down. "But first, I think we should address the big white elephant in the room. I'll start. You have to admit we haven't put ourselves in the most…the best situation, and I want to apologize face to face for my unsavory behavior the other day."

Exactly a week ago today. Did she recall that too? "I didn't find anything unsavory about it." *Exceptional. Special.* A couple more descriptions came to mind. Unsavory not among them. "If you ask me, you're being way too hard on yourself."

"Or making too much out of a one-night stand." The bitterness in her tone gouged a major chunk out of his heart.

"Is that what you'd call it?"

Her face flamed, but to her credit she didn't drop her gaze. "Wouldn't you?"

He shook his head. "Not even close. Granted we didn't exactly follow a traditional path."

"That's an understatement if I've ever heard one."

"I wholeheartedly agree. What do you say we sort of work backwards from…uh…there. See if we can maybe become friends. At least while I'm here."

The light in her eyes dimmed momentarily before she released a tiny smile. "To tell you the truth, having a friend right now is exactly what I need."

"Then consider me a friend."

By all rights, he should put his arm around her to seal the deal. Much as Joel had done with her son. Instead, he convinced himself to be content by her side. Maybe touching shoulders now and then.

"Listening to, I suppose you'd say Flynn's son read those lines with you today as your son." Staring at the

115

well worn floor, she paused to swallow. "Was a lot like listening to Cameron as my son, saying some of the things I truly believe he'd say to me. If he could." She raised her gaze to meet his again. "Does that make any sense?"

At the sorrow seeping into her eyes, Adam lifted his hand. He so wanted to reach out to cradle her cheek. Brush the bad away for her with the stroke of his thumb. Instead he let his palm settle on her shoulder. "He can't blame you for his father's death. No one but God carries that fault."

She released a lackluster laugh. "I would hope he didn't. But I am to blame for the rest of what's going on in his life. Aren't I?"

"If you're asking for my opinion, I'd say probably not. All parents and teens struggle, regardless of their circumstances." He moved his hand to the small of her back to usher her ahead of him. "We can talk as we tour."

For the next twenty minutes or so, they walked side by side. Talking mostly about Cameron and Dak. Once in a while, about themselves. And hardly at all about the property they toured. He'd like to think he'd put her at ease about the two of them and helped her better understand, or at least was a decent sounding board, when she wanted to discuss her relationship with her oldest son. He was sure of it when her gaze brightened as she looked up at him again.

"I have to say, letting Cameron take this acting job has made a big difference in his behavior. If nothing else, it gives me some necessary disciplinary leverage I dearly needed." She took his hand and squeezed. "For that I'll be eternally grateful."

His face broke out in a smile as he squeezed back. "Here's to good things ahead."

"Good things ahead."

With no glasses to raise, they dropped hands to exchange a hasty fist bump before they continued on.

After a little bit more walking, they started to head back to the soundstage, making their way down a hallway where all the yet to be used audio visual equipment, extra camera stands, lights and such were stored. He took her elbow for guidance as they picked their way around some large coils of heavy-duty electrical cords.

Whatever else he wanted to convey to her, he'd best do it in the next few minutes. Before they joined up with the rest of the crew.

"Maybe you, I and Cameron can go over to the food truck to grab dinner later. Given my current limited living conditions, it's the closest I can offer to a home cooked meal. And it will give Cameron a real feel for movie life."

"He would love that." A tentative smile grew as she glanced up at him. "I would too."

"It's a date." His heart warmed the more he looked at her. Until he caught himself grinning like an idiot. The kicker, he didn't really care. "As soon as we finish our tour."

No doubt emboldened by her easy agreement, he reached over to take her hand again as they continued down a little used corridor. He was purposely leading her places he was pretty sure would be all but deserted. The better to be alone with her to talk things out. Get to know each other better.

"What's behind that door?" Still holding his hand

in hers, Madison pointed with the other to a little used back exit they came to.

"It's a short hallway that leads to some stairs and another door that opens on the roof. I'd take you down it, but it's not very well lit and has a few uneven boards on the floor. I stumbled and fell more than once filming one of Flynn's escape scenes in there. We went through twenty some takes before I made it from one end to the other without mishap. It shouldn't be locked."

Turning the knob, he pulled the door open then stepped back.

She came forward to peek into the dark corridor. "Sounds tedious."

He took a moment to savor the spring flowers and pure woman scents of her closeness before speaking. "And painful. I was more than a little black and blue by the time we got done."

Leaning in for a further inspection, she took a couple more steps forward. "Oh, I see some of the obstacles you're talking about."

"Be careful. Don't go too far in." He put a hand on her back as he cautioned.

"Hey, Adam. Cindy said to say hi." Frank's baritone was unmistakable as it rumbled over him from Lord knew where. Before Adam could respond, the stunt man went on. "And Regina made us promise to bring you with us the next time we go bar hopping. She said she had a blast with you the last time."

"And Whitney said she sends her love." That higher pitched voice definitely belonged to Rafe.

Adam shook his head as a few chance encounters from a month ago came back to haunt him. Those rare times he had gone out for fun. When loneliness and boredom took precedence over good sense. There was no use trying to defend himself. Counter what these two were saying. Anyway, he was too busy just now. Concentrating on the muscles between Madison's shoulders winding up with more and more tension. Like a spring about to break.

"I'm assuming Tina told you about having to cancel our date this afternoon." He found his voice at last to call out an answer, and, holy hell. *That came out all wrong.* He brought his muddled attention back to address Madison who had backed out of the door and looked at him with a boatload of questions in her eyes. "I was supposed to rehearse a fight scene with our stunt guys this afternoon. Looks like they tracked me down anyway."

"I see." The same wariness she'd started out with when she and Cameron first arrived closed over her features as she stepped away from him. "Don't cancel any plans on my...on our account."

Crap. Any strides they'd made in becoming friends was slipping away from him...from them. He was about to begin a rigorous effort to get it back when the two stunt clowns appeared from around the corner...and pulled up short once they spied Madison. Adam took some measure of satisfaction from their dumbfounded expressions.

"Oh, sorry." Rafe whipped off his ball cap.

"We thought you were alone." After a moment's hesitation, Frank stuck out his hand toward Madison.

Adam had no choice but to make the necessary introductions. "Madison, these are Frank and Rafe, the stunt guys I mentioned."

"I see." Her voice remained cautiously neutral as

she shook hands with each of them. "Nice to meet you both."

"She brought her son in today for a table read. Cameron. The teenager we hired to play Flynn's son." Though he didn't necessarily care too, Adam felt he needed to elaborate. "We were just taking a brief tour before wrapping up for the day."

He could only hope they'd take the hint and leave.

"Oh, yeah. Type casting, you could say." Frank nodded, obviously speaking before he thought it out. "Say, Adam. If you're wrapping up, and you've got a minute now, Rafe and I came up with a couple of moves we'd like to run by you."

With a grimace, Adam automatically swung Madison's way. "Right now? I'm a little…"

Her hand on his arm stopped him mid-sentence. "You go ahead. I'll go find Cameron. Tell him about our plans."

Just like that, she'd taken the decision away from him. Given him no choice, as the four of them headed back to the storage hallway. "Okay then. But just for a minute. You guys go ahead. I'll be right there."

"We'll be waiting." Frank spoke first. "Nice meeting you, Madison."

Rafe tipped the hat he'd put back on his head before looking from Adam to her. "Welcome to the crew."

"Thank you. Nice meeting both of you."

Was it Adam's overly sensitive imagination, or had her voice suddenly taken on a hesitant edge? Not that he could dwell on that when there were more important things to accomplish at the moment. Turning back to face her when they were thankfully alone, he reached for her hand again. Which she also hesitated to give as freely as before.

"Just to be clear. The scheduling changes today were not on your account. But, Joel's. He's the one who set up the table read with Cameron without telling me about it ahead of time. Not that it's a bad thing. The read was successful. Cameron got his feet wet with an idea of what to expect out of this whole thing. You and I got a chance to talk."

If her suddenly cleared expression was any indication, his strategy to reclaim her trust was beginning to work.

"That's true."

"It will only take me a minute with those two. Why don't you go touch base with Cameron? Then I'll meet you back here."

"Sounds good. I'll be waiting."

I like how you think. He could get used to her waiting for him on a regular basis. As she walked away, her shoulders were looser, her stride not nearly as stilted. Her hips swung free and easy. He tilted his head to one side to get a better view. *In the most tempting way.*

As Madison went around the corner and out of sight, Adam shook his head and smiled. Here he'd worried for nothing. This whole situation wasn't going to be a problem, after all.

"How's tonight for that little dinner you promised me?"

At the familiar voice from behind him, he straightened and drew a quick breath. Then needed a second to collect his thoughts before he turned around.

"Tina."

"Yes?"

The instant he faced her, she closed what little distance remained between them.

He tamped down the urge to back an equal space away. "Tonight's not good."

Immediately, she stuck out her lower lip. "That's too bad."

"Yeah. It is. Look, Tina…" He hadn't finished his sentence when she moved nearer.

Adam was at the end of his rope with this woman. How many times did he have to politely refuse before she took the hint? Didn't no means no apply for guys too?

"I said yes, Adam."

Taking another step, she pitched forward. On reflex, he caught her in what amounted to a bear hug. As he was about to set her upright, she clinched her arms around his neck.

"My foot's caught." Her face smashed against the side of his neck. Her words came out strained.

When he tried to loosen his arms, she teetered farther into him. Her grip around his neck tightened. He bent his head into hers in an effort to get away. She lifted her face at the exact same moment, to bring their lips close to connecting.

He couldn't hardly pull back far enough to ask if she'd freed her damned foot yet.

"Oh. Excuse me. I didn't mean to interrupt."

Adam glanced up in time to see the sheer desolation cross Madison's face. Quickly replaced with absolute disinterest.

"Madison…I…" Somehow, he managed to get that much out.

Dumbstruck, he reached up to unlatch Tina's arms from their death grip on his neck. Except, she wasn't about to make it easy for him. In fact, she seemed to be doing her damnedest to spin the moment to her favor. Keeping one friggin' arm fastened to his neck as she righted herself, the woman had the gall to rest her hip against his junk when she turned, casually, Madison's way.

"Can we help you?"

"I just came to tell Adam I couldn't find Cameron yet. He must still be with Joel." All Madison's faculties, especially her mouth and brain, were serving her fine.

Thankfully, he retained the presence of mind to reach up and extricate himself from Tina once and for all. Wonder of wonders, she remained upright without his support.

He was even able to take a step or two back and address Madison again. "No telling where Joel may have taken him. Did you check outside?"

"No." Her brow furrowed. "I should do that right now. Nice seeing both of you today."

"You too, Madison." Boasting a big smile, Tina spoke up.

He didn't. Just stood there incredulous watching Madison take off.

Taking advantage when Tina again stepped back, he put more distance between them, once and for all. "For future reference, when I say no, I mean no. Got it?"

Her mouth fell open and she blinked. "I think so."

"Good." He didn't give a rat's ass about her crestfallen expression. Acting on pure instinct, survival instinct, he took off, too.

"Wait. Madison, wait." He kept his tone low. Why call undue attention to what was going on?

She moved fast. He moved faster to catch up. Until a hitch deep in his hip from the stunt injury caught up with *him*. Pain jabbed into his bone like a mad mother. His limp became more pronounced with each agonizing step until he had to slow down.

"Madison, please." A raspy stage whisper was his only option as they neared the door to the soundstage.

Nothing.

In a last-ditch effort, he lunged forward, primed to grab her arm, or something, before she got too far away. "Madison...I...ooof!"

His palm slapped wood before he nearly did a face plant against the door she slammed shut behind her. He backed up then struggled with the knob to open it again. There were still a few feet of empty hallway before she made it into the entrance to the soundstage and a possible audience. If he had any prayer to state his case, it was now or never.

"Madison. Wait up for me. Please." He was still careful to keep his tone controlled. Draw as little attention as possible, in case anyone stood on the fringes.

Stopped short, she turned to face him. "Oh, Adam. I didn't realize you were behind me."

All he could do was draw up before barreling into her. More than a little slack jawed at her bold-faced lie.

"About what you..." At a loss how to describe the unfortunate encounter, he let a thumb jerk over one shoulder suffice. "About that."

"You certainly don't owe me an explanation for..." She paused to swallow then raised one hand palm up.

"That."

He ignored her second deviation from the truth. "I think I do."

Squaring in front of him, she raised her chin to look him in the eye. "Go ahead then."

"I had no idea she was going to walk up to me then trip over some cables like she did."

With her lips pursed, she nodded as if in agreement. "Trip over cables?"

"Yeah." Even though he sounded like he was manufacturing his *own* rash of bullshit, he kept going. "Which, I have to tell you, was I'm sure somewhat calculated on her part."

He proceeded to give her a little bit of background on previous encounters with the woman. Then continued with similar excuses until he flat ran out of them.

"I believe you."

He pulled his lower jaw up from where it had dropped as her response registered in his somewhat screwed up mind. "You do?"

"Uh-huh." Her small smile oozed innocence. "Why wouldn't I?"

She's got me there. "You shouldn't. You definitely shouldn't. I mean should."

"Something else I didn't get a chance to tell you back there." She mimicked his thumb jerk of a few moments before. "I'm afraid we can't stay for dinner. I forgot I promised Dak and my mother Chinese takeout. Dak loves sweet and sour chicken. Sometimes he'll even eat a piece of carrot that comes with it."

Though he strongly suspected she was feeding him her version of a rash of bullshit, with no real proof, he couldn't call her on it. "Maybe some other time."

"Maybe." She reached out to gently pat his arm. "I'm glad we got to talk though."

"Me too."

"Thank you for…" Her lips curved up ever so slightly at the corners. "…that."

Turning, she walked away from him and into the soundstage, where she proceeded to collect Cameron first, then her purse. Making pleasant small talk with various crew members the whole time.

"Thank you, Joel. Nice meeting everyone." She gave a broad wave to the group in general.

About to follow her again, Adam skidded to a stop, as a chorus of *nice meeting you too* soon followed. Punctuated by a couple of good job, Cameron comments.

Replying with more kudos, she scanned the room with a polite smile that immediately fell when her gaze landed on him. Leaving no doubt in his mind, he wasn't included in the list of niceties.

Why would I be?

"Let's go, Cameron." Her stare strayed Adam's way once more. "We'll pick up Chinese to take home."

By all indications, she hadn't believed me after all. Coming forward to explain himself, in front of this crowd, was out of the question. Same with following her to the parking lot to plead his case.

Yeah. That'd work great in front of Cameron.

He contemplated climbing the spiral stairs in the far corner to the balcony then jumping. The fall would probably be sufficient to, if not kill him outright, do great bodily harm. Render him temporarily unconscious.

Glaringly aware of his inability to rectify the situation, he watched the door close behind her as everyone else went back to doing what they had been doing. Leaving him to stand there with more unused lines of apologies and explanations left in a hopeless tangle at the back of his throat. Primed and ready to choke him to death.

Which, at this point, might not be a bad way to go either.

Chapter Seven

Madison pulled to a stop in the parking lot of Dexter's Shop and Save. As a recently discovered freedom settled in, she shut off the engine, unbuckled her seat belt, closed her eyes, and proceeded to simply breathe. After months, years even, of grief and turmoil, her life was beginning to settle down.

Dak was doing well in school. Cameron was coming around. She was slowly getting her late husband's final affairs in order. And, maybe most important, she had made peace with someone who, if not necessarily a dream come true for her, was at least a positive influence on her boys' lives. Which was all that really mattered anyway.

Oh, and her mother was in town for a visit.

As her eyes opened, she cracked a small smile. *So, okay, still a decent, positive, average.*

Lifting her purse from the passenger seat, she extracted two items before she hid the brown leather shoulder bag in the console. After shoving a long grocery list, keys and her wallet containing a debit card and her driver's license in her coat pocket, she got out and locked the car.

The gray of a bleak sky loomed above, with greenish blue storm clouds billowing on the far horizon. Even the dismal weather couldn't drag down her mood. She strode through the sliding glass doors to join the throng of cart pushing shoppers who, like her, were there to stock up for the approaching Thanksgiving weekend. Another smile tipped her lips as she rattled a wheeled cart from the stack. This year, she was determined to do whatever it took to assure their dwindling family enjoyed themselves on the holiday.

Scarcely more than a half-hour later, her shopping basket mounded with a variety of items, she waited with several others to check out, surrounded by the bleeps and dings from busy tills. Unloading her groceries quickly, she set the second large package of boneless, skinless chicken breasts on the conveyor belt, then pushed the now empty cart in front of her as she stepped up to pay.

"Does it show I haven't been to the grocery store in a while?" Reaching into her pocket for her wallet, she laughed as she made small talk.

The thin blonde woman ringing up her purchases smiled in return. "You have no idea how many times a day I hear that."

"I imagine."

As she continued to scan produce, cereals, canned goods and meats, her cash register pinged its acceptance. Madison had her debit card out by the time the last article, a bag of frozen peas, was scanned and bagged.

The cashier's ponytail bounced as pleasant eyes met hers. "Your total is one eighty-three seventy."

"I'll need to get some cash back, too." She inserted the chip end of her card into the reader and tapped her fingers on the counter, waiting for the machine to do its thing.

Then waited. And waited. Then waited some more.

"I'm sorry. That card's been denied."

Her mouth dropped open at the news. "That's not possible. There's more than enough money in the account to cover this. I'm sure of it."

How many times a day did she hear that particular line too?

"It's been denied." Obviously unmoved, the woman shrugged.

Madison couldn't bring herself to give up. "There must be some mistake."

"If you want, you could take this up with someone at the service desk." Ms. Ponytail flipped a switch. The square opaque light above her cash register blinked continually on and off as if sending out some universal distress signal.

Though heat flared up her neck, Madison stood her ground. On either side of her *bleeps, blips and dings* continued unabated. "Let me try it again."

"Do you have another card you want to use?" The clerk shifted to the other foot, showing her impatience.

"Perhaps I can help."

At the familiar tenor voice, for an instant Madison ceased to breathe. Cheeks already flushed in humiliation grew piping hot as two one hundred-dollar bills were laid down in front of her.

"Oh, no. I couldn't." She moved to pick up the bills with every intention to return them.

A warm hand covered hers. "Please."

Electric sparks tingled up her arm and down to her fingertips before she could pull away. She didn't need to turn to identify the speaker, nor his touch, but did so anyway. As usual, the baseball cap rode low over his forehead, all but hiding his eyes. Minus the aviators, there was no mistaking the owner of those eyes. Cool blue, intense, and zeroed in on her. She made herself ignore their hypnotizing effect as she diverted her gaze. Stubble that must have been at least two days in the making peppered his chin and circled his mouth. For a split second, she wondered how those lips, surrounded by a cushion of whiskers, would feel on hers. Then their outer edges tipped up and sanity prevailed.

"I can't take your money." Opening her mouth to lodge another protest, her gaze fell on the line of customers building behind them, and she bit her lip.

A frazzled mother with a crying baby in the seat of her overflowing cart had a thumb sucking toddler beside her, clinging to one hand. A good old boy with no cart hefted a couple twelve packs of beer. A stooped, white haired lady behind him had such a white-knuckle grip on the handle of her cart, you'd think she'd topple over without its support.

Responding to a tongue click of disgust from behind the register, Madison tried to recall how much cash she carried. At the end of the counter, the bag boy, wearing a pained expression, leaned on the basket he'd already loaded with her groceries.

The cashier who waited for the money she was due planted one hand on her hip. Her expectant gaze alternated back and forth from Madison to Adam then back to Madison again. Beseeching one of them to make a decision. *Please.*

"All right. But only to keep these nice people behind us from having to wait any longer." The smile she flashed backward wasn't returned by any one of those *nice people*. "I'll pay you back when I get this mess straightened out."

The cash drawer opened with a loud ding. Only the thumb sucking toddler reacted with a high-pitched wail. Heat spread up her neck all the way to her forehead and into her hairline as Madison faced forward. Scooping the bills off the counter, the cashier flip flopped both through a counterfeit detector, then dropped them under the metal drawer she banged back down.

"Who gets the change?" She held sixteen dollars and a couple of coins aloft.

"It's his money." Cheeks flaming, Madison stepped to one side as Adam reached over.

In addition to the pleasant aroma of aftershave he carried, another, headier scent, she remembered all too well, moved in with him to tease her. Given the limited space between the conveyor belt counter on one side and racks of impulse items on the other, his shoulder brushed hers. Providing a firm and solid refuge she fought an overwhelming urge to lean into.

"Move it along, lady. You're not the only person in this world, you know."

At the rude comment from beer man with no basket, Adam pivoted to face him.

"Show a little courtesy. We're getting there." His delivery was calm and direct.

"Sure as hell not fast enough to suit me."

The toddler directly behind them started in on another howl as he looked up with tear filled eyes running over.

"Hey, little guy. It's okay." At Adam's soothing tone, mouth open in awe, the child stopped crying to stare. "That's better. You'll be out of here soon, too."

He flashed a smile at the child's mother before setting a package of lunchmeat and loaf of bread on the belt, along with the ten he still held. Coming to the end of the counter, Madison clutched the handle of her fully loaded shopping cart with both hands to push that, and herself as quickly as she could to the exit. Returning his wallet to the back pocket of his jeans, Adam caught up to walk beside her as they passed by the controlled commotion of more cashiers and shoppers interacting without incident.

"Well that was beyond embarrassing." Eyes still forward and focused, she whispered from one side of her mouth.

As is this. It had been difficult enough a few days ago to remain calm and, above all, civil after hearing about the playboy's previous romantic exploits. Then seeing him, literally, entangled with some woman as some cruel visual reinforcement. All while pain and anger were taking turns in a heated battle to claw their way out of her.

Now this! Of all people to run into…

"I'm sorry you had to go through that." True compassion colored his voice to scatter her thoughts.

She paused until the sliding glass doors they came to opened. "I have no idea why that happened."

A cool blast of November wind shot over them as they stepped outside. Not only that, sleet-like raindrops pelted everything in their path with a rat a tat rhythm. All courtesy of those storm clouds, formerly on the far horizon, now settled in directly above.

Lowering her head, Madison kept moving as she flipped up the hood of her parka. Now that she'd escaped the grocery store humiliation, another form of indignity took hold. How to gracefully leave this man who seems to be the master of saying one thing and doing another.

To be fair. She let out a breath as her ever present rational side came to the fore. *He did take the time to explain the circumstances of what you saw at the studio.*

"Winter is definitely on its way." Burrowed deeper into his bomber-style jacket, Adam kept up with her hastened pace as they approached her car. "If this cold air is any indication."

As if to prove his point, a sudden gust blew her hood off then cycled through her hair, like icy fingers doing a scalp massage. Shivering, she kept moving.

"It is that." She pulled the keys from her coat pocket with a gloveless hand and hit the unlock button on her fob.

"Where do you want the groceries?" Adam picked up two of many beige plastic bags from the cart.

"In here is fine." Opening the back door, then tying the tops closed as she went, with Adam's help, they soon had all her bags transferred.

Metal wheels rattled against pavement as he rolled the empty basket to the nearest cart corral. Madison took the opportunity to hurry into the driver's seat. A welcome shelter from the rain and wind. Another sharp gust slammed the door shut just as she pulled in her left foot.

The icy shower pitter-patted on the roof and windows like so many tiny needles. Her breath puffed out in plumes of frost as she leaned forward to start the engine. Pulling out her cell, she looked up the bank's number and connected, encouraged when the virtual hostess answered on the first ring.

'We are currently experiencing an exceptionally

high volume of calls.' Irritating canned music immediately funneled into her ear.

"Oh course you are." Disconnecting with a scowl, she returned the cell to her purse.

When Adam approached her side of the car, she rolled down the window.

"Thank you again for…helping me out of that little financial jam. I'll get the money I owe to you as quickly as I can."

"No rush." Sliding his lone plastic bag securely on to one wrist, he thrust both hands in his coat pockets. "It's not like I'm going anywhere for a while."

"I can bring cash to you at…where you're staying." She switched the heater on full blast. Surely the engine had warmed up enough by now.

"You don't have to do that."

"Yes, I do." Her words carried on a cloud of vapor that touched his cheek.

"Okay, but now's not the best time to discuss it." He hunched into his jacket as tiny streams of water dripped from the bill of his baseball cap. Lifting his gaze, he hunkered down even more. "I don't know about you, but right now, I'm feeling a little chilled."

"Oh, I'm sorry. I'll let you get to your car. We can figure out the semantics later."

A strange expression crossed his face as he glanced around. "Yeah. Okay."

"Where is your car?" Her gaze followed his around the parking lot.

"Back in Detroit." He made the admission with a sheepish smile. "When the weather was decent around here, I walked everywhere."

"You walked here?" She mentally calculated the

distance to the historical site. "That has to be well over a mile."

"Mile and a half." The sheepish smile returned. "I used a GPS program on my watch to measure it."

"You never bothered to rent a car once you got here?"

He answered with a small shrug. "I meant to. I just never got around to it. Never thought about where I might want to go. Until now."

Madison's mouth fell open with no idea what to say. Then something clicked. "Well, for heaven's sake. You can't walk that far in this weather. Get in. I'll give you a ride home."

As if he was just as conflicted as she was, Adam didn't move right away. For some reason his reluctance made her more secure in the offer.

"Seriously."

"All right."

A gust of rain-soaked air whooshed through the car as he climbed in beside her. He shut the door with a thud. Any more cold drafts that may have come in with him were quickly gobbled up by the car heater running on full blast.

"Walking over here seemed like a good idea at the time." His cheeks and nose were already a little pink. He sniffed then shook his head, shedding more droplets of water. "I wasn't expecting rain."

A slight shiver followed as, fingers extended, he placed his palms against the gushing heat vent. She studied the hands splayed out in front of her, memories of their firm yet gentle touch floating into her mind.

Her heartbeat fluttered unevenly as he caught her gaze and flashed a full-fledged smile. Wave upon wave of rolling, hot air surrounded her, thick and suffocating. Which was nothing compared to the spirals of inner heat she suddenly dealt with. Though it would be rude to shut off the rushing warmth when Adam was so obviously enjoying it.

As discreetly as she could, she opened the zipper on her parka halfway down.

The minute he lowered his hands and sat back, she reached out to dial down their own personal blast furnace. The roar of the blower immediately gave way to silence broken only by the steady hum of the engine.

"What brought you to the grocery store in the first place?" A rather inane comment found its way out of her mouth.

"Boredom mostly." He peeled off the hat and leaned toward her to set that and his bag on the back seat. His jacket pulled deliciously tight over the expanse of his chest. "The company shut down production for the Thanksgiving holiday. Everyone but me went home."

"Why didn't you, too?"

"Nowhere to go." Another shrug, if meant to show indifference, didn't quite meet the mark.

"Everyone has somewhere to go." The follow-up absurdity was released before she could stop it.

"The lucky ones, maybe." For the first time since he'd gotten into her car, he glanced away from her and out the side window.

Not sure what to say, she studied the back of his head. Until she felt obligated to fill the silence growing between them. "You did a nice job with that upset child."

"I learned how to make good use of tact early on in

my academy days."

"Academy? You went to military school?"

He shook his head. "Not hardly. The way I grew up. Most of my valuable learning took place at the police academy near Detroit."

"I didn't realize you used to be a policeman."

"Not used to be. Am. This movie thing is temporary."

"You don't enjoy what you're doing now?" She didn't want to dwell on the combination of Adam and temporary.

"Not really."

When he offered no more, she glanced over at him. "What's the movie about? A buddy film of the good cop, bad cop variety I'll bet."

"You'd lose then. You'd definitely lose." His tone was suddenly thoughtful, his voice low, his gaze focused on the tan leather dashboard in front of him. "Don't get me wrong. The guy I play is your typical Hollywood style cop who plays by his own rules. Though he's definitely not unhinged or unpredictable. People seem to love a cop who plays by his own rules. And Hollywood loves to deliver. So long as it takes place in fantasyland." Emotion seeped in to cloud his voice, and he swallowed. "Being a cop in real life is totally different. Even with all the crap we sometimes put up with, I'm itching to be done with this acting stint so I can get back to a job that defines who I really am."

An icy chill crawled up her spine with enough force to encase her heart. She sat up straighter and cleared her throat. "My, uh, my first husband, Dave, the boys' father, was a police officer like you." She pressed her lips tight together as memories flooded in to clog her throat. "I can't tell you how many times I kissed him goodbye before he left to start his next shift, hugged him tight around the stiff bullet proof vest he wore, and wondered if the boys and I would ever see him again. If he'd come home safe to us when his shift was over."

Lifting her chin, she breathed deep through her nose as emotion threatened to sweep her away. It had been a while since she'd been free to talk about Dave, though his presence in her thoughts and her heart was constant. Joe certainly didn't want to hear about him. Or much of anything else that had occurred in Madison's life prior to their involvement.

"All families worry about their loved ones. Law enforcement especially." The lack of emotion in his tone surprised her.

While she was hard pressed to keep the passion from her voice, he seemed to find it equally difficult to bring the passion into his.

"I'm sure your family shared with you how hard it sometimes was."

"No. Not really." His tone hardened, and he looked away.

Without really thinking about it, she reached up to shut off the engine. In many ways, she welcomed the opportunity to speak about Dave. Share the things she remembered about him. In other ways, she would have preferred to not relive the still raw pain at losing him.

"What's your character's name?"

"Kyle Flynn."

"What's he like?"

"He's a dedicated cop who's lost everything he values in his personal life." His voice became solemn, and he didn't look at her. Preferring instead to concentrate on a family of four hurrying by. A father and mother each holding the hand of a youngster.

She joined him in studying them. Two parents, not one. Caring for two children.

Like us at one time.

"Flynn's wife and their unborn child died in a drive by shooting. He soon finds out he was the target. A formal police investigation goes nowhere. Eventually, Flynn takes matters into his own hands."

"Has anything like that ever happened to you in real life?"

He shook his head. "No. But then, I've never had anyone who meant so much to me."

"Never?"

"Maybe a few women I dated over the years who came close."

A tremor ran through her as visions of happier times with Dave filled her mind. "Losing someone you love is like losing a part of yourself. A part you never really get back when you've given your heart to someone." She dropped her gaze as additional words failed her.

"He must have been quite a remarkable man. With a lot to give." The sincerity in his voice reached out to draw her in.

"He gave everything, both personally to me and our boys, and professionally to his department. He took his job very seriously."

"We all do. What was his rank?"

"Lieutenant. He was in his fourth year. There was talk he'd one day be chief. He had mixed feelings about that. Though he loved his job, he loved his family more." A flood of sadness, regret and pride, gathered at the back of her throat to pinch it closed.

"I'm not sure anyone can love a job. Be devoted maybe."

"My late husband, my second husband, would be the exception. To him, work was the be all and end all of life. As far as families go, Dak and Cameron were never...didn't take Joe's last name. He didn't seem to mind." Drawing a deep breath, she glanced up, willing away tears that threatened. "To tell the truth, though I took Joe's name when we married, I can't begin to count the number of times I was tempted to give it back."

"I think they call that divorce."

"I think you're right." The corners of her mouth tweaked up. "And I've never told anyone before you."

"Your secret's safe with me."

"Thank you. I appreciate that."

They exchanged pleasant smiles before each fell to their own thoughts.

Madison was the first who couldn't stand the silence any longer. "What's being on your movie set like? In general, I mean. It seemed friendly enough the other day, but I thought maybe that was because Cameron and I were there." She glanced over to make quick eye contact.

He quirked a brow in response. "For your benefit, everyone was on their best behavior?"

"Were they?"

"You want to make sure your son doesn't get into something unpleasant. Run into raging egos and temper-tantrums."

She stared at him as he read her mind. "Exactly."

"As movie sets go, those I've been on anyway, you could say ours is pretty boring. Not a lot of drama. No professional feuds or torrid affairs going on. Take that production assistant you saw me tangled up with the other day. Tina."

She held in a fierce grimace at the unpleasant memory. "What about her?"

"She's flirted and suggested we get together I don't know how many times. Don't get me wrong. She seems to be a nice enough person." He paused to shake his head. "Just leaves me kinda cold. For whatever reason. And, no I haven't slept with her. Not once."

"I never…." Looking aghast, her shock face crumbled and she grinned. "So okay, I wondered."

"Now you know for sure."

She couldn't hold back her next question. "Anyone waiting for you back home?"

"No." The single word hung between them for a few seconds. "I'd like to think if there were someone back home, she'd be here on location with me, rather than trying to make things work while we're apart."

"You don't believe in long distance relationships?"

"Nope."

The immediacy of his answer caught her by surprise. "That sounded pretty final."

"It's all about stability, especially if children are involved. A belief I've come by honestly."

Though she wanted to, Madison didn't press. If Adam meant for her to know more, he'd tell her in his own time.

"Stability wasn't exactly my mother's strong suit when I was growing up. Hell, a normal middle-class home life wasn't even on her radar. She bounced around from town to town with the guy who she said was my father." He faced forward to focus his attention out the windshield. "Then he took off for good when I was about ten. At the time, I figured our gypsy lifestyle would end. It didn't. We landed in Detroit when I was seventeen. She took off about a year later. I stayed put. With a high school diploma and making good money working on the line in the auto plant, I was more than able to support myself."

Another family came by. A mother and father, each pushing a cart with a toddler in the seat. He watched them until the children were placed in the car and the parents began loading their groceries. Even then, he was slow to turn her way again.

"For now I'm making a lot better money than my patrolman's salary. More than enough to support a decent sized family. If I'm ever lucky enough to have one of my own."

"You seem to have a lot of love inside of you." On one hand, she had no idea why she said that, and on the other, knew exactly what prompted the line of thinking.

"The capacity maybe." Regret entered his eyes before he looked away. "I've never really had the chance to put into practice."

"Is your mother still alive?" Madison clenched her fists in her lap, thinking of how much better a life she'd had with hers.

"She is. We stay in touch when it suits her." He cleared his throat. "To this day, I'm not sure what she looked for all those years. And I still doubt she's found it with the current man she lives with in Florida."

"You don't seem bitter. I'm surprised."

His gaze changed to reflect a sense of peace. "She

robbed me of a lot of my childhood. Why allow her to take even more now that I'm an adult?"

"Makes sense." Her hand was covering his before she even realized. The need to touch him, make simple human contact, was that strong.

He glanced down as he securely twined their fingers.

She glanced there, too then up at him. "That may be some of what Cameron is feeling. Being dragged around against his will. I met Joe at a real estate convention in Chicago where we're from. Sold a house I couldn't afford anyway after Dave died. Brought my boys here."

"That's a little different than the jumping around my mother did with me."

"Is it?"

"I think so. From what I've observed, you're more involved in your boys' lives than my mother even pretended to be in mine. Anyway. What she did to me is old news that doesn't matter anymore."

She wasn't totally buying it. "Some hurts never go away. Do they?"

"Not completely. You just learn to live with them."

"Here's hoping that's true." She shook off some melancholy about her own past. "You said you weren't going home for Thanksgiving."

"I said I had nowhere to go. As far as I'm concerned, home is a relative term."

She didn't try to decipher the meaning behind his words. Nor did she bother to ask. Instead she leaned forward to start the engine again, then dove in before losing her nerve. "We're having a family Thanksgiving at our home." She made sure to say home rather than house. "You're welcome to join us if you'd like. Though our celebration will definitely be low key this year, I can promise you a pretty traditional family gathering."

"Just you and the boys?"

"Along with my mother."

"Will that make it hard to explain my presence?"

"Not if you're introduced as Cameron's friend. He'd love it."

"As Cameron's friend. Right."

"Right." She smiled.

"As long as you're having turkey, I'm in."

"Good." Putting the car in gear, she concentrated on backing up, then drove forward without glancing his way again.

Afraid the look on his face would persuade her to do, or say, something she might later regret.

Chapter Eight

Adam stood on the expansive front steps of the elegant brick and mortar, okay he'd go ahead and say it, mansion. Neoclassical style, if his limited knowledge of architecture was correct. He tipped his head back to take it all in.

Sporting four fluted, white pillars across the front, three regal stories rose before him. Probably with scores of bedrooms and an equal number or more of bathrooms. Where only three people lived presently. Four if you counted Madison's mother.

He should have expected the grandeur when the gated driveway he drove down in his newly rented Denali was longer than most of the streets he lived on growing up.

May as well get to it.

Taking a deep breath, he squared up in front of the stained-glass double doors and pushed the lighted doorbell on the left. Even the resulting chime that reverberated within echoed impressively. He stepped back, darned near at attention, to wait. And all he could think about was how this was so totally and completely out of his league. Even with the extra income his movie contract brought.

Tipping his head back again to look above him, he waited some more.

Probably because some stuffy old butler had to find

his way down from a third-floor ballroom or something to answer the door. Being that the maid was busy dealing with setting the table for a five course Thanksgiving dinner. And the cook was similarly occupied.

As time ticked by, his gaze fell to the lone bottle of Chardonnay he cradled in one arm for the adults. Along with the liter of punch for the boys. Madison hadn't given him any guidance when he called to ask what he could bring. Beyond her flippant 'just you would be fine,' he was on his own. It wasn't as if he had any traditional family recipes to share. Making store bought beverages his best option.

Even though the porch area was somewhat sheltered, a substantial breeze was swirling snow from a minor shower earlier in the day. A dusting of the cold stuff slapped its sting across the back of his neck. He scrunched his head down into the collar of his leather jacket as he began to question the wisdom of coming here in the first place. He'd originally thought dinner might be nice. Especially on a national holiday. After all, how long had it been since he was part of an established family unit? Even as a guest?

Too long to even remember.

Rocking back on his heels, as he was about to hit the bell again, or simply turn around and travel back to the solitude of his trailer, the door opened.

"Well, hello, you must be Adam Pride."

A tall woman with lighter coloring, but definitely Madison's expressive eyes, stood before him.

"Hollingsworth, ma'am. My real name is Adam Hollingsworth."

Ignoring the hand he extended in greeting, she

pulled him into a quick hug. "Regardless, it's so very nice to meet you." She let him go and stepped back but kept a tight hold on both his upper arms. "My grandsons can't stop talking about you, Adam. It's okay that I call you Adam, isn't it?"

"Of course. I'd prefer it."

"You'll have to forgive me. I'm a little star struck here." Smiling, she fluttered a hand in front of her face.

"You shouldn't be. I'm nothing special." As he returned her brilliant smile, he accepted a stab of disappointment Madison hadn't been the one who couldn't stop talking about him. Though he burned to inquire whether she'd mentioned him at all, he didn't chance it. "It was nice of your daughter to invite me."

"Sorry to keep you waiting when you rang the bell. I had to take my pies out of the oven." She wiped her hands on a bright red apron with *TIP THE COOK AND KISS THE WAITRESS* spelled out in bold yellow script. "Oh, by the way, my name is Kay. Kay Carmichael. I'm Madison's mother, but you already figured that out."

"Nice to meet you, Kay. Dak and Cameron are a couple of very nice kids."

That elicited an even broader smile. "I'm their grandma. You don't have to tell me that. But why are we standing out here in the cold. Come in. Come in."

With no maid or butler in sight, she swept him over the threshold with an arm around his back then shut the door. A collection of savory smells inside made his mouth water. Basted turkey, stuffing, and whiffs of cinnamon, ginger and nutmeg. The sweet scents of an apple pie or pumpkin. Maybe both.

"These are my contributions to dinner." Offering

the beverages, he wished he'd had the foresight to pick up a bouquet of flowers as well.

"Why thank you." She set the drinks on a long, mahogany table in the two story, marble-tiled foyer, then turned back to face him. "Let me take your coat."

"Thank you."

When he obliged, she hung it in a nearby closet then led the way to a huge, elegantly furnished living room.

"Madison told me all about the filming you're doing. And as for the opportunity Cameron has. My grandson is over the moon about that."

"The director was prepared to put out a nationwide casting call, which would have held up production. Luckily Cameron was a good fit."

"Fortunate for both of you then." She hefted the two bottles off the table. "Let me put the wine and punch in the fridge and I'll be right back."

"I'll be here."

He stayed where he was when she hurried out. The better to study the landscape. Two light blue suede couches faced each other from across the massive room, with cherry wood end tables on either side of each, and a matching oblong table in between. A couple of plush wing chairs, covered in a rich, and he'd bet expensive, darker blue fabric, flanked a fieldstone fireplace. Complete with a crackling fire that, judging from the uniform nature of its flames, was of the artificial gas variety. Which didn't take away from the inviting mood it created. Paintings and a few family pictures were hung on the walls around the room. A desk and chair were tucked into an alcove of sorts behind one of the couches.

"Have a seat." Kay bustled back from the kitchen before he knew it.

"Thank you." Adam pulled his gaze away from the elegant décor to do as she instructed. Choosing to sit right in the center of one of those impressive couches. Opulent or not, the house had a true, homey feel to it.

Sitting on the couch opposite, she wiped her hands on the apron. "Madison and the boys aren't here right now. Obviously."

He glanced at the huge grandfather clock in a corner by the spacious picture window. Nearly two-thirty. "I was sure she said to be here any time after two."

"I'm sure she did too."

When she seemed to await a response, he gave her one. "Did something come up?"

"Only of her own making." Lifting her shoulders, she drew a breath. "First, her ex-brother-in-law John called to say he was going to the cemetery to pay his respects and did she want to go with him. Some kind of family tradition. Or so he claimed. If it had been me, I would have told him to pack sand. But, then my daughter always has been nicer than I am. She let Dak and Cameron go to a movie earlier today with Phil Something."

"A friend of Cameron's."

"Yes. Have you met the boy?"

"Only briefly." He looked up as the clock chimed.

"At any rate, she said it wouldn't be too far from the cemetery, so she planned to drop her boys off at Phil's house on the way. Saying they didn't need to take time out of their holiday for a cemetery visit. A decision I fully agreed with. Phil's father is going to bring the boys home." She glanced at the imposing clock then back at him. "She did plan to return before you got here. But you know what they say about the best laid plans. Although I suppose you and I could both get in line for her attention these days. After John talked to her, Hayden something or other called, but she'd already left. That character had some business thing to discuss, he said. I gave him what for, bothering her on the holiday." Chuckling, she shook her head. "He didn't seem to like that. Too bad."

"I'd say you did the right thing."

"Well, thank you." She favored him with a high-beam smile. "I do what I can to defend my little girl."

You and me both. He smiled back rather than speaking.

Not only was her smile that infectious, he liked her immediately. Maybe it was the fierce way she protected her family. He'd always held a certain admiration for women who put their offspring first.

"The holidays notwithstanding, I came out here partly to help with the boys. Then I had dinner to prepare today. Not that I mind or anything. Madison was the one who put the turkey in the oven. Set the alarm and got up early to do it."

"Everything smells terrific." He maintained the presence of mind to make the polite, and truthful, response as a vision of Madison fresh out of bed came to mind. Or newly awake and still under the covers. Eyes soft and dreamy. Beckoning smile on her face.

"Well, if my daughter may need some work in sprucing up her manners, I should probably brush up on mine. Can I get you anything? Maybe a glass of that wine you brought?"

Deep sixing the daydream, Adam shook his head. "No thanks. I'm fine. Let's wait until everyone else is home."

"In a way, it's partially my fault they aren't here. She originally told the boys no about the movie, then relented when they argued with her. And I sort of took their side when maybe I shouldn't have. I tell you, she's walking a fine line between overindulgence and restrained discipline these days. What with everything that's happened."

"Losing a spouse has to be rough." He made the only fitting response to come to mind.

"You have that right." Her eyes misted over as she stared straight ahead. "Madison's first husband, Dave, died of acute leukemia only six short weeks after being diagnosed. Quite suddenly and brutally, I'm afraid." Tears welled up, and she cleared her throat. "Madison was beside herself with grief. Needless to say the boys were devastated. She suppressed her feelings to tend to theirs. As any good mother would, of course."

"Of course."

"If nothing else, my little girl is a wonderful mother."

"I'll bet she is."

"Those boxes contain Christmas decorations she got out." She pointed to an assortment in a back corner. "Then, to quote her, didn't have it in her to put up just yet."

Though his reasons were somewhat different, Adam could identify with her reluctance. "One holiday at a time, I suppose."

"That would be one way of looking at it."

Before she could respond further, the huge clock

chimed again to signal two forty-five.

"A wonderful mother, maybe. But, I'm afraid a lousy hostess." She frowned as she glanced over at the clock. By the time her gaze came back to him, her smile was intact. "So how did you get into acting, Adam?"

"Actually, I'm a police officer by profession."

"Really?" Her eyes lit up even more at that piece of information.

"For close to fifteen years now. I work at a precinct near Metro Detroit."

"My first husband was from Michigan. Sault Sainte Marie in the Upper Peninsula. The other end of the state from you." Folding her hands in her lap, she leaned toward him. "So whatever are you doing up here in the mountains of Colorado? Making a movie of all things."

"It started with a personal escort detail a couple of years ago. A bigwig movie producer was in town for a local premiere. I was assigned…"

"…to protect him, I'll bet."

"Pretty much. Anyway, we spent most of the time in my squad car stuck in traffic and got to talking. Long story short, when he asked, I offered some advice on a television show he was involved in at the time. A police drama. One thing led to another, and he hired me, on a part time and occasional basis, to work as technical advisor on the series."

"And given the fact you are devastatingly handsome, they came to their senses and cast you in a starring role."

Throwing his head back, he laughed out loud, even as some self-conscious heat climbed up his neck. "Not exactly. I ended up doing some stunts for a couple of the supporting cast members. When the time came to film scenes on location, I was hired by default."

She blinked at that but said nothing as she kept listening.

"The actor they originally hired for the role I'm in quit over a salary dispute or something. Since I knew most of the lines and all of the stunts, I was asked to step in. More to help out than anything else."

"You don't find this kind of work glamorous and exciting?"

He was taken by surprise at the understanding that entered her eyes. It was as if she'd sensed how he really felt about his current situation.

"The travel and unpredictable hours, gypsy-style living arrangements. Those things, for me at least, overshadowed the glamour and excitement pretty darned quickly."

"You're yearning for more stability in your life." A gaze wiser than his bore into him.

"Something like that." He relaxed back against the cushions. "Living like a nomad with no roots takes its toll."

"Do you have family back in Detroit?"

He shook his head. "Not anymore. My mother lives in Pensacola, Florida with her husband." *Number five, or was it six?* He'd lost count.

"Do you get to see them often?"

"Not lately." No need to share he hadn't been invited down there in a while. "How about you?"

"Divorced long ago."

He caught her gaze. "I'm sorry to hear that."

"Don't be. It was for the best. Madison was in college. We haven't heard from him since."

"That has to be hard." Though always sad when a

family split apart, regardless the reason, he had to admit the knowledge made him feel closer to Madison in some way. Gave them something in common.

"As I said, for the best." The smile she produced was wistful. "I've had a few promising suitors over the years. Nothing terribly, terribly serious, though, I'm afraid." She glanced away then back at him. "In some ways I count myself more fortunate than my little girl. Widowed twice now. And in such a short amount of time."

"She mentioned that." Bringing his arm down from the back of the couch, Adam sat forward.

"Joe Clark isn't, I should say wasn't, the boys' father. Thank God." She covered her mouth with the palm of her hand. "Though maybe God Himself will get me for saying that."

"Or He may just give you a pass."

She looked right at him and another smile bloomed. "One can only hope. Madison married Joe, I think, on the rebound. After her beloved David died." Her eyes took on a distant cast. "Those boys have been through so much. Madison too, of course. I'm taking Dak and Cameron back to Chicago for a Bears versus Lions football game weekend after next. My brother-in-law got us tickets. He's a big Bears fan."

"They should enjoy that. Though I have to say, my heart is with the Lions. Even in those years they don't deserve my loyalty."

"To each his own." She grinned at him then put a hand to the edge of her mouth, as if prepared to divulge a deep family secret. "If you ask me, it will do Madison and the boys good to get away from each other for a change."

The grandfather clock erupted into its customary tune, and she jumped then let out a self-deprecating laugh. "I swear I'll never get used to that irritating thing. Joe was big into appearances. Madison wasn't." All of a sudden, the wistfulness returned to cloud her expression. "Though I would dearly love to see my little girl get the happiness she deserves. The boys too."

Kay offered him a small smile when she finally quit speaking. As if lobbing the conversational ball over to his side of the court.

"She's a strong woman. I expect she made the best of the situation."

"She really should have been back by now. Almost an hour ago, actually." She stopped talking to stare at him as if she wanted to let that sink in. "Ordinarily, I wouldn't be this concerned, but when I tried calling, her cell rang in the kitchen. She'd plugged it in to charge and forgot to take it with her. She was a little frazzled after spending most of yesterday trying to figure out some issues with her bank. I'm not sure about the particulars."

"That has to be frustrating." Adam said no more. Not his place to let on he did know a few of those particulars Kay spoke of.

"Though, I suppose with everything else going on in her life, she can be excused a little carelessness."

You have that right. All his serve and protect genes that had been latent of late suddenly rushed to the forefront. "You said she went by the cemetery. One near here, I assume."

Though he didn't have concrete facts to back it up, running on pure instinct, he suddenly had an uneasy feeling something wasn't right.

"Pine Grove Memorial Gardens, a ways down the highway. Madison said no more than twenty minutes from here." Alarm crept into her voice. As if she too shared his concern. "I certainly hope she didn't get a flat tire or something."

"She's probably fine." Regardless of what he said, Adam stood.

Kay stood too. "Not that it's particularly relevant right now, but the turkey is done. I need to take it out of the oven soon or dinner will be ruined."

Then it'll be ruined. "Why don't I go out and see if I can find her. If she's been held up somewhere by car trouble, at least we'll know for sure."

"I'll stay here. In case something did hold her up and she manages to get to a phone."

"What's your cell number? I have Madison's." He programmed hers into his phone then dialed it to give her his. "I'll call as soon as I know something."

"You be careful." Following close behind, she watched as he retrieved his coat and walked to the front door.

"It's not storming or anything. The roads aren't at all icy." Slipping his phone in his jacket pocket, he put all the reassurance into his tone he could come up with.

"That's true." She twisted her apron in trembling hands.

"Don't worry." As much as he wanted to head out on a dead run, he paused long enough to pat her on the shoulder. "I'll find her."

"I hope so." She shut the door behind him before he had to say any more.

A hearty gust of frigid air slammed into him as he stepped onto the porch. A perfect match to the sudden chill sliding over his neck and down his spine. Nearly losing his footing on the brick stairs, he hiked up the collar of his coat and ran to his car.

By the time Adam drove to the end of Madison's driveway, a stronger wind gust buffeted from the north. He gripped the wheel with both hands as he navigated out on to the deserted street. Only three turns and two miles later, he was headed down the narrow highway. Just shy of twenty minutes after that, he came to the entrance of Pine Grove Memorial Gardens. Impossible to miss, with the name spelled out in wrought iron script across an arched gateway that spanned a two-lane boulevard leading into the place.

Observing a five mile an hour posted speed limit, he wound through several evenly spaced rows of headstones, pillars, statues and neatly groomed trees. Though he ran across the occasional car and visitor, Madison wasn't among them. Nor did he see any sign of her pale green Lincoln.

Finally, he came to a stop when he circled around to the entrance again. Drumming his fingers on the steering wheel, he sat back to contemplate what to do next. Gray skies shrouded the landscape in gloom and shadows as he peered first one way then the other down the winding mountain road. Another sharp gust blew through the trees, fluttering the peaked tops of tall pines.

He started to accelerate and turn to head back the way he'd come when his cell went off. Slamming on the brakes, he punched the blue tooth button on the steering wheel.

"Hello. Hollingsworth here."

"Adam?" The woman's voice was meek and

tentative. Also familiar.

"Kay? Have you seen her? Is she home?" Releasing a breath, he relaxed against the seat.

"No. That's why I'm calling. Have you?"

He bolted upright. "No. Nothing."

"I was afraid of that."

He tried to not hear the dejection in her voice. And failed miserably. "That doesn't mean she isn't okay."

"Where are you now?"

"Just coming out of the cemetery."

"She wasn't there?"

He peered into the rearview mirror at nothing but more gloom and shadows. "I'm afraid not. Doesn't mean she wasn't earlier."

"I'm getting very worried, Adam."

I am too. "I'm sure she's fine." When Kay didn't reply, he continued, "I understand how you feel, but there's no reason to suspect foul play. Is there?"

"I suppose not. While I wasn't terribly fond of Joe, John has been nothing but supportive of her since Joe's death."

"It's too early for real concern yet. But unless I get off the phone to keep looking, I never will find her."

"Don't say that."

He gritted his teeth at his own dumb ass word choice. "I'll call you when I do find her."

"I'll be waiting."

Ending the call, he took cursory glances to his left then right before pulling back onto the highway. Flat, wide spreads of land soon gave way to a narrow roadway with steep drop-offs on either side. Daylight was quickly giving up the fight to dusk, filling Adam with an urgency he couldn't seem to shake.

By necessity, slowing to negotiate a hairpin curve, he eased the steering wheel one way then the other. Partly focused on the road ahead, at the same time he scanned from side to side along both shoulders. On his trip out to the cemetery, he'd been hell bent to get there. Period. On his way back, he could take his time. Be on the lookout for anything out of the ordinary. As tires hummed on pavement, he kept his gaze going right, center, left. Left, center, right.

After a mile or two, a flash of metal at street level caught in his headlights. Slowing to a crawl, he aimed the car slightly right. Bent at the center, what had been a speed limit sign picked up the light again.

His tires crunched on gravel as he pulled onto the shoulder. Turning the ignition off and the flashers on, he stepped out on the pavement. More chilling gusts pummeled him as he slammed the door shut and walked around the front of the car.

Primed to take full advantage of what little daylight was left, he walked over for a closer look. Though rough under his fingertips, the metal surface didn't have one spot of rust. Plus, the post supports were bent. Mangled. Not rusted or broken off from everyday wear and tear.

In the distance the yowl of a coyote competed with the wind howling in the treetops.

Cursing himself for not being better prepared, Adam yanked out his cell then issued a sigh of relief to find it was fully charged. With the flashlight app flicked on, he scanned its beam along the rugged terrain of the roadside. Slowly and methodically, taking one careful step then another, he strained to discover something.

"Come on, damn it. Give it up. Send me a clue."

Navigating on pure instinct, he blinked as a wicked blast of cold air stung his eyes. He brushed at the resulting tears with the back of his free hand.

Concentrate!

Blinking away more wind induced tears, he kept his single-minded focus on the ground. Suddenly, the small stones and pebbles up ahead of him were separated in a linear pattern.

Tire tracks! Two sets. Running parallel to the shoulder.

Strands of fear prickled their way up his spine to the back of his neck. The hairs all along the way rose up as a sickening chill slid over his flesh. A chill that had nothing to do with the strengthening wind.

Along the shoulder, dual distinct tire marks dwindled to a single track as the one on the far side disappeared. Farther along, the solitary track vanished too.

Over the edge of a steep embankment.

Skidding sideways, half running, half leaping, Adam made his way down the ridge until he came to a stop at a thickening clump of trees. A collection of saplings, their narrow trunks bunched together to form a distinct barrier, hid whatever lay beyond.

He blinked several times to clear his vision then held the phone light up to eye level as he peered as far down the mountain as the beam would allow.

A sliver of lighter green was discernable just beyond the conglomeration of trees. He angled the light from left to right. More pale green showed up. His heartbeat spiked as he strained to make out what, exactly was down there.

A car! Madison's car!

Stones, twigs and other debris rustled and rattled down the mountain and out of his way as he slid then jogged and slid some more in a hasty descent. Pushing through the jutting bare branches of larger trees, his head notched back and he cried out as the spikey finger of a limb sliced across his cheek. More surprised than injured, he kept going. Surging adrenaline made him immune to pain as he rounded a small blue spruce growing at a horizontal angle.

Madison's car rested with its nose tilted downward on a large, flat expanse of land. The front passenger door was buried against a scraggly pine tree.

His blood chilled.

Rushing to the driver's side, horror took over for expediency as he stared at a severely cracked window. Madison's head lay still against its surface. Fear and apprehension, dread and alarm all rose up to collide into a twisted mess in the center of his gut. Going rigid, he brought flailing emotions under control and took careful stock of the situation. The air bags never deployed. Several saplings must have gradually slowed her descent until she came to a stop.

Better than being jolted to a halt by the side of a cliff. Or worse.

He shuddered at the grotesque vision as he maintained the presence of mind to circle the car. All four wheels were firmly planted on solid ground. *Thank God.*

Jabbing nine-one-one into his cell, he listened for a response.

"Nine-one-one what is your emergency?"

"I'm out on Highway thirty-four. East of the Pine Grove Memorial Gardens." He quelled the panic he hadn't kept from his voice and gave a brief description of the circumstances along with his best guess of GPS coordinates. "My car is on the side of the road with the flashers going. A dark blue Denali. Texas license MJT 721. It's a rental."

"Stay on the line, please."

Whatever. Keeping the call open and on speaker, he shoved the cell in his pocket. Hurrying back around to the driver's side, he rapped lightly on the glass. Had he detected movement? Or were growing shadows and a strengthening wind playing tricks on him?

Sending forth a silent prayer, he rapped again. His heart jumped as he truly did detect movement. Her head lifted briefly. Rebounded down, then rose again. Relief rushed through him on such a torrent, his knees nearly buckled. Gripping the door handle, with a shaking hand, he pulled then braced his body against the side panel when the latch gave.

Her hands had slipped from the steering wheel and rested one on her lap and one on the seat beside her. Her face was turned away from him. The seat belt was in place around her, tight and secure.

"Madison." His voice came out raspy. He tried again. Making it stronger. "Madison."

She raised her head. *"Hmmmmmm."*

The groan she released both thrilled and terrified him. "It's me. Adam."

"Adam?" Her voice was frail, somewhat muffled as she lifted her gaze to his. "What are you doing here?" Closing her eyes, she shifted on the seat.

"Don't move." Willing his fingers not to shake, he placed a firm but gentle hand against her left shoulder at the same time sending up a huge note of gratitude she was able to move at all. Her neck and back seemed intact. Hopefully a sign nothing was broken. Or too badly damaged.

"Where does it hurt?"

"Nowhere." Bringing her gaze level with his, she shifted her head side to side then raised one tentative arm and the other. As she rested them back on the seat, she groaned first then sighed. "And everywhere."

Relief washed over him again as her speech remained measured and coherent.

No indications of shock.

"What happened? How'd you get down here?" He silently chastised himself for bombarding her with questions. "You do know you're at the bottom of a shallow ravine."

She nodded, and Adam sucked in a breath he held on to.

"Does your neck hurt?" His fingers barely made contact as he probed her cervical vertebrae.

A wind gust whipped through the opened door, and she shivered then shook her head.

"No. Should it?"

He slowly released his next breath. By all indications she was in one piece. "I guess not."

"Nothing really hurts except my arms and elbows. I stiffened them and held on to the steering wheel when I lost control and went off the road. I didn't dare let go until the car came to a stop." As she relived the ordeal, she shivered again. "I must say, that was one heck of a ride."

Leaned against the door frame more to support himself in case his knees buckled again, he blew out a weak chuckle. "I don't doubt that."

"A big white truck coming from the other way, swerved into me. It happened so fast."

A series of questions immediately came to mind. *Did you get a license number? Can you describe the driver? What make of vehicle was it? Late model? Older? Any distinctive markings?*

One by one, he dismissed them all as he simply reached for her hand. "Don't try to do anything right now. An ambulance is on the way."

"Are you sure that's necessary?" Even as she asked, she stayed still.

"I'm sure." Holding her hand, he stroked his thumb along the inside of her wrist. But only after he made sure he'd quit trembling. "Just relax, Madison. I'm also sure you'll be fine."

Chapter Nine

"You're very fortunate, Mrs. Clark. No broken bones and no evidence you suffered a concussion or any serious injuries." The dark-haired woman who had introduced herself as Doctor Winters returned the stylus to the right breast pocket of her white lab coat and closed the laptop that contained Madison's electronic medical record.

"Tell that to my aching muscles. I'm not sure they got the message." Madison offered a weak smile as she settled her head against the small pillow and wiggled her limbs into a more comfortable position. Not an easy task on the thin, plastic encased cushion that passed for a mattress. Even if it was covered in a clean flannel sheet.

The tall, slender doctor smiled and rested her hand on the metal railing that encased Madison on one side. "It's perfectly natural to have a certain amount of muscle soreness following an accident like yours. Whether we're aware of it or not, we automatically tense up in that kind of situation. It ties in with the fight or flight reaction our bodies naturally go into when we're faced with imminent danger."

"Your car traveled a good hundred or so feet over some pretty rough terrain." Adam spoke from nearby. "It's no wonder you're hurting. You must have been bounced around quite a bit. Although knowing why you're sore probably doesn't make it hurt any less."

Madison glanced over at the man who had not left her side or let go of her hand, except when he was forced to, since he first found her a few hours ago on the side of that mountain. Who had even helped her fill out the myriad of papers and forms they needed signed before anyone would even look at her.

As she inadvertently squeezed his hand, he smiled at her and her heart warmed. Right now, his calm, easy-going manner did more to ease her discomfort than all the efforts of Doctor Winters and modern medicine combined.

She shifted her limbs again, then winced when tingles of pain ran along her shoulders and down the middle of her back. *So okay. Once again, he stepped up to rescue me.* This was fast becoming a habit she'd have a hard time to break when the time came.

"Time. You'll feel better in time." The doctor tucked her laptop under one arm. "Until then you're restricted to acetaminophen as needed for any discomfort, and rest. A woman in your condition needs lots of rest." Though her words were for Madison, Doctor Winters looked directly at Adam before bringing a benevolent gaze back to her. "You were very, very lucky."

"I know." Without thinking much about it, Madison found her eyes straying again to Adam. Again she squeezed his hand. "I know."

"I'll send the nurse in to go over your discharge instructions. Have a nice remainder of your holiday." Twisting her wrist, she looked at her watch as she headed for the door. "What's left of it anyway."

"Thank you. We will."

Adam and Madison spoke in unison, then glanced at each other and laughed.

He too checked his watch. "It's almost nine thirty. When I talked to your mother an hour ago, she said Mr. Ratcliff brought the boys home, and the tow truck company had called to confirm where your car was taken."

Even though she really wasn't in any horrible physical pain, Madison winced again. "I am not looking forward to working with my insurance company on all of this. I've had it up to my eyeballs dealing with various financial and insurance institutions since Joe's death."

At the mention of her late husband, she could have sworn Adam grimaced. Or maybe she imagined hearing Joe's name bothered him. Possibly as much as it bothered her to speak it. Before she could decide, there was a light tapping at the door.

"Yes?"

After a couple more taps, the door was pushed open. "Everyone decent?"

Recognizing the voice, Madison glanced up. "John. What are you doing here?"

"Your mother filled me in on what happened after we left the cemetery. I got here as quickly as I could." Talking as he entered the room, he came to a stop beside Adam.

"You didn't need to bother coming down here." She softened her words with an appreciative smile. "But thank you for caring."

"Of course. I wanted to see for myself how you were doing." Glancing at Adam first, he quickly looked back at her with one brow lifted.

It took a moment for realization to dawn. "Oh. I forgot. You two haven't met."

After she made the introductions, along with a brief description of how each of them fit into her life, Adam released her hand just long enough to shake John's.

Emotions she couldn't discern flitted across his face as, retaking her hand, he stayed where he was at the head of her bed. "The doctors say there are no serious injuries from her ordeal."

She didn't mind one bit when he saved her the trouble of filling John in on the details of her condition. Only adding one more thing when he was finished. "The police came here to fill out the accident report."

"That's good." Though he'd clearly heard Adam, John didn't take his eyes off her. "Did they find who ran you off the road?"

"Unfortunately, no. I'm afraid I wasn't much help to them in identifying the truck." Plastic creaked as she shifted on the narrow gurney. "The doctor says I'm in good enough shape to get out of here. Although I'm afraid I ruined Thanksgiving."

"You did that." John laughed outright at her feeble attempt at humor. "Kay did say she's keeping dinner warm for you."

"Speaking of which, she's probably made enough food for a small army. She always does." She glanced from John to Adam then back to John. "Stop by next week for leftovers."

The ghost of a smile played around his lips, and his eyes lit briefly. "You know, I just may take you up on that offer. As much as you've raved about your mother's cooking."

"We'd love to have you."

"Then it's a date. As my work schedule allows. I have a couple of jobs out of town. You could say the demolition business is booming." Again he laughed. This time at his own joke.

Madison glanced at Adam. "John owns a construction company which specializes in demolition projects. Done Right Demolition."

"Must be interesting work." Adam nodded but said nothing more.

"Pays the bills, as they say." His attention swung from Adam to Madison. "I'm glad to see you're okay." His gaze strayed back to Adam. "I see you don't need a ride home."

He nodded and, whether he realized or not, his grip on Madison's hand tightened. "Yeah. I've got this."

"And your car and everything—"

"Got that too." Adam didn't let him finish.

"Well. Again, it's good to see you're okay." Leaning forward, he reached out a tentative hand. Then, as if wondering what to do with it, he ended up patting her shoulder. "I'll touch base with you soon."

"Thanks for checking on me, John."

"Anytime." Backing away, he nodded to Adam and was gone.

"Well, I sure didn't expect a visit from him." She pulled her gaze away from the closed door to look at Adam. "But I shouldn't really be surprised."

"I understand he's been there for you in all this."

"He probably feels guilty. John was at the cemetery when I got there. He said a few words about Joe. I said a few, very few. We talked briefly about some of Joe's good points." She glanced away then back at him. "Such as they were."

"Anything else you remember? Did someone follow you when you left the cemetery?"

"To be honest, I didn't pay attention. I was focused on getting home to celebrate with the boys, my mother…and you."

"We should get someone in here to help you dress." He reached under the gurney for the plastic bag containing her clothes and placed it on the bed, then left without saying more.

As the door bumped softly closed behind him, Madison rested her head against the postage stamp sized pillow and closed her eyes. So much for the low key, traditional family holiday she had hoped to share with the boys…and promised Adam.

Taking a second to draw a breath, the next thing she knew her throat started to burn. Unbidden tears bubbled to the surface, and immediately spilled over. Dropping her chin, covering her face with one hand, before she could do anything to prevent it, deep, heartfelt sobs erupted out of her. Though she tried her best to keep them from becoming too loud. God forbid she call more attention to herself than she already had.

Making very little sound at all, she let loose. Her chest rose and fell, and her shoulders trembled as she gave herself up to a good cleansing cry.

"They're in the middle of shift change right now, so it's going to be a while until…hey…Madison…what are you doing? What's wrong?"

Adam was across the room and beside her bed, taking both of her hands in his.

"I don't…" She hauled in a breath that shook her, head to toe.

Readying more words of explanation, she never got

171

the chance to use them as strong, capable arms gathered her close. Pulled her fast against a solid chest. Gripping the smooth front of his dress shirt, she burrowed into unbelievable comfort and let more sobs convulse out.

"It's okay. It's okay." The tenderness in his voice was like a cherished and familiar blanket as it floated over her.

Saying no more, simply hanging on, with her next exhale all the pent up sadness and tension flowed away. She rested her head against him to just be, soothed beyond measure by the constant rhythm of his heartbeat.

Don't get too used to this.

"I don't know why I keep doing that, but it has to stop." Pushing away, she coughed self-consciously into her elbow, then gave a few clumsy swipes to both cheeks.

"I'd say you're entitled." Adam stepped to a counter for a box of tissues he passed over.

"Thank you." Unladylike or not, she didn't care as she grabbed a handful and blew her nose with a blast that would make a moose in the wild proud. Pulling out a few more sheets, she dabbed at her eyes and blotted her cheeks.

"These might work better." Rushing back to the same counter, Adam brought over some pre-moistened cleansing wipes he found.

"Thank you again." Turning her full attention to opening the pack, she ran the cooling, scented clothes over her face and neck. "That feels a lot better."

"Let me take care of those." Springing into action again, he gathered the disposable towels he tossed in the flip top trash can by the door.

He'd no sooner returned to her side when a twenty something man, clad in running shoes and navy blue scrubs with a stethoscope draped on his neck, strode in.

"Mrs. Clark, I assume. I'm Tony, here with your discharge information."

Making sure her gown was securely closed, Madison swung her legs over one side of the bed. "I'm listening."

Adam stood straighter, hopefully to do the same.

"Doctor Winters recommends a follow up visit with your family doctor in the next week to ten days." The nurse flipped, one by one, through the packet of papers he'd brought in with him, explaining pertinent details of each. "If you have any immediate issues, the direct line to the nurses' station here on the floor is in there too. Do you have any questions?"

Madison accepted the sheets of type-written instructions and laid them on the tray over her bed. She did have questions. Lots of them. He'd gone through the whats and what nots so quickly, she'd followed some but hadn't retained much.

"No. No questions." When she got home and her brain defogged some more, she could read through the papers and figure everything out.

"You said a no lifting restriction."

Relief rushed in when Adam picked up the sheets he began to slowly leaf through. She made sure to pay close attention when he ticked off a few items for clarification.

"Just so we're clear."

"Of course." Nurse Tony glanced up, not seeming to mind as he patiently went through the better part of the list again.

When he finished, Adam got one more item clarified Madison hadn't even thought about then nodded. "Thanks. I feel a lot better about taking her out of here now."

"Oh, one other thing. Who's emergency contact?"

He glanced up expectantly at Adam, who immediately rattled off his personal information the man copied down.

"Now just sign here and here." The nurse set more papers in front of Madison. "Then you can get dressed." He glanced from Madison to Adam as he backed toward the door. "I'll send an escorted wheelchair in when one's available."

"Thank you."

"Do you want me to go get a female nurse to help you?" Adam indicated the white plastic bag he'd long ago set at the foot of her bed.

She shook her head. "I think I can handle it on my own."

"Sounds good." On his way to the door, he paused and turned back. "I'll be right outside if you need me."

"I know."

Their gazes locked and a shimmer of unity seemed to pass between them. Only to be gone just as quickly when Adam walked out and closed the door behind him.

As it happened, Madison was entirely capable of dressing herself. Though not without a touch of frustration when she struggled to get the top button of her sweater fastened at the back of her neck. Which, after turning her arms into a couple of pretzels, she eventually accomplished. Slipping into her shoes, she got up to walk across the room and open the door to summon Adam. As promised, he was just outside. Along with the wheelchair and escort.

"I'm ready. Let's go home."

Her next car ride was blessedly uneventful. Walking into her house, with Adam's help, and the waiting arms of her overprotective mother was another story entirely.

"Madison. Sweetheart. Thank God you're okay." She was immediately crushed into an intense embrace.

"I'm fine, Mom. Just a little sore is all."

As if taken at her word, she was immediately let go.

"Adam! How can I ever thank you for bringing my girl home safe."

If Madison's welcome home hug had been intense, the one Adam received appeared to be even fiercer. In fact, she actually heard the whoosh of air rush from his lungs once Kay Carmichael decided to take hold.

"I'm just glad nothing more serious happened." Leaned down to her mother's level, he briefly returned her embrace and stepped back.

"What you did was so wonderful." Her mother took both his coat and Madison's and hung them up. "We can never thank you enough."

"There's no need." Adam turned his gaze on Madison. "The fact she's fine and relatively unhurt is thanks enough for me."

"Mom! You're okay!" Dak tore down the stairs and launched into her arms. "I was so afraid you wouldn't make it home." He kept his arms clamped tight around her waist.

Her mother caught her eye and mouthed, 'he was inconsolable'.

Tears welled up, as her heart squeezed. "But I did come home to you, honey. I would never leave you."

She put her hand on Dak's head to hold him close as she raised a watery gaze skyward. Dak seemed upset enough. Why add to it with a mother who couldn't control her emotions? The last thing he needed was to see her blubbering away.

Clearing her throat, Madison swallowed her tears, then nodded and willed her voice to come out strong. "Adam came and found me and brought me home."

The words had no sooner left her mouth when Dak released her and flung himself at Adam. Arms wrapped securely, head burrowed tightly. Much as he'd embraced her.

This cannot go on forever. Would she and the boys ever recover?

"Hey, Buddy. It's okay. Your mom's fine." Adam gently stroked the back of Dak's head.

Lowering her chin to her chest, Madison let her own shoulders slump as she drew slow, shaky breaths. She simply had to pull herself together. If only for the sake of her children.

"Take it easy. It's okay."

Adam's voice reached out to fold her in, much as it had in the hospital. While he still held on to Dak with one arm, he circled her shoulders with the other to bring her close. Warmth seeped in from his body to hers. Exactly what she needed, exactly when she needed it.

"The important thing is we're here together with a few hours of Thanksgiving Day remaining."

At her mother's voice, Madison lifted her head. And found herself looking directly into Cameron's dry eyed gaze. His forehead creased further as he glanced from his mother to Adam then back at her.

"Hey. I'm home." Stepping away from Adam, she gathered her oldest in for a quick hug. Surely all he'd allow.

"I'm glad you're safe." He whispered just before she released him.

"Thank you, sweetheart. I am too." Gratitude filled her heart as the smiles they exchanged took care of any more tears that may have been left in her.

"Who's hungry?" Again her mother spoke up.

Good old Mom.

"I know I am. I haven't eaten since breakfast." Adam was the first to get on the family food train.

"Me either." Though Madison hardly had the appetite for a big turkey dinner, she was willing to give eating something a try.

"I could eat again." Dak let go of Adam to follow his grandma toward the kitchen, his fears about losing his mother apparently put on the back burner for now.

"Cameron. I know you could eat again." As her mother passed by her oldest, she rounded him up with a sweep of one arm. "Boys your age are always up for another meal. I will confess the boys and I did eat a little something while you two were still at the hospital." She called out over her shoulder as she hustled Dak and Cameron toward the kitchen ahead of her. "Once we knew you were okay, of course. Then we reset the table while we waited for you to get home. You two sit down in the dining room. After the day you've both had, you deserve to relax."

As the door shut behind them, Madison glanced up at Adam. "But first…" She walked over to the table in the entrance for her purse and the two hundred dollars she handed over. "I had planned to give this to you when you got here today."

Surprise crossed his face as he accepted the cash. "I'd forgotten all about this."

"I hadn't. Keep the change."

He glanced up at her as if unsure what to do with the money. "You're sure you can…"

"…afford to pay you back? I'm sure. It was a bank error that was easily resolved." Spouting the little white lie, she closed his hand over the bills. *After nearly half a day on the phone with them and the promise of my soul.* "But thank you for helping me out."

"Anytime." He flashed a smile as he slipped the money in his pocket.

"So now. How about it?" Setting her purse back on the table, Madison extended her hand his way. "Dinner?"

"Sounds good to me." Coming forward, he wrapped his fingers over hers and squeezed.

A sense of contentment and well-being flowed up her arm to settle directly around her heart. "Thank you for comforting Dak the way you did."

"What else would I do?" The fingers holding on to hers loosened. Releasing her hand, he ushered her in front of him into the dining room. "Whatever is going on in that kitchen smells pretty awesome."

"It does, doesn't it?" Another little white lie escaped from her lips as she sat in the chair Adam pulled out for her.

"I'll say." He took a seat beside her.

"If you ask me, the best part of any Thanksgiving feast is the leftovers." Her mother entered with Dak and Cameron close behind. Each of them carried a dish heaped with a traditional menu item. "And we do have plenty of leftovers." She set a steaming plate of white and dark turkey meat in front of Adam. Then a bowl of rich, moist stuffing beside it. "We're about to give new meaning to the term midnight snack."

"Only babies go to bed early." Cameron added his bowl to the table with a thunk. One mounded with mashed potatoes glistening with butter.

All the rich and succulent flavors and smells made her stomach roil, and Madison swallowed.

"Ooops." Gravy slopped over the side when Dak fumbled the white china boat onto the table. "Sorry."

"No problem, sweetie." Of course, Grandma intervened immediately. "I probably got that dish too hot for you."

The thick liquid pooled on the light blue tablecloth. A small ring of grease immediately formed around it. Madison's stomach flip-flopped before she averted her gaze.

"This all looks great, Kay." Adam swept his napkin off the table. "And guys."

"Green bean casserole is yet to come. It's in the microwave." Her mother put both hands on her hips as she surveyed the spread. "What else?"

"You forgot the rolls." Madison was out of her chair in a heartbeat. "I'll go get those."

"Grab the casserole too, dear, if you would."

"Sure."

Whatever she had in her stomach, which wasn't much, churned to the back of her throat as Madison bolted for the kitchen. Once in there, and alone, she went immediately to the sink and gripped the counter with both hands. Lowering her head, she concentrated on taking slow, even breaths. Eventually, she turned on the tap to cold and reached in the cupboard to her left for a crystal tumbler. Cool, clear water splashed and bubbled from the faucet into the glass. The queasiness of her stomach eased in response.

Even so, small, deliberate sips were all she could handle as she kept a tight hold on the counter edge with her free hand.

"My goodness but you certainly did shoot out of there...Madison..." Her mother was beside her in an instant. "Are you okay?"

"I'm fine." Straightening, she set her glass on the marble counter with a clink. "Just feeling a little woozy is all."

"From the looks of you, it's more than woozy." The back of her mother's hand was pressed to her forehead. Cool palms landed on her cheeks. "You don't feel warm...but...maybe we should call that hospital back. I'm going to get Adam."

"No!" The sheer power in her voice surprised both of them.

On her way to the dining room, her mother swung back around. "What do you mean no? Or I should say, that was pretty definitive." To her credit, her mom kept her voice down as she walked toward her.

Releasing her grip on the counter, Madison made her way over to the carver blue breakfast nook by the bay windows to sit on one end of the blue and yellow flowered cushion.

"No doubt the result of today's ordeal." Taking the seat directly across, her mother set down the glass of water Madison had neglected to bring with her.

"Thanks." She clutched the tumbler with both

hands and swallowed a couple of healthy sips.

"Plus so many emotions getting to you?"

She glanced out at the backyard dotted with an assortment of bare-branched elms illuminated by strategically placed flood lights. Several of the blue spruce on the outer lot had recently been neatly trimmed. Thanks to John.

"Something like that. I am actually feeling much better now." White lies three and four came out with very little effort.

"You're fortunate to have met Adam. Very fortunate he cared enough to come looking for you."

Though her mother voiced the same thoughts that had been running through Madison's mind of late, all she did was shrug. "Most anyone would have done the same thing."

A hand rested on her arm. "Not with the determination I witnessed in those beautiful baby blues of his today. When he headed out the door."

"Maybe so." Madison glanced down. "Too bad this will be the end of it. Coming to my aid once certainly doesn't translate to a forever relationship."

Her mom inclined her head until Madison could do nothing but look up at her again. "Give me one good reason why it wouldn't be the beginning of something wonderful for you."

"How much time do we have? I can provide several."

Kay Carmichael didn't flinch. "I'm listening. And I have all the time in the world."

"For starters." She ran a finger around the rim of her glass. "We've been over this before. Two husbands within a three-year span is bad enough to make me feel like I carry the curse of a Black Widow. Why subject Adam to my apparent string of bad luck."

"Who said anything about another husband? I certainly didn't." Thin brows arched above knowing eyes. "Why did you?"

Madison picked up her water she brought slowly to her lips. If only to buy time to come up with a feasible answer. "I'm not suggesting marriage, per se."

"What other kind of marriage is there?" One corner of her mouth quirked up, almost in challenge. "And I ask again, why did *you* even suggest it?"

Glancing up, she toyed with the ridged surface of her glass. "Do you want to hear my answer or not?"

"I'm sorry, sweetheart. Go ahead." Folding her arms on the table, she leaned forward. "Except, I think it's very telling you classify Adam in the same league as two other men you actually cared enough for to marry."

"This isn't a forever relationship. He's here in town temporarily for possibly another month, maybe two."

"That's his commitment to the production company. Not a schedule for the rest of his life."

Madison remained silent, allowing a pointed stare to speak for her.

"I'm sorry, sweetheart." Her mom closed her mouth and made a locking the door motion in front of it with her thumb and forefinger.

"Aside from the Black Widow Syndrome that seems to be following me around, and the lack of permanence that Adam seems to be offering, there are my boys' feelings to consider."

Her mother made an elaborate show of unlocking her once sealed lips. "You mean those boys who absolutely adore the man. Those boys?"

"Yes. Those boys. Adam has also made it very clear his first love is police work. A job he wants to get back to as soon as he can. All the way in Detroit. He hasn't exactly asked me to pull up stakes with the boys to follow him there."

"Not yet anyway. If you don't recognize everything he's done for you and the boys as interest, there is something seriously wrong with that head of yours." She considered her daughter with wise eyes. "Or I should say your heart."

Madison brought her right hand over to cover the left side of her chest. "Not that far-fetched that something's wrong with either one of them, especially my heart. It's been broken enough times." She rubbed her fingertips lightly over the badly bruised organ. A slight stab of regret seemed to confirm her words. "I'm not sure how much more damage it, or I, can take."

"Oh, sweetheart." Standing, she came around to wrap Madison in a hug. "You have been through more heartbreak than most women twice your age. And come through remarkably well."

"Thanks, Mom." Madison sank into her mother's familiar warmth. "Sometimes, most times, I wonder about the remarkably well part."

"You and the boys deserve stability and happiness in your future."

"I won't argue with that."

"And one Mr. Adam Hollingsworth might be just the answer."

Madison blew out a breath. "If only that were true."

"Hey. Where's the green bean casserole?"

Cameron burst through the door.

Both of them jumped, then jerked their gazes up at him with their mouths open.

"What?" Her mom found her voice first.

"Adam says he loves green bean casserole. Though I have no idea why." Since Cameron didn't, he made a face of disgust. "I told him I'd get it for him."

"Here." Apparently finding her wits about her first too, her mother jumped up, then reached in the microwave and handed over the towel wrapped casserole dish. "Take this in to him. Your mother and I will be there in a minute. Once we get the rolls in a basket."

That was Madison's call to action. Hoping Cameron hadn't overheard even one tiny syllable of their conversation, she hurried over to the warming oven and opened it.

"Tell Adam we'll be there in just a minute. Like Grandma said."

Casserole in hand, Cameron headed back to the dining room. "Yeah. Sure. I'll be sure to tell…" The mumbled comment was cut off as the door swung shut behind him.

Madison stared at where Cameron had been, before she feverishly loaded rolls into the wicker basket she'd pulled down from a top cupboard.

"Let's go." Her mom already stood by the door making a subtle head tilt toward the dining room.

Thankfully, Madison's stomach was acting as if it was willing to cooperate. The roiling had subsided for the most part, and the back of her throat was no longer burning with whatever was down there struggling to come back up. Walking over to the table, she picked up her glass for another swallow, more like a gulp, of water then set the tumbler down too hard. The glass clinked then wobbled. Steadying that, she took a deep breath in an attempt to steady herself.

"Okay." Straightening, she silently vowed to keep from looking at the greasy spot of gravy. Which surely must have dried by now.

"We have a guest waiting."

"Not. A. Word." Madison more hissed than whispered as she passed by. "Nothing about what we discussed. To anyone out there."

"Moi?" A look of pure innocence followed as she led the way to the dining room.

"I won it once. And only once." Adam leaned toward Dak and Cameron who sat across from him.

"How?" Both leaned forward too, eyes wide. Mouths even wider. "Neither one of us can get beyond level eight."

They were obviously talking about some video game Madison knew nothing about.

Adam turned when she and her mother came into the room. "Everything okay?"

"Peachy." She set down the rolls then took her seat beside him.

"That's good." He looked away to return to his original conversation, and hopefully didn't see how flushed her cheeks were. "I'll show you guys a few of the secrets I learned."

"Tomorrow?" Dak was the first to pipe up.

Adam glanced at Madison. "Maybe not that soon. But soon enough. In fact…" He swung his gaze back to the boys. "I'd invite you both over to my place to play, but I'm afraid where I'm living these days is a little

185

cramped for a gaming tournament."

He went on to explain a few details about his 'place' Madison remembered all too well.

As Adam occasionally caught her with a keen eyed gaze, she tried to swallow, only to find the inside of her mouth had gone bone dry. As echoes of her mother's words rang in her ears.

Chapter Ten

Bright and early the Monday after Thanksgiving, all the cast and crew had returned to Colorado to get back to work.

"Piece of cake." Frank stood beside Adam on the roof's edge of the highest point of what was originally built as a church. "Your typical long jump maneuvers. Run up, take off, flight, landing." As he spoke, he ticked each item off on the fingers of one hand. "Push off, leap across the short chasm between the buildings, and end up on the roof over there." He indicated the main mansion. "If it's not a perfect landing, they pick up the scene from there. Or however Joel wants to film it."

Short chasm my ass. Adam peered across the empty expanse that, in his estimation had to be a good thirty feet in length. With its three story drop to nothing but jagged rocks and unyielding pavement.

"It's twenty-three feet eight inches from here to there. Rafe and I measured it yesterday." Frank's voice was calmly matter of fact.

Adam shifted his gaze from across to down. "How far to the ground?"

"No more than forty feet max. Give or take." His stunt buddy didn't even bother to look when making the calculation, which wasn't comforting in the least.

"You didn't bother to measure that?"

"Why would we?" Brow creased as he glanced over, Frank shrugged. "Not a calculation we need."

"Might be nice to know." Adam eyeballed the distance he then tried to calculate.

"Jumping higher to lower is the saving grace of this stunt. You get the advantage of two, three feet easy."

"That's horizontal right? Not vertical."

"Of course horizontal." The man who had taught Adam everything he knew about stunts stared off behind him. "You're gonna need at least forty feet of runway. Sixty would be better."

Which means maybe eighty would be best. Adam stayed silent as he studied the flat portion of the roof behind them, doing his best to figure how much 'runway' he actually had. Obviously Rafe and Frank hadn't measured that part just yet either.

"One thing to remember is to start as far back as you can to get enough forward motion behind you. Then jump more out than up. Maybe do a hitch kick while you're airborne. We'll work on that. You don't want to waste any trajectory energy." He raised his hands in a brief illustration. "You'd probably be better off to tuck and roll as you land safely on the other side. They can always edit that out. Since the scene calls for you to keep running right to the door."

Safely on the other side. Right.

"You're less likely to break your neck that way. Or a limb. So long as you remember to pull your arms in. And, of course, protect your head."

God yes. Protect my head. So far, Adam had been concentrating on the ways to prevent any broken bones and major bruising of vital organs. He hadn't even considered the probability of more serious injury. Like maybe a concussion. Severe brain damage. Death.

"Yep. This should work pretty well."

"*Should* work, *pretty* well?" Adam parroted his friend's words. Emphasizing those that left him feeling less than supremely confident. "Gotta tell ya, that's not terribly reassuring."

"You'll do fine." The stunt master thumped him on the back.

To reinforce the supposed encouragement he was spreading? "Uh-huh."

"We'll do all the rest of the measurements to be sure."

"Sure of what? How far I'd have to fall to break my neck?"

Frank's hearty laugh was followed by another back thump. "Something like that."

"The fact you're failing to make eye contact doesn't mean anything. Right?" His self-preservation instinct had been activated the moment they'd climbed up here. All fifty-four stair steps. Adam had been very particular in counting them. Three frickin' stories.

"Yeah. Right." Still not looking directly at him, Frank stepped closer to the edge. No doubt the better to see straight down. When he turned again to look behind him then stared down once more, Adam joined him. Even though he wasn't exactly sure what they were evaluating.

"I read the part of the script this stunt plays into." Adam didn't take his eyes off the ground below. "The bad guys are holding Flynn's son hostage in the mansion." He spread an arm out. "On the other side of the little chasm, as you so eloquently put it."

Frank let out a chuckle but said nothing, so Adam

went on.

"The room they're holding him in is ringed with windows aka our converted ballroom slash soundstage. The only way in without being detected, is down from that roof. That's how it's written to fit the layout of this site."

"Listen, if Joel wants it, we'll make it work."

"If the resolve in your voice is designed to be convincing, it's definitely not working. You still haven't made me feel any better."

"Don't sweat the small stuff. You'll wear a harness. You don't make it all the way across, you don't fall that far and we haul you back up."

Yeah. The small stuff. I got this.

"We'll figure out all the trajectories and angles." Frank turned to leave the rooftop. "Then we practice. Practice. Practice."

"Be still my heart." Adam thumped himself on the chest with a closed fist. "I can't wait."

A roar of laughter echoed up the enclosed staircase as they descended to street level. "They want to shoot the scene within the next two weeks. We have our work cut out for us."

As they walked outside, a bright sun overhead had no clouds to interfere with its warmth. Even with the bite of a light northern breeze filtering in.

Frank put a hand on his shoulder. "I'll let you know when we're ready to start those practice runs."

"I'll be waiting."

With one last smile, more of a smirk, and casual salute, Frank turned left as Adam headed right. Hurrying across the center courtyard toward the base camp, he was anxious to reach the solitude of his trailer.

He hadn't gone far when his cell went off. Its distinct ring alerted him one of his brothers in blue was calling.

"Hey. How's it going?"

His greeting was generic. No matter which of his three best friends this was, Brad, Vince or Luke, he truly did want to know how they were doing.

"My life is shit right now. How about yours?"

Luke, the maverick of their close foursome, known for getting the job done, proper procedure be damned, must have gotten himself in hot water with the brass yet again.

"What happened now?"

"Not much. For once *I* didn't do anything." A quiet sigh followed. "Chelsea and I broke up. Rather she walked out on me."

"Gee. That's tough. I'm sorry to hear that."

"Yeah, thanks." Another sigh came out more like a groan. "Tell me women are poison."

"If that's what you want to hear. Women are poison." Adam sat on a stone bench in front of the church, leaned back and stretched his legs out in front of him.

"I can tell by your tone you're just humoring me. Care to share?"

"Not if you called to talk. Go." No need to add he wasn't sure what exactly it was he had to share anyway.

"Here I thought I'd started a trend getting engaged and all. Then Brad hooked up with Jenny, Vince found Sydney. I was convinced you were going to end up the last man standing."

"Yep. It's you and me now buddy." Even before he spoke, he wasn't sure he could keep the promise.

"I'm gonna hold you to that." Luke let out a chuckle. "However, that's not the only reason I called. Vince asked me to give you a heads up on the Hawthorn case. Official notification is coming your way, but he says plan on flying home day after tomorrow. The Department can make the arrangements. Notify you by email."

"I'll wait to hear." He looked across the complex toward the house Joel used as an office. The lights were on. "Listen. I'm going to have to let you go."

"Okay."

"I hate to cut you off. Call me later if you need to talk about your breakup. Right now, I want to talk to my director before he gets too holed up going over the dailies from yesterday. I need to secure the time off, because, believe me, I am going to be there to testify."

"Sounds good, buddy. Talk to you soon."

"See ya." Adam stuffed the cell in his pocket as he stood.

As he'd assumed, Joel was totally engrossed in staring at the computer screen. He looked up briefly when Adam walked in. "Hey. What do you need?"

May as well come right to the point. "Time off."

"Have a seat." Joel depressed a button on the keyboard and the action running across the screen froze. "We'll talk about it."

Adam stayed on his feet. "Nothing to talk about, Joel. I need the time off."

His director leaned back in his chair. "For what?"

"The voice mail I left you?" Taking in the blank stare he got in return, Adam went on. "The case I told you about. The one I worked on nearly a year ago back home has a trial date. It's set to start this week. I fly out day after tomorrow."

"You have to be kidding." He had Joel's full attention now. Intense glare and all.

Adam put his hands out, palms up. "Short notice, I know. That's how the criminal justice system sometimes works."

"I'm not sure that's possible. We're deep in production here and—"

"It has to be possible. It's my job. My testimony is crucial to getting a conviction."

"Thought this was your job. That's what the contract you signed says." He reached toward the keyboard as if their discussion was over.

Adam came forward to put a hand on his arm to stop him. "I'm going, Joel. I don't have to stay for the whole trial. Just long enough to give my testimony. Probably no more than a week."

"A week?" The director damned near came right out of his chair. "That long?"

"Hopefully not. But, I promise, I'll make it up to you."

Letting out a sigh, Joel lowered his head. "I don't know. Did you get a subpoena?"

"Not yet. One's coming. Even without it, I'd go anyway."

That made him look up again quickly. "Without being legally forced?"

"It's my obligation as a peace officer."

"As opposed to your obligation as a member of this production."

"The two don't even compare."

"Really? I think they do."

Adam wasn't about to back down. After a little

more arguing, he was forced to share some of the particulars in the case. A pointless road rage incident that resulted in the death of a child. "That's why it's so important."

"I can see that. Okay, we'll shoot around your scenes, but be aware." He raised one finger he aimed at Adam's chest. "You owe me."

"Yeah. I do. And, believe me, I'm good for it."

Once back outside, Adam finally made it to his trailer and the solitude he craved. Picking up the remote, he just sat down when someone knocked. "What now?"

The tuner set aside, he stood then opened the door. Tina looked up with some papers in her hand.

"Hey."

"Adam. Good, you're here."

Without waiting for an invitation, she was up the stairs, giving him no choice but to step back to let her in.

"Joel wanted to make sure you got these."

Adam took the mini sheets she held out. More frickin' pages of script revisions he set on the table then glanced over his shoulder. "Thanks. I'll let him know if I have any questions."

"Or." She stepped farther in, shutting the door behind her with a click that echoed unreasonably loud. "If you want to go over the changes now, I'd be happy to run lines with you."

"I don't think…" He turned to reply and damned near bumped into her. "I don't think I'll go through them until later. I'm a little tired right now."

This time no lie.

Tossing and turning until the wee hours the night

before, he finally gave up at four AM, and got out of bed to go for a run. Five miles of heavy breathing and sweat soaked clothes. Then a cold shower to top off the morning's enjoyment. All because of some uneasiness he couldn't quite get a handle on. The only thing he knew for sure, his disquiet had something to do with Madison.

"I really planned to just chill the rest of the day."

He turned to take the three steps necessary to make it to the couch. She stayed right on his heels. All he wanted was to sit down and relax. Instead, he remained standing, knowing full well if he sat, she'd sit. Making it even harder to get rid of her.

"Did you have a nice Thanksgiving?"

Adam stared at her, unsure at first how to answer. "Yes. I did."

"Where did you go?" She glanced down at the cushions of his couch. A silent signal he and she should sit…together. Get comfortable.

He wasn't about to take the bait. "Local friends."

"You've met some of the locals?" Curiosity sparked in eyes rimmed by liner.

"A few."

"I suppose being the star and all. It's easy for you to be recognized. Strike up conversations."

His first instinct was denial, until he realized she was right. His position, notoriety if you will, was how he'd met Cameron…and led to his introduction to the boy's mother. "Being a cast member of this production does have its benefits I suppose."

"Hollingsworth. You got a visitor here."

At the holler and accompanying rap on the door, Adam glanced that way. Still standing face to face with

Tina, he gingerly stepped around her.

"Hollingsworth. Are you in there? You home?" More rapping followed. Harder this time.

"Yeah. Yeah. I am." Adam had his door opened to the welcome diversion in two seconds flat. "Hey, Woody. What do you need?"

"Had someone up at the front gate looking for you. I decided to escort him to you personally."

Call it a cop's intuition they shared. Adam was pretty sure the security guard had a good reason to bring whoever someone was directly to him. He registered his colleague's perpetually serious face first. Then his visitor stepped out from behind him.

"Cameron. What are you doing here?"

"Hey, Adam." With the lit up eyes and easy grin Adam was used to seeing on him whenever they met, Cameron bounded up the stairs. "I brought the copy of my birth certificate my mom said you needed."

"That's great." Adam had no choice but to step out of the boy's way to let him by, then stuck his head out the door. "Thanks, Woody. I owe you."

The ever-efficient officer simply raised a hand in the air as he ambled away. "My pleasure. Have a good day."

I will now. He turned back to his guests. "You know Tina."

"Sure. Hi, how are you?"

"Good, Cameron. And you?" Folding her arms over her chest, she offered the half smile of someone thwarted on a mission.

"She brought me some script revisions. Someone's always changing something in an effort to make things better. I think they want to start shooting your scenes soon. They said your part of the script would be sent to you after all your paperwork is properly filed."

"Yeah, my mom explained all that to me."

"How's your mother doing? Feeling better I hope."

"She's good, I guess. Stayed in bed a lot on Friday and Saturday."

"Is that right?"

"I didn't see her much."

He burned to ask for details, provided Cameron even had any, but kept his mouth shut. Though that did fit with what he knew, first hand, about her condition. She'd mentioned being tired when he called to check on her Friday afternoon. Then stayed on the phone with him for a few minutes talking about a Christmas program Dak was involved in at school. Not seeing her in person over the rest of the weekend had given him time to step back and think about his relationship with Madison Clark. Which was taking off at a zero to sixty speed he hadn't anticipated. Leaving him, more or less, along for the ride.

"I told the kids at school you came over to our house for Thanksgiving. They were pretty impressed."

At Cameron's voice his thoughts scattered, and all Adam could do was nod. "I had a good time."

Surprise settled onto Tina's face as she digested that tidbit of information. "Well, apparently I'm finished here in more ways than one."

While Adam would have preferred to execute a fist pump, he refrained. "Make sure this is properly filed with the studio. Please."

Backing toward the door, she paused just long enough to accept the certificate Cameron handed her. "Of course. It's my job."

"Thanks, Tina. For all your help." A pang of conscience hit as she turned. Though there was nothing he could do about it. He couldn't make himself feel something he didn't. Any more than he could keep himself from feeling something maybe he shouldn't. "Thanks, too, for bringing by the script changes. I appreciate it." He ended up speaking to the door she closed firmly behind her.

"Well, I guess I better head back." Cameron stood with his hands in his pockets. "I'm not sure how long it will take me to get home."

"You don't know?" *WTH?* He was certainly old enough to calculate the time and distance back to his house. "Why?"

Guilt leaked into his eyes and washed over his features before he firmed up his lips. "I…uh…hitchhiked over here."

"You what?"

"Hitchhiked. Phil's dad was supposed to give me a ride, then he couldn't." He shrugged. "What was I supposed to do?"

Sure as hell not that.

All of his knowledge about children and cars and strangers and dangers rushed to mind. Keeping his mouth shut, he held off on the lecture. Especially when Cameron's face all of a sudden had challenge written all over it. He sure as hell wasn't going to lead with *Does your mother know?*

He gritted his teeth and nodded. "That's one way of getting here."

"Mom would have a fit if she found out."

"Tell me about it." Though exasperated beyond measure, he held in a sigh as he pulled his jacket from a rack by the door. "Come on. I'll give you a ride home."

"Great! I…" Momentary elation turned to suspicion. "You aren't going to tell my mother, are you? About how I got here?"

Finally, a sigh did escape before he shook his head. "Not this time. But don't do it again. Okay?"

Cameron nodded. "Okay."

Whether wise or not, he couldn't just leave things at that. "Promise me, Cameron. It's never a good idea to hitchhike."

True remorse crossed his features as he looked Adam in the eye. "I promise."

"Good. Now let's get you home."

Letting Cameron go first, they walked out the door and got in Adam's rental. Adam gave Woody a small salute when they passed his guard station as he drove out of the complex while Cameron talked a mile a minute.

"My friend Phil got hired too. He got a part in a crowd scene. Nothing like mine."

Adam heard loud and clear what Cameron didn't say. The pride in his voice was evident. He was feeling important. And, maybe, just maybe, Adam could take credit for a little piece of Cameron's turn around.

It wasn't until he pulled into the driveway at Madison's house, put the car in park and killed the engine, that he managed to get a word in edgewise. "What are you guys doing this afternoon? Any plans?"

"My grandma said something about wanting to go to a movie."

"Any one in particular?" He followed Cameron toward the house, figuring he may as well go inside with him. Check on Madison face to face.

"Grandma's a huge sci fi fan. Dak too. They probably want to see the Star Galaxy Episode Eight."

Adam nodded. "It's supposed to be good."

"That's what we heard. Grandma didn't want to go last night for the opening. Which would have been so cool. She said it would be too crazy busy."

"Understandable."

"Welcome back, Adam. It's good to see you again." Kay's cheerful voice exploded from the living room before he barely got through the door.

"Same here, Kay."

"This will be perfect." She didn't bother to explain herself, just looked at her grandson. "Adam, you do have time to come in for a while."

Taken slightly aback, he readily agreed. "I don't have any other plans."

Grinning at his response, she shut the door. "Let me take your coat."

Adam handed over his jacket. She'd obviously decided he had plenty of time to stay. Who was he to argue? "How's Madison?"

She smiled at his question, then grew serious. "Cameron, I have cupcakes in the oven and my timer's about to go off. Would you get them out so they don't burn? I'll hang up your coat."

"Sure, Grandma." Giving her his jacket as well, he headed straight for the kitchen.

"Then when they cool you and Dak and I can frost them." She waited for him to disappear, then turned to Adam. "As well as could be expected. I'm not going to lie to you and say fine. That incident took a lot out of her. In fact—"

"Grandma. Can I start frosting the cupcakes?" Dak

called out from the kitchen.

"I told him no." Cameron's voice came next. "That they had to cool first."

"Your brother's right, Dak."

"But I want to."

"Wait. Don't do anything. I'll be right there." Kay raised her voice, quickly hung up Cameron's jacket then again turned to Adam. "We can talk later. Make yourself at home. Madison should be downstairs soon. She was taking a nap but is up now. I just talked to her."

"Okay." Adam walked into the living room as Kay hurried off. "I'll wait for her."

Visions of Madison sleeping came to mind as he sat on the nearest blue couch. More specifically, Madison in bed. *Waiting for me?* He closed his eyes on a silent moan. *Not in this lifetime.*

"Adam. What are you doing here?" Her voice filtered down from the top of the stairs.

Glancing up, he stood and gravitated toward her. "I gave Cameron a ride home."

"Oh. I thought Phil's dad was bringing him home." She took hold of the bannister to descend the steps.

"He was unexpectedly called away." The lie flowed out of him as naturally as water running downhill.

Reaching the bottom step, she walked beside him back to the living room. "You talked with him then. Mr. Ratcliff."

Her question made him blink. "Not exactly. Cameron told me. How are you feeling now that you've had a couple of days to recover?" Even as he asked, he took in subtle signals to assess for himself. There was a slight discoloration beneath her eyes. A sure sign of fatigue. And she seemed to be moving a little slow.

"I'm feeling okay."

"Cameron said you've been tired." Needing the contact, he took hold of her hand as they made their way over to the couch.

"I've been a little sore. Which, as we both know, is to be expected, so I laid around a bit the past few days."

"Rest is always good for what ails you."

"What have you been doing since we saw you last?"

Was she just making polite conversation? Or did she genuinely want to know? *Waiting to see you again.*

"Memorizing lines. Receiving instructions on a few upcoming stunts. The usual."

"You're not relishing your time in the movie making business?"

"Not as much as I thought I would."

"Well, that's too bad."

All he could do was shrug. "Not a big deal. It will be over soon enough."

She withdrew her hand from his as they sat. "When do they plan to wrap up shooting?"

"I haven't been given an exact date. Another month or so I'd guess."

"I see."

Everything in him wanted to say more. Reassure her his leaving when their production was done, didn't mean he was necessarily leaving her.

"What are you going to do after..." She stretched her hands out in front of her as if striving for nonchalance. "...you leave here?"

"Go back to work at my department. I took a

temporary leave of absence for the picture."

"Law enforcement is your first love then, as you've said."

He was nodding in the affirmative even before she quit speaking. He hadn't realized until recently how much he missed it. "Always has been."

"I get that." Nodding briefly, she took a moment to study his face. "Something else is bothering you. What is it? Trouble with the production?"

"If only it were that easy."

Even though Adam had barely realized it, Joel's reaction to his request for time off still bugged him. Assuming he'd blow off something as important as testimony for the prosecution. *Did you get a subpoena?* Yeah right. Before he knew it, he'd related the entire story to Madison. Who listened patiently until he finished.

"He just doesn't get how important my real job is to me."

"Back in Detroit."

"Yeah." Adam caught her eye and nodded. "Exactly."

"You have to do what's right for you. He can't penalize you financially, can he?"

Finances hadn't even been on Adam's radar. "He probably could, but I don't think he would. He has a lot of leeway in what and how he films different segments. He could do a lot with me gone, even if it's longer than a week."

"We both know you're going to testify regardless." She laid a hand on his arm.

"Yeah. We do. He just doesn't get that. Between playing make believe and real life, real life wins every time."

"You're certainly right there. After all, it is your future. Not his."

"Absolutely." Adam sat back. Another thing he hadn't realized. How good it would feel to talk to someone who understood. What better someone than a woman he was really starting to care for? Given that admission to himself, may as well take things one step farther...with her. "So how about you? What do you see in your future?"

Her eyes softened. "My immediate future would be, of course, raising my boys."

He couldn't help but press. "And after that?"

She hunched her shoulders. "I have no idea."

"Any chance you'd want to spend time together?" He again reached for her hand.

"With you?"

"That's kind of what I had in mind."

"Spending time together would be nice. At least as long as you're still in town."

He opened his mouth to assure her his interest in her and the boys extended beyond however long he *officially* remained in town.

"Galaxy Raiders are so much better than plain old Frontier Troopers."

They both looked up as Dak came backwards into the room, nose to nose with Cameron.

"The Troopers always kick their butts." Cameron poked his brother's chest.

"Dak, sweetie. Look behind you. Watch where you're going." Bringing up the rear, Kay called out as she extended her arms. "Careful with the roughhousing, you two."

Among grunts and grimaces, the two boys gripped arms as they staggered in lock step one way then the other across the living room.

"Would not."

"Would, too." Cameron raised a leg he looped behind his brother's to take him down.

"You boys be careful you don't get hurt." Kay again reproached from behind.

Dak bobbed and tilted but remained standing. Quick as a flash, he executed a reverse move. Cameron's eyes grew large as he staggered then fell.

"The champion!" Straddling his brother in triumph, Dak raised both arms in the air.

Cameron jerked upright and led with his shoulder. Suddenly, Dak flew backward.

Adam was on his feet. Lurching forward, he grabbed for Dak. Stretching already extended fingertips, the best he could do was graze a corner of his t-shirt. An instant too late as the material slipped through his hands.

"Watch out!"

Tumbling forward, Dak landed sideways with a thump, square on Madison's lap.

"Dak! Honey! Watch—" The squeal she let out was cut ominously short. "Ooof!"

In the same instant, Dak bolted upright and Madison fell backward against the couch as if they performed one of Adam's carefully choreographed stunts.

Though she didn't make another sound, Madison's deep wince broadcast she was hurt. Drawing her legs up, she recoiled on the cushion into a tight little ball. Adam stayed on his feet to remain in front of her like some sort of guardian.

"You okay, Buddy?" Taking Dak's arm as gently as he could, Adam hauled him away from the couch.

"Yeah." The boy spun around as Madison righted herself. "You okay, Mom? I didn't mean to fall on you."

"I'm fine." Though her voice was tight, she looked up at her son and smiled. "You're growing, but you haven't gotten that big yet."

"I didn't think I pushed him that hard." Deep grooves of uncertainty marred Cameron's forehead.

"She seems okay to me." The concern clouding Kay's eyes debunked her words as she kept a keen gaze on her daughter. "That's exactly why we rough house outdoors."

"We got it, Grandma." Cameron shoved his hands in his pockets.

"See that you do." A smile softened her words. "As long as everyone's okay, our movie starts in a half hour."

Madison glanced up at her mother. "Like I told you, Mom, I don't think I'll go. I didn't sleep well last night."

"You don't have to explain, dear." Kay shook her head. "We understand. Don't we, Boys?" She didn't give her grandsons a chance to answer. "And since Adam stopped by, I'm sure he won't mind staying with you while we're gone. It's a good thing you put both of us on the agreement to drive that rental car." She smiled, the picture of innocence, as she looked from her daughter to him then away from both of them. "Dak, Cameron. Let's go. We want to get there in time for the previews."

"Shotgun!" Apparently still a bundle of pent up energy, Dak bolted toward the back door.

"Each of you pick a number between one and ten. That's how we'll decide." Intent on getting her brood out the door, Kay gave a quick wave over her shoulder.

As the last of Madison's family filed out, shutting the door behind them, Adam could see no reason to move from where he'd ended up. Beside her on the couch.

"Oh. Listen." She sighed then grew silent.

Adam did as she asked but heard nothing. "For what exactly?"

"It's quiet for a change." Smiling his way, she spoke in a whisper.

"Nothing was what I was supposed to hear?" He kept his voice hushed like hers.

"Exactly. You have no idea how much I covet sitting in the quiet. It happens so seldom."

"I'd leave, but I don't think your mother would appreciate me if I did."

"I don't think so either. Not after the fuss she made, practically forcing you to stay."

"No coercion involved. I was happy to do it. I wanted to see for myself how you were."

"That slide down the mountain may have done more damage than I realized. I must have really tensed up as I went over. My lower back has been especially sore." She sank more deeply into the cushions as if to prove her point. "Even before Dak fell on me."

He was about to ask if there was anything he could do for her when the phone on the desk rang to startle them both. Being closer, Adam stood to pick up and brought it over.

"Hello. Yes, this is she." Madison immediately sat straighter. "Yes, Doctor Winters. How are you?" Her gaze strayed to Adam. "A little sore, is all. Which, I'm sure is to be expected. My appetite? Decent, I suppose. I'm a…yes…what?" Eyes widening, she flicked another glance his way as the breath seemed to be sucked from her voice. "You're sure. Absolutely sure? Yes, to the address you have on file. Thank you. Goodbye."

Even as the dial tone droned from the other end, she kept the phone to her ear, a death grip turning her knuckles white.

The hairs on the back of his neck lifted as a chill washed over him. "Madison? Is something wrong?"

She didn't answer, nor did she seem to notice when he lifted the phone away from her to replace in its cradle.

Chapter Eleven

Stunned, Madison remained stock still, letting the information she was given sink in. A simple phone call forced her to bring to light at last what she'd put so much energy into keeping hidden in the darkness of denial.

Vaguely conscious Adam had taken the phone from her hand, she mindlessly placed both palms on her stomach. There was no more denial now. She'd soon be getting the test results through the mail in irrefutable black and white.

Pregnant. I'm honestly and truly pregnant.

"Madison. Talk to me. Please."

The urgency in Adam's voice cut through the fog that had taken over her brain.

"I'm okay. Really. Doctor Winters just called to check up on me. Nice of her."

Looking directly into concern-filled eyes, Madison kept up the monologue while her mind took off in a completely different direction.

Pregnant…pregnant…pregnant.

If there was one consolation, the arrival of another child to join their family would, in some way, be a constant in her life never to change.

Unlike the man responsible.

"What else did she have to say?"

Her thoughts dispersed at Adam's question. "Say?

Not much."

The eyes staring intently into hers broke contact. Chin dropped to his chest, shaking his head, he scoffed before he spoke. "Yeah. Right."

This can't be happening. On top of everything else.

Her physician's exact words came back like some steam of consciousness lines. *The test they ran, hCG, was a very accurate blood test that detects pregnancies a mere six to eight days after ovulation and...*

"Whatever she called about seemed to upset you."

More of what Adam said filtered in to shove all other thoughts aside. But did nothing to quell a rising panic. Like a churning tidal wave about to come crashing down on a relatively peaceful shore.

"She said they ran some routine tests as a matter of course." Her hands remained on her abdomen. She snatched them away to set on the couch cushion on either side of her.

Adam's gaze followed her movements, his brow furrowed in concentration.

He noticed!

"And...?"

She studied the unease reflected in his eyes. When she didn't respond right away, unease edged over to the beginnings of alarm. Until she couldn't bring herself to look at him any longer and diverted her gaze.

"Madison. Talk to me. Please."

"I'm pregnant." Even as she heard her breathy admission, she still couldn't believe it.

Almost on its own, a hand came up to cover her mouth. She hadn't meant to say the words out loud. Too late now. There was no way to take them back. When she finally worked up the courage to meet his gaze, gauge his reaction, she got more than she bargained for. The wide eyes and gaped open mouth said it all. He was as dumbfounded as she was.

With his jaw still open, he continued to stare. "You're what? Are you sure?"

A myriad of emotions played across his face. Shock. Wonder. Disbelief. So many and so swiftly, she couldn't hardly catalogue them all.

Let alone ponder their possible significance.

One thing was for sure. She refused, absolutely refused to ask in any way shape or form—*what should we do now?* What he chose to do was irrelevant. What she chose to do would make all the difference. Because whether Adam was in the picture or not, or any other man for that matter, she would have this child she'd raise on her own. Single mother families were becoming the norm. Madison and her boys, along with her newest child, would fit right in.

"How far along do you think you are?"

She glanced up as he spoke then shrugged. "Not too far. As I understand, blood tests are very accurate."

Though his eyes were still wide, by now his mouth was closed. That was something. She waited for him to do the mental calculations. Next would come a personal favorite from those of his gender. *Are you sure it's mine?*

"How do you feel? Physically?"

Her mouth dropped open on that one. Not the question she'd been geared up to answer.

His somber expression remained. "Seriously, Madison. How do you feel?"

She lifted one shoulder. "Fine."

He didn't even twitch. "You can do better than

that."

"I'm not sure I can." All she could do was shrug again. "I really don't feel any different. A little confused, maybe."

"Don't take this wrong, but if you didn't feel any different…"

"I was given a pregnancy test, Adam. Those things don't lie." On a sigh, she dropped her chin to her chest. "And neither do I."

"That's not what I meant." He raised her chin with gentle fingers. As he grabbed hold of her gaze, his expression cleared, and his eyes lit up. An ear to ear grin graced his mouth. One that stretched his cheeks and caused his eyes to sparkle. "I'm going to be a father. What do you know?"

Had she even heard him right? No argument? Just acceptance?

She stared at him for the time it took to find her voice. "That is not exactly the reaction I expected. You act as if this was something we were trying to do. On purpose."

No way did she care to hide the sharpness in her tone. That didn't keep regret from tugging at her heartstrings when the elation on his face dissolved.

"What now?" He didn't wait for her to reply. "I'm sure no expert, but I do know pre-natal care is key to a healthy baby and mother. Do you have an obstetrician already? Probably not. We can ask around and find you a good one. Or you could find one on your own…if you'd be more comfortable without everyone knowing…yet."

Again, she didn't utter a word, just allowed him to keep talking. The adrenaline she'd lined up to prepare her for a confrontation drained away. Already he was acting like a doting father. Why had she really expected anything less of him?

He flashed another grin, only adding to her consternation. Then his eyes darkened.

"When Dak fell on you. Did he hurt you?" He moved forward on the couch to get closer then rubbed one hand lightly down the side of her arm. "Are you okay? Should we call the doctor?"

"No. Yes. And. No. I'm fine. I'm sure I'm not that far along." *Talk about the understatement of the century.*

"Well, that's good."

She sat very still. "This is a lot for me to absorb."

"Tell me about it." A small laugh rumbled out of him. "It's one consolation we at least have some time before you deliver. Or even begin to show."

"Not necessarily as much as you might think. I popped out quick with both Dak and Cameron."

"No evidence yet." His voice continued to hold a sense of awe. "I still can't believe this."

"Believe it." She was obviously going to be the more pragmatic of the two going forward.

But then, she had been through this before. As far as she knew, Adam never had. Pulling back, she chanced a quick glance his way. At the gaze still focused on her mid-section, disbelief still evident in his eyes. Similar to how Dave reacted when they'd received the news Cameron was on the way.

"I'll do my best to be a good father."

Her first husband's promise from that special time entered her mind with incredible clarity and she momentarily closed her eyes.

True to his word, Dave *had* been a good father. One of the very best. Involved in his sons' lives at every juncture. Very hands on. As both boys grew, he'd used a soft mix of discipline and companionship to guide them.

Much like this man does with them now.

"My life insurance policy will have to be changed."

Adam's voice invaded her thoughts. She blinked and looked over as his kind face came into focus. "What?"

"The life insurance policy I have with the Department. I'll have to change the beneficiaries." He glanced upward in thought. "Right now I only have one. Policy that is. I should probably get more."

Madison let out a sigh as her heart swelled. *Exactly something Dave would think about.*

For the first time since she'd gotten the confirmation of her pregnancy, Madison was able to relax. Even give in to a small smile.

"There's plenty of time for you to do that." She placed a hand on his arm. "And thank you for thinking about it."

"No real thinking involved." He put his hand over hers. "It's kind of a no brainer."

"However, you're looking pretty far into the future, don't you think? Who knows what can happen a few years down the road."

"I won't change my mind. If that's what you're getting at."

"You don't understand how completely having a child changes your life."

"I would assume as much. You act as if you don't want me to be part of our child's life."

Our child.

A situation that would bind Madison and Adam together forever. *From this day forward. Until death do they...*

She brought her thoughts to a screeching halt.

"Do you?"

She caught the urgency lingering in the depths of his voice and her heart squeezed.

"That's not it at all, Adam. I would expect you to be a part, a big part, of our child's life."

Madison had a hard time believing what she was even saying. She still couldn't fathom she was actually going to share a child with this man. Someone she'd met only a short time ago. And become intimate with almost immediately.

"And your life as well."

"We'll always have a connection through this child." She closed her mouth as emotion stole her voice. Clearing her throat, she went on. "In a perfect world, this would be so much different. In a perfect world, you meet, become friends, fall in love, get married *then* have a child together. We did kind of get to this point, as my grandma used to say, bass-ackwards."

The sound of his laughter warmed her. "I'd say grandma made an excellent call."

A sweet smile continued to light up his eyes. Reflecting, if not love, a definite affection for the child they shared...in addition to the child's mother? Her lips curved as she smiled back.

Bringing two fingers under her chin, he gently rubbed his thumb along her cheek. "Just because we started out that way, doesn't mean we can't arrive at the same end-game." He gently brushed her lips with his. "Does it? Even without this child between us, as I think I mentioned before, I'd want to look forward to some kind of a future with you."

"I liked your line about exploring a future with me, child or not."

"No line. Only truth." When his tender gaze landed where their child grew, undeniable caring she never expected seeped in. Brought on, in part by the absolute protectiveness that had suddenly crept into his eyes. "But, what do we do now? In the immediate future?"

"We don't necessarily need to *do* anything." *No more than has already been done.* "I know one thing for sure we aren't going to do. Not right away."

"What's that?"

"We are not going to make this public."

"Tell me something I don't know. That kind of goes without saying, don't you think?" His tone was surprisingly gentle.

She let its comfort wash over her before lifting her chin to meet his gaze. "I especially don't want Dak and Cameron to find out until I'm ready for them to know."

"Did they tell you when the baby is due?"

"Probably eight and a half months from now. Doctor Winters said the test could prove fertilization after only a matter of days after…um…"

Her voice trailed off, and her cheeks flamed. No need to finish. They both knew all too well how that sentence would end.

"Within as little as two weeks? That's pretty amazing." He drew a short breath. "I promise you I plan to be very involved with this child. No way will I be an absentee dad. One per family is more than enough." His voice took on an edge and roughness she never saw coming.

"What makes you say that?" The words were out before she fully thought them through.

"I know first-hand about the devastation of growing up without a father. It's not something I want anyone else to go through. Especially my child."

She covered her abdomen with clenched fingers. He was talking so possessively of something, no someone, growing inside of *her* body. Surely she had a right to some say in how the birth of this child would unfold.

"You're being just a tad bit possessive." The strength of those hurtful words were out before she could stop them. But they needed to be said.

If her intention was to put him off, the stricken look flashing across his face proved she'd been successful. She stood and walked across the room to put some distance between them.

"Are you saying I don't have that right?" His voice was sharp, yet tinged with pain.

"I'm saying." Turning, she threw up her hands. "I'm not sure what I'm saying. I've never been in this situation before."

"You think I have?" He rose and came toward her.

When she retreated, he stopped to simply stare.

"I didn't say that."

"Be aware, I will be a part of this child's life. Even if I have to use force to do it."

Stunned by his message, she took a few steps backward, until her legs came up against the opposite couch, effectively trapping her in place. "I think you should leave."

"Well, I don't." Though he no longer advanced on her, at the meaning of his statement and his vehemence in making it, a ribbon of fear trickled through her.

Fear she had no choice but to meet head on. "Are you threatening me?"

The raw resolve in his expression slipped away and he pulled back. Neither of which prevented him from meeting her determined stare with one of his own.

"No. I'm not threatening you, Madison." The intensity in his voice spoke otherwise. Until he drew away and glanced down. "I wouldn't threaten someone I'm close to. Especially you." His gaze lifted to capture hers. "Especially now."

His voice had softened considerably to its usual, soothing tone, but she wasn't convinced its volume wouldn't pick up again. Fueled by emotion as opposed to common sense. For her as well. Right now she wasn't up to the daunting task of engaging in a highly charged discussion. Making decisions that would change her life and the lives of *all* her children forever.

"I think you should leave." She said it again. This time, with more resolve. When he gave no immediate response, she went on. "I'll make some excuse for you having to do so. Maybe I'll tell them Joel called with something that couldn't wait."

"You think your mother would take 'because Joel said so' as enough reason for me to leave you alone? Because I know I wouldn't."

"Regardless." She was treading on shaky ground and each of them knew it. "I'm asking you to leave so I can be alone…to sort through this."

She didn't wait for an answer. Couldn't, or she was in grave danger of changing her mind. Relenting, and asking him to stay. Maybe even plead with him to remain by her side. If only to bring some sense of sanity to a life spinning more and more out of control.

"If that's what you think is best."

"I do." Though her nod of assent was emphatic, her inner commitment waned. Even threatened to desert her altogether. "Now, please."

Turning to make her way up the stairs, she never looked back. Increasing her pace when she got to the second-floor hallway, striding directly through her bedroom to the sliding glass doors and the veranda beyond them.

Nippy early winter air swirled up to cool her flushed cheeks. The sturdy, black wrought iron railing was cold beneath the grasp of her fingers. Standing still and rigid, she embraced the chill. Eagerly drew it into her lungs to slow the erratic *thump, thump, thump* of her heart.

Alone at last. The huge ceramic planter beside her in one corner the only company, closing her eyes, she swayed with the circling breeze.

"Oh no!"

The words flew out of her as the railing creaked then tilted. She lurched forward. Arching her spine, Madison heaved backward for all she was worth. It didn't help. On instinct, she splayed both hands out to grab on to something, anything, to regain her balance. Her fingers slid along the smooth surface of the planter with nowhere to take hold. The heavy urn simply teetered in response. In the midst of her scrambling, the rail jolted and groaned. Bent over at an awkward angle, she caught sight of the solid, unforgiving patio two stories down. Dread took over for shock as she squeezed her eyes shut. Braced for the inevitable.

A weak, mewling cry of alarm had no more than left her lips when strong hands gripped her shoulders then moved down to clutch around her waist. With one swift motion, she was snatched up and placed, none too gently, on solid footing. Her back came up against an incredible length of hard muscle.

"What on earth are you doing?" Adam's words were sharp as he held her close. "If the idea of me being involved in the future of our child drives you to do this, I swear, I'll give up any rights. Sign whatever papers you ask me to. Whenever. Now if you want."

The more he talked, the more his voice shook. Until he gave in and quit. All the while, his hold on her tightened until she was challenged to draw her next breath. Giving in to a shudder, she allowed him to lead her back into her bedroom. The sliding door was whooshed shut behind them.

"That's not what I was doing." She finally pulled in enough oxygen to speak.

"I started to leave as you asked, then I just couldn't."

Yielding to the obvious fact he wasn't about to let her go, she wedged her arms up and between his then struggled to turn and face him. "I just need to catch my breath." Squirming out of his hold at last, she plopped down on the bed.

He plopped down right beside her, lifting his arms as if ready to, once more, gather her in. "Only if you're sure you're okay. Not going to try anything else."

"The railing collapsed. I had hardly leaned on it at all." Shock and disbelief gave way to anger and irritation. "Do you truly believe I'd try to kill myself, leave my boys without a mother, over something like this?" *Don't flatter yourself.*

A thump then crash rumbled from behind her as what must have been the planter fell and shattered. Madison flinched. *That could have been my body hitting the ground.*

When Adam settled his arm firmly around her shoulders, she took full advantage and leaned into him. His strength drifted over her like a familiar blanket.

"I have no idea why that railing wasn't stable. Except that it's an older house. Screws work loose. Though nothing like that has ever happened before." Envisioning herself sprawled, face down, on the patio stones, she momentarily closed her eyes and shuddered again. "Thank you for being here. Not leaving when I told you to get out. I was feeling overwhelmed."

"I couldn't leave. I hoped against hope you really didn't want me to." He stared into her eyes with a passion and intensity that held her momentarily awe struck. Until he broke eye contact again. Lowered his head. Again. "This all couldn't have happened at a worse time though."

The blanket of well-being was swiftly ripped off. She pushed away from him to sit upright. "Worse as in inconvenient?"

"No, Madison. Not at all inconvenient." Frustration was evident in his voice as he stood.

Cold air washed over her as the sliding door opened then closed. A short time later, more cold air rushed in before he shut the door and came back to sit beside her. Took both of her hands in his.

"It appears as if the anchors simply pulled out of the cement." Even as he offered the explanation, a measure of skepticism entered is tone.

"It was an accident."

"Pretty much." The hands holding hers squeezed tighter. "And I wish I could stay here and make sure...help you see to the repair. But, I can't."

"You're not making any sense." Was he already second guessing his avowed commitment? Deciding she and their child would prove to be too much of a burden after all?

He glanced at the ceiling on a sigh. "That testimony I told you about. I'm due back in Detroit day after tomorrow."

"Oh." She fought to hold in the sadness swamping her. At the very least, keep the disappointment from showing up in her voice. "That shouldn't be an issue. I'm sure I can handle things on my own."

"I should only be gone for a few days."

At this point in my life, I've been on my own for so much longer. "We should be able to cope with a few days apart."

"You would think." He lowered his gaze to meet hers.

"I would know." Bringing out a small smile, she also brought out the reservoir of grit she'd used when Dave had needed her to be strong. "I'll still be here when you return. We all will."

"That's all I can ask."

"We'll miss you though."

"No more than I'll miss you."

The moment she looked up at him again, his lips took possession of hers. Lightly at first, as if seeking permission. When she shifted closer and brought her hand up to rest on his collarbone, he wrapped her more securely in his arms. Tilting his head slightly, and on a low moan, he deepened the kiss. Taking her breath.

As if of one mind, they reclined on the mattress, shifting somewhat until they were both more comfortable side by side. She sank into him as Adam held her, treasuring their newfound emotional connection as well as the physical pleasures they shared. Breaking their kiss at last, the corners of his mouth tipped up as he gazed deeply into her eyes.

Further words became unnecessary as he again covered her mouth with his. A strong, able hand slid effortlessly along the outside of her thigh and over her hip to rub lightly over her stomach. All while his lips continued to touch hers. Drink her in. Hold her as his own. Moving both hands to her back, the clasp of her bra was easily undone before Adam brought his palms around to…

"Mo-o-o-m. We're home." Dak's voice pierced the quiet. "Where are you?"

Adam pulled back first, guilt awash on his features as color filtered over his cheeks.

Madison smiled at his innocence and yet again her heart warmed. She turned her face toward the door. "Upstairs. We'll be down in a minute."

"I think I'm going to need more than a minute to…uh…compose myself." Standing, Adam helped Madison to her feet.

A small giggle escaped as she reached around to refasten her bra.

"Mom!"

Glancing at the open doorway, she snickered again. "Sorry. A minute is all you're going to get. If that."

On a head shake, he blew out a breath. "So be it."

They left the room hand in hand, until Adam quickly snatched his back and gave her a weak smile and small shrug.

"What were you doing?" Dak stood at the bottom of the stairs staring up.

Madison took in the collection of faces below them. Her mother's holding a definite smirk of approval. Dak oblivious to anything but the fact she and Adam came when he called. Cameron, on the other hand, with his running rampant adolescent hormones, gave Adam a knowing look then nod.

"The railing on the veranda off my bedroom came loose and I almost fell. I'll have to call someone in the morning to fix it. Don't you boys go out there. You either, Mom."

"Now why in the world would I go out there off your bedroom?"

"She just wants you to be careful, Kay." Adam added the cautionary note.

Madison detected a bit of guilt behind his tone. Something he needed to work on, but he'd learn. When he actually became a parent in his own right. Halfway down the stairs, she paused at the thought and smiled.

"How was your movie? Any good?" Adam's voice was somewhat improved. Less guilt infused. More confident.

"Better than any of the previous episodes." Her mother managed to speak around a huge grin.

"Yeah it was."

"Uh-huh."

The boys concurred in unison and went on to provide graphic details.

"You missed something really special, Adam,

staying here." Dak's voice held a note of reprimand.

"His loss." His grandmother's grin remained as she chimed in with her two cents.

"Sounds like you all enjoyed it." Still descending the stairs beside Adam, Madison spoke up while he remained silent.

As if they'd choreographed their next actions ahead of time, the second Madison and Adam reached the living room, each pretty much went their separate ways. She to accept the hug Dak ran up to give her.

Adam, assuming an extremely casual air Madison was positive he hardly felt, walked across the room and took a seat in one of the wing chairs beside the fireplace.

Chapter Twelve

For Adam, an uneventful flight back to Detroit led to an equally uneventful arrival back at his apartment.

After more than two months away, he figured it would feel really good to be home, but wasn't surprised to discover the opposite to be true. Dropping his duffel bag by his bedroom door he headed for the kitchen area, still holding the manila envelope he was given when the rookie picked him up at the airport. Setting that aside on the counter, he reached in a top cupboard.

His phone went off as he stood at the sink downing a large tumbler of water. He put the glass down with a clink and quickly swallowed as he dug in his pocket.

"Hello."

"You in the city yet?" That was Vince. Straight and to the point.

"Already home." He glanced around the open concept space, taking in its emptiness. And quiet. So absurdly quiet. "Just got here."

"You testify Friday?"

"That's what the subpoena said. I plan to be there by ten. Most of the reports I have to go through I wrote, so it's just a matter of refreshing my memory."

"That's usually how it's done. Use your frag notes if you have to."

"Definitely. Either way, I'll help get that conviction. It's basically a pretty cut and dried case.

The suspect was known for being a hot head. Even those witnesses who are the most adamant in claiming they didn't see anything come forward when there's an innocent child involved."

"As it should be." There was a moment of dead air. "Seems like you've been gone a lot longer than two months. I gotta say, though, you sound a little off. Everything okay?"

"Pre-testimony jitters." He came up with the answer he was sure Vince would accept without question. "Happens every time. You know how defense lawyers do some real character assassination. Trying to discredit witnesses for the prosecution."

"Yeah. In that sense, testifying is always tough."

"Just doing their job, I suppose." Adam moved to the living room. Sitting on the plain brown leather couch, he glanced at the sole picture on the wall. A painting of a street scene that caught his eye at a charity function a few years ago.

"Like we do ours. If you're not doing anything first thing tomorrow, how about meeting us at Bernie's. All you can eat. Remember?"

"Not something I'd easily forget." Their favorite local mom and pop eatery. Bernie's Famous Pancake House on Dequinder. Home of the lightest, fluffiest pancakes on the planet. With an all you can eat special held every weekday, six am to noon. Even thinking about them made his mouth water. "Sounds good to me."

"Great. I'll call, Luke. He's got the day shift tomorrow like I do. And Brad's back in town."

"He is? For what?"

"Taking some refresher training the chief set up for

him. He's got a job up at Cascade Lake as the county undersheriff. Plans to run for the top job next election cycle when the current sheriff up there retires."

"Glad he's one of us again. I didn't expect he'd do that bounty hunter thing for long."

"I don't think it was so much coming back to police work as wanting to figure out a way to stay in Cascade Lake after he met Jenny."

"Understandable." Adam leaned back against the cushions. "He's settled down for good like you have with Sydney."

"Pretty much. Speaking of which, I need to let you go. I promised to be home early tonight. And I have a slew of paperwork to go through before I do."

"Enjoy your evening."

Vince let out a low chuckle. "Thanks. These days, I always do."

Adam winced at what he was missing. "I'll look forward to seeing you all tomorrow." *Since my evening isn't going to be all that great.*

"And, eating pancakes. Don't forget the pancakes."

"Yeah. The food. Not the company."

Vince's laugh echoed back as he hit disconnect. Returning the phone to his pocket, he stood then surveyed his empty apartment for a moment before deciding on Chinese take out for dinner. Probably turn in early.

Maybe seeing his three best friends the next day would help him feel less at a loss.

One could only hope.

As it turned out, morning for Adam couldn't come fast enough. Not because he was worried about his upcoming performance on the witness stand. Because he was sick of tossing and turning, missing Madison, as well as the boys. In and around what little sleep he did get the night before, he'd made a decision to work with Madison on a future arrangement everyone could live with. Keep him involved, without overtaking their lives. Or having the same done to his. For now, at least. Until they were both ready to make a final decision about the future for all of them.

Madison and their situation remained foremost in his mind as he showered, shaved and dressed. Then, despite battling the last remnants of rush hour traffic, he arrived at Bernie's only a few minutes after the rest of them.

"Well there he is."

Brad, Vince and Luke stood as he walked up to what the group had always deemed their table, a big round in a back corner of the restaurant. Amid greetings and smiles, handshakes soon became brief hugs before they all sat back down to catch up on each other's lives.

Which didn't take long since they all communicated on a pretty regular basis. The more in-depth discussions would begin after they put in their orders.

"Pancakes all around." Ruby Gage, sometime waitress as well as the owner's wife, gave them all glasses of water. "Anything else?"

To a man, they each ordered a large orange juice.

"Coming right up."

Before long, she returned with place settings and beverages, including an initial round of coffee, then was back again to deliver plates stacked with pancakes in front of each of them.

"It's been a while since all four of you together

have been in here." She took two plastic bottles of syrup out of her apron pockets she set on the table. "You've all been friends for a long time now."

"You have that right." Vince, their unofficial leader, was the first to speak. "Since we met at the police academy, what, about fifteen years ago."

She stood back to survey her handiwork as they dug into their food. "That long?"

"That long," Luke added with a nod. "Then we were all lucky to get hired at the same department in Waterton, and worked together as a pretty darned good unit until Brad left for that stint as a bounty hunter."

"Bail Recovery Agent. Get your facts right." Brad sat forward, a smile taking the sting from his words.

Luke smiled in response. "Whatever you call it, glad you realized the error of your ways and came back to the fold. Even if you are taking a job up north."

"Not that far away." Brad took a swallow of his orange juice and set down his glass. "My wife does own a bed and breakfast in that little resort town. I'm sure she'd give you a discount on room rent if any of you decide to come up."

"Sounds good to me." Vince, of course, agreed first.

"Can do."

Luke and Adam each added their two cents.

"We should figure out a future date that works for all of us."

A chorus of affirmative comments rose up at Brad's suggestion before they commenced eating again.

Luke speared a forkful of cakes. "If my current shift is any indication, they're out today, and it isn't even a full moon. Meeting you guys for my meal break is good for my sanity."

The rest of them settled back in their seats to listen.

"I made a traffic stop where a woman was driving with a toddler on her lap, letting him steer. On the expressway." Blowing out a breath, he shook his head. "Said he was getting bored in the back in his child seat."

"Some people." Adam joined Luke shaking his head in disbelief. "They just don't think."

"Tell me about it. But there's more." Apparently their colleague was just warming up. "Then there was a shop lifting incident on Fifth and Harrison. A couple of little punks stole some beer and cigarettes. When I got on scene, the store owner ID'd them right away. Neighborhood kids who didn't have the sense to go rob someplace where they weren't known."

"Takes all kinds." Vince chimed in. "Guess we can call it job security."

"Fifteen years. Has it been that long?" Having had his fill of pancakes, Adam folded his arms on the table.

"Time flies, as they say." Vince took a drink of his coffee. "A few more for me and I'm going to retire. Sydney wants to travel."

"I'll be glad when my role in the trial is over so I can head back to Colorado."

"You're anxious to get back to the movie making business?" Luke eyed him over the rim of his cup. "Thought the last time we talked, you'd decided that was getting kinda old."

"That part of it has." Adam responded without thinking. At the resulting silence, he concluded the unfiltered answer required follow up.

"That part of it has?" Brad parroted the answer as

he opened the second of two creamers he dumped in his brew. "What other parts are there?"

"I've…uh…met this family."

His beginning explanation was met with more silence. This less from curiosity and more from respect. These brothers knew how badly Adam wanted a family of his own.

"And?" Brad leaned forward to stare across the table.

"This woman, a recent widow, has these two fantastic boys, nine and fifteen. From what I've seen of her relationship with them, she has to be the best damned mother ever created." He glanced over at Vince. "Not counting yours, of course."

"Of course," his friend deadpanned.

The widow of a police officer, Vince's mother 'got them.' In that sense, she was group mother by default.

"This woman, she's a good mom." Vince paused long enough to glance around the table at each of their other friends. "Anything else?"

Adam picked up his cup to take a slow, unhurried sip. Although bursting to fill his best friends in about the impending birth of his first child, out of deference to Madison, he kept his mouth shut. She deserved to let people know in her time. Not his.

"Nope. That's about it."

As if rehearsed beforehand, each of his friends creased his brow in turn, yet no one pressed him for additional information. *All in good time.* He'd eventually let them in on these new developments in his life. Once he figured them out for himself.

"More power to you if you can make it work." A shadow fell over Luke's expression as he pulled out his wallet. "It's time for me to get back to the streets."

"Me too. Now that we're all stuffed." Vince dropped a five on their table for the tip. The three others did much the same.

"Thanks, Ruby. We'll be back as soon as we can." Luke lifted a hand to wave as they all rose and shrugged into their coats.

"I'll look forward to that."

"No offense, but not me." Brad smiled as he waved too. "I can't wait to get back to Cascade Lake. And Jenny."

"No one can blame you for that." Vince zipped up his jacket. "I'm glad I don't have that far to go to get home to Sydney."

"You boys sure have settled down since you started coming in here all those years ago." Ruby scooped the bills off the table she shoved in her apron pocket then cast a critical eye in Luke's direction. "Most of you anyway."

"What can I say? I'll get it right one of these days." He put his hands out, palms up, then jerked a thumb over to indicate Adam. "How come you're not picking on him? He's single too."

Ruby's smile became huge before she turned oddly serious as she glanced at Adam. "I have a good feeling about him. He's carrying that pleasant, settled vibe." She brought her hands up to air quote then glanced back a Luke. "But don't worry. As you said, you'll get it right, too."

Discussing the merits of Ruby's comments, the foursome filed out as Adam held the heavy wooden door. It shut behind them with a thump.

"See you tomorrow, Luke." Vince was the first to

speak as they formed a loose circle on the sidewalk to say their goodbyes. "Adam, good luck testifying tomorrow."

All eyes landed on him as others made similar supportive comments.

"And don't forget to—"

Blam! Ping!

Wood splintered on a nearby telephone pole.

"Get down!" Vince hollered.

All four crouched low, scrambling to get out of range. Sidearm drawn to a man, they all dove for cover behind a giant dumpster on one side of the building.

"Shots fired!" Luke spoke into the radio mounted on his shoulder, then gave their location.

"Where'd they come from?" Adam pushed flat against the hard, metal surface. Unforgiving cold seeped into his back.

"Not sure." Luke took up a position beside him. Firearm gripped and ready.

"Drive by." Back to back with Vince, Brad peeked out from behind their cover.

Tires squealed and screeched as the dark green, late model sedan careened around the corner. From a distance, a boom reverberated. Immediately followed by the crash and crumbling of metal and glass.

"They hit a pole." Vince yelled the obvious.

"Just another day at the office." Luke peered through an opening where the dumpster lid was ajar. "One of them bailed. I'm taking him." His body low to the ground, he took off.

More bullets flew. Spinning around, Vince rose up to return fire.

"There's one on his tail."

Adam registered the shout from Vince, saw the dark figure closing in on Luke.

"Cover me. I'm going after him." Brad took off as well. Firing one shot then two.

A cry of pain. The thud of a body to the turf.

"Got him in the leg." Relief colored Brad's tone as he shouted back at them.

Firearms aimed, he and Brad ran up to the prone, squirming figure on the ground.

"Stay down!" Rushing forward, Adam roared the order. With a backward kick, he cleared the assailant's weapon from the immediate area as Brad knelt down beside the man.

Vince appeared on his left, holstering his sidearm. "He injured?"

Not budging his stance, gaze and Glock trained on the suspect, Adam nodded. "Collins winged him in the leg."

As if just now aware of his injury, the guy on the ground twitched and moaned.

"Luke! Where are you?"

"Back here. I'm okay. I got the other one collared too." His voice was sharp and breathless. "Didn't even wing him though. Tackled him instead."

Sighs of relief echoed between Vince and Adam.

"Dumbass." As usual, Vince spoke first.

Adam nodded his agreement. "Taking off after him like that. Coulda been killed."

Sirens wailed, their mechanical screams rising in volume as the squad cars drew closer. Soon, red, white and blue lights spiraled into the sky around them. Four uniforms piled out from two separate vehicles, their sidearms drawn.

"Don't shoot. Vince Miller. Waterton PD."

"Brad Collins, Cascade Lake Undersheriff."

"Luke Simms, Waterton."

"Adam Hollingsworth. Waterton, too."

Hands in the air, one by one, they barked their identities as backup swarmed all around.

With the two offenders subdued, all four brothers kept their revolvers aloft and in open view as the chaos soon became a tightly controlled crime scene.

"Jesus Christ." Chief Lambert strolled into the center of the action as the suspects were being led away. "Hollingsworth. Welcome home."

"Yeah. Thanks." Adam nodded. Despite the situation, it felt good to hear his real name.

"You guys all okay?" The chief's voice was gruff as he scanned the four of them, his gaze concerned.

Vince took stock of the other three along with him. "Seem to be."

"Unfortunately, this is the new reality. We've had a few similar incidents around the city lately. Totally random, this bullshit of taking pot shots at law enforcement. You ready to testify tomorrow, Hollingsworth?" The chief again keyed in on Adam with an abrupt change of subject.

"I am. I'll get you the conviction. Promise."

"Good. That's what we're paying you for."

"I'll let Ruby and her customers know what happened. That it's safe to come out." Vince left the group to head back into the restaurant.

The four brothers regrouped back on the sidewalk a few minutes later, then headed for their cars and headquarters. It didn't take long for the accused gunmen to be processed and jailed. After Adam and his brothers each filed separate reports about the incident, they were free to go. Temporarily, of course. As one of the shooters, Vince was put on paid administrative leave. In keeping with protocol, the other shooter, Brad, had been instructed to remain in town until notified otherwise. All pending the results of an official investigation by the Michigan State Police.

"You may as well stay with me while you wait." Luke addressed Brad as the four of them walked out to the parking lot behind the Waterton PD station house. "Lord knows I have plenty of extra room since Chelsea moved out."

Adam wondered if he was the only one to pick up on the undertone of sadness in Luke's otherwise wise-cracking voice. Maybe because he could so relate. The ache in his gut told him he missed Madison and the boys like crazy. Even, he had to admit, the no nonsense Kay.

In a very short amount of time, they'd all become like a family to him. Especially the soon to be born little one he and Madison were expecting. His heart seemed to enlarge in his chest at the prospect of being a father. He'd be a darned good one, too. That he knew for sure.

"Earth to Hollingsworth. Anyone in there?" Luke landed a couple of light taps on Adam's forehead. "Hey, Man. Where'd you go?"

"Huh?" Bringing his pals into focus, all of them staring in his direction, Adam shook his head. "Uh. Just thinking about getting back to Colorado."

"So you've said." Brad smiled.

Adam shrugged. "That's all."

"That's all?" Luke honed a tight gaze in on his

face. "We're back to that again, are we? Sorry. I'm not buying it. The last time I talked to this guy, he couldn't wait to be done with his stint as a movie idol. Now you claim you can't wait to get back to it."

"What can I say?" Adam hoped his shrug was sufficiently casual. "I miss those kids I told you about."

"Ah yes. The kids." Stepping over to him, Brad put an arm around Adam's shoulders. "The kids." He proceeded to grin ear to ear. "Anyone else you'd care to tell us about?"

"Their mother, Madison, is pretty special." *As is my unborn child.*

Again he wanted to shout his upcoming fatherhood to the world. Again, he made himself keep his mouth shut.

"Special." Luke thumped him on the back this time. "Gotcha."

"I'm leaving right after I testify." Giving cursory hugs to each one of them, Adam promised to stay in touch. "Though I may talk to some of you before that. Especially to learn how these two shooters fare in the investigation."

He pointed to Brad and Vince.

"We should be good." Vince spoke for both of them as Brad nodded his agreement.

"Hang in there, Luke." Adam gave one final slap on the back for his newly single pal. Then acknowledged the others with a head nod as the group broke up. All of which only made him yearn that much more for some real permanence in his life.

Walking across the parking lot, he thought about Dak and Cameron rough housing one on one, or just as lively playing video games. Kay in the background with that satisfied little smile she always wore lately. Madison front and center in his life.

The radio came on as soon as he started the car. Ironically, issuing a report of the shooting. He postponed his phone call to Madison long enough to listen.

"A major gun battle erupted on Dequinder, involving four local police officers. Two were on duty at the time."

Adam turned up the volume as, one by one, the officers were identified by name.

"…and Adam Hollingsworth, also an officer with the Waterton Department though currently on leave of absence for an unknown reason."

"Jesus." Scoffing, he pulled out on the street. "Check your sources. Get it right."

"A motive for the shooting has not been revealed at this time. Two suspects, one injured but not critically, were taken into custody. According to information obtained, the shooting appears similar to some others perpetrated on law enforcement around the country."

"Just one more in a series of random acts of violence." Lips tight, Adam shook his head.

"On the national news front…"

Reaching over, he flicked off the noise and gave verbal instructions to dial Madison's number. Then, navigating through traffic, waited for her to come on the line.

"Hello."

A smile formed. "Hey. How are you?"

"Adam? It's good to hear from you."

"It's good to hear your voice, too." *What an understatement.* Its effect on him was swift. His shoulders lowered a good inch or two from their perpetually tensed up position. His grip on the steering wheel relaxed so blood flow actually returned to his knuckles. "How are the boys doing? Cameron having any more trouble with that one teacher?"

"Not lately. He says they're doing okay since he took your advice."

"One day he'll appreciate you. Much the same way I do."

"Thank you for that." She let out a small laugh. "It's nice to be appreciated by someone. Oh, and Dak was invited to spend the night at his friend Liam's Saturday, but declined."

His brows raised on that one. "Dak declined a sleepover invite?"

"Unbelievable, right? I heard him on the phone explaining how you were coming over when you got back and he didn't want to miss seeing you."

"He said that?" Something in his throat thickened up, but he swallowed around it.

"I wasn't surprised. You're very important to him."

"You have no idea how much that means to me." His response didn't nearly match what he felt in his heart. Before he could share how miserable he was, she was talking again.

"John came over today."

Adam sat straighter. Just when he thought he couldn't feel worse. "He did? What for?"

"Just to see how I was doing."

"That's nice of him." He should be thankful she had someone near to look out for her when he wasn't available. *Why aren't I then?*

"I told him about the veranda off my bedroom. He

seemed pretty upset. Very upset actually. Sometimes, I don't know what I'd do without him. He's been so helpful since…lately."

"Sounds like he has everything under control." Adam tamped down on a sudden urge to rush back and replace this John.

"He offered to take charge of getting it repaired for me."

"That's good he's there for you." *Exactly where I'll be as soon as I can.*

"He kept going on about how tired I looked. I…um…I finally told him I was pregnant."

"You did?" He refrained from asking why. Revealing the news was her prerogative. He'd already decided that. "What did he say?"

"That he was happy for me."

Me? Not us? He refrained from asking about that, too as he accelerated to get around a slower moving semi.

"I…um…didn't tell him…well, you know."

"Yeah. I do."

"He just naturally assumed the baby is Joe's. It would have been beyond awkward to explain otherwise."

"Understandable." His brows drew together and something in his gut shifted. *Doesn't mean I have to like it.*

"He really didn't stay long. Mom and the boys had gone to another movie. He left shortly after they got home."

"Nice that he stopped." Slowing when brake lights came on up ahead, he swallowed. "Uh. Something happened shortly after I got here." After clearing his throat, he gave her a brief run-down of the shooting incident. "In case you see something on the news." She needed to hear the real story from him.

"I'm glad you're okay." There was no mistaking the strain in her voice. "All part of it."

"Unfortunately, yes." It meant a lot, how completely she understood him...and the job. Not every woman he'd been involved with before had her insight. Probably one reason, a main reason, those relationships never progressed beyond a few dates. "Luckily, I wasn't one of the shooters or I'd be cooling my heels here in Detroit for Lord knows how long. As it is, my friend Brad is going to be stuck here for a while. He's the undersheriff in Cascade Lake, a resort town in Northern Michigan." He took a breath. "Poor guy. He's recently married to a lady from there. Bet he's missing her like crazy right now."

"I would imagine he is."

"I'll be headed your way again as soon as I'm done testifying."

"You're still coming over when you get back to Colorado?"

"Wouldn't miss it."

"We'll see you then."

"Count on it. I'll talk to you before."

"I hope so. Good luck with your testimony."

"Thanks."

"Good-bye, Adam. Take care."

"Good-bye, Madison. You take care too."

Silence filled the car as he pulled onto the exit ramp to his apartment complex a few minutes later, and he flicked the radio back on.

The following day, Adam put all he had into being

a witness for the prosecution. That day, and the next three days he remained on the stand the following week. In between, a weekend spent without Madison and the boys turned out to be brutally long. Several times throughout, he'd call her just to talk. Catch up with what he was missing. Until finally the prosecution and defense each rested their cases.

Leaving the courthouse after he was finally released, Adam had never been more anxious in his life to get on a plane. He sure didn't plan to stick around to wait for the verdict. Vince could fill him in on that.

A quick trip to his apartment for some minimal packing, a cab ride to the airport, and he'd be on his way back to where he belonged.

Chapter Thirteen

"Adam! You made it!"

Madison stood back beside her mother as both boys, Dak in particular, mobbed Adam the second he walked into the house.

"I told you I would." His grin was huge as he accepted a fierce hug from Dak and a more sedate fist bump from Cameron.

"We're glad you're home."

At the comment from her oldest, Adam flashed another grin. "Thanks. I am too."

"Yeah. We're glad." Dak stepped back, keeping his eyes glued to the large paper shopping bag Adam had with him. "What's in there?"

His grin grew wider, if that were possible, as he reached inside. "A few things I picked up. These." He pulled out two plastic wrapped video games he distributed to each of them.

"Galaxy Blaster!" Dak held his out in front of him and simply stared before hugging the game to his chest. "We gotta play this. Now!"

"Yeah, we do." Again Cameron's reaction was more subdued. "Thanks, Adam."

"You're welcome."

Kay nudged her youngest grandson. "What do you say, Dak?"

As he mumbled the proper words, Adam spoke up.

"Hey, he gave me a hug. Gratitude at its finest."

Almost immediately, both boys jabbered excitedly about the game.

"I've heard it's awesome," Cameron promised. "Graphics like you wouldn't believe."

"We gotta play!" Dak went back to caressing his. "We gotta. All three of us."

"Okay. Okay." Adam chuckled. "Go set them up, and I'll be there shortly."

Despite smiling, Madison shook her head as both immediately complied without argument.

"Glad you had a safe trip." Her mother got into the act next to give him a quick squeeze. "Welcome back."

"Thanks." The grin remained as she let him go, then he dipped his hand in the bag again. "This is for you."

"Chocolates. And the good kind too." Kay accepted the gold foil box with the sparkly bow, then grinned as she glanced up. "Do I have to share?"

"Not if you don't want to." He lifted a similar box. Briefly. "I brought another."

She put her hand on his cheek. "You do think of everything."

"One more for you. A cookbook with lots of space to take notes." Setting the bag down, he fluttered through the pages of the spiral bound book he pulled out. "I know how you like to personalize your recipes."

"You're right there. Thank you, Adam." She tucked her box of candy and cookbook under one arm. "Well, I have noodle dough waiting I don't want to dry out. Then I'm making the boys' favorite, Macaroon Brownies, for dessert. Which reminds me. Madison, where do you keep your sweetened, condensed milk? I couldn't find any."

"I probably don't have any. I rarely buy it."

"I can't make the brownies without it." Her mother's free hand landed on her hip.

Madison was quick to acquiesce. "I'll run to the store to get some. I have a few other items to pick up anyway."

"Okay. I don't need it right away." Hurrying toward the kitchen, she glanced over her shoulder. "You are staying for dinner, Adam."

"Yes, Mother." Madison finally made it through the commotion to stand in front of him. "Of course you're staying for dinner."

Looking directly at her, a definite sparkle lit his eyes before his gaze softened. "I'd love to stay for dinner."

Her heart filled with joy as she gazed up at him. "I'm glad you're back."

"Me too."

They remained face to face for a couple of seconds before Adam made the first move. Slipping an arm around her shoulders, he drew her in. She clung to him, savored him. Readily offered her lips for his kiss. Closing her eyes, she eagerly accepted the pressure of his mouth on hers. Relished the familiar scent that was his alone. Shuddered at the knowledge of how deeply she'd missed him. Loved that he kept his arm around her when, eventually, their lips parted.

Cherished how he'd come home to her once again.

"So, aside from your shootout..." She stopped to swallow. "...how was your trip?"

"Long. It's good to be ho...here."

"How'd your testimony go?"

"Pretty well." He nodded. "I'm relatively sure the prosecution got what they needed out of me."

"I'm glad to hear that. I know appearing in court isn't most officers' favorite part of the job. Dave used to hate it."

"Of course, the defense attorney tried to discredit me from the get-go. Cited my current occupation. Said there was no way I took my police work seriously if I was on leave of absence to do something frivolous. His words, not mine."

"How'd you handle it?"

"Told him the movie stint was my way of bringing credibility about our profession to the public. Portraying police officers as we really are. Doing the job we believe in, then going home at night to the kids and wives who love us."

It was a moment before she spoke. "Do you think he bought it?"

"I don't know. But I'm pretty sure the jury did." He was over talking about him. "Aside from you and the boys, and of course, Kay, what else did I miss while I was gone?"

Her smile turned to a grimace. "Not much else except for the pounding and drilling when they fixed the railing on my veranda."

"That was fast." His brows creased as he looked at her.

"It was a safety hazard, and when John agreed to take care of the particulars. I let him."

"Hey, Adam. Come o-o-o-o-n-n-n." Dak's ten-decibel voice erupted from downstairs. "We're ready to go."

"In a minute." He lifted his head to carry his voice

then lowered it to glance back at Madison. "I'm having too much fun where I am."

"Nice to return to a little peace and quiet?" With a quick wink, she smiled up at him.

"Something like that." Bending down, he retrieved the shopping bag and reached inside. "In addition to another box of candy. I brought you this. I didn't know…"

"Thank you." She held the larger, gift wrapped box in front of her. *Pamper Her* was written across the top in pink script. Slippers and a satin neck pillow were visible through the clear plastic wrapper. "I'll get a lot of use out of these."

"I hope they're okay." He rubbed a hand along her shoulder.

"They're perfect."

"A-a-d-a-m! Come on!" Once again, Dak's megaphone tone blasted up from downstairs.

Shaking his head, he laughed. "All right. All right." Brushing the top of her head with his lips, Adam reluctantly turned away. "See you in a few."

"Okay." Madison set her gifts on the table in the entrance.

"Move, Cameron."

"No, you move. I'm playing Adam first."

The poor man was barely out of sight when her boys' latest dispute burst forth from the family room. Shaking her head, she was all set to make her way down there to intervene.

"Guys. Guys." Adam's controlled and steady voice rose above the fray. "We'll get all the games in. We have plenty of time."

We have plenty of time. Madison broke into a smile

as she bypassed descent to the family room in favor of walking toward the kitchen. The phone rang behind her, and she reversed course.

"Hello."

"Mrs. Clark. It's Hayden Riley."

Her smile morphed to a frown. "Yes. Hayden."

"I wondered if you'd had time to look into the Concord situation." If he noticed the impatience in her voice, he didn't let on.

Closing her eyes, she counted to five. "Not yet. My hus…Mr. Clark's lawyer has been out of town. He's scheduled to be back sometime next week."

"I don't suppose you'd care to call him sooner."

"No, Hayden." She shook her head for emphasis. "I truly wouldn't." At the dead air that resulted, she went on. "Right now I'm home with my family. Plus I'm about to head to Dexter's grocery store to pick up a few things for dinner." It didn't hurt to further her argument she had had more important things to do than his bidding. "I'll be in touch with you at the proper time."

He blew out a breath before responding. "Fine. I'll wait for your call."

Hanging up the receiver, she let out a low growl before gritting her teeth. "What a pain he is turning out to be."

When will this all be over?

"Come on, Adam." Cameron's excited voice came at her from the family room. "You can beat him."

"Bet me." The chortle of Dak's laughter was unmistakable.

A few more joyful shouts, chuckles and outright guffaws followed, and her irritation was easily forgotten. Heart lifting, she smiled, all the way into the kitchen.

"Those are sounds I haven't heard in a while. Especially coming from Dak and Cameron." Sliding on to a bar stool at the island, she addressed her mother who was wrist deep in preparing homemade noodles.

Eyes the identical green as hers glanced over. "Music to my ears, too, knowing my grandsons are going to be okay."

"We all are." Madison rested her elbow on the counter and cupped her chin in one hand.

A wistfulness entered her mother's gaze as her hands stilled on each handle of the rolling pin. "That's what I care about the most. You're all on the way to being okay after so long. It's wonderful Adam came into your lives when he did."

"I think you may be on to something."

"I know I am." Adding a touch more flour to the counter surface, she continued her methodical flattening.

"Come on, Adam. You've almost got him."

The excitement in Cameron's tone did a world of good to Madison's heart. "It's been even longer since that boy has sounded even marginally happy."

"Go, Adam. Go!!! No. Not that way! He's coming up behind you. Look out! Noooo!"

She and her mother glanced up to exchange smiles.

"I absolutely love that excitement." Putting her rolling pin to one side, her mother picked up the pizza cutter she expertly wielded to cut the dough into strips. Setting that to one side as well, she carefully laid her noodles on the big counter by the double door refrigerator to dry. "There. I made extra so you'll have plenty of leftovers when the boys and I are gone next weekend. I'll make a double batch of brownies too."

"The leftover chicken and noodles yes. The brownies, I don't need. Take those with you."

"Provided I could get them on the plane, I would." She narrowed her eyes. "I'll leave them here. I'm sure Adam would enjoy them."

"Probably." She grimaced as the mere thought of the homemade, gooey treats made her stomach turn.

"Well, that was quite a face. Was it in response to my mention of Adam or the brownies?"

Madison smiled up at her to soften what she was about to say. "The brownies, I'm afraid. For some reason the thought of rich desserts doesn't appeal to me these days."

"You don't say." Soon after her mother spoke, Madison became the object of some rather intense scrutiny. "As I recall, you've felt the same way before this. From time to time."

"It has happened before. Only occasionally." On reflex, she looked away then back. "And only when I'm confronted with certain foods."

"Confronted with… You're pregnant!" The woman who had given birth to *her* was by her side and hovering in an instant. But then just stood there. "You have to be pregnant."

Madison rushed to bring shushing fingers to her lips. From what had started from her mother as a squeal, she lowered to a whisper. A gleeful whisper, but still a whisper.

"How long has this been going on?" No way would Kay Carmichael be put off now.

She held up four fingers.

"Is that months or weeks?"

Madison thought fast. "Months."

"Sounds about right." Smiling, her mother nodded. "Think about it, sweetheart. Think about how you felt, what your symptoms were, with both Cameron and Dak."

"My pregnancies with Cameron and Dak were very different if not emotional. With Cameron I was sick as a dog the entire nine months. With Dak, I breezed through with hardly a hiccup. Except for being emotional all the time." She gazed up into wise eyes focused on her. "But, you were there. You know all this."

"I do know. I just wanted to make sure you remembered, too."

Her mother's gentle tone nearly drove Madison to tears she absolutely refused to shed. This weepiness at the drop of a hat had to stop. She took a breath she held on to while she counted to ten.

"I remember. Believe me." The words rushed out of her, and she hauled in another helping of air. "I remember."

"Dave hovered over you the whole time. Both times." Her mother's eyes became reflective.

"He felt bad I was so miserable with my first pregnancy." Madison smiled at the pleasant recollections of her kind and caring Dave. Holding her hand. Waiting on her when he was home. Calling to check on her when he wasn't.

Despite the different circumstances, much as Adam did when I told him.

"It is Joe's, I assume."

Madison cringed then swiftly recovered. "Of course it's Joe's. I haven't…" She immediately put a stop to saying, 'been with anyone else'. "Of course it's Joe's," she repeated. There was also nothing to be gained by sharing how seldom she and Joe actually slept together.

"Do the boys know?"

"Not yet." Sitting straighter, she faced her mother head on. "Adam knows. He was here when the doctor called."

"What did he say?"

"What could he say? He was supportive of my situation." She let the little white lie stand, laid both hands in her lap and looked down. "Adam is a kind and thoughtful man."

"Who adores you and the boys. Especially you."

"We'll take that for what it's worth and go from there."

"Sounds like a plan to me."

"Oh no!"

"Watch out!"

A chorus of cheers followed the sudden outbursts from below. Madison glanced in the direction of the noise and couldn't help but smile.

"The winnah!" Dak's excitement was hard to miss.

Soon, all the noise and chaos from downstairs burst into the kitchen.

"You've had more time to practice than me."

"Admit it. You're a level lower than I am."

"I demand a rematch." Adam's exuberant voice wove into the hoots and heckles happily provided by the boys.

Just like with Dave.

Madison blinked away any tears before they had a chance to gain any traction, breaking into a smile instead.

"I won fair and square." Dak puffed out his chest where he directed both thumbs. "But I wouldn't mind playing you again. I'd probably beat you worse."

"I bet he would, Adam." Cameron sported a huge grin. "You better be careful."

"I'm getting robbed here." Adam aimed a mournful look toward the other adults.

Madison's heart lifted as she and her mother merely glanced his way and laughed.

"You're getting everything you deserve." Her mother turned around from the sink, drying her hands. "Trash talking my grandsons the way you did. Don't think we didn't hear all that went on down there."

"She's no help." Adam plopped down on the stool beside Madison "How about you?"

Concentrating on the heat flowing into her as their shoulders touched, unlike her mother, no glib answer sat anywhere near the tip of Madison's tongue.

"From the sounds of it, you were all having a really good time." When in doubt, speak the truth.

"Things did get a little rambunctious, but, damn, we enjoyed ourselves." Taking hold of her hand, his expression softened. "Much as I enjoy just being back here again."

"It is nice." She stopped just shy of admitting how terribly she'd missed him. Just squeezed his hand.

"I'm planning your favorite for dinner. Chicken and noodles. With Macaroon Brownies for dessert. Don't you boys go and spoil your appetites."

"We won't, Grandma." Cameron spoke for both of them as they stood in front of the opened refrigerator, scanning its contents.

"Right now I could use a water." Adam flattened his forearms on the counter.

Cameron stooped toward the bottom shelf of the refrigerator. "Here you go. Catch." With the flick of one wrist he tossed a plastic bottle Adam's way, though his aim had it coming directly at Madison's face.

"Cameron. Be careful." His grandmother hollered a warning. You'll hit your mo—"

Adam stretched out one hand. The bottle landed in his palm with a slap while Madison didn't even flinch. "Thanks."

"Nice catch." Cameron beamed as he shut the refrigerator door. "My dad used to do that."

Suddenly, it was as if the room itself gasped in surprise. Her mother raised her head, and her mouth fell open. In a similar pose, Madison said nothing. Simply stared. Even Dak froze with a cheese stick halfway to his mouth. Only Adam seemed unaffected as he cracked the bottle open. Except to draw down his brow as he took note of everyone else's reactions

How would he know? For the first time, since his father's death, Cameron mentioned him without his voice trembling in grief or cracking in anger. The best part, her son didn't even seem to notice.

"Very cool." He smiled as he bit into a mini-bagel.

"Left over skill from my high school baseball days." Tipping the bottle, Adam took a long drink.

"Well, I'm on my way to the store." Madison jumped off the stool so fast, she practically fell on her butt.

Much as he had in coolly palming the water bottle, Adam rose with a steadying hand on her upper arm. "Easy. We don't want you to fall."

"We certainly don't." Her mother quickly added two cents worth.

Without further comment, Adam slid his arm around to circle Madison's waist. For the duration of a breath, how they remained.

"What brand do you prefer?" She addressed her mother, pushing free to stand on her own two feet.

Adam resumed his seat.

"Either one of the name brands. Not the store's. There is a difference, you know." She crossed her arms over her chest. "I pride myself on my baking successes."

"Culinary skills I'm afraid your daughter didn't inherit." Madison lifted her jacket off the hook by the door to the garage and picked up her purse from a shelf beneath.

"If you hold up for a minute, I'll go with you." Adam set down his water bottle.

"Okay." Turning, she waited.

"Don't go with her." Dak let out a loud protest. "You promised me a rematch."

"Right now?" Palms flat on the counter, he started to stand.

"Yes, now." Charging forward, Dak grabbed his bicep and tugged. "Right now."

"I guess you're taken." Slipping into her jacket, Madison couldn't resist adding something meant for Adam alone. "For now."

He accepted her comment with a wink. "Seems as if I am. For now."

"It won't take me long at all to run to the store." Hiking her purse onto one shoulder, she smiled at their private joke. "I'll be right back."

Closing the door, she made her way down the three cement steps. After she hit the remote, the garage door rolled up to reveal sunshine glistening off freshly fallen snow. Rims of water pooled where some of it had already melted on the cement driveway. She was barely out on the street when her cell phone buzzed, and she automatically depressed the button on her steering wheel to connect.

"Hello."

"Madison? John here."

"Hi, John."

"I'm calling to check on that railing repair. Did my guys get there to repair it?"

She nodded before she spoke. "They did. Yesterday. The foreman came to the door about four to say it was all fixed. Though I didn't have a chance to check it out for myself."

"Can you do that now? I just want to make sure it's been done right."

"I'm on my way to Dexter's to do some quick shopping." Braking at the corner, she checked left then right before pulling forward to turn on to Skyline Avenue. "As long as the railing is back up, I'm not too concerned. I won't be going out there again for a while. At least until it gets warmer."

There was no need to tell him after the scare she'd had nearly falling, she was fine staying away.

"Okay, then. As long as you're sure. I'll stop by myself in a few days. Your mom and the boys still going to Chicago?"

"Sounds good, John. Yes, they are. Thanks again for handling the repair arrangements."

"No problem. You take care now. Goodbye."

"Bye." Ending the call, she accelerated as she came to the highway.

Quite a few vehicles were in the massive parking lot when she arrived at Dexter's a few minutes later. As she stepped out of her car, the sole of her well-worn running shoe landed on slick pavement. She lurched forward, clutching the side of her opened door with both hands to keep upright.

Just what I need. Having to call home from an ambulance and tell them I broke my leg.

She shut the door snickering, and found solid footing the rest of the way into the store. Soothing elevator music surrounded her as she slowly pushed the metal cart she'd picked up near the door down one aisle then another. Rows of neatly arranged cans of peas, corn and carrots flowed into similarly arranged cans containing various fruits. Gathering the gallon of milk, loaf of bread and carton of eggs they needed, she set out to find the item she'd come for.

"Where in the heck do they hide the sweetened, condensed milk?"

Coming out of one aisle by the cash registers at the front of the store, Madison leaned on the cart to change direction and head down another. This one containing stacks and stacks of cellophane wrapped toilet paper, paper towels, boxes of tissues and the like.

"I'll never find it at this rate." Picking up her pace, she and her cart *clickety-clacked* to the back of the store. At the end of that aisle, she rounded the end cap again.

Wonk! Wonk! Wonk! Wonk!

Continual short blasts reverberated off the ceiling and echoed along the walls.

"Your attention, please. The fire alarms have been activated. Please exit the store in a calm and orderly fashion." The unknown voice went on to boom further instructions.

"Fire! I smell smoke. There's a fire in here!"

The anonymous shout was all it took to incite pandemonium. A number of screams rose up all around her. From somewhere nearby a baby began to cry. Carts clanged against shelves as shoppers abandoned them to flee. Several people pushed by her in their rush for the exits.

Detecting the unmistakable odor of smoke, Madison let go of her cart, more than ready to join them. Before she took even one step, a blow to her shoulder from behind careened her forward. A man in a dark jacket had plowed into her and kept going. Thrown up against a display of boxed graham crackers, her shins rammed the bottom shelf. Red and blue boxes flew in all directions.

"Agh!" Waves of pain spiraled through her calves as she slumped sideways. *"Oooff!"*

In the distance, familiar bells went off. She righted herself and started to turn around. The cart slammed her in the stomach, and she doubled over.

My baby!

From the corner of her eye, she caught sight of the cart advancing at her a second time. Somehow, she maintained the presence of mind to twist sideways then kick at the oncoming crush of metal. Bells pealed from far away, clashing with the cries of customers. Near her side, the cart clanged as it hit a stationary pole then ricocheted off.

As if someone were purposely directing it. The

thought arrived just before the cart raced toward her yet again. This time, grazing her on the right hip. As she struggled to stand, a massive palm struck her shoulder to once more throw her forward.

The shrill whine of a siren came on the heels of deep and pulsating horn blasts.

"Clear the area! Everybody out!" Excited shouts, and the clomps of heavy boots reverberated toward her.

Bucking upward, she grasped the edge of a nearby shelf and tensed, awaiting another assault. One never came. Looking around, she glimpsed the dark jacketed figure making a hasty retreat. Her fingers closed over more solid metal and she leaned into it to get her bearings. The cart stood to one side, unmoving and harmless. Pulling it toward her with an outstretched hand, she curled her fingers on its handle to steady herself as she pushed toward the door.

Right foot left foot. Right foot left foot. Right foot...

A fully clad firefighter charged to where she struggled halfway up the aisle to stop directly in front of her. "Ma'am. Take it easy."

"I...I..." She blinked to make out the concerned features below a tarnished yellow helmet, its visor pushed up and away from his face. "I was nearly trampled by someone in their haste to get out of harm's way."

Anger flashed in otherwise kind, brown eyes. "Let's get you out of here. Can you walk?"

"I think so." Making a liar out of herself, she sagged slightly as he loosened her death grip from the cart.

Before she could steady herself, she was swooped up and bundled against the thickness of his jacket. The scent of smoke and canvas assailed her nose, but she let her head slump into it, the scratchy material rough against her cheek. Her rescuer pivoted with very little effort, and heavy boots thump thumped a short distance across the tile floor and out sliding double doors into the late afternoon sunshine.

"Stretcher!" The command vibrated from under the thick coat.

She lifted her head. Cool breezes washed over her face, and she greedily guzzled in huge gulps of untainted air.

Suddenly alert, she scanned the crowd milling around the parking lot for some sign of her attacker. A woman clutching the hand of a small child talked excitedly on a cell phone. An elderly couple, wispy white heads bobbing, appeared shocked and disoriented as they stood, wide-eyed, beside a massive fire truck. Its engine rumbled as waves of steam spurted up from a silver front grill, leaving glistening beads of water on the bright chrome surface. Reflectors flashed white and red lights off damp, shiny pavement.

"Appears to have started in a storeroom. Blaze contained." The information crackled from a two-way radio one of the responders held as Madison was hustled by him.

"Roger that."

"Stretcher!"

She flinched at the deep shout next to her ear. Almost immediately she was lowered onto a firm, plastic mattress. Her head was settled onto an even more rigid pillow.

"Oh, my God, Madison! What happened?" Warm hands took hold of hers.

Forcing her eyes open, she blinked away some residual tears until Adam's face came into focus. Concern etched deep lines into his forehead and on the edges of his eyes.

"Madison." He clutched her hands between his. His breath floated over her cheeks.

She savored his closeness then shook her head to clear a fogged up mind. "Adam? What? How?"

"You'd been gone for a while." He broke in before she could fully express her thoughts. "Dak had the tv on. They broke in with a report."

"Excuse me, sir."

"What?" Adam jerked his head up as an EMT appeared on the other side of her.

"We need her vitals."

Small plastic jaws were clamped on the index finger of her left hand. A long, thin thermometer was inserted in her mouth.

"You need to know she's pregnant." Adam kept his gaze on her as he blurted the information.

"Mmuh." Madison stared at him, wide-eyed.

She would have preferred to be more discreet in divulging her condition. If she'd chosen to divulge it at all.

Her assessor didn't seem to care. "Any cramping?"

"Mmuh." Unable to speak, she shook her head.

"Other discomfort?"

Another negative motion from her. *Thank God.*

A tiny bell chimed and the device was removed from her mouth. The clamp taken off her finger.

"Eighty-seven and ninety-nine point two. Close enough."

Before Madison could comment, Adam picked up

her hands again. Lines of concern furrowed his brow and drew down the corners of his mouth. "Do you need to get to the hospital?"

Not again! Shaking her head, she put a hand on his shoulder to rise then sit up. "No. I'm fine. Someone was just overzealous in evacuating the store. I got caught in their crosshairs."

He seemed to accept her explanation as he said no more.

Before she could provide a few details of her ordeal, a police officer approached. "If you don't mind, we need your name, address and phone number."

Madison blinked before she answered. "For what reason?"

The officer didn't flinch. "This incident will have to be investigated. To determine if the alarm was falsely set. We're collecting a list of witnesses."

Adam glanced from him to her. "They don't mess around with that kind of thing."

Nodding, she complied with the officer's request.

"Thank you, Ms. Clark." He flipped his notepad shut when she finished. "We'll contact you if need be."

"Before you leave." Adam reached over to put a hand on his arm. "Ms. Clark needs to file a report of her own."

Chapter Fourteen

Adam parked in front of Madison's house and sat back, anxious to get off the phone with Joel. Even if his nit-picky director was in the middle of apologizing for giving him such a hard time about going to Detroit.

"I shouldn't have made you bust your ass to get back here now that the shooting schedule has been changed."

"Not a biggie." Adam didn't have the heart to reveal his real reason, check that...*reasons*, for busting his ass to get back here had little to do with the shooting schedule, changed or not.

"We're suspending location shooting for this weekend and the following week to do some aerial establishing shots higher up in the mountains. Right away." As Joel continued on...and...on, Adam rolled his hands in a 'wrap it up' gesture. *Get to the point.* "Wouldn't you know all the drones and other equipment we need would be available this week and not next like I'd originally asked. Bottom line, I got nothing for you to do until we return."

It took a second to realize the man had stopped talking. *Finally!* "Don't worry about it. I'll keep myself busy."

He eyed the white plastic bag on the passenger seat. His mouth watering at the delicious aromas coming from inside. Catered meals he'd picked up to share with Madison. Just the two of them. By now she'd surely be alone.

With her mother and the boys well on their way to Chicago.

Smiling, he made a mental note to bring Kay a huge bouquet of flowers when she got back in a few days.

Madison had sworn him to secrecy about all that had taken place at the grocery store.

"The lease we have with the Concord properties is still in force." Joel was at it again. "So you can stay out there in your trailer at Base Camp. That hasn't changed."

"Like I said, don't worry about it. Hell, I'm still getting paid. Right?"

"Yes, of course. That hasn't changed either. Just the damned drone availability."

"I understand you gotta go for the outside shots when the opportunity presents itself." Opening the car door, he lowered his left leg and tapped his sneaker clad foot on the pavement. *Let's wrap this up.*

"Yeah. That's exactly it. Hey, thanks, man for being so understanding. I'll see you in a few days."

"Sounds good, Joel. See you."

Adam was out of the car and onto the porch in record time. Package in hand.

About to ring the bell, he changed his mind and keyed in the security code Madison had given him to unlock the front door. Why wake her if she was sleeping? According to Kay and Cameron, she'd been doing that a lot lately. As far as he was concerned, she was entitled. When the latch yielded, he stepped inside and set the food on the table in the entrance, recalling her exact words about the grocery store incident.

'If my mother finds out what really happened, she'll cancel their trip. I know she will. I won't do that to my children. They deserve to start living their lives as normally as possible, no matter what happens in mine.'

There was no arguing with her. She'd been adamant, before they got in their respective cars to drive back to her house. He could still hear the fervor in her voice, as clearly as if she stood before him now. Shaking his head at the memory, he turned around to open the closet door and hang up his jacket.

"It's going to be nice to be able to think of myself for a change."

Hearing Madison's voice for real, Adam froze with his right arm still in the sleeve.

"You're a vital adult woman." A deep, male voice came next. "You should think about yourself more. And not just at times like this."

Doffing his jacket, he scrambled to hang it up and closed the closet door. Then simply stood there with nowhere to go. He hadn't noticed a strange car out front. *Probably because it's parked in the garage.* The better to keep it hidden.

"Adam!" The utter surprise on Madison's *vital adult woman* face would have been priceless. Under different circumstances. "What are you doing here?"

Damned if I know. "Hey." Getting that out with a weak smile, he remained rooted to the spot. Totally poleaxed. "I wanted to see how you were doing."

"That was nice of you." She kept walking down from upstairs with her male companion to her rear.

Pun intended.

"What are you two up to?" He clamped his mouth shut after that idiotic release.

What he meant to be an innocent bit of small talk sounded more like a command for her immediate explanation.

Eyeing the stocky dude who remained directly behind Madison, it was all Adam could do to not get right up in his face. Demand to know what the hell he was doing here, of all places. With her of all people. By the time he advanced to the bottom of the stairs, his more sensible side managed to squash irrational jealousy…somewhat.

Through it all, Madison kept her gaze on him. "I wasn't expecting you today."

That's damned obvious. He made sure his mouth remained shut tight so that particular phrase wouldn't escape.

"I thought you had to work."

After Madison spoke, he figured it was his turn next. "Change in plans. You were sleeping when I called this morning. Your mother said you were still pretty sore. I wanted to see for myself how you were doing."

He scanned her from head to toe as proof, then searched her face for even the slightest trace of guilt. Seeing nothing but cool, calm and collected set his teeth on edge.

"Adam Hollingsworth, this is Ray Ratcliff, Phil's dad."

His attention snapped back around as he shook the hand extended his way. "Oh. I…"

The dark-haired intruder planted his other hand on Adam's shoulder. "How's it going?"

267

You tell me. "Nice to meet you." He couldn't keep his eyes from narrowing.

Phil's dad. The very man she purported to have very little use for. Which begged the question, what, if anything, had changed?

"Hope I'm not interrupting anything." *Smooth, Hollingsworth. Way to fish for information.*

Madison's initial response was a single quirked brow.

"Hey! Adam! You came to tell us goodbye."

He jerked his head up toward the top of the stairs just as Dak raced down them to launch into him. His chin dropped a good two inches as his mouth fell open. With no time to react, other than to catch the squirming little body that pressed up against him, he held Dak tight and thought fast.

"And to tell you have the very best time."

"Don't help with the suitcases, you little dork." A scowling Cameron lugged two medium sized suitcases down with him.

His friend Phil, close behind, toted a slightly larger one.

"You can go back up and get your backpack." Kay followed, hauling her own bright purple bag. "I swear with all this luggage, you'd think we were going for a month."

Adam jumped into action, meeting her halfway. "Here. I'll take that."

Once he had her suitcase in hand, he wasn't exactly sure what to do with it.

"Ray offered to drive us to the airport." As if aware of his dilemma, Kay clued him in to what was going on, then made a point of sniffing the air. "Something smells delicious. And I don't think it's anything I cooked."

"I brought lunch." His smile was weak, but a smile nonetheless. "For Madison and me."

"Well that was certainly nice of you." While Kay spoke, Madison stared at him with her face clouding up as if she was about to cry.

Now WTF? He had no clue what to do about her unexpected reaction. If there even was anything he *could* do. Not that he wouldn't try.

"That was very thoughtful, Adam." Emotion clogged her voice by the time Madison responded. "Thank you."

Kay settled her purse strap more firmly on her shoulder. "Well, as *nice* as it would be to stand around and chat, if we don't get moving, we'll be pushing it to get through security to our gate on time. Even if traffic might be lighter since it is Saturday."

"Sounds like a plan." Being in front of her with the suitcase, Adam automatically headed for the front door.

"This way." Madison pointed toward the kitchen. "Ray parked in the garage to make it easier to load everything." She put a hand on his arm as if he needed the extra guidance to where they were going.

Well that explains it. Sad to say, he heaved a sigh of relief as he walked beside her while the others trailed behind.

After a few luggage rearrangements, the car was loaded. Hugs and goodbyes were exchanged in a flurry.

Ray wove his way through the throng and back to Adam. "Nice meeting you. The way Cameron speaks about you, I'm already a real fan."

"Thanks." He stuck his hand out for another firm shake. "Nice meeting you, too."

More waves and goodbyes followed until the car and passengers were down the driveway and gone. The garage door lowered to the cement. Stepping into the kitchen, he and Madison were alone. Standing side by side, staring at the recently closed back door.

"I hope they have a good time and…" Her voice cracked and she grew quiet.

Adam slipped an arm around her shoulders to draw her close. "They will."

She remained silent, resting her head against his chest as her arm came around his waist.

"Did you ever tell your mother about any of what happened the other day?"

"Are you kidding me? I did not." Raising her head, she looked up at him aghast before she returned a wistful gaze toward the door. "Except, now that they're gone, I sort of wish they weren't."

"It's only for a few days."

"You're right. They'll have a great time." Straightening, she stepped away from him. "What did you think of Ray?"

"He seems like a nice enough guy."

"Actually, as it turns out, he's not half bad as a person." She cast a long, lingering look toward where they'd all made their exit. "Not bad at all."

He was unsure how to take her comment. "What makes you say that?"

"I don't know. He seems very sad. I have a feeling maybe his recent divorce wasn't totally his idea. If he had any say in it at all."

"Did he tell you that?"

She shook her head. "Not in so many words. He didn't have to."

"How come?"

Her gaze strayed back to the damned door again. "Didn't you notice how he carried himself? Head lowered, shoulders slumped."

You obviously didn't see him following you down the stairs. "Maybe he has back problems." Adam couldn't resist a snarky comment. "Most older men do."

"He did apologize for not being able to help with the suitcases." A smile played around her mouth as she glanced up at him. "If I didn't know better, I would say you're a little jealous."

"Possibly. I will admit I wasn't sure what to think when I…when you and he first came strolling down the stairs."

"Strolling down the stairs?" Eyes twinkling, she made no secret of giving him a slow and sassy, head to toe inspection. "Really?"

"Keep looking at me like that and I will disavow all responsibility for my actions." As if to prove it, he rubbed his hand across her shoulders and up the back of her neck.

"I have only one thing to say to that." She rested her head against him at the same time as she tightened her arm around his waist.

He responded in kind, pulling her closer still. Enjoying the heat where their bodies touched. To the point he almost forgot he owed her a response. "And what would that be?"

The corners of her lips curved up as she lifted her head to gaze into his eyes. "What did you bring me to eat? I'm starved."

Talk about deflating his ego. While he stood there contemplating his losses, she'd already slipped out from under his arm and was well on her way to the front entrance. Where their steaks had been sitting for too long already.

Before he got very far after her, he reversed direction to again follow as she breezed by him carrying the white plastic bag back into the kitchen. Digging eagerly inside, she set the two covered plastic plates she pulled out on the island counter.

"Whatever you got me, I love it. It smells heavenly."

Adam had to admit his mouth watered too. "I figured it wouldn't hurt to have a big lunch. Maybe lighter dinner later on. Hope you like your steak medium rare."

The confidence he'd arrived with dipped as it suddenly dawned on him his menu choice wasn't without risk. *What if I guessed wrong?*

"Perfect. Medium rare is the only way to eat a steak."

Turned out she hadn't lied about that. After Madison pulled some utensils out of a drawer, sitting side by side, they each ate with enthusiasm. Talking some, but not much. No more than a half an hour later, Adam shoved their empty trays in the trash while Madison put the silverware they used in the dishwasher, then wiped off the counter.

"Can I interest you in some wine? I have red Shiraz." She pulled a serving sized bottle of club soda out of the refrigerator. "This is my beverage of choice these days."

He smiled at her reminder of the event that changed his life forever. For the better. "I'll have what you're having."

Her return smile of appreciation said it all. "Another club soda it is."

As they walked into the living room, beverages in hand, Madison placed her other hand on the small of her back and arched against it.

"Helping the boys, and then my mother pack, took more out of me than I realized. Plus, the doctor said no heavy lifting."

His water bottle hit the end table with a soft thud as he set it down.

"Why don't you sit and put your feet up. Better yet, lie down." He grabbed a plush throw pillow from the center of the couch to position at one end for her. "Can I get you anything? A heating pad maybe?"

"Thanks. That sounds good. There's one upstairs in my bedroom."

"I'll go get it for you." Turning on a dime, he immediately headed that way.

"According to a book I have, a heating pad is a good option to use on isolated parts of your body when you're pregnant. As opposed to a hot tub or sauna, which can raise your core temperature."

Halfway up the stairs, Adam nearly lost his footing as *his* core temperature shot up considerably. At her mention of a hot tub, a fairly explicit image came to mind. Madison surrounded by nothing more than clear, bubbling warm water. Eyes half closed and dreamy as he approached to join her. A soft smile curving her lips. Beckoning.

"Which isn't necessarily good for the baby." Her voice reached out to him from downstairs.

Stumbling again, he shot his arms out to regain his balance as he tripped his way to the second floor. With all thoughts banished but those pertaining to his mission, he headed straight for her bedroom. As soon as he cleared the doorway, he spied what he was after. The pink covered pad sat on top of some pillows propped against the headboard. Following the cord to where it was plugged into the wall, he knelt beside the cherry wood nightstand. His gaze immediately landed on an eight by ten photo in a gold filigree frame, and his hand stilled.

With a younger Dak and Cameron in the foreground, Madison stood behind wearing a smile broad enough to extend to her eyes and set them sparkling. Beside her was a man with features similar to Dak's. The brightness of his smile rivaled Madison's. His arms were wrapped firmly around her waist. Love shone in the gaze he focused on her and their boys.

Her first husband Dave.

Suddenly feeling like an intruder, he pulled the plug, gathered the pad, and left. All the way down the stairs, he vowed to bring a smile of that magnitude to Madison's face once again.

"Here it is. Let's get you comfortable."

In short order, he had the heating pad plugged in and rested against her back. Handing over her bottle of club soda, he grabbed his next and sat down beside her.

Taking the cap off hers, she took a sip then set the bottle aside. "It's going to be quiet around here for the next few days."

"You still aren't alone, you know. I'm here." Sliding closer, he raised her chin with the thumb and forefinger of his free hand. "If that's okay with you."

"It's more than okay. I don't know what I'd do without you."

The message in her gaze told him everything he needed to know. Her eyes fluttered shut as he lowered his head to claim her lips. Kissing her tentatively at first, he brushed his mouth at one corner of hers then the other, loving it when she trembled under his touch. When he finally covered the warmth of her mouth with his, a sigh escaped her he willingly accepted for his own.

As she slid her palms over his chest and clasped her fingers together at the back of his neck, he fumbled his bottle onto a nearby table, then wrapped his arms around her back, pulling her softness more tightly against him. A tiny murmur of acceptance coming from low in her throat, was more a delicate vibration from her soul to his.

On an answering groan, he lifted his mouth briefly before taking possession of hers again. This time with an urgency and want he could no longer contain.

"You're very important to me, you know." His voice came out husky with need he didn't try to hide as he trailed a chain of kisses along the side of her throat. "Let me rephrase. You're more than important to me. You're very much vital to my very existence."

The cross between an easy giggle and delicate sigh flowed from between her partially opened lips. "My thoughts exactly."

Tucking her closer still, he gladly held tight and, when she shifted to recline against the cushions, followed her down. As the heating pad dropped to the floor with a swish, she didn't seem to notice. The oversized couch was more than ample to accommodate them as they lay side by side. Even when, still holding on, he shifted to his back, pulling her to settle on top of him.

Pleased when she came willingly, totally immersed in one Madison Clark, he relished the taste of her lips. The heat of her body. Suddenly stiffening, she brought her arms down from around his neck as she started to pull away. More disappointed than perplexed, he quickly moved to draw her back in. When she still resisted, the trill of a ringing telephone registered as it began to penetrate his testosterone charged brain.

"It might be important. The boys or my mother." The devastation *he* experienced was evident in her voice. "I need to get that."

"Yeah." Breathlessly, he agreed. "You probably do."

Reluctantly, he let her go.

The kiss she planted on his cheek was totally unexpected. "Stay here. I'll be right back."

"I'm not going anywhere."

Smiling wider than ever, she pushed off him to stand.

"Hello." Her voice traveled back to him from the desk in one corner. "You what?" Slowly, she lowered into the high-backed leather chair. "When?"

Adam was on his feet and by her side in no time.

"Okay. I'll wait."

"What's this all about?" He laid a hand on her shoulder. "Are the boys okay? Who is it?"

She tilted the receiver away from her mouth and looked up at him. "I'm on hold right now. It's the police." Sitting straighter, she placed her free hand over his. "Yes. I'm here." The hand covering his suddenly grew damp then squeezed. "Now?"

"What is it?" He was about to take the phone away

from her and put it on speaker.

"No. That's fine. Mr. Hollingsworth is coming with me." She glanced briefly up at him before returning her focus to the conversation. "We can be there in an hour. No. It's no problem. I want this creep brought to justice even more than you do." Growing quiet, she listened, closed her eyes then nodded. "Yes. Of course. Thank you. Goodbye."

Adam waited as long as he could after she hung up the phone. "Well?"

"That was Officer Hardy."

"Who took the police report the other night." Adam had liked the patrolman immediately. He seemed like a real straight shooter. Though not quite as anal as his pal Vince, they'd bonded in a similar way when Adam had identified himself as a fellow officer.

"They want me down at the police station." As if in some sort of trance, she stared straight ahead. "To possibly identify…" She stopped. Swallowed. "…to possibly identify the person who assaulted me." Her voice trailed off as she raised her worried gaze to meet his.

The same unbridled fear he'd seen in her eyes the day it happened had returned to settle deep within them now. Minus the benefit of an adrenaline rush and maybe a little shock to help cushion the unpleasant effect.

"Are you up to it? You don't have to do anything if you're not up to it."

As she remained seated, he circled both arms around her to wrap her up tight.

She readily grabbed hold to lean into him. With her head resting on his shoulder, she released her next breath on a shudder. "As long as you're with me, I'm up for anything."

"Then you're up for anything. Because I'll be with you, no matter what."

Madison wasn't saying much more as they drove down to the station, and Adam was at a loss how to fill the void. Her silence continued once they arrived, parked and stepped out of the car. Unable to take it anymore, he stopped them on the sidewalk out front. The pulse pumping at the side of her neck made her skin quiver. By now, she had both arms crossed in front of her and hugged herself tight.

"You sure you're ready for this?" He turned her toward him. In one swift movement, he pushed her arms apart and pulled her close.

"I'm sure."

Not totally believing her, he stood there and held her. For as long as she needed him to.

Her cell pinged, and they both jumped. She had it out of her purse in a heartbeat. Staring at the screen, her anxious expression cleared.

"It's a text from my mother. They're in Chicago. Heading for my uncle's house." She moved her fingers over the virtual keyboard. "I'll text back thanks for letting us know. I can call them tomorrow."

"Whatever you want to do."

Straightening, she returned the cell to her purse then walked to the door leading inside. "Let's do this."

"Let's."

Officer Hardy met them at the reception desk and proceeded to take them to the two-way mirrored surveillance room to view the line-up.

A tall, balding man stood the second they entered.

"As counsel for the accused, I protest anyone but the witness being in here."

"Sergeant Hollingsworth is a police officer from the Detroit area." Hardy spoke up immediately. "Professional courtesy."

If the colleague sought to ingratiate him to the man, Adam wasn't sure that was the best way to go about it.

"In no way am I connected with the case in any professional capacity." Adam moved to offer the attorney his hand. "Only as a friend of the vic...of Mrs. Clark."

"And I suppose you're going to coach her to identify my client."

"Hardly, sir." *Wasn't this guy a real piece of work?* He glanced at Hardy to help give credence to his next statement. "I have no idea who your client is. Like I said, I'm simply here to support Mrs. Clark."

"Fine." Eyes mere slits, the man glanced at Madison then back at him. "Just make sure that's all you do."

"I'll make sure."

Ignoring a number of chairs set out in the room, Madison and Adam remained standing as one by one, the four subjects, all male, all roughly the same height and build, filed in. Apparently hitting their marks on the floor, they all stopped.

"Face forward." Hardy spoke into the microphone mounted beside the two-way glass.

Four subjects complied. Adam immediately recognized two of them. Patrolmen he'd met when he first arrived in town and stopped by the station to introduce himself. The other two he'd never seen before.

"I'm…I'm just not sure." Madison stepped back to shrink against him.

"Take your time."

He and Hardy each issued the identical message.

Standing behind Madison, Adam made himself refrain from touching her. He had a feeling not even a fingertip rested on her shoulder, if only for moral support, was allowed. He'd just have to endure doing nothing as he watched the rigid set of her neck atop hunched shoulders.

"I just don't know. I can't be sure."

She spent another few minutes staring through the two-way glass. From Adam's close vantage point, her reflection was crystal clear. Including the tell-tale lines of fatigue around her eyes and unmistakable strain drawing down the corners of her mouth.

"It's hard. Everything happened so fast."

She leaned into him and reached for his hand. He readily accepted the contact. Even went so far as to place his other hand lightly on her shoulder. A hand she immediately covered with her own.

"If you aren't sure, you aren't." Adam made eye contact with counsel for the accused. Daring him to object.

To his credit, he didn't come out and tell Adam to back off, or physically remove his hands. Though he did look rather pointedly at their placement.

"He's right, Mrs. Clark." Hardy's voice was calm. "You need to be sure."

"Number three, maybe." Stepping from what amounted to Adam's embrace, she again approached the glass. More assuredly this time. "I was more concerned about protecting myself than I was thinking about making a positive identification."

"You're doing great, sweetheart. Take your time." Adam risked another warning glare as he stepped forward too.

"Could I see him from the side, please?"

Speaking into the intercom, Hardy gave the instructions for that suspect to step forward. Turn left then right.

All the while, Madison's focus on him didn't falter. Until she lowered her head on a sigh. "I'm sorry. I just can't be sure."

Adam had his arm around her in a heartbeat. This time he wasn't about to let her go. "Then you can't be sure. And that's all right."

After thanking Hardy for the effort, and ignoring the counselor's self-satisfied sneer, he and Madison were soon in his car, headed for her house. For most of the way, she sat, chin in her hand, staring out the side window.

Reaching over, Adam covered her other hand with his and squeezed. "I'm sorry."

"I had such high hopes going down there." Letting out a sigh, she didn't even bother to turn toward him. "I was so sure I'd be able to…" Another sigh whooshed out. "…not have to worry about that creep coming after me again."

"What makes you say that? I thought the attack was random. Someone, albeit an extraordinary jerk, freaked out when the fire alarm went off."

"I know. Still, the entire situation creeped me out."

"Anyone who might have an ax to grind with you?"

"Not anyone I can think of." She gave her head an emphatic shake. "Except maybe Hayden Riley. But he's really more an annoyance than threat."

"You don't have to face this alone, you know. I've told you that."

"I was staying strong for the sake of my boys. Now that they're gone…" She turned her head to give him a weak smile.

"It's normal to feel violated after what happened to you. Even if you weren't a specific target. A random act of violence, intended or not, is still violence. I don't think you should stay alone for the next few days."

"Is that your professional opinion?"

He could have sworn her smile strengthened. "Professional and personal. Mostly the latter."

Taking the time to study him for a long moment, damned if she didn't grin outright. "I was hoping you'd say that."

"That's all I needed to hear." Adam spun the car around, glancing over as he righted the wheel. "I'll stop to pick up a few things from my place before we go home to yours."

Chapter Fifteen

Madison shuddered as a chilling blast of early December air blew in with them when she and Adam entered her house. "What happens now that I was unable to positively identify my attacker?"

"That depends." He set down his duffle bag and shut the door with a solid thump. A click as he slipped the lock into place was no more than a delicate echo. "There's no question a positive ID from you makes for a stronger case, but chances are they can still get a conviction with whatever circumstantial evidence they might have based on the surveillance tapes."

"That's something."

"However, it's still a misdemeanor. Right now they have him on a petty suspected battery charge. Non-aggravated because only minor injury was caused. To you." A fierce scowl took over his features. "If he'd hurt the baby, I would have had to kill him myself."

Momentarily struck by the fury in his voice, a rage she never expected rose in her as well. "My sentiments exactly."

"Thankfully, that didn't happen."

She ran a hand over her belly. "It's still terrifying to think about."

Stepping forward, he gathered her in his arms. "Then don't. What happened is over."

He seemed to know she needed another moment or

two in order to collect herself and didn't move. Didn't speak. Simply held her. Splaying his palms flat, he rubbed gently up and down her spine and across her shoulder blades. Her eyes closed almost on their own as he massaged away the stress of the last few hours. Once tight and rigid muscles became relaxed and pliable under the gentle pressure of his hands. All the tension that held her captive in its merciless grip didn't stand a chance and slithered out of her.

"You'll be okay, sweetheart. I'm with you." He dropped a light kiss on the tip of her nose.

"I'm looking forward to getting a good night's sleep." Resting her cheek against his chest, she eyed his bag by the door. Maybe she was wrong, but to her way of thinking, he seemed to have packed a lot more than a few things as he'd claimed on the drive over. "I hope moving in here won't compromise your shooting schedule."

"That's not my main concern right now. You are. Even if it wasn't, I'm not included on the shooting schedule for the next few days."

...next few days.

Before the enormity of the thought could truly take hold, Adam was speaking again.

"So, another of my major responsibilities as a soon to be parent is to protect my future offspring. And his mother, of course." He squeezed her tighter. "And thank her, from the bottom of my heart, for giving me the opportunity to do both. I know this is probably old hat for you. You already have two great kids. But for me." He spoke low, his words circling her heart. "I've never had much of a family before. Never had anyone who truly belonged to me."

"It never becomes old hat, Adam." Her voice was an intimate whisper in honor of the wondrous miracle they shared. "Never. Ever."

Wrapped in his arms, all the amazing emotions she'd once felt with Dave bubbled up. Emotions she wasn't capable of dealing with, until just now.

After so, so long and so much heartache, maybe, just maybe, life can be good again.

Another thought hit soon after, and she couldn't resist sharing as she pulled back to look at him. "He? What makes you so sure this baby is a he?"

His mouth fell open for an instant before his eyes filled with mischief and he grinned. "You mean there's the possibility of another one like you? Sign me up."

"Be careful what you wish for." Her teasing response rode on the ribbon of her laughter.

"Trust me. I know exactly what I'm doing." Another smile lit up his eyes as he squeezed her shoulders. "Now that that's settled, where do you want me to sleep?"

She blinked and her mouth dropped open. *Where indeed?* "What?"

His lips quirked up yet again and his eyes danced. "Where should I put my things?"

"I'll show you." As he went to retrieve his bag, she turned to lead him up the stairs.

They soon arrived at one of two guest rooms, with its mint green walls and pink, green and white rosebud patterned bedspread and matching, lace trimmed, curtains.

"This is your room." She almost laughed at his look of pure consternation at the feminine décor as he poked his head in to scan the interior.

"A king-sized bed. That will be a nice change from the barely double-sized number in my trailer back at the lot." He dropped his duffel at the foot of it, then splayed his hands out on top of the mattress and pushed down a few times. "The mattress in my trailer isn't near as plush. Lucky for me, my living quarters are only temporary."

...only temporary. A gray cloud filtered in, casting a shadow she did her best to ignore.

"And your own bathroom." She walked over to open the adjoining door and reveal the white gloss, free standing soaker tub, large enough for two, beside a more traditional sink and toilet. "Sorry there isn't a shower."

He came to stand behind her and peeked over her shoulder. "Not what I'm used to, but I'm sure I'll do just fine. I can be very adaptable."

His warm breath blew over the back of her neck. On a slight shiver, she closed her eyes. "It's really quite comfortable."

I should know. It's where I stayed most nights, alone, when Joe was still alive.

She banished the bad to concentrate on the good and opened her eyes to glance up at him. "Everything you need should be in there. Otherwise, let me know."

He looped an arm around her waist to pull her in. "Everything I need is already here."

"For me too." Her words came out a whisper.

Warmth spread through her everywhere they made contact. Standing on tiptoe, she sought his lips. All it took was his mouth to cover hers, and the once ominous cloud lost its power, floating farther and farther away. Only to disappear entirely.

Clutching the hard muscles of his back and shoulders, she poured in all the promise of a brighter future as she returned his kiss. Right now, only the two of them, together, mattered as she willingly sank into him, fitting her newly relaxed body to his firm and solid strength.

After a time, his mouth lifted and he rested his forehead on hers. Gazed into her eyes. "For that good night's sleep you talked about. Do you want to go to your room?"

"No." Her response was immediate as her blood heated. "That other bedroom holds not so pleasant memories for me."

"I'm sorry to hear that. As far as I'm concerned, you deserve nothing but good memories."

Captivated by the true affection shining in his gaze, she nodded her agreement. "Besides, it's a shame to let that big soaker tub go to waste unused."

For the breadth of a second Adam froze. "Is it okay? I mean I thought you said hot tubs weren't good for…" He shut his mouth as anxiety entered his eyes.

She let out a soft giggle, her heart soaring at his concern for their child. "A hot tub yes. Soaker tub is something else entirely."

Relief flashed in the gaze that remained on her. "I have to say this is the most enjoyable personal protection detail I've ever been on."

Backing slightly away from her, he pulled his shirt over his head he deposited on the chair in one swift motion. With his hands positioned at the top button of his jeans, he stopped and smiled at her. Her return smile quickly became a grin as he undid the fastenings and slid them off.

Never breaking eye contact, she slowly and deliberately walked toward him. "And since you are personally protecting me, I can put aside any cares and worries to concentrate only on us. Tonight. Together."

She finished on a murmur as she eagerly touched his lips with hers. Bringing her arms around his neck, as he circled her waist to draw her against him, she ran her palms over his shoulder blades, savoring the warmth of bare skin, the sheer power of hard muscle.

"Aren't you feeling a little overdressed?" He whispered against her lips.

Another soft giggle preceded her answer. "As a matter of fact, I am."

"Since it's my room, I'll go get things ready for us."

Disappointment when he let her go only fueled her need to quickly rejoin him. With rushing water as a backdrop, she slipped out of her clothes, setting them in a jumbled pile on top of his. Steam glistened on the mirror over the sink as she entered the bathroom and shut the door. Standing by the tub, Adam turned. Smiled. Heat funneled along her skin as his gaze slowly and thoroughly lingered on every curve and angle.

Adam stepped in the tub first, then offered his hand. "Careful. I don't want you to fall."

"I'll be careful."

"Warm, not too hot." He nuzzled the side of her neck.

Water splashed and gurgled as he sat, resting on the sloped end.

She slid in to settle against him. "You're referring to the water, I assume."

His chest swelled on her bare back as laughter

erupted. He clenched her more tightly between his legs. She ran her hands along the tops of his thighs, smiling at his swift inhale. Squeezing body wash into his palm, he rubbed his hands together briefly, then began to rub the suds over her shoulders and the back of her neck, across her shoulder blades and down her spine. Pausing at its base to massage over her sensitive skin, his touch sent fluttering pulses through her until she rolled her head back against him on an extended sigh of pleasure.

"If only I could turn around." Her voice was no more than a hasty exhale. "I'd be happy to return the favor."

"Why would you want to mess with perfection?" Dipping his hands in the water, he gently rinsed her off, then slid his palms along her hips and up her ribcage.

She drew a breath as he captured her in a loving caress. Losing all control, the only thing she could do was arch into him. Turning sideways as best she could, she offered her lips for a lingering kiss. Finally, unable to stand it any longer, she twisted her body until she was on her knees facing him.

Meeting the desire in his gaze, she joined her mouth to his, then plunged her tongue inside while she slid her palms along the smooth surface of his chest to the hard ridges of his stomach. She let her hand slip below to stroke between his legs.

Hauling in a sharp breath, he broke their kiss on a moan. She smiled at the power of her touch.

"There's more beyond this." She whispered her promise.

He met her gaze and smiled. "Much more."

Clean and towel-dried a short time later, they lay side by side between soft sheets. Their bodies and hearts a jumble of marvelous connections. Lips touched lips again and again with immense longing, as if they'd never get enough.

Releasing her mouth when they'd had their fill, Adam drew back to gaze into her eyes. So deeply, she was awestruck at its power to glimpse the very depths of her being.

"The last time we did this, neither one of us was in the proper state of mind to be truly conscious of what was going on. This time, I want both of us to be fully aware of what it is we're doing…" His words were a delicate vibration upon her skin as he feathered a trail of sweet, tiny kisses along the side of her throat. "Who it is we're doing this with."

Her breath caught at his truth and honesty. Once again gazing into his eyes, she marveled at the depth of caring she found there. "I promise to remember every touch. Cherish every nuance."

With that, his lips found hers again. They meshed so perfectly and completely, it was impossible to tell where she ended and he began. He slid his palm along the outside of her thigh, up over her hip. She sucked in a breath as strong palms moved over the sensitive flesh on her belly. All the while with his mouth pressed to hers.

A sigh of pure contentment was all she had in her at the intimate contact. She squirmed and twisted to get closer to him. Lips that brushed over her ear lobe traveled a slow and sensuous path along the sensitive skin down her neck as he held her tight.

A small whimper of need crept forth from low in her throat. His heartfelt groan of longing answered. Shivers of desire overtook her as she opened in acceptance.

He began with mild and tentative movements, she was sure were in loving homage to her 'condition'.

"It's okay, Adam. I'm not as delicate as you think." She whispered against his skin. "Honestly."

His response was as swift as it was thrilling. She clung to him, riding higher and higher on precious waves of pleasure. Letting go when she reached the very top. Adam soon followed, stiffening as he murmured her name.

Lying side by side after, he trailed his fingers over her arm and across her breast, then down her rib cage to her stomach where he settled his palm in a gentle caress.

"From now on, we'll always be a part of each other. Always."

"Always," she replied.

The sweetness of their union brought tears of joy to her eyes, and love to fill her heart.

****

Madison lay on her back. The previous night's dreams slowly giving way to awareness and remembered pleasures as a welcoming warmth filtered over her. She stretched out to move closer to its source. Smiled as a kiss feathered over her temple. Twisting her head to one side, the smile remained as she lifted sleep-heavy lids.

Adam's face, mere inches from hers, came slowly into focus, his sleepy gaze full of softness and caring.

Her breath caught and her smile broadened. "Good morning."

"Morning." He dropped a kiss on her waiting mouth.

The weight of his arm wrapped around her waist to roll her toward him. His warm palm splayed across the sensitive skin at the small of her back to draw her against his heat.

"I have to tell you, I could easily get used to this." His breath brushed, light and sensual over her mouth.

With a smile curving her lips, she shifted to more fully face him. "My thoughts exactly."

For the next few moments, neither spoke as they relished just being together. Holding. Kissing. Touching.

Loving.

"What would you like for breakfast?" She drew back slightly but kept her arms around his neck.

"You." He proceeded to capture her mouth again. Then again. And again.

Quickly rendered breathless, she was more than ready when he rose above her. Joined their bodies as one. Though their lovemaking was less intense than the night before, that didn't make it any less sweet. Same with the afterglow as they held each other in silence, while minute after minute slipped lazily by.

Until her cell went off, and she was obligated to slip it off the nightstand.

"Hello."

"Madison? It's Mom."

"Hi, Mom."

Glancing up at Adam, she instinctively held her breath. Momentarily startled at being caught in bed with him, she soon realized that wasn't the case. It wasn't as if she had face-timed or anything. *Thank God.* Though he too had gone noticeably quiet.

She fought to find her voice. "How was the flight?"

"Relatively smooth. The boys seemed to enjoy it."

"It's been a while since they've flown."

"They went to get doughnuts with Uncle Harry a few minutes ago. I took the opportunity to give you a quick heads up. Dak's been a little homesick. I told him he could call you anytime he wanted. So far he's refrained."

"Probably best then if I wait until he calls me."

"That was my thought. Just so you know."

"I appreciate that."

After a few minutes of idle chit chat, Madison hung up. Knowing he'd be interested, she shared some of what her mother said.

Firming his lips, Adam nodded. "Poor little guy."

"Hopefully he'll eventually adjust."

"It will just take time."

"Thank you for being here for me. For us."

"No other place I'd rather be."

Nestled in the crook of his arm, she lifted her head to look at him, then reluctantly rolled away to get up. "Nice as this is, we can't stay in bed forever. I'll go make us something to eat. After I take a quick bath."

"Don't use all the hot water. We need to preserve some for tonight."

She turned to look at him, then grinned at his wink. "Don't worry. I wouldn't think of it."

A few minutes later, finger combing her hair to dry on its own, she stepped out of the bathroom wrapped in a towel. "Your turn. And I left you plenty of hot water."

"Thanks. I'll be quick like you." He touched her cheek as he walked by.

A simple act, yet intimate. And endearing.

Once she was dressed in yoga pants and long

sleeve top, all the way down the stairs, Madison relived the special moment in her mind. Gratified at how nice it was to be part of someone's life again.

Setting the cell she'd brought with her on the end table, she gazed upward at the sound of the water shutting off.

He wasn't that speedy when they bathed together.

Smiling to herself as she walked into the kitchen, she grabbed the carton of eggs out of the refrigerator. Styrofoam squeaked as she opened the lid. Setting the container on the counter, she paused. She'd neglected to ask how he liked them cooked.

From somewhere in the house, a door opened. Adam coming out of the bathroom. *No worries. He'll be down soon enough.*

Bending to a lower cupboard, she slid out the large, silver electric waffle iron. Busy putting fresh water and grounds in the coffee maker then hitting the brew button, at a creak in the floor behind her she turned, fully prepared to greet the man who had spent the night.

"John!" Shrinking back, she slammed a hand to her chest at the last person she expected to see came up behind her. "You scared the daylights out of me."

Eyes wide, he stood as if frozen to the spot only a few feet away. Totally astounded, as if *she* had just scared the daylights out of *him*. Shoving something in his jacket pocket, he didn't respond right away, but looked over her right shoulder as color drained from his face. Prodded by his stunned expression, she spun the other way to discover its cause.

Adam stood in the doorway. Barefoot and in jeans and a T-shirt. With his hair combed but still obviously wet, there was no question where he'd just come from.

Where he'd been.

She whirled back to John, who had yet to take his gaze from Adam. The coffee maker sputtered.

"Well, I just…" A stupefied grin spread over his face as a deep flush rose up his neck. "I came to check out the veranda repair when I noticed you were in here." For the first time, he shifted his gaze toward Madison then back to land on Adam.

"We were just about to have breakfast." Her tentative regard swung Adam's way as he walked over to stand beside her.

"I see that." John lifted an arm toward the waffle iron.

"I was called down to the police station late yesterday afternoon to view a line up in connection with the incident at the Shop and Save I told you about."

Finally taking his intense stare off Adam, he again glanced back at her. "Did you identify anyone?"

She shook her head. "Unfortunately, I couldn't. Positively anyway. They do think they have the right person in custody, though."

Adam slipped his arm around her shoulders. "They're going through more surveillance tape."

"That's good." Despite his words, he scowled. "That they have more tape to look at, I mean."

"I was a little rattled, to say the least. Adam offered to stay with me at the house. So I wouldn't be alone." Madison kept her voice strong. If he somehow viewed Adam's presence as a betrayal of his brother, though unfortunate, that was his problem. Not hers. "Oh, and I finally got a hold of Mr. Conklin."

"Joe's lawyer?" The lines in his forehead

deepened. "When did that happen?"

"Last week. I know you had taken on the task of making those arrangements for me. But you've done so much. I decided to take on some of the responsibility."

"It wasn't a problem." His voice came out sharp. Almost resentful. "I told you that."

"John, it wasn't a big deal. We meet tomorrow."

"Yeah." His voice moderated somewhat as he addressed her. "It's not. Well, as I said, I was checking out the repair from the backyard." Seemingly recovered, most likely from the surprise of seeing Adam, John grinned. A definite return to his old relaxed self. "If it's okay, I'll run upstairs and make sure they fixed it right from inside too, then let the two of you get on with your day."

Saying nothing, Adam immediately deferred to Madison with a head nod.

"It's okay with me. Then you're sure you won't stay for breakfast?" Hoping he'd refuse, she still felt obligated to make the offer.

"Thanks, but no." Headed across the kitchen, he paused in the doorway. "I have a long day ahead of me, too. Lots to get done. I'll just let myself out."

Without further explanation, he slipped out the door and was gone.

Chapter Sixteen

Madison looked up at Adam with a sheepish smile. "That was somewhat awkward."

He glanced toward the empty doorway. "If I'd known he was down here, I would have stayed upstairs until he left."

She shook her head. "It's not a big deal. He surprised me was all."

Even so, he'd put her in an embarrassing situation that could have been avoided. "I didn't hear the doorbell."

"There wasn't one." She took a can of cooking spray from the top cupboard. "He came in through the back door. Walked in unannounced. That's what threw me."

"Really?" A deep crease furrowed his brow. *Unannounced? Were they that familiar?* He shook off both questions. Who was he to judge? "You're comfortable with him being upstairs alone?"

"Of course. He's been nothing but helpful since Joe died." Plugging in the waffle iron, she flipped the toggle switch on its front. A green light blinked on. "Seeing to minor repairs around the house. Taking care of some of the finances of Joe's business dealings. Keeping me sane."

A pang of jealousy hit he couldn't ignore. He reminded himself the man was in Madison's life before he came along.

It didn't help.

"Have you—"

"The repair looks fine." This John character hollered from outside the door.

Madison glanced up then turned. "Okay. Thanks for checking."

"You're welcome." The reply was muffled as if he was walking away. "I'll let myself out. Call if you need anything else."

"I will." When the front door shut with a thud, she smiled at Adam. "Sorry for the interruption."

His face softened as he moved toward her. "No need." Taking her in his arms, he planted a kiss on her forehead, then with two fingers under her jaw, tipped her face closer to his. "This was how I planned to greet you this morning. Except he kind of threw me off." Without further comment, he covered her lips with his, loving how fresh and inviting she smelled.

A smile curved up the second he lifted his mouth. "It's a great way to be greeted. One I could definitely get used to."

"You and me both."

Despite the smile, a cloud seemed to filter into her eyes, but was gone before he could be sure it had been there at all. When she turned away so abruptly, he had no choice but to release her as the coffee maker beeped.

"There's coffee. Help yourself." Busy setting flour, sugar and an assortment of other ingredients on the counter, he assumed for their waffles, she no longer faced him.

Which bothered him no end. After very little soul searching, he'd reached the decision to ask Madison to become a permanent part of his life. No complicated arrangements. No restrictions. Unfortunately, she was in no mood for any discussion beyond the superficial. It might be best to not bring up the subject just yet. He could wait.

Though not for long.

"Can I get you a cup?" He took two red ceramic mugs off a rack on the wall.

"Yes. Thanks." She nodded acceptance of the one he put in front of her. "Do you want eggs too?"

He filled his own mug he set down after taking a sip. "I'll make those. Where do you keep your frypan?"

"Right here." She pulled one from a lower cupboard she handed over. "I prefer mine over easy. If that's okay."

"As a matter of fact, my specialty."

While they set about preparing breakfast, she seemed to relax. Some.

After coating the waffle iron with cooking spray, she spooned some batter onto the surface and closed the lid then turned to face him. "Hard to believe my mother and the boys will be back tomorrow already."

Even harder to accept. Adam fielded a flash of guilt at being selfish. So shoot him if he enjoyed being alone with her. Not that he didn't miss the boys, too. "That's kinda how weekends are. Two days long. Three if you're lucky." *Either way, too damned short.*

"The bank still hasn't given me a decent answer as to why my account was temporarily frozen. Makes no sense."

He dumped a pat of butter in the pan he'd put on the front burner. "If you need…"

"…a loan? Thanks but no. I have my own money I

kept separate that Joe didn't know about." She glanced down for a moment then up at him. "Possibly not my finest hour, but now I'm glad I did. Thankfully, Joe at least had the foresight to put my name on the house, so that's not an issue. Until I can sell it and go back home."

"To Chicago?" He couldn't hide his surprise at the certainty in her tone.

"Yes. Chicago. Why?"

Butter sizzled, and he turned down the heat. "I had assumed…"

Before he even finished his sentence, she was all over it.

"That the boys and I would…" She caught a breath and swallowed. "…maybe move to Detroit?"

"Yeah." The stupidity of his assumption began to dawn on him.

"Or you could move to Chicago."

He couldn't help but wince at the very idea.

A reluctance she noticed. "I rest my case."

The timer on the waffle iron beeped softly. She stopped staring at him long enough to open the lid and fork out a fragrant crisp cake.

Turning back to the frypan in front of him, he lowered his head. Here he'd hardly opened his mouth and, already, he'd lost their first disagreement. "You're right. I'm an idiot. Sorry."

"You're not an idiot by any stretch, Adam." She poured in more batter and shut the lid. "Chicago is where all my ties are. My family."

While his only ties to Detroit were his job and a few close friends.

"You and the boys could move in with me." That

made a lot of sense.

Her abrupt laugh indicated maybe she didn't agree. "And that's all there is to it, right?"

"Well, yeah."

"Not when children are involved."

She had a point. Now that he thought about it, there would be adjustments to make he hadn't considered. For starters, he'd have to get a three bedroom apartment. Maybe four. There were some in the complex where he lived. At least he thought there were. There had to be.

When she came over to take both his hands in hers, he stared down at her. "I guess this is all more complicated than I realized."

Staring back, she took a breath as if what she was about to say required an extra dose of courage. "We could stay here until the boys are out of school. With Christmas coming up, it would make things easier."

The hope in her eyes tugged at his heart. This was what he'd wanted all along. A family. If not all his own, certainly close. Now that it was offered, why would he hesitate to take it?

"You make a lot of sense. I'm sure we can work out the logistics. I can talk the Chief into extending my leave of absence. Or." He raised his voice as she opened her mouth to, he was sure, lodge some kind of protest. "Give me a letter of recommendation so I can hook on to a department somewhere else. Illinois, maybe."

"You think?" She considered him from beneath hooded lids before a smile spread across her face.

Releasing her hands, he brought her into his arms. "I'm sure. As I said, we can figure this out. Get input from Cameron and Dak."

She looked up at him with the huge grin still intact. "My thoughts exactly. Thank you so much for thinking about my boys. That's not something Joe would have thought to do." Putting her head on his chest, she hugged him tight.

"As you once said, with our child as a connection we'll always be together."

"Always."

When she glanced up at him again, he cupped her face in his palms and gazed into her eyes. "I love you, Madison Clark."

She pressed her lips to his. Briefly, then pulled back. "I love you too, Adam Hollingsworth."

Behind her, the waffle iron dinged. Brushing another kiss on his lips, she turned away.

That major question settled between them for now, sometimes talking, sometimes not, they soon had a respectable breakfast on the table. Fresh coffee, warm waffles, just right over easy eggs.

He took his seat at the table. *A beautiful and caring woman sitting across from me to share it with.*

Adam poured orange juice in her glass than his. "So what are your plans for today?"

He knew full well how he'd prefer to spend this Sunday.

"I only have one thing to attend to today." She grimaced. "The bank is supposed to call. I think the branch manager is trying score brownie points, agreeing to address my concerns today. Through a phone call, but still. Then, you heard me tell John I have an appointment with Joe's attorney first thing tomorrow. What a way to start the week." She laid a pat of butter in the center of her waffle. "He's been out of town the past couple of weeks on a family emergency. Now that he's back, I'm anxious to get the estate settled once and for all."

"I don't blame you. It's a huge responsibility."

She cut a piece of waffle she dipped in syrup then brought to her mouth. "The economics involved don't bother me so much as wanting to just be done. Put all this behind me. Get on with my life."

Giving in to an urgency to touch her, he set down his fork and reached across the table to take both her hands in his. "Call me selfish, but I'm anxious for you to get on with your life too."

"In such a short time, you've become a big part of the rest of my life." Glancing up at him, she smiled. "For that I'm very grateful."

He rubbed his thumb along the ball of her palm. "I'm the one who's grateful. For you."

The caring in her gaze nearly did him in. It took all his self-control to stay where he was. Not carry her upstairs and make love to her. Show her through the tenderness of his touch, in addition to his words, how much she meant to him.

"Not to take advantage, but I have a favor to ask."

"What?" Coming out of the enormity of his thoughts, it took a moment to comprehend her comment.

"It would be a huge help if you could pick up my mother and the boys at the airport tomorrow. Their flight gets in at eleven thirty. With the attorney and all, I can't be in two places at once."

"Sure. I can do that."

"Thank you. I appreciate it. Though this has been,

is nice, I miss Dak and Cameron."

"I've missed them too." Without a second thought, he spoke from his heart. *Maybe even as much as you.*

"Sometime this week we can, hopefully, get around to decorating the house for Christmas. The boys have been after me to do that. Especially Dak."

Swallowing a mouthful of waffle, Adam smiled. "Now why doesn't that surprise me?"

For the next half hour, after finishing their meal, they lingered over coffee, making plans for decorating. Each sharing traditions they held dear. Because, as far as both were concerned, spending the upcoming holiday together was a given.

Finally, Madison stood. Starting to gather their dishes, she leaned down to drop a kiss on his forehead. "Here's to happier times for all of us."

"That's for sure." Before she had a chance to pick up his plate, he reached an arm out to wrap at her waist and pull her against him. Right now, a peck on the forehead simply was not going to cut it. With a gentle jerk, he drew her onto his lap.

"Adam...I..."

She squealed then laughed as she landed with a thump. Holding her in place, he buried his face into the sweet scent of her hair as playfulness became the farthest thing from his mind. This was no game. Never had been. What he and Madison were working to discover, was as serious to him as it was essential. As he sought her lips, her response was all he could hope for. Turning into him, she wrapped her arms around his neck, then squirmed to get closer. Pressed her lips more firmly to his.

The tempo of her breathing was quickly rising to

match the rhythm of his. Kissing her, running his palms along her sides and across her back was never going to be enough for him. He contemplated whether the kitchen table was sturdy enough to sustain both their weights.

Chime. Chime. Chime.

Chime. Chime. Chime.

Of one mind, they both froze, mid-kiss, as the doorbell echoed.

Planting her palms on his shoulders, she sat upright. "Who could that be?"

With a ragged sigh of regret, he relinquished his grip as she pressed against him to stand.

"Whoever it is, they have piss-poor timing." He stood too. Moving to adjust the front of his pants.

She looked back at him with an apologetic smile as she lowered her gaze from his face. "I'm sorry."

"Not half as sorry as I am."

Chime. Chime. Chime.

Chime. Chime. Chime.

"It doesn't sound like they're going to go away." He gestured toward the living room. "You get that and I'll start cleaning up in here."

"Then maybe we can pick up where we left off." Standing on tiptoe, she brushed a quick kiss over his lips.

"I'm going to hold you to that promise."

"I certainly hope so." Her laughter stayed with him as she scurried out of the room.

Picking up their plates, he allowed himself a heaved sigh of frustration as he ambled over to the sink. He had the door to the dishwasher open when he heard Madison give a short greeting to whomever had arrived.

"We've talked about this before." Suddenly her voice rose. "I've explained the realities involved."

"I don't think you're taking all that's going on out there seriously enough."

As an agitated male voice responded, Adam was out of the kitchen like a shot.

A man he'd never seen before stood between the entryway and the living room. Medium height, lanky, fair complexion and balding. Madison faced him toe to toe, effectively blocking him from getting farther into the house. Both he and she glanced over as Adam entered.

"Who are you?" The encroacher spoke first.

Adam didn't bother to answer. When he moved to strong arm Madison behind him, she dodged away to remain at his side.

"To be honest, Hayden. The situation at the Concord property is the least of my worries." She glanced at Adam. "Not that I would be concerned anyway. Because I can assure you I have it on excellent authority the movie company is taking very good care of things. And will leave it in the best condition when they finish."

Adam stepped forward. "Is this about the estate where we're currently filming?"

"It is." Asshole gave an abrupt answer.

"I have an appointment tomorrow with my late husband's attorney. I promise you I will discuss the use of the Concord estate with him and learn all I can to address your concerns."

The man scowled. "I don't think—"

"That will have to be good enough." Adam couldn't resist interrupting.

On the Make

An accusing gaze strayed his way. "There are items out at the site that are irreplaceable if they should be lost or stolen."

Narrowing his eyes, Adam chose not to answer.

"So noted, Hayden." Madison stepped by them to open the door. "When I know something, you will too."

It took a moment for this intruder to take the hint. With a sniff, he raised his head and walked toward her. "See that you do."

"You're welcome." Smiling through clenched teeth, she shut the door behind him then leaned against it. "That man is beyond irritating."

Adam placed his hands on her shoulders as he began to knead away the tension. "From what I saw, you sure don't owe him any special accommodation."

"I know that." Raising her head, she rested back against him. "Aside from being enormously rude, he's basically harmless."

"That doesn't mean you have to deal with him." He circled her waist.

She rubbed her palms along his arms, then settled her hands over his. "I know that, too. At first, I tried to be nice. I talked briefly with John about this property. He calls it nothing but a big, asset sucking albatross. Says it's been in the family for generations."

"And you end up having to manage it."

"Yep." Turning in his arms, she clasped her hands behind his neck. "But as I told him. Not until tomorrow."

"Which means we still have the rest of today."

Bending to kiss her, he planned to use his next breath to invite her to do something to celebrate. Like maybe spend the rest of their day between the sheets.

The chirp of her cell phone from the end table cut that idea off at the knees.

She pulled away with a sigh. "Not again."

"Seems so." *Am I ever going to catch a break today?* He dropped his arms to allow her to step back. But not before taking another, albeit brief, kiss.

"It's the bank." Scooping up her phone, she glanced at the caller ID then up at him. "Hopefully, I'll get some answers. But first I need to get the notes I left upstairs." She spoke over her shoulder as she hurried away.

"I'll finish up in the kitchen until you get back."

"I shouldn't be long. Then we can pick up where we left off."

Adam stared after her. Then shook his head as he glanced down at the front of his pants. "Definitely."

A short time later, closing the dishwasher door when he had it loaded, Adam wiped down the counters and rinsed out the coffee pot. Smiling at the thought of what a great house husband, and father, he had the potential to become, he walked into the living room. He was about to take a seat, maybe find the remote and surf through some channels, when the nearby phone rang.

Since Madison was still upstairs, after one more ring, he walked over and picked up. "Clark residence."

"I'm calling for Mrs. Madison Clark." The person on the other end was female.

"She's not available at the moment. Can I take a message?"

"No. I…"

It's possible the police had news. "Who am I speaking with, please?"

"This is Doctor Winters."

"Doctor Winters." His body tensed. "Is something wrong?"

"I'm not sure I can share that."

"This is Adam Hollingsworth. We met when you treated Madison after her car accident." He closed his eyes, praying she'd remember him.

"Oh, yes. Mr. Hollingsworth. Just a minute. I…"

In the abrupt silence, he could only listen to the echo of his heart pounding in his ears.

"I'm sorry. My computer is slow today. Oh yes. Here it is. You're a listed individual on her Authorization for Disclosure so I can tell you. I'm afraid there was an error made on the results of her hCG pregnancy test."

"Yes." Adrenaline shot through him. He clutched the receiver in a vice grip as he fought to stay calm. "What error exactly? Is she not…pregnant?"

His question was met with a dignified chuckle. "Oh, she's pregnant all right. However, in cross referencing, we found out the test result was different than we originally thought." The sound of papers being shuffled came next. "Medical science and all the insight it offers can be a wonderful thing. But sometimes good old Mother Nature has to be factored into the equation."

Madison's physician went on to elaborate about some false positive ratio statistics. Inevitable fallacies in clinical testing.

Tightening his hold on the receiver with one hand, he nervously drummed his fingers on the desktop with his other.

Bottom line. Give me the bottom line.

"It was discovered she's actually further along in gestation than we originally reported. That will move her due date up considerably."

Be careful what you wish for.

"Which means?" he prompted.

"Which means she'll be able to welcome her child into the world more than a month sooner." In the same tone, she went on to apologize for any inconvenience.

Are you fucking kidding me?

"Thank you for letting us know." At the import of the news, somehow Adam maintained a relatively serene voice. He thanked her again and promised to relay the information to Madison ASAP.

"Have her call me if she has any questions."

"Oh. Yes. Definitely."

He didn't figure she caught on to his sarcasm. But then, he really didn't care.

Dropping the receiver in the cradle, he reared back as if from the force of a gut shot. It had happened to him once in a domestic call gone bad. Even without an actual bullet ripping into his flesh, the tearing of his insides was no different. Burning pain that didn't go away for a very long time. If at all.

Just like that, his entire world turned upside down. How would Madison take the news? Would their mutual agreement to somehow be together change for her? Now that a future he'd begun to envision with some form of clarity had gotten all murky again.

"That's the best I'm going to get."

At Madison's voice from the top of the stairs, his jumbled thoughts fell apart. He stood still for a second then bounded her way as she walked down to join him. Not even thinking straight in his haste to share the news with her. *There's been some mistake.* Part of him was driven by the irrational hope she could somehow

310

change the facts. Make this burden of reality go away. Or be somehow different than what it was.

He struggled to find his voice. "No luck?"

"Nope." Shaking her head, as she walked toward him, she stared at her cell as if by doing so she'd somehow miraculously receive the answers she sought. "They still aren't sure what happened, though this guy assured me they were taking steps so this never happened again." Glancing at Adam with a wry smile, she set the phone on an end table. "Yeah. Right."

Before he could respond out loud, she was in front of him with her arms around his neck

"Now tell me. Where were we?"

Smiling, she dropped a kiss on his cheek, then pulled her face back, brow furrowed when he didn't react as she might have expected.

"Doctor Winters was on the phone." He stopped to clear his throat. "The home phone."

"Something in your behavior tells me that's not good." Her eyes widened as she took a breath. "Is the baby okay? Am I?"

"No. Yes. It's nothing like that. You're both fine." In need of physical contact, he took her hand. Sitting, he drew her down beside him. "But there is more."

He thought about putting his arm around her then didn't, keeping hold of her hand instead. Things were different between them now. Very different. Though Madison didn't know it yet, *they* were different. And nothing in the world was going to change that fact.

She stared at him, cocking her head to one side. "What's wrong, Adam?"

As gently as he could, he relayed the information he was given. At first she listened with concerned interest. *How else would she?*

Fighting to keep his voice from cracking, the more he explained, the more her expression fell to one of despair. Still holding his hand, she stared off in the distance when he finished.

"Oh, Adam. I am so sorry." The hushed apology came out in a rush.

For you or for me? His question wasn't fair, so he never asked it.

She gave her head a slight shake. "I never saw that coming."

"Me either."

"I'm not sure what to say."

"What is there to say?" He spoke softly as he rubbed his palm on the top of her hand.

"I didn't want it to be this way." The anguish on her face and pain in her voice were twin daggers to his already damaged heart.

"Neither did I." When his voice failed him, he took a deep breath. "I guess I just didn't want to believe it."

"I didn't either. I wanted the baby to be yours."

"Too bad wanting doesn't necessarily translate to getting." For the first time since they'd started this conversation, a hint of sarcasm crept into his tone.

She raised her gaze to meet his. "It is too bad."

It doesn't change things between us. He couldn't bring himself to utter the words he was sure she so desperately needed to hear. Why do that to her? Promise something he wasn't sure he could live up to.

"But that's just the way it is. This doesn't change things between us." He got the promise out, finally, unsure he could believe it himself.

"No." Her reply was wistful. "I had...I..." She

stopped and started over. "I assumed the lab work was correct. That you actually were this baby's father."

When she ran a hand over her stomach he followed the motion as something inside his chest twisted.

Closing her eyes, all of a sudden she leaned forward.

"What's wrong? Are you okay?" Full of alarm, he wrapped her in his arms.

"I'm fine. Just a little spasm. Don't worry."

"That's not easy for me. Not to worry." He let her go as he spoke. "It's not your fault or my choice I'm out of it. It's just the way it is."

"The way it is." Whispering, she turned toward him as tears erupted.

"Don't cry. It's not so bad." The quiver in his voice betrayed his words.

"You're right. This could be much worse. Though I'm not sure how, we will get through this." When he made no reply, she went on. "Adam, I'm so sorry."

"I'm disappointed. A little sad. No. A lot sad, but not angry. Not at all angry. That kind of blows my mind."

Her gaze met his. "I wanted to believe this baby was yours as much as you did. Probably more."

I doubt that. Looking down, he discovered he held her hand.

Funny. He didn't remember taking it.

In the context of actions so natural they became second nature, maybe, just maybe, there was hope for them yet.

Chapter Seventeen

The next morning Madison opened her eyes as peaceful dreams of sleep inevitably gave way to drowsy cognizance. On the window beside the bed, the full-length draperies fluttered and swayed as heat flowed from the floor vent below them. Sunlight filtered in from between the panels as she turned her attention to slivers of beams dancing on the ceiling.

What do you know? The sun had risen as it always did. Bringing daylight after the dawn, as it always did. But, unfortunately, no change to the new reality Adam and Madison found themselves in.

His slow and steady breathing, the warmth of his body along her skin, affirmed his presence beside her. A physical testament to the fact they were both trying hard, very hard, to not acknowledge the abrupt shift in their relationship.

That was not to say the time they spent together since the devastating news wasn't pleasant. Exciting even. That hadn't changed. Much like their lovemaking the night before. Pleasant. Exciting. Not necessarily lacking in the passion and resulting satisfaction of previous times.

Just different.

Because *they* were different.

Or am I the only one so profoundly affected?

"Good morning."

At the deep voice close to her ear, her thoughts flew apart. She closed her eyes as his arms surrounded her, basking in the sheer delight of his touch. Yet yearning for a return to the lightheartedness they'd shared as recently as the morning before.

"How did you sleep?" Maybe if she asked a common everyday question, things between them could at least seem to be more normal.

"It never fails. I always sleep better beside you."

Tears welled up at his sweet reply. Before she could respond, his lips pressed to hers. Squeezing her eyes shut so no unnecessary waterworks would escape, she responded enthusiastically. Hungrily. As if she was starving, and he offered the last available food.

She still wasn't properly sated when he gently pulled away.

"What time do I have to be at the airport?" He checked his watch, not looking at her.

Why did that bother her so much? "Their plane lands at eleven-thirty."

"I'll want to get there early. Find a parking space. Go inside."

"My mother will appreciate your courtesy." She responded in a decidedly sterile tone that infuriated her even as she did it. Still bowing to this relationship correctness they were on. "The boys, I'm sure, will be thrilled to have you pick them up."

Madison could only wonder if he noticed the absurdity too. How, lying side by side in the intimacy of a shared bed, they kept up the ordinary, everyday conversation.

"My appointment with the lawyer is at ten this morning. Though his office is about forty minutes away, it's only a short distance from the main branch of my bank. I'd like to leave early and stop there first. As long as I'm in the neighborhood."

"Makes sense." After a sidelong glance, he smiled briefly. "That plane is going to land whether I'm there or not. And you have things to do too. We should probably get up and get moving."

"Probably." What else could she do but agree?

Since she had to leave first, in further everyday dialogue, they mutually decided she'd get ready while he made breakfast. A short time after getting out of bed, going their separate ways for a time to bathe and dress, they sat together once again as they ate. And, bowing to the inevitability of their new normal, made mindless small talk.

She took a sip of the orange juice he'd given her. "With all of the unanswered questions surrounding my current bank account, I'd like to close that one and open another."

"A good idea to get rid of the old. Start fresh." He set a bowl of oatmeal dusted with brown sugar and dotted with raisins in front of her.

"This looks delicious. Thank you." Picking up her spoon, she spread out the toppings then added a splash of milk.

Get rid of the old. Start fresh. Is that what they were doing? *Without consciously thinking about it?*

Her thoughts continued as they ate for the most part in silence. Caught off guard when Adam reached over to take hold of her hand, she glanced up. Concern filled eyes met her troubled ones.

"You have a lot going on now. I get that. Don't worry about anything but taking care of what you have to today. I'll do the same. Meet you back here when we're done."

"Sounds like a plan to me." She used a flippant answer to hide her dismay.

His response was a simple squeeze of the hand he still held.

And so it went, until, a short time later, she had her purse strap over one shoulder, ready to leave. Placing his hand at the small of her back, he walked with her to the back door. Then they both stopped. Stood face to face.

"Once I get to Mr. Conklin's office, my appointment shouldn't last long. He mentioned the disposition of most of Joe's holdings were pretty cut and dried. As I understand, inheritance rights of a surviving spouse are very strong in Colorado. Most of my responsibility will lie in filing proper, final tax returns." When he said nothing, simply nodded, she went on. "I'd like to be home by the time you get back from the airport. Before even. It's only been a few days, but I'm anxious to see my boys again. I miss them."

"I'll get them back to you as quickly as I can."

"I appreciate that." More polite sterility rolled off her tongue. "Thank you."

"Consider it done."

It doesn't have to be like this, Adam. It doesn't. She screamed the words in her mind as, in total betrayal, her head nodded complete acceptance.

Notching her chin up, she lifted her lips to within inches of his. As if daring, yes daring, him to kiss her. A challenge he readily accepted. His mouth covering hers was incredibly soft and sweet. Much as most of their morning had been.

"I'll talk to you when we get back here." She spoke the second he ended their kiss.

"Sounds good to me."

With no further comment, he ushered her out the door he shut gently behind her. Gentle enough to barely register he'd done so until she stood in the garage alone.

Once settled into her car, she'd no sooner backed out of the driveway to head down the street when her cell chirped. *Maybe Adam regretted our stilted goodbye. Was calling to check on me as he had before.* Immediately following the first time they'd made love.

Which seemed so long ago.

Hope rising, she pushed the button on the steering wheel with her thumb to engage the call. "Hello."

"Mrs. Clark. Hayden Riley here."

Disappointment momentarily stole her voice. The last person she cared to deal with just now. "I'm rather busy, Hayden."

"This simply couldn't wait. I'm calling you as a courtesy, actually."

How did you get my cell number? The question ran through her mind, but he was talking again before she had a chance to ask.

"I understand the movie people have abandoned the property."

"Not exactly, Hayden. They—"

"Since they're gone, I'm going out there to make sure nothing was damaged. I'll report back to you if I find anything has."

She again tried to get a word in to correct him. "They aren't gone. In fact…"

"Just so you know, those are my plans."

"You don't need to…"

"It's my duty, for the good of the people and their history."

"Hayden, I…"

Gripping the wheel, she clenched her teeth as he interrupted her to detail a few of what he considered larger problems.

I so do not need this just now.

Unfortunately, the man who had just elevated himself from minor irritation to full blown burden gave her no choice. She wasn't going to allow him to take charge of something she was responsible for. Something that didn't need to be handled in the first place. As owner of the property, she had an obligation to head him off. Protect the possessions of her renters. Not allow some self-appointed idiot make decisions he had no right to make.

She glanced at the clock on her dash. If she ditched her planned side trip to the bank, stopped out at the Concord Estate to give him what for and make him leave, she could still make it to the attorney's office in time. Provided she hurried.

"I still don't think there's anything to be concerned about. Just to prove it, I'll meet you at Concord." She slowed to make a U-turn. "Don't do anything until I get there."

'Call ended.'

Shortly after, Madison let up on the gas pedal as she steered around a particularly tight curve on the two-lane highway. Sunshine today was a nice change from the haze of fog and darkness that had hung over the hilly area on her last trip through here. Wide shafts of light sparkled off what few snow piles remained on the side of the road.

Holding in a shiver, her gaze strayed to the ever-narrowing edge as she came alongside the dreaded spot where her car ran off the road. As memories swirled, all she could do was grip the steering wheel more tightly and ride it out. Literally. Once beyond the accident site, the warmth of relief flowed in to replace ice cold anxiety.

Much as it had the Thanksgiving afternoon when Adam came for me.

Accepting the sudden hitch in her heart at what now may never be, she completed her trip without mishap.

The security hut was unoccupied as she pulled into the main entrance of the Estate a short time later. *No surprise there.* Adam had said shooting was suspended. Not abandoned as Hayden claimed.

Following the curved driveway around to the complex of buildings, she glided to a stop in front of the main one. Right beside Hayden's vintage Buick Wildcat. Physical proof he was there already. And had no doubt embarked on his so-called quest for the good of the people.

"Because it would have been way too convenient to wait outside for me." Setting the gear shift into park, she cut the engine. "Jerk."

The keys she dropped in her purse sank to the bottom with a soft clunk. Hiking the leather bag onto her shoulder with her right hand, she used her left to lever the door open. Her low heels tapped softly as she made her way across the asphalt and up the wide cement steps.

Pushing her way in, she closed the heavy paneled

door with a thump and paused, waiting for her eyes to adjust from bright sunlight to darkly paneled foyer.

"Hello, Hayden. Are you around?"

Silence.

To her right, the door to the study stood ajar and she peeked inside. More dark paneling and red velveteen floor to ceiling curtains drawn tight made it nearly impossible to make out anything in the shadowy gloom.

"Hayden?" Her voice echoed eerily back at her.

A curtain edge flapped as if it had somehow been disturbed. Icicles of fear rode a thin trail up the back of her neck. She immediately retreated and closed the door. Not sure where to look next, she checked her watch. A few minutes past nine thirty. She'd misjudged her time. Whether she found Hayden soon or not, she'd be late getting to Mr. Conklin's office. *Dammit.*

Fishing in her purse, she pulled out her cell. Since he'd been nice enough to provide her with his private number, she dialed that to bypass his administrative staff. Fortunately, he picked up on the second ring.

"Mr. Conklin. Madison Clark."

After exchanging a few pleasantries, she immediately apologized for having to postpone their meeting.

"Not a problem, Mrs. Clark. I understand how things sometimes come up that can't be helped."

Relieved at his understanding, she wasn't surprised. In her limited dealings with him, she'd found him to have a keen sense of fairness and integrity.

"I appreciate your indulgence."

"Actually, what we have to get through shouldn't take that long. Especially if we're only minimally delayed because…oh, excuse me, I have another call coming in I have to take. We can talk about this when you get here."

"Yes. Of course." Reluctant to hold him up more than she already had, she readily agreed. "Again thank you for understanding."

Disconnecting, she slipped the phone back into her purse then stood there, unsure what to do next. Though her eyes had adjusted to the gloom somewhat, she still wasn't confident enough to venture too far into the building.

"Glad you could make it."

Her heart thumped against her ribs. The male voice was shockingly familiar. Though not Hayden's. Hand to her chest, mouth open on a gasp, Madison wheeled around. Peering into the darkness, she couldn't make out anything more than an undefined form.

John!

The name formed in her mind at the same time as the man stepped from the shadows to materialize in front of her.

Dropping her hand, she shook her head on a little laugh. "John. You scared the bejeebers out of me." *Yet again.*

"Did I?"

"Yes."

"Sorry about that." With an offhand shrug, he advanced toward her. His unusually intense stare never leaving her face.

"What are you doing here?"

"Hayden called me about what he was up to. I started thinking it might not be a good idea for you to meet him out here alone." He came to a stop before her.

"Thank you for that. Though I'll admit the man can be…is irritating as hell, I'm pretty sure I can handle him. I'm sorry he bothered you."

"I didn't mind." His tone was oddly deliberate. "Doesn't hurt to be cautious."

Reaching behind her, he flipped on the old-style wall switch. The huge crystal chandelier high above her head flooded the area with light. She blinked at the sudden glare.

"His car's out front, but I can't find him anywhere." All of a sudden it occurred to her John's car hadn't been out front when she arrived. *But why?*

"I can take you to him if you like."

His voice startled away her thoughts.

"That would be great. Thanks."

"This way." He swept an arm out then tilted his head to indicate she should go ahead of him. "You first."

The hallway he ushered her into was not only dark, but oddly cold. Obviously, the heat had been dialed down with the building deserted.

…the building deserted.

The hairs on the back of her neck lifted. Squinting, she willed her eyes to see more than they did. Reveal to her where she and John were going. She'd been escorted down this hallway before. At that time, modern, bright lights had shone down from the ceiling. When she brought Cameron here to read parts of the script with Adam.

…with Adam.

Again the words of her thoughts echoed in her mind. Immediately followed by a sudden yearning to have him with her. *But why?* There's no reason he should need to...

"I don't know who you think you are."

As they made their way toward the soundstage, Hayden's unmistakable voice grew louder.

"He's no doubt belly aching about something he's found amiss." Madison dropped back to walk beside John.

"No doubt."

When he said no more, she grew silent too.

They came into the large, nearly empty ballroom that was converted to a soundstage. Unlike the time she was here before, the floor length draperies were closed. She could barely make out the conference table at one end surrounded by several chairs. At what she saw next, Madison stopped in the doorway so abruptly, John bumped into her. Hayden wasn't going through artifacts at all but sat in a chair on one side of the room, hands tied behind his back.

"We were in this together. Partners." Jerking his head up, he glared at John, not acknowledging her presence at all.

She still hadn't moved. "What's he talking about?"

Unable to process the reality she'd stumbled into, she spun toward John, seeking answers. An unexpected glint drew her gaze downward. She recoiled with a gasp at the barrel of a handgun aimed directly at her stomach.

John?

Her mind formed the name, but nothing came out of her mouth. She couldn't take her eyes off the deadly weapon he kept trained on her...and her child.

"Tempting. So very tempting." At his ominous tone, she returned her gaze to his face.

"What?" No more than a breathy rasp escaped.

"It doesn't matter now."

What?

She didn't dare ask again as chilling threads of terror worked along her backbone and into her limbs.

"You told me once she was scared off, and the movie crew went away, our group could have the property back." Hayden strident voice rose from behind her. "For life. No strings."

Face to face with John, Madison didn't dare move a muscle as Hayden's litany of accusations continued.

"I can't help it if you were stupid enough to believe me." John's response was flat. Dismissive. As his gaze never strayed from her midsection.

Shock and fear had rendered her virtually helpless. Unable to even think. Let alone plot out a possible escape. She no longer knew this man. Had no idea what he planned to do.

He flicked the gun barrel toward Hayden. "You. That way."

Stiffened legs somehow supported her as she had no choice but to comply. John followed, step by step. When her knees threatened to fail her and she faltered, he slammed his palm between her shoulder blades to propel her forward. A few stumbled steps later, the same hand pressed hard on her collar bone to push her into a chair beside Hayden. When John moved behind her, she squeezed her eyes shut, expecting the explosion of a bullet to enter the back of her head. Execution style. Her heart hammered. Its out of control beat thrummed in her ears with the fury of a jackhammer. She was at a loss what to expect from the man she'd thought to be her friend. Hot tears scalded her cheeks.

From the corner of her eye, she caught him bent behind Hayden.

"Darned right you'll loosen those bindings and let me go." Hayden's words were insanity enough. His high and mighty tone was downright suicidal. To a man who held a loaded handgun on both of them. "And don't call me stupid." His shrill retort echoed off the walls. "Stupid is to not realize the value of this marvelous estate."

"Don't kid yourself." John stood and stepped back. "I realize all right. Although not in its current form."

"You can't mean your plan is to blow up this building like you have so many others. The jewel of the complex."

At Hayden's words, Madison swung her gaze to John. Surely he'd deny such an absurd charge.

"True. The family albatross is worth more to me blown to smithereens. Which would be exceedingly more efficient than an unwieldy wrecking ball."

She glanced wildly around. Now that she knew the truth about John Clark, she wouldn't put it past him to have planted dynamite or whatever he used to ensure destruction all around them.

"Too bad that would be too obvious."

An odd sense of relief washed over her. Relief that was short lived as she turned to look at him.

"Why, John? Why are you doing this?" Flirting with insanity herself, Madison gave in to the misguided notion it was possible to reason with him. Reach out to somehow reclaim the person she'd once known so well.

The person she'd once believed him to be.

Much like her marriage to his brother, her pleasant rapport with John was one more grotesque charade.

"This Concord property is been in the family for generations." His nostrils flared on a deep breath as he glared at her. "Long before you got on scene, and I—."

"Your family decreed long ago that this property be maintained and preserved as a designated historical site." Hayden spoke up to interrupt. "Your mother promised."

"The Concord Estate passes hands through a blood inheritance, and only through blood inheritance." John seemed to recite from some legal documentation. "The oldest progeny of each generation receives the property. Upon their death, the next sibling in age would inherit. Provided the eldest deceased had no issue."

Madison's head spun. Blood inheritance. Eldest deceased. No issue. *Joe's child.* Looking down, she found her hands already splayed, protectively, across her stomach.

"Concord has always passed through generations to the eldest surviving sibling. How it's been. How it's always going to be. At long last, the eldest surviving sibling is me." He turned on her, hatred reflected in dark eyes. "Until you ruined everything."

"The property can belong to you." She willed her voice to come out with a strength she desperately sought. "We'll figure out how to make the legal transfer. There must be a way."

"That's impossible." There was no mistaking the menace in his tone. "Joe made sure of that."

"That was Joe." She closed her mouth to breathe. "I'm not him. I have no desire to stand in your way."

"As I said. It's too late. Joe prided himself on being quite the stud. His marriage to you a prime example. He taunted me with the fact he planned to knock you up.

Create the heir to prevent me from inheriting our family's legacy. Our family. My family. Not yours. Or that brat you told me about. After I—"

"Brat? What brat?" Hayden's shrill cry cut him off.

"She's pregnant, you dimwitted asshole." John's tone remained flat. Unemotional. Chilling.

"The plan was to scare her off." Hayden wasn't done. "You didn't tell me there was a baby involved. I didn't sign on for that."

"You didn't care what you signed on for. At first my plan was to scare her off. Get her the hell away from here. If she died in the process. No big deal."

Tears burned her throat.

"Why can't you just take over the property and be done with it?" It was a monumental feat to keep the desperation from her tone. She paused, breathed, and went on. "I won't stand in your way."

"Maybe not. But I can't chance that." As he leaned forward, his snarling words assaulted her ears. "Nothing will keep me from inheriting what is rightfully mine."

"You're insane."

Hayden, shut up. Madison held her tongue.

John's laugh was pure evil. "Everyone's entitled to their opinion. Even you."

"You can't do this." The veins on either side of Hayden's neck bulged as he continued the useless rant.

Unmoved, John glanced up with nothing more than an innocuous smile. "Try me."

Hayden refused to budge. "I never signed up for this."

"You didn't care what you signed up for. And now you're paying the price. The ultimate price."

Facing forward, Madison closed her eyes, powerless to shut out the madness all around her.

"You don't deserve this property. The people do." As if himself insane Hayden once again taunted John. *"Aggghhh."*

Expecting a gunshot to echo beside her, she held her breath. But heard only the sickening whack of metal hitting flesh.

"You're lucky I need you alive. For a while anyway. Or you'd already be dead."

Hayden didn't respond.

Madison steeled herself for the worst. Opening her eyes, she glanced over. Slumped in the chair, his head had fallen forward, chin resting on his chest. A trickle of blood ran from his temple down his cheek. His eyes remained closed. Only his still shackled hands kept him from falling to the floor.

"Idiot. Look what he made me do. Now we have to wait until he wakes up." John jabbed the gun between her shoulder blades as if blaming her as well.

She winced at the pain but refused to give him the satisfaction of crying out as he strode around to stand in front of her.

"Joe should have listened to me when I told him about the vein of gold discovered nearby. He's my brother, I thought. Surely with this development we'll share in the wealth. Pool our resources to excavate. But, oh no. Big brother would have none of it. Greedy bastard."

"You have to believe me, John. I had no idea about any of this. Joe never confided in me."

"He had to die. As do you."

"You killed Joe?" An adrenaline rush pushed

words out better left unsaid.

"No. I can honestly say I didn't. Not that I wouldn't have if fate hadn't intervened to beat me to it." Spittle flew out of his mouth in his zeal to tell another story. "His death was purely serendipitous. A definite sign from above, don't you think? Imagine my good fortune when, as we argued, he clutched at his chest before his free fall to the carpet. Such a beautiful sight, him dying like that." Wild eyes lit up as a grin split his face in two. "Who knew I'd be so fortunate. Then my only problem became how to properly deal with you. Dispose of you really."

Like an unwilling witness to some horrific accident, she stared into the eyes of a madman. It was as if he believed spilling his guts to her when she was destined to die would justify his actions. Hot bile surged to the back of her throat and she gagged as John went on with his raving diatribe.

"Hayden was somewhat right though. This is quite the spectacular room. With its, as I understand, perilous balcony so very high above us." His voice took on a melancholy tone, making what he said even more terrifying. "Not quite as, shall we say, as picturesque as an accidental tumble from some bedroom veranda to cement. Or slide down a treacherous mountain. But it will have to do. Especially when that idiot falls on top of you. Then again, once you climb up the stairs on your own, perhaps I'll shoot you. Then him. To make things easier. More complete. Leave the gun behind. Murder suicide anyone?" He stopped to take a harsh inhale, release a diabolical laugh. "I have no doubt I could make the scene believable."

For the sake of her unborn child she had to keep

fighting. "I would have gladly given you the property. Will give you the property."

"Madison. The blood inheritance rule is iron clad." He drew another loud breath. "This is the only way."

She had no idea if what he said was true or not. He'd long ago lost all sense of reason. Any measure of sanity.

"We both know I can do properly grief stricken after your tragic and untimely death. Much like I did during Joe's memorial. Quite a performance, don't you think?" He didn't wait for her reply. "In this case, though, how can we possibly keep the site as is after it's been the place where a murder was committed? The entire complex will have to be demolished. Which, for me, is easy enough."

You can't do this.

Angry tears flowed freely over her cheeks and jaw to trickle down her neck as she grieved a monumental loss. Not so much the loss of her own life, but at leaving her children without a mother.

Including the child who would die with her.

Chapter Eighteen

Adam wheeled Kay's suitcase to one side as he punched the security code into the keypad on Madison's front door, mildly alarmed she hadn't met them on the porch. Earlier that day, she'd been adamant about being home in time to greet her family.

"We had a good time." Kay came up to stand behind him. "But it's also nice to be back here with these two."

His thoughts dispersed as he glanced over at her. "Madison will be happy to see them. And you too."

When the latch clicked, he opened the door.

Preceding him inside, she paused in the entrance. "Dak especially." She glanced back to where the two boys unloaded their bags from Adam's rental. Jabbering as they did so. "I called Madison Sunday morning. He had quite a bout of homesickness that first night. Though little trouper that he is, he did his best to fight it. For a while there, I was afraid I'd have to put him on a plane early to get him back here. Or have her fly to him."

"That has to be tough." He got that much out before she went on.

"His father's death has been so hard on him." Her voice became a whisper as she set her purse on the table then turned when the boys came in. "Dak. Cameron. Take your things straight up to your bedrooms, please."

Dak pushed by them to clamber toward the stairs. "Mo-om! We're here. Mo-om."

Silence.

Adam glanced over at Kay.

Her forehead creased before she lifted her head. "Madison! I brought your boys back."

Her try met with stillness as well.

"Where's my mom?" Dak dragged his suitcase into the living room then stopped.

Kay and Adam exchanged puzzled looks.

It was Adam who decided to answer. "If she's not here now, she'll be home soon."

A renewed sense of unease crept in as he made the promise.

"I want to see my mom."

"Adam just told you she'd be here." Cameron came through and headed for the stairs. "I need to update my computer."

Kay issued a short laugh. "Look out social media. He's baaaccckkk!"

"Where's my momma?" Dak's face started to crumble as he barreled into Adam.

Taken by surprise, he wrapped his arms around the boy. "I'm not sure. Don't worry. She'll be here soon enough."

Calling on his de-escalation training, he kept his voice low.

Dak nodded as he stepped away. "Okay."

When his cell went off, Adam had it to his ear in a heartbeat. "Hollingsworth."

"It's Hardy."

The hairs on the back of his neck lifted, an adrenaline surge nearly knocked him off his feet. With

Dak and Kay watching, Adam kept his composure. If something had happened to Madison, all the de-escalation training in the world wouldn't do him any good in keeping calm.

You don't know for sure that she's in danger.

The optimistic side of him, the one that didn't know any better, stuck its nose in.

Yeah. Fat chance of that.

He caught a glimpse of Dak's hopeful expression before he turned away and lowered his voice. "What can I do for you?" It sounded a sight better than *Why the hell are you calling?*

"It's what I can do for you." Clearing his throat, Hardy went on. "Professional courtesy. I wanted to update you on the Shop and Save occurrence Mrs. Clark was involved in. We don't think the attack was random."

Walking away, Adam missed a step then stopped, as if a wrecking ball had swung in to land in the middle of his gut. "How so?"

"The store's company headquarters finally released the rest of the surveillance tapes from that night. But before that, our investigators determined that fire was intentionally set. We think as a diversion. Mrs. Clark was the only person on premises who wasn't able to exit the store without incident.

He didn't need to elaborate for Adam to figure out the details. "Kidnapping attempt?"

"That's what we're thinking. The way she described the attack, it fits she was targeted."

Adam kept walking into the kitchen and through the sliding glass door to the outside patio. No way did he want Kay or Dak to hear what he was about to say.

334

"Actually, I have some information to share with you, too."

Opening the gate to the backyard, he shut it behind him with a click. Over the next few minutes, he filled his colleague in on Madison's absence.

"It could be nothing, but then again, it could be…" He couldn't bring himself to finish.

"…something. We can always waive the waiting time needed to file a missing person report. If you think she might be in danger."

His hand shook as he kept the phone to his ear. "I'm hoping that's not it."

"Your call."

"Thanks." He lifted his gaze as he spoke.

A gray sky held all the indications of snow. The tops of the evergreens that ringed the property along the lot line rustled in a now and then breeze. Bare branches of other nearby trees barely moved at all. The whole area seemed almost sterile. Well-groomed and stark. Even the hedges growing up against the house had been trimmed to perfection. In the wintertime no less.

As if someone almost had an obsession going on.

"The guy we thought we had in that line up turned out to be a dead end. Though we were able to hold that one on an unrelated charge. But there's more."

Adam was all ears. "Which is?"

The new surveillance tape also revealed someone wearing the same clothes Mrs. Clark described her assailant wearing getting into a truck."

"Yeah? And?" Unable to remain still, he paced the perimeter of the yard.

"We haven't been able to identify the person in question, but we got a clear picture of the license plate of the truck. Commercial. The vehicle is registered to a company called Done Right Demolition. Ring any bells?"

Adam stopped short, leaning against the brick wall at the property edge as his knees nearly buckled. "Playing a whole damned dissonance. Her ex brother-in-law owns that company."

There had to be a connection. But what?

"Not sure what that means."

"You and me both. But I plan to find out. Thanks for the update."

"No problem. Call if you need anything from us."

"I may just do that."

Adam was walking back across the yard by the time he hung up. Then something made him turn to again check out the perimeter. More to put off returning to the house than anything else. He'd run out of excuses to explain Madison's continued absence to her family. Plus, it went against everything in him to simply do nothing but wait.

Coming to a stop by a carefully groomed pine tree, he scrolled through his phone to Madison's number and dialed. What he should have done when they first returned to an empty house.

Damn! He gritted his teeth when his call went straight to voicemail.

Tempted to heave the damned thing toward the trees, he glared at the screen before returning the cell to his pocket. Turning in a one eighty, he surveyed the pristine grounds yet again. A piece of cloth caught the corner of his eye. Protruding from underneath a stone border, it flapped back and forth in a strengthening breeze. *Out of place.* An unusual blemish on an otherwise flawless landscape.

With nothing else to do, he walked over to pick up the litter. His fingers were inches away from it when he froze. Finding a decent sized stick nearby, he used that to poke at the cloth until he pulled out a sack of some kind. He awkwardly maneuvered the stick until he was able to dump out the contents. When he did, the blood pumping through his veins instantly chilled. Then froze solid when his heart stopped.

Duct tape, jumbo sized zip ties, a hood of some kind. That and more spilled out in front of him. He jabbed the stick at a solid steel bar. Shorter in length, but thick enough to do major damage to someone's skull.

Rolling it one way then the other, he leaned down for a better look when an engraving on one end caught his eye.

DONE RIGHT DEMOLITION.

Etched in bold letters along one side.

Jerking upright, he gazed skyward as more clues fell into place. All of them having to do with John Clark.

Madison run off the road after he called her to meet him. Nearly falling from a veranda with a faulty railing. A gunny sack hidden in the bushes outside her kitchen he walked into unannounced a few days before.

Thank God he was there at the time.

Adam stared at a grotesque assortment of tools— weapons really—as the hairs on the back of his neck and along his arms rose in one continual wave of alarm.

The string of accidents that had befallen Madison, so called random acts of violence, were calculated events. Deliberate.

He should have suspected someone wanted her scared off, out of the way. Or…

Squeezing his eyes shut, he refused to finish the thought. The realization was a gut punch that doubled him over. Staring at his shoes, he hacked up some nasty junk that surged from his stomach to his throat. Wiping his mouth with the back of his hand, he straightened then stood.

Though there were no eyewitnesses, he possessed enough circumstantial evidence to make a positive ID of who was behind it all.

On an all-out run back to the house, he slowed his pace to make sure by the time he got there, to walk coolly inside.

Kay met him in the dining room. Her face was pale. Her eyes filled with worry.

"That attorney of Madison's called while you were outside." She kept her voice so low, he had to strain to hear her. "He wondered if she was here. She never made it to their meeting."

A bolt of fear shot straight to the center of his heart. Opening his mouth to reply, she spoke again before he could.

"She had called him though." Her voice trembled so badly, she stopped to draw a breath. "Said she'd been held up and would be late."

"I know she planned to stop at the bank."

For fleeting seconds he thought of robberies. Hostage situations. *Which is absurd.* The radio was on in the car on their way from the airport. Surely something would have been reported. Didn't mean he wouldn't check it out.

"Hey, Grandma. Look at this." Dak called from in

front of the TV.

"Coming, sweetheart." Her tone was surprisingly even as she glanced up then back at Adam. "We've been here before, and it turned out okay."

"Yeah. We have." Much as he wanted to, he couldn't offer much more assurance.

"We have." She squeezed his arm before rejoining her grandson.

Adam hit redial on his phone to call Hardy, all the while thinking how useless this particular quest was. Would the bank even know for sure if she'd been there or not? When voicemail picked up, he left a message asking Hardy to check anyway. For all the good it would do. After he hung up, another thought arrived.

There were always surveillance tapes to study. If it came to that.

As he stood there contemplating what to do next, a shaking hand clamped onto his shoulder from behind. He turned to face a wide-eyed Cameron.

"Anything from my mom?"

"Not yet." Adam's heart broke to say it.

"Where is she?"

No idea. He shrugged. "What does it mean when a call goes directly to voicemail?"

"Without even ringing once?"

"Yeah."

Fear streamed onto Cameron's face. "You tried calling her cell and that's what happened?"

"Yeah."

So what if he was becoming a monosyllabic idiot.

"Either the phone's turned off or in a dead spot."

"That's it?"

"Yeah."

"And the GPS would be useless. Like my phone was. That night at the casting call."

"Not necessarily." A kind of concern Adam couldn't quite read replaced the fear.

He grabbed Cameron's arm as hope soared from a terrified heart. "What do you mean?"

"I…uh…"

At his sudden hesitation, Adam was tempted to take him by the shoulders. Shake the information out of him. He leaned closer.

"How, Cameron?" He spoke through clenched teeth to keep from shouting.

The boy cast a sheepish glance toward his grandmother. "I put an app on her phone. A hidden one. Phil dared me."

"Never mind the excuses." This time, he did grab on to shoulders he gave a hearty shake. "Tell me where she is."

At his little brother's laugh from the living room, they both glanced that way. Kay looked up at them then back to the old cartoon rerun Dak was engrossed in.

Cameron worked something on the screen of his phone. "According to the coordinates here, she's out at that place where you're filming."

"Concord? Where exactly?"

Shaking his head, Cameron kept his fingers moving over the screen. "I don't know exactly."

It's a start. Gritting his teeth, Adam silently waited.

"It looks like that main building out there. This is a conversation she had earlier." Pushing a few more icons, Cameron handed over the phone. "Maybe it'll help."

Adam held the cell to his ear. Listening to nothing at first. Creasing his brow, he looked at the boy, shaking his head. Then voices came on.

Madison first, saying hello.

'Mrs. Clark. Hayden Riley here…'

Adam barely breathed until the conversation ended. He handed the phone back.

Empty threats from a whack job? Or something far more dangerous?

"Is that the guy who's been giving my mother a hard time?"

No way could he lie to the kid. "It is."

He hung his head as his shoulders began to tremble. "I can't believe this. It's not real."

Adam reached out to pull him in. "She's going to be okay. I won't let anything happen to her." He forced absolute conviction into his voice, even as what he promised could be nothing more than a glorified line of bullshit.

No time to dwell on that now.

He looked Cameron in the eye as he let him go. "You stay here. Take care of Grandma and Dak. I'm going to Concord. Tell your Grandma why, but not in front of Dak."

"Okay."

Cameron nodded as Adam headed for the front door.

A light snowfall dusted the streets as he drove like a man possessed. Made a quick call on Bluetooth. Tires squealed as he made the turn into the Concord complex damned near on two wheels. He rolled to a stop on the side of the road. Behind where Woody had parked.

"I told Joel he needed someone to remain on site

341

when everyone else was gone, but no. He knew best."
The security guard didn't bother with the formality of a greeting as they met by his back bumper. Both wore holsters on their hips holding identical Glock nine millimeters.

"What can I say? He's a civilian."

"Got that right."

"Thanks for meeting me here."

"What else was I supposed to do after you called?" Woody didn't wait for him to answer. "I sent the smaller drone out. There are two cars parked in front of the main building. A white truck is parked behind, near some trees."

"Unfortunately, we try going in the front. With all those windows, there's no way of sneaking up on them."

"If that's where she is."

"I don't plan to take that chance. Where else would she be?"

"Since her car's there, she wasn't brought here against her will."

"That doesn't mean she's not being held against her will now." Adam ran a hand through his hair as he shared more discoveries he'd made. The implication of John Clark being behind it all.

"We need to call the police." Woody spoke up as their eyes met. "Except there's no guarantee they'll get here in time. So I guess I'm the next best thing. You do have extra ammo, I assume." He opened his trunk and reached inside.

"A couple of extra magazines. Though I doubt I'll be able to reload."

"Probably not." Pulling out a pair of compact

radios, Woody shook his head. "At least take this. It'll allow us to communicate. Give me the green light when you're inside."

Trying not to think about what might lie ahead, Adam strapped the radio to his shoulder. "Here's what we need to do."

Adam filled Woody in on his idea as, leaving their cars, they trotted into the complex. Straight up to the roof of what had at one time been a church.

"You can't do it. You can't." Woody was shaking his head. "Frank told me about this stunt. Said once you got into it, he had second thoughts. Decided it might be too dangerous. Plus, all the rigging, the safety net has been removed. Joel was afraid someone would steal it."

Adam only half listened as he went over to the edge and looked down. It sure was a long way to the concrete below.

Woody came to stand beside him. "What with this feathery snow, if the temperature drops even one or two degrees, you're looking at the possibility of ice. That's going to impact your footing. And your take off."

He glanced across to the other roof then back at his colleague. "You got any better ideas."

"No...but..."

"It's settled then."

"You're insane."

"Not now, but I will be if I lose one of the most important people in my life."

"Why not wait for the real cops to get here?"

In his gut, Adam knew waiting on the professionals was the right thing to do. How many times had he, on the other side of a situation like this, admonished civilians for taking matters into their own hands?

When they lived to be admonished.

He couldn't risk any kind of wait. Besides, he was a professional too. In his other life anyway.

"You gotta do what you gotta do." Woody's voice broke into his thoughts. "I'll get a posse here stealth for back up."

"I'll let you know."

"I'll be waiting." He spoke over his shoulder as, pulling out his cell, he headed back down the stairs.

Ice water pulsed through Adam's veins as he stood there, then reversed direction to crawl up the back of his neck. Several hairs rose on end in their wake. He lifted his foot to stomp on the lip of the edge. Simulate a hard landing on the adjoining rooftop. Pieces of cement broke off and rattled down the side as it fell. And fell. And…

Finally, the last of the pebbles settled on the ground and silence returned. He took a breath.

Purging everything from his mind but Madison and her unborn child, he backed up as far as possible, said a small prayer, and took off. Once airborne, he stretched his arms out and kicked for all he was worth to propel forward. Maybe buy a few more inches of distance. The bite of the wind slapped his face. Within seconds, his feet grazed the raised cement lip on the edge of the far roof. One foot landed solid. The top of his trailing foot caught on the ledge, pulling at him, and he stumbled. Started to fall. Flinging his arms out, he lunged forward.

Tuck and roll. Tuck and roll.

After two full body rotations across the roof, he was again on his feet.

With no time to deal with tiny spikes of pain

rippling up his legs and across his back, he flung open the heavy metal door, offering a murmur of thanks the latch gave so easily. Once he slipped through to the dark, cool corridor, he eased the door shut so it wouldn't make a sound.

"I'm telling you, you won't get away with this."

"And I'm telling you, try me."

Two male voices echoed down the deserted hallway. One deep. One shrill. Faint, but discernible.

Adam strained to hear more of the petty exchange. Desperate for evidence Madison was even in the room. Not daring to take the chance she wasn't. The two idiots arguing had to be John Clark and that Hayden character, but he couldn't determine who was saying what.

"You're insane. You know that."

"You think so?" A scoff escalated to laughter. "No one will know it was me. This complex was mine. Until she came along. That brat she carries doesn't deserve to live."

Adam fisted his hands. His body vibrated on a non-stop collision of anger and adrenaline. He slammed his back against the unyielding wall. Momentarily trading pain for helplessness before he took off.

In no time, he made his way down the dark corridor he'd navigated so many times. An opened door into the sound stage his ultimate goal.

Arriving at the entrance, Glock in hand, cocked and ready, Adam craned his neck to chance a peek inside. A revolver was aimed at the historical society president by a wild-eyed John Clark. He strained forward a little more and caught a glimpse of Madison in front of both of them.

Quickly pulled back to analyze the situation, he needed to create a diversion. Something to make Clark drop his guard.

"You can't possibly believe you'll get away with this." The trembling behind the shrill tone of that Hayden jerk set his teeth on edge.

"Oh won't I?" John Clark spoke next. "How many times did you proclaim to anyone who would listen that if your precious historical society couldn't have the property, no one could?"

"I didn't mean it like that."

"No one cares how you meant it. The important thing is you said it. And I'll be more than happy to swear to it. Thwarted in your efforts, you went off the deep end. Attacked the woman you'd been pleading with to help you. Chased her up to the balcony then pushed her off in a fit of rage. Used too much force and fell with her. No. More. Stalling. Get up those stairs. On second thought, maybe I should just kill you both before I go. Then push your lifeless carcasses off myself." An empty chuckle followed. "Kinda hard to find bullet holes when the skulls have been smashed."

There was no time to wait for back up. The door clanged against the wall as Adam flung it open.

"Adam!" Madison screamed.

He hit the floor as a volley of bullets erupted over his head. Counted four. *Two left.*

"You bastard!"

The barrel of a handgun was leveled at his chest. From a prone position, for a split second, he entertained visions of a single blast pinning him to the floor in a bloody mass of shattered flesh and bone.

"This is not going to end well." That asshole

Hayden spoke. And thank God he did.

John's attention was diverted. Adam scrambled up.

"John! Don't do this. Please!" Madison screamed again.

"Don't tell me what to do."

When Clark stupidly twisted away to glance toward her, Adam took full advantage of the opening to lunge. He chopped at the assailant's gun with his free hand. The barrel dipped downward. A forward kick connected. The crack of bone. A cry of pain and the gun clattered away. Adam grabbed hold of his shirt front. Had him spun around and spread eagle against the wall in seconds.

"Adam, be careful!"

"Ow! Hey! You're hurting me."

Ignoring the complaints, he turned to concentrate on Madison. "You okay?"

"Yes." Her voice broke.

"Woody. Send in the troops." Adam spoke calmly into the radio as he leaned his full body weight into John.

"Ahhh! That hurts. What the hell."

Both front doors flew open as a collection of uniforms arrived. Guns poised and ready. "Police! Nobody move!"

"Don't shoot!" Adam's voice rang out. "The suspect's been disarmed. His firearm is over at two o'clock."

One officer moved in to commandeer his prisoner. Holstering the Glock, Adam rushed over to Madison. Pulled her into his arms.

"This guy's an accomplice." He jerked his head toward Hayden who had remained frozen in place the whole time.

"Nobody said anything to me about a baby. I swear." The man spouted a litany of excuses for his actions as another officer snapped the hand cuffs into place on his wrists. "I just naturally assumed the property would revert to the surviving spouse. I did this for the good of the public domain. That nasty John Clark lied to me."

Gripping his shoulder, the arresting officer turned him around. "You have the right to remain silent."

"I'm telling you, this wasn't for me alone."

"If you give up that right, anything you say can and will be used against you in a court of law."

While two officers remained behind to secure the scene, the rest of them filed out with their prisoners.

Hugging her tight, Adam slipped an arm around Madison's shoulders as they turned to follow. She slid her arm into place around his waist when they walked into the crisp air of a December afternoon. Pausing for a second to simply breathe, they headed down the stairs to the parking lot where a cluster of squad cars, white, red and blue lights spinning, tossed pulsating reflections on the glossy pavement and surrounding sky.

"John Clark said if we got rid of her, he would be able to restore our precious Concord Complex to its original glorious stature." Hayden's voice pierced the chilly air. "Undo the damage done by years of neglect."

"You have a right to an attorney…"

"You better believe I'm not done talking."

And talk he did, continuing his rant as he was led to a waiting police car. The verbal implications of his cohort going non-stop. As he was ushered, butt first, into the backseat, the door was finally shut on his tirade.

Tires rolled on pavement as most of the squad cars pulled away. With the bubble lights of the one remaining turned off, a quiet calm settled over the area.

"It's hard to believe John was behind what we now know were attempts on my life." Madison huddled close, releasing a shudder as she buried her face against him.

Heat flowed from his body to hers, then circled back again to spiral inside and wrap around his heart. Her belly brushed against him, and a heart that had come so close to breaking, swelled to fill with such an abundance of love, he could barely contain it all.

"It's over now." He held her tighter. "Are you okay?"

"To be honest, I've been better. But I'll be fine."

The words between them rode on sparkling clouds of mist.

Remaining beside her, he rubbed his palm across the tenseness of her neck and upper back. She immediately released a deep sigh as rigid muscles eased beneath his touch. Even as she firmed up her hold on him. He flexed the arm wrapped on her shoulders to grasp her more securely. As always happened with this woman, her mere presence swamped his senses.

He thanked God for that as she snuggled into him. Made herself at home.

"As much as I want to forget the nightmare, there are still issues I need to confront."

"All in good time." His voice trembled, but he didn't care. "I'm so thankful you're safe. You and boys are very important to me."

"You're important to them too. To us. All of us."

Her true meaning wasn't lost on him as she huddled nearer. "And, while I can't wait to see my kids, right now I hate to give up this moment."

"Then don't."

"If only that was possible." With a sigh that shook both of them, she pushed back to look up at him while still careful to stay connected. "If not for Hayden Riley striking again."

"How could he?" Hadn't they just witnessed the man being hauled off to jail?

"The way he was going on and on about a baby."

"Oh."

Both their gazes settled on her mid-section.

"What if some of it somehow gets picked up by the local news? I'd hate to have my family, Cameron and Dak especially, find out that way. I want to tell them myself."

"I see your point." He drew a long breath, about to take the high dive of his life. "Do you want me to be with you when you do?"

"That would be nice. Why?" Her voice held an edge of caution as she stared at him through narrowed eyes. "Why? Don't you want to be?"

"What? No definitely." His words tumbled over one another in his haste to get them out.

"Truth is, Cameron would probably take the news better coming from you."

He smiled at that. "It might be best if we had a definite plan before we talk to them."

"Does that mean you have an idea for one? Because, I'm sorry, but I'm not sure I do."

"Wouldn't it make the news be easier for them to accept if we also told them something else?"

"Such as?"

He wrapped her in his arms and held on tight. "Even before all this, I'd been doing some thinking. A lot of thinking."

"About us?" Her response was weak, and his heart squeezed.

Momentarily losing his voice, at first, all he could do was nod. "The five of us."

"Us?" She lifted her face to meet his gaze.

"Yes. Us."

Deciding then and there to jump right into the deep end, he sprung off the board with ease. And hoped to hell he wouldn't end in a painful belly flop.

Letting her go, he dropped to one knee. "Marry me, Madison. Make our family complete."

Her mouth fell open as she stared at him. "Are you serious?"

"Never more serious in my entire life." Standing, he once again gathered her in his arms. Partly because she looked like she was about to fall down. "I know you may have reservations. Given the circumstances of your last marriage." He didn't give her a chance to utter a sound. "I promise to do everything in my power to prove my love for you is real. That I'll cherish your boys and your baby the same as I'd cherish my own."

She pulled back far enough to look up at him. Initial disbelief in her eyes melted into the beginnings of joy. "As long as you put it that way, what else can I say but yes." Wrapping her arms around his neck, she kissed him long and hard before letting him go. Tears glistened as a smile stretched her cheeks. "I accept your promise. And your love."

"Now we have something more to tell the kids."

His heart enlarged even more as he dropped a kiss on her open mouth, then put his arm around her to lead them to the car. "Our kids."

"Our kids," she breathed.

A few minutes later, she was strapped into her seat belt with Adam behind the wheel. Their drive home was blessedly uneventful as they made plans for their upcoming arrival. Cameron, Dak, and her mother were in the entrance when he opened the door to her house, and they walked inside.

Dak sailed into his mother's arms the second she crossed the threshold.

"Momma! Momma! You're home."

"I am, sweetheart." She bent to gather him close.

Cameron circled her in a hug from behind. "We missed you so much."

"It's so good you're home." Standing to one side, Kay gave Adam a quick squeeze before stepping forward to embrace her daughter and the boys. "Both of you."

She came back to slip her arm briefly around Adam before letting him go, too.

Smiling through her tears, Madison continued to hug her sons. "I missed you, too. So much."

"You did it, Adam." Pushing away from her, Dak grabbed hold of him. "You brought my momma home."

"Of course I did. Have I ever lied to you?"

The child pulled back far enough to look up and shake his head. "Un-uh. Never."

"And I never will. Ever."

"Me too, Adam. Thanks." Cameron moved away from Madison and toward him, then hesitated as if not sure what to do next.

Grinning, Adam reached out to her oldest, wrapping his arms around both children as if he were holding his own. In that instant, he glanced up to lock gazes with the love of his life, and a slow smile of pure contentment lifted his lips.

"Dak. Cameron. Mom." Never taking her eyes from his, Madison stepped forward to take his hand. "Adam and I have something, two very special somethings, to share with you."

A word about the author...

A big city girl turned country woman, Margo is an award-winning author of contemporary romance and romantic suspense. Her short stories and human-interest articles have appeared in national publications. When not writing, she can be found in the company of family and friends, on long walks in the woods with her super supportive husband, or sitting quietly somewhere, reading.

For more about Margo and her writing, please visit:
www.margohoornstra.com